AWAKENED AND BETRAYED

THE LOST SENTINEL BOOK 2

RUSSELL TRASK

Copyright © 2019 Ivy Asher

All rights reserved. This book or parts thereof may not be reproduced in any form, stored in any retrieval system, or transmitted in any form by any means—electronic, mechanical, photocopy, recording, or otherwise—without prior written permission of the author, except in cases of a reviewer quoting brief passages in a review.

This is a work of fiction. Names, characters, places, and incidents either are the products of the author's imagination or are used fictitiously. Any resemblance to actual persons, living or dead, businesses, companies, events, or locales is entirely coincidental.

Edited by Denise Krekling

Edited by Robin Lee at Rainy Day Editing

Cover Design by Nichole Witholder at Rainy Day Artwork

DEDICATION

For everyone who got back up after the world tried to break them.

1

The last of the forest's untamed trees flash by my window, suddenly replaced by manicured landscapes and the brick visages of Solace's town center. On my previous visits to the heart of this caster town, I found it idyllic and homey. Now, I don't find any comfort in the tidy images left behind in the wake of our moving SUV. Knox squeezes our interlaced fingers, the supportive action his attempt to break me away from the melancholy of my thoughts.

"What should we do when we're done with the elders?"

The guys all shrug their shoulders at Knox's question, but Valen's eyes find mine in the reflection of the rearview mirror. We stare at each other for a couple seconds before he refocuses on the road, leaving Knox's question hanging unanswered in the air.

It's been three days since the lamia attack. Three days since I lost Talon. I've spent every second of those three days holed up in my room with the guys, avoiding everyone else at all costs. I've been unfazed by the visitors or their banging on the door. Unmoved by the words and apologies shouted through the wood and stone barrier. Everything outside of my room has been met with silence.

That is, until yesterday, when a summons was slipped under the door demanding my presence at a meeting called by the Elders Council. It seems their patience has finally run out at my offering zero answers and my refusal to see anyone but the guys. The summons didn't exactly say *be there or else*, the wording was more flowery and embellished, but the underlying message was obvious.

The SUV dips down a ramp, and Valen navigates into a parking spot. We pile out of the vehicle, our movement and the shutting of car doors echoing throughout the underground parking structure. The guys circle themselves around me as we file into a stairwell and start to make our way up.

I don't know if their positions are a conscious or unconscious decision, but it makes my bruised heart swell with tender affection. Valen and Bastien fall in behind me, Ryker is to my left, Knox to my right, and Sabin leads the way. Based on how they've surrounded me and the looks on their faces, there's no question that I'm being protected. Everything about their countenance shouts, *you'll have to go through me to get to her*.

I activate the runes on my sternum to allow how I feel in this moment to flow into them. This is the first time I've activated these particular runes since we discovered what they could do on the night the guys got their Chosen marks. But I need them to feel all the affection and gratitude I have for what they're doing, for what they've *been* doing for me.

From the minute I was lifted out of the blood and ashes in the back of the car, I have been cared for, patiently listened to, and supported in ways I've never experienced before.

I've spent so much of my life picking myself up off the ground when the world got in a solid hit. With the exception of Talon, it's been me relying on me. But that's changing now. I'm learning that I can share my grief and heartache. That it doesn't have to be me against the world. Not if I don't want it to be.

Letting the guys in on what I'm feeling right now seems a million times better than any words I could string together to express what they're coming to mean to me. Acknowledging smiles sneak across everyone's faces, but each of us stays quiet and alert.

We make our way out of the stairwell, and I quickly deactivate the runes.

A solitary caster awaits us. He gives a slight nod in greeting then instructs us to follow him. I take a deep breath and slip my game face on. I'm not looking forward to what's about to go down. I don't want to fucking describe what happened or answer any questions they may have about it.

I relive it enough every day.

I'm sure the elders have gotten detailed accounts from the others that were there that night. I'm not sure why my version of events is so necessary. What is it they think I'm going to add that they haven't already been told?

The guys and I figure that this has less to do with my version of events and more to do with the Elders Council wanting details about my abilities. Unfortunately, there's a strong possibility that they could want more information about what a Sentinel is, too.

As much as I'd hoped that the binding on my reading would keep what I am under lock and key, I'm pretty sure the fucking lamia just blew that hope right out of the water. If Enoch and the others were paying attention, the questions will start piling up for them. I suppose there's a slim chance that the *Baby Sentinel* nickname Faron was throwing around in that cellar will stay buried down there, but I'm not holding my breath.

Between the weird pet name, Talon's dying account of where I come from, and the display of some of my abilities, I doubt any of that is going to stay in the shadows like I want. Enoch looks like the kind of guy who doesn't keep secrets from dear old dad. It just sucks that his dad happens to be a council member, and the jury's still out on just where I stand with that lot.

The caster that's leading us pushes through an ornate set of black doors, and we follow him into a room that seems to be an odd combination of courtroom and amphitheater. To my left, seated in a row of elevated desk-like tables, is the Elders Council. I recognize the three that I've already met.

Elder Balfour, portly and balding, looks back at me with an air of *I've got better things to do.* Elder Nypan's smile is friendly and gleaming, and the overhead lights wink at me from his completely bald, ebony head. He really needs to have a talk with Elder Balfour about embracing the *bald is beautiful* movement. While Elder Nypan looks like Seal and makes bald look good, Elder Balfour looks like a plumper version of George Costanza.

Elder Cleary watches me as we all settle in, his bright blue eyes accentuated by short, expertly styled, white-blond hair. I see pieces of Enoch in his father's face, but it's just touches here and there, and it makes me wonder what Enoch's mother looks like. There are two other elders I don't recognize; one is Elder Kowka and the other Elder Albrecht, but I couldn't say which one is which.

I pull my gaze from the raised position of the elders and find Lachlan and his coven of paladin seated in a type of jury box off to the side. It's the first time I've seen any of them since they clustered around the back of that black suburban. My eyes connect with Aydin's and Silva's fixed stares, but I'm quick to look away and shut myself off. Enoch, Nash, and Kallan sit in a matching jury box on the opposite side of the room. Enoch gives me a head nod, and I answer the gesture with a slight lift of my chin.

The guys and I are escorted into the room until we're standing dead center in front of the elders. Everything about this setup oozes intimidation and power. I'm forced to look up at the elders on their raised throne-like chairs that are tucked neatly behind a long table. There's no doubt in my mind that they want us to feel small and less significant in this room. *It's all mind games,* I tell myself as Elder Balfour instructs the guys to have a seat behind me.

"Welcome, Vinna. We are glad you could make it and that you are looking much better than the last time we saw you," Elder Balfour offers in greeting.

We assess each other for a second before I decide he's waiting for me to respond.

"A summons is a summons, or so I'm told. I'm sorry the blood and ash weren't to your liking. Here I was thinking I pulled it off," I deadpan.

A couple of chuckles bounce around the room, and Elder Nypan starts to cough. I catch the smile on his face before he brings a fist up to his mouth, covering it up. Elder Balfour isn't as amused, judging by the way the skin around his eyes crinkles when he narrows them at me.

"Vinna, we've requested your presence here today to address an issue that was brought to our attention."

He pauses dramatically, and I wait for him to elaborate.

"Would you please tell us why you were found walking on the side of the road with no shoes, means of transportation, or a way to contact anyone?"

I tilt my head to the side as I stare blankly at Elder Balfour and process why he's asking this question. My eyes flit to Enoch of their own accord, and I conclude that he or his coven is the source of these insignificant details. Enoch suspiciously avoids looking at me.

"I had a couple of flat tires and only one spare. I didn't have my phone, so I was walking back to get some help."

"And how is it that you found yourself driving around with no shoes and no phone?" Elder Balfour asks, leaning forward a little too eagerly in his chair.

"I'm sorry, is that illegal here?" I ask, confused, my eyes bouncing from one elder to the next. "Who cares why I didn't have a phone or shoes? What would any of that have to do with you or what happened with the lamia?"

"Vinna, we've been made aware that your current living situation may not be safe for you. What Elder Balfour is asking will help us determine whether that is the case or not." Elder Nypan calmly informs me.

His smile is kind, and he folds his hands patiently in front of him while I contemplate what he just said. I look at Lachlan. I'm not sure why it matters, but I want to see just what he thinks about this line of questioning and the accusation that now hangs heavy around his coven's necks. His posture is stiff, and his focus never wavers from the elders. A mask is in place, hiding any emotion, but I can sense the anger rolling off of him in waves.

He has to feel my eyes on him, but he doesn't turn to meet them. I don't know why, but for the briefest of seconds, I thought he would. Maybe it was the glimpse of compassion I saw in him in the back of the death-soaked SUV. The way he looked at me that night, with empathy and brutal understanding, it's been fucking with the *unredeemable* category I have him in.

"Two days ago, did you contact a Lucy Barton and

request her assistance in finding and purchasing a property?"

My head snaps to Elder Cleary at his question. How the hell does he know that? I sense the shifting bodies behind me, and I'd bet the guys are wondering the exact same thing.

"Yes," I answer, offering no additional information.

Aydin shoots up out of his chair. "Vinna, please, you have to hear us out!"

"*Quiet!*" Elder Balfour bellows across the room.

Aydin looks pained and beseeching, but he sits back down and does what he's told. The look on his face stings. The hurt that I see there calls to me, but I try to ignore it as I brick up my defenses even more. No matter how I look at things, analyze them, hold them up to the light hoping there's more that I'm just not seeing... The truth is I can't trust them, and without that, there's no hope to remedy anything.

His pleading eyes look for cracks in my armor. What right does he have to look at me that way? Like I'm the one inflicting injury. Fuck him. Fuck them.

"You are underage, Vinna, and until you've had your awakening, you are not allowed to be on your own," Elder Nypan politely tells me, pulling me from my thoughts.

Fucking hell, not this again! I'm twenty-two, an adult in the eyes of the country we live in, shouldn't that be enough?

"I've been on my own for a long time now; I can take care of myself. I have the means and ability to do it, and I don't see what the problem is. The situation with Lachlan and his coven has become...complicated." I look at each of the elders imploringly. "No matter what you say, I'm not planning to stay there much longer."

The room goes silent with my declaration. The elders look over to Lachlan. "Will you rescind your claim on her?"

As soon as they ask Lachlan that question, my hope that the elders just might see things my way crumbles into nothing. Lachlan growls out a resounding, "No," and it's punctuated by the frustrated sigh that escapes me. Why can't he just let me go?

2

"We challenge Lachlan Aylin's claim on Vinna Aylin and ask to submit our own."

Valen's smooth voice fills the room from behind me. I look back at him over my shoulder, and a small smile sneaks across my lips at his declaration. I track Valen as he steps up to my side, his new proximity causing warmth and comfort to wash over me. It's like lying in a pile of clean clothes fresh out of the dryer.

"My coven and I would like to submit a Bond Claim. We know the council likes to wait until all parties have achieved their awakening, but exceptions have been made in the past, and we request an exception be made today."

Valen briefly looks at Silva and takes in a deep fortifying breath before continuing.

"My coven and I agree that living with Lachlan and his coven is not a good place for Vinna to be."

Valen barely finishes that sentence before Silva, Lachlan, and the rest of them are on their feet, shouting at him. The guys answer the attacking indignation with their own, and aggression floods the room. I watch my guys defend me and shout out the coven's offenses against me. I'm grateful that they have my back, but I also feel shitty that this is what it's come to.

I can't grasp why Valen's statement bothers them so much. Lachlan and the others are delusional if they think they haven't earned this. Yeah, this *Family Court* scenario with the elders is extreme, but how did any of the paladin think I would stay and keep putting up with their shit?

Shouts reverberate through the room, and Elder Balfour's demands for *quiet* aren't having any effect. Other paladin have rushed into the room, in an attempt to reclaim some semblance of order, but their sudden presence is adding to the chaos.

The large Polynesian-looking elder, whose name I still don't know, stands up and snakes out a hand toward the upheaval. A white rope of magic shoots out of his palm toward Lachlan and his coven, and it wraps itself tightly around each of their necks. They immediately fall silent. The elder lifts his other hand and sends out another rope of magic, this one moving quickly toward my guys.

"Oh no you don't," I mutter as I reach out and grab the rope of magic as it attempts to flash by me. The thought of someone choking my Chosen into submission—which is exactly what is happening to Lachlan and his coven—pisses me the fuck off.

I yank on the cord of magic in an attempt to get a better grip on it, and surprisingly, the white cord snaps from the elder's palm. It whips back toward me and then winds itself snake-like up my arm. I stare at it, waiting for the magic to move up to my throat and start choking me too, but it's still.

I shake my arm around like I'm trying to get something *icky* off, but the super badass move doesn't budge the milky coil. I look up to the elder responsible for my new magical cling-on. I'm about to ask him to *get it off,* but the whiny question sticks in my throat when I take in the look on the elders' faces.

I see different versions of shock staring back at me from behind the long desk-like table they're perched behind. Slowly, loaded looks are exchanged, and it becomes clear that some kind of silent conversation is taking place amongst them. The extra paladin who poured into the room at the onset of the shouting match position themselves in front of the elders. Their protective movements making it clear that they now identify me as a threat.

Well, shit.

Snapping himself out of his shocked stupor, the Polynesian-looking elder releases his choke hold on Lachlan and the others. He slowly resumes his seat and clears his throat, his eyes flicking from the stolen magic on my arm to my face.

"Sorry," I offer sheepishly. "Do you...um...want it back?"

I hope he's cool with me just keeping it, because I'm not sure how the hell to give it back if he answers *yes*. The weird ass shit that I do is mostly instinctual. It surprises the hell out of me most of the time, and I couldn't tell you why something works the way that it does. It just does. It's an in-the-moment thing. Later, when I try to replicate the things I've witnessed my magic do, I can't. *Fickle fucking magic.*

Even though I'm just as in the dark about my abilities as everyone else, I feel compelled to offer this armband of magic back to its owner. Maybe it has something to do with the look he keeps giving the magic clinging to my arm, like it's betrayed him somehow. But before he can respond, the runes on my arm light up and begin to absorb the constricting magical cord.

Well, this is awkward.

In the past, when offensive magic has been thrown my way, a shield or two pops up to deal with it, so I'm not quite sure what to think of my runes' new desire to *eat* the magic instead. I try to act super nonchalant and unfazed about whatever the fuck just happened.

The fact that the elders have front-row seats in witnessing some of my *unique abilities* is not ideal. I don't want to be categorized as more of a threat, and I don't want them more curious about me than they already are.

Really, magic? I scold, and then I give it a little pat. It did keep the guys from getting choked out, so I can't be too mad.

Elder Balfour breaks the weighted silence and begins to call everyone back to order, chastising Lachlan's coven and the guys for their unappreciated disruption. A sudden flash of pain keeps me from tracking what he and the other elders are saying. I try to pant through the burning onslaught discreetly, and thankfully it ends after about ten seconds, which is the fastest it's ever taken for me to get new runes.

Relieved that no one seems to be noticing my sudden pain-induced distraction, I casually look down and find a single new rune on the sides of my hands. *Please don't tell me I've somehow unknowingly connected myself to this fucking elder?* I silently plead with my magic.

I scan the mystery elder's hands, but I don't spot any marks on him. The fact that he didn't start shouting from a sudden attack of pain supports my hope that the new rune is only for me. The weight of someone's stare pulls me from my introspection, and I find Elder Cleary watching me shrewdly.

Nothing to see here, I repeatedly chant in my head before I try to ignore him and check back into what's going on around me.

"Thank you, Conscript Fierro, for your candor. We will accept your petition for a Bond Claim and review its merits."

I turn excitedly to Valen, but the look on his face tells me that I've missed something. My smile falters, and the use of my name pulls my attention back to the elders.

"Paladin Aylin, your claim on Vinna Aylin is hereby severed. Until this council makes a decision in regards to the Bond Claim submitted by Conscript Fierro on behalf of his coven, a temporary claim will be assigned. Brothers, please speak your recommendations now."

I wait anxiously for the elders to start discussing what they're going to do with me, but it doesn't take long to realize that the conversation is once again taking place in their heads. I shoot a panicked look at Valen as the room fills with a heavy silence. He runs his finger discreetly over the runes behind his ear.

"Don't worry, Vinna. This will probably only be for a couple of weeks. They don't take long to decide on Bond Claims. You'll be back with us soon."

His words do nothing to lessen the panic rising inside of me. An orange crackle of magic moves over my palms, and I ball my hands into fists to hide it. Two weeks of living with who the fuck knows, and that's if the elders accept the Bond Claim. They could reject it. Then what the hell am I supposed to do? Before I can mentally shout any of this at Valen, Elder Nypan's voice slices through the quiet.

"It is agreed; temporary claim will be given to Elder Cleary until a decision is made on the Bond Claim petition."

"What the fuck?" I exclaim loudly.

My outrage is drowned out by a flurry of activity as the elders hurry from their thrones and quickly rush out through a door behind them. *Better run, you fucking cowards.* As the last elder scrambles out of the room, I turn to go to my Chosen. A large group of strange paladin are surrounding me, blocking my access. *What the hell?* I spot Ryker between the shoulders of the two paladin directly in front of me, and I see that a separate group of paladin are herding him and the others away.

Panic floods me, and my magic answers its call. Orange, pink, and purple flashes skate over my skin, and I quickly track my options for escape like a cornered dog.

"Stop!" Ryker shouts, but he's ignored and pushed away. "She's going to lose it, you moon-cursed assholes, just let me talk to her, and then I'll leave."

I reach for the magic in the runes for my short swords. The guy to my left is about my size and looks like the weakest link. I formulate a plan to take him out first.

"Squeaks, stop!"

Ryker's voice is closer than it was before, and I pull my eyes from my first intended target. I was already moving toward him, and I hadn't even realized it. I stop the advance and find Ryker. The paladin around him won't let him get any closer, but they're no longer trying to force him out of the room. "It's okay. Don't fight. It'll just make things worse if you start killing people."

Someone gives an incredulous snort, but I don't pull my eyes from Ryker's fixed sky-blue stare to glare at whoever it is.

"Just go with them, Squeaks. Call us when you get settled."

He nods at me reassuringly, and I mirror the movement, even though I am anything but reassured at the moment. If he's telling me not to fight, I'll listen—for now.

"It's going to be okay."

Ryker gives me a sad smile and taps his chest with two fingers, right over the runes that sit between his pecs. Then he turns and walks out of the room, surrounded by paladin as they escort him away.

3

I stand staring at the door that Ryker left through. Images of my Chosen being forced away from me begin to mix with the memories and helpless feelings of losing Talon and Laiken too. It takes me a couple of minutes to get a hold of myself and rein in the loss that's slamming into me like a tsunami. One of the paladin surrounding me gets impatient with my lack of movement, and a hand settles on my back as if the owner thinks he can herd me away with a simple guiding touch.

I whip around to punch whoever the fuck is touching me, but he jumps to the side, avoiding the full force of my hit. I still manage to clip him, and he stumbles into the paladin on his right, causing a domino effect of faltering bodies.

"High five for having quick reflexes, but if you touch me again, I will fuck you up."

I glare at the blond male, who doesn't look much older than me. He tilts his head to the side and then, with exaggerated slowness, clasps his hands behind his back. He hikes his eyebrows up and gives me a look that asks, *happy now* before a smartass smile takes over his face.

"Watch yourself, Paladin Rock; you've heard what Aydin's been saying about her," a stocky paladin to my left warns.

"That's doesn't even include what we all just saw happen with Elder Kowka," another paladin warns the cocky blond asshole, who responds with an amused chuckle.

Well, I guess that clears up the mystery. Elder Kowka is the elder I just magicjacked. I fix my stare on the cocky blond idiot.

"Better listen to your buddy, *Pebble,* he seems to have more sense than you do."

A chuckling paladin in front of me starts to move toward an exit, and I follow like the good girl I'm not. The group of warriors around me fall into step with one another, and I'm led through several sets of hallways to an underground garage. This one is different than the one the guys and I parked in earlier this morning, and I can't get my bearings or figure out exactly where I am. I climb into a black Range Rover and try not to shudder at the brief flashback that surfaces.

I've about had my fill of black SUVs. The paladin that's driving maneuvers us out of the parking garage and pulls out onto the roads of the town. He then begins to drive like we're being chased by something. I take a couple peeks back behind my shoulder just to check that we're not, in fact, being tailed, but there's nothing there. I look to the faces of the others in the car, but they don't seem alarmed by the Grand Theft Auto reenactment.

After thirty minutes, and more turns and winding roads than I can keep track of, the SUV pulls through a set of gates and comes to a stop in front of a house that's sleeker and more modern than anything I've ever seen before. A giant wooden door that's double the size of any door I've ever seen opens, and out steps Elder Cleary, Enoch, Nash, Kallan, and another young caster I've never seen before.

I blow out a frustrated sigh and quietly mumble a string of colorful swear words. *Well, let's get this shit show started.* I let myself out of the back seat, slamming the car door behind me, which silences the growing laughter filling the car in my wake. I guess I wasn't as quiet as I thought in expressing my displeasure about this situation.

My eyes automatically narrow at Elder Cleary's calculating smile, and my angry look makes its way down the line of casters waiting for me by the front door. Gravel crunches under my feet, and I begrudgingly trudge toward my new *hosts*. The paladin escorting me catch up and match my steps. I hadn't even noticed any of them get out of the car.

"Vinna, we're delighted that you're here."

Elder Cleary's blue eyes sparkle, and his overly welcoming voice booms out at me. I stop a couple of feet away from him. I don't say anything. I just stare at him emotionlessly until he squirms from the uncomfortable lack of response. I'm not sure what's really going on, but I don't believe for one second that all of this stems from a genuine concern about my safety.

"Well, let's give you a tour and get you settled in. I've already arranged to have your things moved over here. I expect boxes will start arriving by this afternoon," Elder Cleary announces as he turns to make his way through the oversized door.

I absently follow everyone into the house, tuning them out as I'm guided around. It's very different from Lachlan's mega-mansion, or any other place I've ever been, and I'm not sure what to think about it. The floors are polished concrete, and the space is open and encased by huge windows everywhere. Warm wood tones and textured carpets help break up the cold concrete and white walls, but there's a definite masculine feel to everything.

It's not a huge house, which surprises me. I don't know Elder Cleary that well, but I assumed his home would be more ostentatious and showy. The tour takes me into a room that I'm told is now mine. A large bed sits against the wall in the middle of the room, a gray, tufted fabric headboard at its crown, a sofa in the same color set against the foot. The bedding and other décor in the room have been done in shades of purple and sage, and there's a huge TV mounted on the wall across from the bed.

It's clean and comfortable looking, and I've definitely stayed in worse places. Alarm bells go off as I take in the feminine decor. Either this is some other female's room, or they've been preparing for me for longer than the thirty-minute drive it took to get here.

"I'll leave you to get settled in, Vinna. Please let Enoch know if you need anything."

I ignore Elder Cleary as I continue to look around, but my lack of communication or acknowledgment doesn't seem to bother him as much anymore, and he turns away.

"Enoch, I'll see you on Sunday for dinner. Be sure to let Straten know of any dietary restrictions she may have."

"Dad, she's right there, just ask her yourself," Enoch grumbles from where he's leaning against the doorway of my new—hopefully temporary—room.

Elder Cleary swings back toward me. "Vinna, we do a family dinner every Sunday at my house. Is there anything you don't like to eat?"

I stare at him, confused. "Wait, you don't live here?"

Elder Cleary looks around and laughs. "Of course not, this is Enoch's home that he shares with his coven. I thought you'd be more comfortable here." He declares this innocently, like my comfort was simply his biggest concern, but the pieces fall into place for me.

"Delicate flower broodmares," I mumble quietly, shaking my head in disgust.

The guys told me about the elders and how they like to *facilitate* matches that *they* think are appropriate. These fuckers are trying to match me up with Enoch and his coven.

I glare at Enoch. "Did you know that this was what they were up to?"

Enoch looks at me, puzzled. "What who was up to?"

I jerk my chin toward his dad. "Daddy dearest. The other elders." I give an incredulous snort. "Are *you* in on this set up too?"

I don't give Enoch time to respond before I round on Elder Cleary. "Do other caster females let you get away with this shit? Never mind, I don't really care. You can't just point me in the direction of the males *you* want me to choose and think I will just fall on my back."

"Vinna, that's not what—" Enoch starts to say.

Elder Cleary cuts him off. "Whatever I or my fellow elders chose to do, it will always be what's in your best interest. You have a lot to learn about being a caster and all that it entails. This is the best possible fit for your strong magic."

"I don't exist to pop out magic-filled babies at your fucking behest," I growl.

"That statement alone shows just how much you don't know about being a caster, or who we are."

Elder Cleary's reaction and response is cryptic, and it leaves me confused. I can't tell if he's saying that I'm *wrong* in thinking that they only want me as a broodmare. That my incorrect assumption shows just how much I don't know about being a caster. Or that I am *only* worth the children I can give them, and I'm *wrong* in thinking I have some other choice.

Before I can glean any clarification or find my way out of the maze of his words and my thoughts, Elder Cleary is gone. I stare at the now empty doorway, not sure what the hell to do about any of this.

All these people making decisions *for* me is getting real fucking old. They just move me around, arranging me however they see fit, like a pawn in a game of chess. Well, I'm done questioning my next move. I'll sit tight until I know the endgame. Then, I'll flip the chessboard and fuck up all the pieces. *Pawn* is not a label I'm good with.

4

I pull my phone out of my back pocket and try and call the guys. After several attempts of holding it at every possible angle—in every square inch of the room—I concede that the *no signal* indicator is, in fact, not lying to me.

I plop onto the foreign bed and run my finger across the runes behind my ear. Here's hoping the magic in my runes has a better signal than my phone.

"Sentinel to Chosen, come back, over, cuhhhhhhhhhhh-hhhhhhh."

"Killer, you ok?"

"Bruiser, this is not a CB radio; handles are not necessary, and neither is the static noise you are making."

"Bastien, why do you want to spoil my fun? Didn't you hear, I had a shit day...over."

I sigh, and some of my tension sloughs away as their voices sink into me.

"Killer, Knox? Really?"

He laughs, and it does more to wash away the trauma of today than I would have ever thought possible. "What? I like it.

Tough but also adorable, and it's technically accurate, which I thought you would appreciate."

"*I guess it beats Squeaks,*" I grumble, and Ryker chuckles.

"*Come on, you know you secretly love it, Squeaks.*"

I give a playfully annoyed moan and marvel at just how quickly they can pull me from a horrible mood, moment, or memory simply by being themselves.

"What the hell happened today?" I ask. "I thought I was going to be answering lamia and Sentinel questions, not being subjected to a fucked up child custody hearing and forcibly relocated to Enoch's house."

"*What the fuck, they moved you into Enoch's house?*" Sabin shouts into my head, and I wince.

The guys must have said something to him because he quickly apologizes for the volume. I hate that they're all together, and I'm not *allowed* to be there.

"*This whole thing is fucking ridiculous! Why the hell do they treat casters like children until their awakening?*" I ask.

"*Before an awakening, a caster is not in complete control of their magic. It's not safe for them to be on their own before they can fully control their abilities. After an awakening, there are way fewer magical accidents. That's why casters are free to be independent and make their own choices once they have full access to their magic and the control that comes with it. We hate this as much as you do, but like I said earlier, it should only be for a couple of weeks,*" Valen reassures me.

I wish I could argue that I can control my magic and deserve to be on my own. But magicjacking an elder probably wasn't the best example of that. Maybe if I hadn't looked just as shocked as the elders had when it happened, I could have played it off as intentional. I focus on Valen's reassurances that this will only be temporary. One way or another, I'll make sure of that.

"*If you need anything, Bruiser, just use that handy new trick we discovered the other day, and we'll be there as soon as possible."*

I look down at the runes on my ring finger at Bastien's reminder. I immediately feel better knowing that if I need them, I can call on those runes, and they will feel it.

"They told me they were bringing my stuff over; can you guys keep Laiken and Talon with you? I don't want anything to happen to them."

"Already done. We also kept the tablet and folder the Readers left for you. We figured it would be safer with us."

"Thank you, Sabin—"

A heavy knock at the open doorway pulls me from my mental conversation.

"Guys, Enoch's knocking, I'll talk to you later...over."

Bastien chuckles, and a round of irritated goodbyes and promises to see me soon sound off in my head. I run my finger over the runes behind my ear, turning them off and sit up. Enoch presses his palms on either side of the doorway; his sun-kissed skin and muscles flex as he pushes against the frame. His gray-blue eyes run over me, and he seems nervous.

"I want to introduce you to Becket. You haven't met him yet," Enoch nods his chin in the direction of the hallway, the sun from the window catching the white-blond highlights in his tow-colored hair.

He backs out of my doorway, and I follow him to the living room where Nash and Kallan are lounging. I trade awkward waves with them as I'm introduced to the only unfamiliar face in the group. Becket has a very boy next door appeal. Short ash brown hair, straight eyebrows over dark brown eyes, and high cheekbones with a smattering of freckles. He's good-looking, but not in an overwhelming, my-brain-stopped-working-because-he-looked-at-me kind of way.

"Beck is the fourth member of our coven," Enoch explains.

I give him a confused look. "I thought Parker was in your coven?"

Enoch takes a seat on the couch next to Kallan and sweeps his hand out in an invitation for me to sit down, too. I stay standing.

"No, he's a friend we go rock climbing with occasionally. That's what we were coming back from when we ran into you that day on the road."

The room falls silent, and it seems none of us know where to tread when it comes to talking about what happened that day. Just as the silence teeters on awkward, Nash breaks it up, his jovial tone overcompensating for the dark thoughts surrounding the lamia abduction.

"Consider yourself warned," he teases. "After Parker woke up the next day and was told what you did, a heavy dose of hero-worship kicked in." Nash chuckles, and his eyes light up with mirth. It's clear by the look on his face that he has a love for gossip that could rival any sweet tea drinking, rocking chair owning, old Southern woman.

His dark hair is damp, and it makes me wonder when he had time to shower or swim before I got here. Nash is rocking some scruff on his face that wasn't there the first time I met him. He looks tired, and for the first time, I wonder how they've been impacted by what happened. I've been so wrapped up in what happened with Talon and everything he revealed, that I haven't bothered to step outside of my own shit to wonder what new scars the others who were taken might have.

"I didn't really do anything," I offer dismissively, brushing away Nash's teasing. "I'm sure Parker will get over it when he realizes that."

I look around the living room and just catch the shadow

of a figure as it streaks past a window. Curious, I move toward the window to get a better look.

"Um...were we not at the same abduction? Because I don't think what you did could be classified as *nothing*," Kallan tells me, the tone and look he's giving me are incredulous.

I shrug my shoulders, not sure what else to say. I'm tempted to point out that none of them would've been there if it weren't for me, but that's a road full of potholes I don't want to go down right now. I continue to look for whoever just walked past the window when the front door opens, and someone walks in. A familiar blond man smiles at me, as he makes his way into the living room and plops down in a chair. I look from him to Enoch.

"What is Pebble doing here?"

"My name is Elias *Rock*, and I've been assigned as your guard."

My face immediately scrunches up like I just smelled something nasty. The council assigned me a fucking babysitter? I stare at his cocksure smirk and shake my head, letting out a soul-weary sigh. I absently pinch my bottom lip between my thumb and index finger. Everything about this situation suddenly feels really claustrophobic.

"I'm going for a walk."

I move toward the door, but Nash steps into my path, and I stop. I give him an irritated glare.

"Is that a problem?"

He doesn't move or answer, just shoots a quick look to the others. I follow his gaze and notice that each of them is on their feet like they're ready and waiting to spring into action.

"Am I a fucking prisoner here?"

Enoch steps toward me, and I tense automatically.

"Not exactly, but wandering off on your own is probably not the wisest move given what happened last time."

"And who gave you dominion over my *moves* and decisions? I sure as hell didn't."

Enoch takes another step toward me, his eyes simmering with frustration. "By the moon, Vinna, is self-preservation not one of your many abilities?"

My eyes bounce quickly around the room before locking back on Enoch's exasperated gaze. "Guess not," I answer straight-faced and then shove Nash out of my way.

He lets out a surprised yelp as I sprint for the door. I fling it open and dash out into the thick warm air. Curses and shouting sound off behind me, but I don't give a shit. I pump my arms and dig in with my legs, quickly falling into a fast run. I don't have time to assess my surroundings and come up with a solid plan for evasion, because the heavy pounding of footfall is loud and ominous behind me. I'll just have to wing it.

A shimmering green wall of magic shoots up fifteen feet in front of me, and there's no way to avoid it unless I stop. I'm not giving in that easily though. They're going to have to do a hell of a lot more than put up a shiny magic wall and think that's going to be enough. *Come on, runes, don't fail me now.* I angle my body so it'll hit the magic barrier shoulder first, and I continue to charge like a raging bull.

A familiar tingling sweeps over me as I slam into the green-tinted magic. There's enough resistance in the barrier to sting as my shoulder makes contact, and it's probably going to leave a bruise. But it only slows me a little before the barrier shatters all around me as I force my way through. I run for the stone wall that borders Enoch's property. I call on the runes on my legs, coaxing extra power from them so I can leap high enough to clear the ten-foot wall. Suddenly with my next stride, the ground is no longer solid beneath my feet. The hole that just formed beneath my foot throws me off balance, and I trip, smashing into the ground *hard*.

Momentum tries to force me to skid forward through the grass, but something solid is holding on to my foot, and I'm jerked and stretched into a forced stop. It fucking hurts. I feel for whatever's now surrounding my calf and ankle. I look down to find that my foot is surrounded by grass and dirt. *What the hell?* I look like I've somehow grown out of the soil, like a fucking flower ready to bloom.

I can't remember which one of these assholes has elemental magic, but I know I have them to thank for this. *Stupid prick, I could have broken my fucking ankle.* I know Nash could technically heal it, but I'm sure it would hurt like hell before that could happen. I pull on my calf, but it doesn't budge, and I'm aware that the others are running toward me. The lead I had disappears like sand through my fingers.

Thinking back to everything I've read so far about elemental magic, I call on mine and push my palm toward the earth surrounding my foot. Nothing happens. I try again to separate the grass and soil from my entombed leg, but my inability to make anything happen is laughable. I let out a frustrated growl. How the hell can I do half the shit I do, but I can't make the ground willingly release my foot when I want it to?

I give up on trying to force my fickle magic to cooperate and instead focus on muscling my foot out of the ground. I painstakingly pull and jimmy myself free and then flip the bird to the hole left behind in the grass.

I get up, and I get ready. I've got maybe ten seconds until irritated, bossy male casters surround me, and I fully intend to put up at least a half-assed fight. Contrary to how this looks, I'm not actually trying to escape. The fucked up truth is, I don't have anywhere to go. But when each of them stood up to stop me, so sure that I would have no choice but to *obey*, I couldn't fight the overwhelming need to give them, and their attempt at control, a little *fuck you.*

They close in around me, hands raised with magic and ready to keep me at bay. My lack of magical ability is clearly going to put me at a massive disadvantage. The fact that the earth just ate my foot, and I couldn't do shit about it, is a brutal reminder of just how fucked I am fighting magic with magic.

My go-to selection of blades aren't an option, since I'm not trying to kill or maim anyone, and I quickly run through what else in my arsenal might piss them off and give me a leg up without making them bleed...too much.

5

My new prison wardens form a semicircle around me, assessing me and my defensive stance as they come to a stop. Staff in hand, I wait to see who's going to make the first move. I'm met by narrowed eyes and various looks of irritation. In an effort to sprinkle a little more intimidation around, I expertly twirl and maneuver my staff around me in a way that would make Donatello jealous.

Pebble moves toward me but stops suddenly when Enoch and Kallan start yelling at him.

"If you go near her when she has a weapon in her hand, you'll be out of this fight in seconds," Enoch warns him.

Pebble looks back at me, and I can see the doubtful debate going on in his head.

"Trust us, bro, that is a fight you can't win. Use your magic, that's your best bet."

I call on a throwing knife and chuck it at Kallan. I make sure to only hit him with the handle of the small blade, but I throw it with enough force that it will leave a nasty bruise. The hilt connects with his shoulder creating a hollow thunk sound, and the weapon tumbles toward the ground. I let go of the magic holding the small blade solid, and it disappears before it touches the ground.

"What the fuck?" Kallan shouts.

He drops whatever magic he had ready in his hands and massages his shoulder with a wince.

"You're just going to sell me out to Pebble like that?" I accuse him, trying not to grin. "I would have only knocked him around a little. Just enough to wipe that cocky grin off his face."

On cue, everyone looks over at the paladin, where—surprise, surprise—he's smiling that overconfident, smartass smile.

"You could've tried, sweetheart," Pebble challenges, the arrogance in his tone a perfect match for the arrogance in his grin.

I roll my eyes at him. "Please, you would have been on your back in five seconds flat."

"If you ask nicely, I'd be happy to get on my back in three seconds flat. I like a woman who wants to be on top."

I tilt my head appraisingly. "Yeah, I could see that. You seem kind of lazy."

Kallan throws an indignant arm in Enoch's direction. "He warned him too, and I don't see you throwing knives at him!"

"Enoch just told him I was going to kick his ass. He wasn't laying out my weaknesses for a perfect stranger. I guess we're not the battle-tested bros I thought we were," I finish, trying not to smirk.

"At least she missed, what are you whining about?" Pebble comments smugly.

Another throwing knife leaves my hand, headed for Pebble before anyone can even turn my way to track the movement. The blade sinks into the meaty part of Pebble's thigh. He cries out and looks down at the knife and then up to me. Anger slowly replaces the shocked look on his face.

"I don't miss. I'd be happy to continue to prove that for however long you continue to prove that you're a cocky prick."

I turn my focus back on a now laughing Kallan. Nash chuckles and slowly makes his way over to Pebble to heal his new leg wound. Enoch snorts and runs a hand over his face, the tension leaving him now that he realizes I'm not actually making a break for it.

"I thought my dad was going to kill me," he mumbles, mussing up his hair in obvious exasperation.

"Don't worry, there's still plenty of time for that," I offer sweetly as my staff disappears and I brush some stray blades of grass off my shirt and pants. I head back toward my new fancy prison and ignore the soreness in my body from the fall.

"Vinna, it's obvious you're not going to make this easy on us," he tells me, and the glint in his eyes gives me the distinct impression that he just might *like* that. "But we're in charge of your safety. You can't just run off." His tone is imploring, but I sense a deeper question I can't quite identify nestled within it.

"Enoch, *I'm* in charge of my safety. And let's keep it real, thanks to this fucked up world of magic, I don't have anywhere to run. But that doesn't make you, your coven, or dear old dad and his elder buddies, my masters or commanders. Yeah, we went through some shit together, but the truth is you don't know me, and I don't know any of you. If you're looking for promises to be good, or blind faith and compliance, look somewhere else. None of you have earned my respect or obedience. So I'll do whatever I fucking want."

We reach the too big front door, and he beats me to the

bronze knob and pulls the door open for me. I know I shouldn't read into the gesture as anything but a polite show of manners, but I can't help feeling annoyed by it. Any other day, I wouldn't think twice about walking through a door someone opened for me. These fucking casters have me reading into everything like it has some hidden meaning or agenda.

I leave Enoch to his shady door holding and make a beeline for the room they've assigned me. I shut myself in and fume. If the floor wasn't polished concrete, I would be wearing a groove into it from all the pacing I'm doing. I need to work out and expel this angry, restless energy, but fuck if I'm going to ask them where the gym is around here. Of course it's the one thing left off the tour I was given earlier.

My thoughts drift to my guys, and I wonder what's happening at the mega-mansion. What did they go home to after the hearing with the elders? If I hadn't witnessed the fight over Valen's statement, I would have assumed Lachlan and the others would be relieved to get rid of me. But then why wouldn't Lachlan just give up his claim when he was asked to? What was that about? Why keep me when you hate me? It's the Beth puzzle all over again. Although now I know that Beth never wanted me, it was just Talon's compulsion that forced it on her.

The ever present ache in my soul fights to the forefront of my mind at the thought of Talon. Just when I think I'm managing to tread water in my pool of sorrow, something else happens, and I get pulled back under to drown in the desolation. I've replayed Talon's dying words over and over again. I've scoured every detail and exhaustively examined each revelation. Of all the crazy shit I've experienced over the past month, I never saw what Talon confessed coming.

It's rocked me to my core, and I'm not sure how to feel about any of it. On the one hand, I'm indebted and beyond grateful that Talon was looking out for me. I wouldn't be who I am today without him or his influence and guidance. But on the other hand, I'm fucking pissed. I can't help feeling manipulated and angry that he kept me in the dark.

I can accept that he couldn't tell me when I was under Beth's roof, but why the fuck didn't he say something when he found me on the streets? From the first day that Talon introduced himself, he should have fucking told me who and what I was. So much confusion and loneliness could have been avoided if he had just done the right thing. Not to mention all the information he had about my parents, information that's now lost forever.

Voices out in the rest of the house are gradually getting louder, and it yanks my attention away from my troubled thoughts. Who the hell is yelling? I leave the room and follow the angry, raised voices to their source.

"You shouldn't be here. You need to respect what the council decided and back off."

"Leave everything there because you're sure as hell not coming inside the house."

I round the corner ready to lay into Enoch and Nash for yelling at the guys. But I freeze when it's not any of my Chosen at the door but Aydin. He stands amidst stacks of boxes, and as soon as he sees me, it's obvious he's no longer listening to shit Enoch or Nash are saying to him. I fold my arms over my chest, and we stare at each other.

"I brought your things."

"I see that. The question is why are you still here?"

Aydin flinches like my words physically hurt him, and I try really hard to stomp out whatever's inside of me that feels bad for that. I knew Lachlan hated me and that Silva didn't trust me. Keegan was more wrapped up in supporting Lachlan at all costs than forming his own opinions about me, and Evrin was nice but mostly indifferent to my presence.

Aydin was the one who made it easier to let all of their shit slide off my back. He was the one that gave me hope. The one who made me think that maybe someday the others would come around. He was my friend, or at least I thought he could be. But as I sit here, staring at the ginger giant, all I can think is...*liar.*

"I'm not leaving until you talk to me," Aydin tells me.

"Feel free to stand out there for the rest of your life then."

I turn to walk away and try to get ahold of the unstable emotions splashing through me at his presence.

"Vinna, I'm sorry!"

The loud boom of Aydin's shout magnifies the pain in his words and tone. Maybe it's the grief I'm struggling with or the stress of this shitty day, but something in me fractures, and I whirl on him.

"You fucking should be! You pretended to be my friend. You knew what I had been through. You knew because I let you in, let you see who I am, but it wasn't enough for you. You stepped aside over and over again and gave them your silent permission to bleed me dry. You're a fucking coward and a liar. You should be more than sorry. You should be fucking ashamed."

I wipe furiously at the angry tears dripping down my face. Enoch and his coven are positioned by the door, blocking Aydin from coming in. They silently witness the exchange, their eyes fixed on the ground as my pain and rage lash out to where Aydin is standing. I hate that I'm emotionally cut open and exposed in front of more people I'm not sure I can trust.

"I've left the coven. I asked to be reassigned. Evrin has too."

Of all the things I anticipated Aydin could say, *that* was not one of them. *Fucking hell.* Aydin stares at me, broken and begging. I look away from the intensity of the questions I see in his eyes and run my fingers through my hair. I tug at the roots in an attempt to hold on to anything and ground myself, but I suddenly feel drained to the point of emptiness. I close my eyes and give a shuddering sigh. Slow tears, I couldn't stop if I tried, drip down my cheeks to plummet to their end from my jaw.

"What do you want, Aydin?"

I open my eyes and stare at him as the hollow question leaves my mouth. He shifts his weight from one foot to the other, and we take each other in, both of us trying to read the other, gauge what's going to come from this.

"You were right; I let you get crushed under the weight of Lachlan's pain. I let doubts and the past taint my own impressions of you, and I know I failed you because of that."

Aydin's voice breaks, and his eyes well up, but he doesn't allow the tears to fall. I wish I could figure that trick out. I'm starting to get really tired of spontaneously crying. I'll have to add that to the list of things Aydin will never teach me. I'll put it right next to creating fire with magic, and loyalty.

"I just want you to know that I'm still here. I can't take back what I did or the damage it caused, even though I would do anything to be able to. I can't make it right, but I can show you that I have your back the way that you deserve. The way I should have always been there for you."

His words battle against my defenses, but ultimately, they don't breach the pain and betrayal I feel. I shake my head and stare past him into the night.

"I don't think I'm ever going to be able to trust you. I'm just not built for forgiveness."

We stare at each other for a moment before Aydin gives

me a sad nod, and he blinks back tears. Mine continue to flow freely as my admission shatters both of us.

"That's okay," he tells me, his voice choked with heartache and apology. "But I'm still going to be here regardless. I'll earn it whether you can give it or not."

Aydin and I stand there, neither one of us sure what to do now. Eventually, I give him the slightest acquiescing nod. I don't know what else there is to say or do at this point. He watches me a moment longer before he turns around and leaves. I stare unseeing out the open door. I work to unravel the mess of feelings that are tangled inside of me as Enoch and the others carry boxes past me. I don't know how long I stand there, statue-like, before I give up my search for meaning and answers in the empty doorway that frames the empty night.

6
———

Sunshine that's too bright and cheerful for how I'm feeling this morning streaks through the windows. Cutlery scrapes against plates and bowls as we all eat, suffocating in awkward silence. Apparently, my emotional display with Aydin yesterday ramped up the awkwardness around here, and none of these guys know what the hell to do with me now. Or maybe the reality of this fucked up situation has sunk in, and there's not much to say about it.

Milk drips off my spoon as I scoop another bite of cereal into my mouth, and I silently formulate a plan to convince the sisters to come live with me. I've already broken up Lachlan's coven, why not go for the jugular and steal the sisters away too? I'm not sure how long I'm going to have to stay in this house, but when I do get out, I'm going to need the sisters, their loving and calming ways, and their amazing food to help me recover.

"So we should probably go over the plan for today."

Heads swivel in my direction, and I look up to find Enoch talking to me. His eyes look a little bluer and less gray today, and I wonder if the shade changes often and what the catalyst is.

"The elders are going to come by this morning and determine what you need to get caught up with where you should be," Enoch explains. His eyes settle on my mouth for a second and then flick away.

I wipe at my lips and chin, making sure I don't have a trail of milk or something.

"I've got a hundred on her being paladin," Kallan announces.

"I'll take that bet," Becket counters. "I know you guys said she's good with weapons, but if her magic is as weak as it seemed to be yesterday, they won't want her."

"She's a healer for sure. She healed injuries on me that she didn't have direct contact with. That's her strongest branch, no question. She can fight, so I'll bet paladin too," Nash argues.

They look to Enoch and wait for him to weigh in. He looks at me appraisingly and then pulls out his wallet. "I'll wager she's paladin. What do you think, Pebble?"

Pebble rolls his eyes and glares at me. Apparently, his nickname has caught on, and it's thoroughly entertaining to watch how irritated it makes him.

"She's too hot to be a proper warrior. I think Aydin was going easy on her, trying to build up her fragile self-esteem. There's no way she's as good as he says. I'm with Becket."

"Careful, Pebble, your sexist pig is showing," I say and shove another spoonful of cereal in my mouth.

I don't really care what any of them think, and I don't have the energy to be offended or make more of this stupid bet than it is. The doorbell rings, and my eyes narrow at Enoch as he moves from the table to answer it. I suspect that will be the elders, here to fuck with my life some more. I grumble internally and debate for half a second if I should get dressed. I look down at my sweat pants and tank top and decide I don't give a shit. I finish up the last of my breakfast as a large group of casters shuffle in through the doorway.

The rest of the guys at the table all stand up and move over to the group of new arrivals. Boisterous greetings involving back slapping and over-the-top familiarity follow me to the sink where I wash and dry my breakfast dishes. A pang hits me; I miss the sisters. Not just their cooking, but their warmth and playfulness. I double down on my sister coaxing-slash-kidnapping plan.

I turn around to face the group responsible for my current cluster fuck of a situation.

"It's a pleasure seeing you again, Vinna. How are you settling in?" Elder Cleary asks me, too chipper for my liking.

Just like yesterday, I stare at him but say nothing. He smiles at me and brushes off my hostility.

"I hope Enoch has filled you in on what the plan is for today. We're here to observe and help in any way needed to get you brought up to speed as quickly as possible."

Elder Cleary turns to the others in his group and starts introducing the mostly unfamiliar faces.

"Unfortunately, we didn't get to introductions yesterday, but this is Elder Kowka."

The Polynesian elder I magicjacked yesterday gives me a nod that makes the salt and pepper curls of his medium length hair wobble and sway. He's not incredibly tall, but his thighs are the size of tree trunks, and his arms are only marginally smaller. Even though he's not defined in a bodybuilder kind of way, he's clearly solid muscle under his russet-colored skin.

"And this is Elder Albrecht."

Elder Cleary gestures to a man who is obviously related to Becket, the fourth member of Enoch's coven. It's like looking into the future and getting a glimpse of what middle-aged Becket will look like. Elder Albrecht has the same clean-cut ash brown hair and brown eyes. His face is more creased and decorated with time, but the same straight eyebrows and high cheekbones are prevalent. His arm is around Becket's shoulders, and they seem to have an easier relationship than the other father-son duo of Enoch and Elder Cleary.

A well-muscled and scarred man steps forward when Elder Cleary nods at him. His hair is thick and stylishly cut, but the white-as-snow color hints at his age. His skin is darkly tanned and leather-like, with pale scars that streak through his eyebrow, cheek, and lips on the left side of his face. It's not just one solid scar but multiple fine lines that make up the appearance of one. I instantly want to sit and listen to his battle stories, knowing they're probably epic.

"Hello, Vinna, I'm Gideon Ender. The leader of the paladin."

We shake hands, both of our grips firm, and I notice more small lines of scarring on both of his arms. He's about four inches taller than my five-eight, and he's fit and trim. Keeping with my temporary vow of silence, I say nothing to his greeting, and he gives me what looks like an approving nod before stepping back amongst the group.

The last man of the group to be introduced is a dead ringer for Marilyn Manson. White powdered face, black-lined hazel eyes, dark lips, and thin ebony hair meet my gaze as if he's ready to go on stage. I miss what his actual name is, I'm so caught up in the likeness, but he gives me a friendly nod in greeting, and it's all I can do not to start whispering *the beautiful people, the beautiful people* to him. I do catch that he's apparently a very well renowned teacher at the Academy, which is the local caster school, but this doesn't surprise me, Marilyn Manson was always hella smart.

"Well, it's a lovely day out, so should we move this into the backyard and get started? The conscripts have a state of the art training facility out there," Elder Cleary explains, already moving to the large sliding glass doors before anyone can answer.

Everyone files out and follows Elder Cleary past the deck, through the professionally cut grass and down into a small stone arena.

"What does it say about you and your coven that you have a gladiator pit in your backyard?" I ask Enoch as we walk side by side behind the group of visitors.

"It says the guys in *300* have nothing on us," he teases and rubs his abs. "Gladiator pits are all the rage now, get with the times."

I chuckle and give him a look that says *yeah, okay* and watch as everyone makes themselves comfortable on the stacked stone seating on one side of the arena. The enclosed ground is some kind of sand mixture. I trudge to the middle, figuring that's where they'll want me, being that I'm today's entertainment. Marilyn Manson casually walks up next to me and faces the elders, dutifully awaiting their instructions. Standing here facing off against this powerful group of casters feels a bit like standing in front of a firing squad. I have no idea what's about to go down and no clue if it will be one of those days where my magic wants to cooperate or be a pain in the ass.

"Alright, Vinna, we're going to go over what we know about your magic based on the report that Reader Tearson submitted. That will give us a starting point. Then Caster Sawyer will take you through several exercises to test your understanding and ability to use your magic," Elder Nypan tells me, his dark eyes and toothy smile friendly.

I nod my understanding but instantly feel nervous about the report Reader Tearson submitted. Could he have lied to me about keeping the knowledge of my being a Sentinel secret? He seemed so trustworthy and earnest, but what the hell do I know anymore?

"It states here that you carry multiple branches of magic. More specifically that you rank very strong in Offensive, Defensive, and Elemental magic, and strong in Healing magic. It was also noted that you presented some Spell magic, but it was ranked as weak. Is that correct?"

I nod my head and open my mouth to voice my confirmation.

"I thought she was lying when she told us that," Kallan mutters before I can answer Elder Nypan.

The others all trade shocked looks and grumbles before quieting down and staring at me wide-eyed.

"No, Conscript Fyfe, it is true."

"How is that possible? No one has more than two branches of magic, and if they do, it's incredibly rare to rank very strong in both," Pebble throws out.

"Paladin Rock, watch yourself. You are here in a professional capacity, not a personal one," Paladin Ender barks out.

Pebble's posture immediately stiffens and a detached mien shutters over his features.

"Caster Aylin's abilities are unparalleled. She is a lucky find, if not a mysterious one," Elder Albrecht announces, a suspicious bite to his tone, as he flattens nonexistent wrinkles out of the front of his button-down shirt.

I can't help the huff of annoyance that escapes me at the accusation in his eyes. It looks like I've come full circle back to the *threat* bullshit. Marilyn Manson, or Caster Sawyer as he's apparently going by these days, gives me a small knowing smile at my sound of irritation. I shrug my shoulders in a *what can you do* motion, and he chuckles.

"They may think I'm all big scary powerful, but they're

about to find out that I can't do shit with my magic. It doesn't listen to me. It's a very *angsty teenager* and only does what it wants, when it wants," I whisper to Marilyn.

His chuckle grows into a deeper laugh, and his eyes fill with a friendly understanding.

"That's what I'm here for. We'll get it all sorted out today, and you'll be taking over the caster world in no time," he says with a conspiratorial wink from his darkly lined eye.

"Caster Sawyer, you may begin your assessment," Elder Balfour announces.

The low rumbles of other conversations around the elders stop, and all eyes focus in on me and the caster now facing me.

"I know it feels weird to have an audience, but you'll have to try and block them out," Marilyn tells me, his black painted lips lifted in a smile. "Well, Vinna, I'm going to walk you through some visualizations and activities that will help me test your control and command of the power you hold. Now, let's start with how you reach for the different branches of magic you possess. Can you identify the different tones or impressions each branch has inside of you?"

"I've read about all of them before I had my reading; I was trying to figure out what branch I might have..."

"I bet that was confusing," Marilyn says with a snort.

"Yeah, that'd be an understatement. Nothing I felt inside seemed to match what the books said. Now I realize that's probably because I have more than one branch of magic."

Marilyn nods his head in agreement and begins to circle me, looking me over with a critical eye.

"Close your eyes, please, Vinna. Before we can do much as far as the assessment goes, you need to learn how to call each individual branch of magic. I imagine that you aren't having much success at this point with managing your magic because you are feeding your intent with multiple branches of power, not all of which are capable of doing what you ask of them.

I consider his words, and surprisingly, what he's saying makes sense to me. I think back to the times I've tried to use my magic and failed. He's right. When I attempt to do anything outside of using my runes, on purpose, I call on everything in my center and try to force it to do what I want. I close my eyes, and before he can instruct me to, I tap into my source of magic.

"Very good, that's exactly what you need to do," Marilyn tells me, like he's a passenger in my body and can see what I'm doing. "Now that you've given yourself access, let's identify the differences in the branches, starting with Offensive magic. I'm going to list off different ways that Offensive magic users have described their magic, and you tell me which resonates best with yours, okay?"

I nod my head. "Okay."

"Offensive or armament magic is usually the easiest to identify. It feels aggressive, eager, and demanding. Casters usually see it in tones of red or pink. It has a cool feel to it, not icy, but the touch of a cool fall day. It will come willingly when called but can be the hardest to rein in and control."

I visualize the magic in my center, and the image of a squirmy and tangled ball of yarn comes to mind. As I listen to Marilyn describe what I'm looking for, I search through the jumbled cords and find strands that match his descriptions. The Offensive magic in me is magenta, and the deep consuming pink threads have a restless feel to them. There is a soothing coolness that brushes comfortingly through me as I call the magic forward, and I can't help the excitement that flashes through me when the twitchy magenta tendrils listen and come to the forefront.

A staticky buzz flashes haphazardly across my body, and

I know that the magic is lighting up my skin in bolts and streaks.

"Very well done, Vinna. Now, I want you to seize that magic and use it to take away my eyesight."

My eyes jerk open at his request, but I just manage to keep my hold on the magic.

"It's fine. There's no right or wrong way to do this. It's your puzzle to solve and whatever you do will not be permanent," Marilyn reassures me.

I question how smart this is for a second but decide he's the one asking for it, so who cares? I focus in on his charcoal smoky-lined eyes and the rich hazel color of his irises. I picture them clouded over with a white film that keeps all light from penetrating the pupil. I show the magic in my grasp what I want it to do, and when it gets restless, I release it and watch, stunned as Marilyn's eyes are hazel one moment and white and unseeing the next.

"Holy shit, I did it," I say, completely surprised.

Instead of freaking out like I would expect, Marilyn smiles and claps his hands, praising me.

"Excellent! Now, feel for the traces of your magic that are now a part of me because of what you just cast. When you find it, call it back to you, and your casting will lift."

Slowly I work through his instructions and figure out how to do what he's explained. His unseeing white eyes deepen until they're brown again. I pat the deep pink magic that's once again in my grasp and then wrestle it back into my center with the rest. Marilyn Manson gives me a proud smile, and I can't help it when my own mirrors it. Bring on the magic lessons!

7
———

Marilyn Manson and I spend three more hours identifying my different branches of magic and getting them to cooperate when called. My Defensive magic, which is orange and feels warmly protective, comes as easily as my Offensive magic came. My Healing magic, which is a soft teal, is harder to find and hold onto in the tangled ball of magical tendrils at my center. The fact that my Healing magic is such a pain in the ass surprises me. It seemed to cooperate easily when I called on it in the cellar with Nash and the others as we were planning our escape from the lamia. Right now, the magic feels thick, but it slips out of my fingers so nimbly and quickly that I know I have my work seriously cut out to master it.

However, the award for the most stubborn branch of magic currently goes to my Elemental magic. It is by far the hardest to coax into cooperation. It's a lovely Kelly green that reminds me of plants in the forest after a rainstorm. But it acts more like a sneaky leprechaun, teasing and dashing away just when I think I have a grasp on it.

"Hold it! Picture the magic wrapped around your fist and keep it right where you want it!" Marilyn excitedly explains. "It will get easier as you practice, but Elemental magic is wild and has always been trickier to master for its users. Now, try again to reach out for the moisture in the air, and use it to form a ball of water."

I attempt a water ball for the fourth time, but I can't seem to hold the wiggly strand and keep it from escaping while focusing enough on what I want it to do. I open my eyes, exasperated.

"It's not working. I can't weave my intent and the magic together fast enough. It doesn't seem to want to make a water ball," I confess, trying not to be too distracted by my audience and their restless fidgeting. They've got to be bored out of their minds, and I'm sure their asses hurt from sitting on the stone seats. That thought actually makes me feel better, and I hope all of their butts stay numb and asleep for the rest of the day.

"What does it want to do?" Marilyn asks me.

I focus on the restless green magic inside of me, and instead of trying to force it to do what I'm being told to do, I feel for where it seems to want to go. An image of Aydin making fireballs pops into my head, and the next thing I know, floating above my palm and warming me is a small ball of flames. I'm not sure what to think of what just happened. I try not to read into the possibility of a deeper meaning behind what I just did.

"What made you call fire instead of water?"

"I don't know. I've seen it done a couple of times before, but I've never been able to do it. It just seemed like what the magic wanted to do," I explain, leaving out any history that might give this little ball of fire more significance than I want it to have.

Marilyn tilts his head to the side and appraises me. His lips purse, and he clicks his tongue absently. He appears to be lost in thought, and I leave him to it while I stare at the baby ball of flames floating above my hand. I sway my palm from side to side and watch the blazing ball follow the movement like an obedient pet. It's fucking thrilling to have so much control over something so destructive.

Out of nowhere, a heavy and painful pressure seizes me, and my little ball of fire blinks out. The force attacking me is strong and ruthless, and I try to work through the panic to figure out what I did wrong. My magic is going haywire, but I'm too confused to figure out how I should direct it. *What the fuck is happening?* As that question takes over my brain, I realize that I'm not the one doing this. I can't explain how, but I know this is the result of Offensive magic, and it's not mine.

The attacking magic constricts viciously around me, keeping me from moving, and it begins to tighten around my neck. I try not to panic as the pressure cuts off my airway, and my feet leave the ground as I'm slowly lifted in the air and strangled.

It's like an invisible giant is holding me by the throat and languidly lifting me up to eye level so it can watch me die. An image of Laiken flashes in my mind, but I refuse to focus too much on why she's here in this moment. The pressure around my throat is pulverizing, and the shouts going on around me fade to nothing as a loud ringing starts in my ears. I can't reach for any of my weapons, which is my first instinct, and I know if I don't figure something out soon, whatever this is, is going to end me.

I use all my magic to feel for the magic that's strangling me. My Offensive magic seems to resonate with what's wrapped around my body and throat, so I call it forward and follow its lead. My magic seems to latch onto a strange hum, but I can't think much on it as black spots form in my line of sight. The hum grows more pronounced, and before I can register what happens, my magic flashes off somewhere, and with it goes a huge surge of power from me.

My Offensive magic connects with something, and as soon as it does, the crushing force around me pops like a bubble and dissipates. I'm at least five feet in the air, and I drop like a sack of potatoes to the sand-covered ground of the arena. I cough and sputter and work to fill my lungs as I blink away the water in my eyes and grasp my neck to protect it from any further attack.

The whole time, I keep a stranglehold on my magic, and I can feel it now doing the constricting around whoever attacked me. The ringing in my ears dulls, and I look around to see the blue sheen of a barrier surrounding the inside of the arena. Enoch and the others are pounding on it helplessly, their faces a mixture of worry and fury as they hurl different colored balls unsuccessfully at the rippling magic surface. The elders seem to be locked in a heated argument, none of them making any effort to get to me.

I scan the inside of the erected barrier for whoever attacked me, and I still when I see the face of my attacker now floating in the air. Marilyn Manson is now five feet off the ground and turning purple. *This fucker attacked me, but why?*

Stunned at the realization that he's the one who just tried to kill me, I feel my hold on my magic slip, and Marilyn tumbles to the ground exactly like I just did. I call on the runes on my ribs, and two short swords appear in my hands. I get up off the ground and stalk toward the coughing and wheezing instructor from hell.

"Get up, you piece of shit!" I demand, my voice scratchy and painful from the damage this fucker just did to my neck.

He looks up at me pleading, he holds his throat with one hand and lifts the other palm up to beg for mercy. He tries to say something, but I touch the tip of my short sword just under his chin, not interested in his defense or excuses.

"Who told you to kill me? And don't think for one second I'll believe this was all your idea."

He shakes his head frantically, cutting himself on the tip of my blade, as he tries to croak out a response. Someone comes at me from the side and tackles me to the ground. Their arms are wrapped around my waist as they try to force me down, and I immediately start pummeling their head with the pommel of one of my short swords as we fall. I release the magic in my weapons before I crash to the sand, and I roll and flip the large body off of me. I kip-up onto my feet and watch as Pebble scrambles up onto his. *Bring it, you backstabbing bastard.* We start circling each other predatorily, and Pebble runs at me again.

He clearly thinks that his size and brute force are going to win this fight. But it works in my favor that this prick doesn't listen to Enoch and Kallan's previous warnings. I run at him, mirroring his charge. We slam into each other, and I bend backwards to help absorb the force and to control the fall. He's bigger and heavier than me, so I tap into my runes for extra strength and maneuver him up and over me, flipping him so he lands hard on his back. It knocks the wind out of him, and judging by the way his head bounces off the ground, I'd bet he's seeing stars too.

I roll from my back to my chest and scramble to straddle his torso so I can rain blows down on his face. All the rage I feel over being attacked by my instructor and now my supposed guard, boils inside of me, and there's not an ounce of mercy as I beat on Pebble. His skin is purpling, and he's bleeding from his nose, mouth, and a cut to his eyebrow, but my bloodlust demands more. I'm pulled off of him roughly by whoever it is shouting at me, but I don't bother to decipher what they're saying. I am in full beatdown mode, and right now I want everyone to hurt.

I call on a small throwing knife and brutally slam it into whoever is behind me trying to restrain me. Fuck anyone who wants to get in my way. A pained yelp sounds in my ear, and their grip on my torso loosens. I try to twist around so I can take them on when Enoch's voice breaks through my rage-drenched thoughts.

"Vinna, *stop!* You have to stop. It's not what you think. He was just trying to keep you from killing Sawyer!"

Enoch and the others are ten feet away from me, and their eyes bounce from Pebble on the ground, to whoever is behind me, and then back to me.

"You're safe, Vinna. It's over. No one is going to hurt you anymore."

Enoch steps forward from the group but stops after he takes a couple of steps closer to me. It's clear he wants me to focus on him but also to understand that he's not a threat to me. I watch him carefully. No one else approaches, and Enoch never tries to push contact. Somehow, he knows he needs to give me space to evaluate, to settle. His gray-blue eyes are steady and calm, and they help tether me to reality.

Pebble is black and blue, bleeding, and unconscious on the ground. The elders have circled around Marilyn Manson, and Elder Nypan's ebony hands are on him, healing him. I release a small growl of frustration because I want to get to Marilyn. I want to make him bleed and hurt as much as Pebble currently is.

I look around, trying to spot an opening or any more threats, and discover that it's Paladin Ender sitting up on the ground behind me. He's trying to remove my knife from his shoulder, but every time he grabs for it, his hand passes through the magical weapon. I release my hold on the magic, and the knife disappears, leaving a bleeding wound behind. He gasps and looks up at me.

"I can't remember the last time I was taken by surprise. That's quite an ability you have there. Are small daggers and swords the only weapons you can summon?" The paladin leader asks me, interest and respect bleeding through his tone and questioning gaze. He reminds me a bit of Aydin, and I shove that memory away.

I'm a little taken aback by the paladin leader's odd reaction to getting stabbed. He doesn't even seem a little annoyed by it. Then again, maybe he's used to it. I doubt you get to a position like the one he holds from playing it safe. Judging by the mapwork of scars scattered across his visible skin, *used to it* might be a massive understatement. He continues to stare at me, waiting for me to respond to his question.

"No," I croak, swallowing down the pain from the damage to my throat.

I don't answer his question in a friendly exchange of information or an effort at comradery. It's a clear warning, and he gives me a nod that tells me he understands. Movement in my periphery sets me on edge, but when I realize it's just Nash moving toward Paladin Ender, I relax again. Nash's eyes flit back and forth between his leader and me in some kind of silent debate before he finally focuses in on the head of the paladin.

"May I, sir?" he offers, reaching his hands toward the oozing wound on the older man's shoulder.

Paladin Ender nods, and Nash knits his tan skin back together in less than a minute. The fit, white-haired man rolls his shoulder a couple of times and, finding no issues, gives an appreciative nod to Nash. Nash moves toward me, and I flinch and automatically step back.

"It's okay, Vinna. He's just going to heal you," Elder Cleary tells me.

He speaks to me like I'm too stupid to understand what's going on. His condescending tone chases away any calm Enoch's efforts created, and I round on the elder.

"Fuck you. If you think I'm going to let any of you come near after what just happened..."

My voice is gritty but strong. I know I need healing, but there's not a chance in hell I'm going to let any of these assholes near me. Fool me once, shame on you; fool me twice, shame on me. In a mask of casual movement, I brush over the runes on my ring finger and hope the guys can get here soon. If the fucking elders think I pin this attack solely on Marilyn Manson, then they're bigger idiots than I thought.

"Vinna, please. There was no other way to know for sure. Putting you in a threatening situation was the best way to trigger what I suspected," Marilyn Manson pleads as he tries to bypass the circle of elders surrounding him and approach me. Part of me hopes they'll let him through so I can have a clear shot at trying to rip his head off his body.

"And did you acquire the answers you sought?" Elder Kowka asks the caster.

"Yes. She's without a doubt a mimic."

"What the hell is that?" Enoch shouts as he moves to stand near me.

I back away from him, and I don't miss the flash of frustrated resignation in his eyes before he turns a narrowed gaze on his father.

"I've seen the use of weaker mimicry amongst rare casters, but nothing on this level, not outside of books and not for centuries," Marilyn responds enthusiastically.

I could probably sink a throwing knife in his throat right now, but quick is not how I want this piece of shit to die.

Marilyn Manson continues with his explanation, completely unfazed by my rage. "A mimic has a very rare ability to see or feel *any* kind of magic and then replicate it. Reader Tearson mentioned that she had underdeveloped Spell magic. But I would venture if Vinna worked on it with an experienced caster, she would be able to mimic their abilities and absorb a stronger affinity for that branch too."

"So, trying to kill me answered your question how?" I seethe.

"I wasn't trying to kill you. I was trying to see if you could replicate the level of magic that was being used against you."

"You could have just asked me, you fucking psycho. I would have told you that I can see things and then do them. It's not a trade secret or something I'd take to the grave. But again, you would know that if you fucking *asked* me." I point to Marilyn. "You better watch yourself. If you ever come near me again, you're not going to like what happens, and you better pray I never catch you alone."

He looks instantly regretful, but he'll learn the meaning of regret if he doesn't take my warning seriously.

"Caster Sawyer is who we selected to tutor you," Elder Balfour announces, wiping sweat from his partially bald head like somehow his statement should erase everything they just allowed to happen.

"Yeah, try again because that isn't happening."

"You have no reason to fear. You weren't in any real danger, and you can rest assured that you are safe," Elder Balfour continues, oblivious and condescending.

Without warning, I send a surge of Offensive magic out at Elder Balfour. I lace the magic with the same cast that Marilyn Manson just used on me. Elder Balfour starts to sputter, and then all sound is cut off as he begins to turn red. His arms are pinned to his side, and his fingers claw uselessly at his thighs. Elder Albrecht is the only one who reacts right away, and he throws something maroon and flashing at me. My shields burst open when the magic makes contact, and it fizzles out harmlessly. I let go of the magic choking Elder Balfour, and he immediately bends over wheezing and trying to fill his lungs again.

"How dare you attack an elder, you insolent little shit. I could have you put to death for that!" Elder Balfour spits out between wheezing coughs.

"What? You're telling me that you didn't feel safe in that moment?" I tut condescendingly, my tone mirroring the one Elder Balfour was previously speaking to me with. *Arrogant prick.* "I can assure you that you weren't in any danger and are perfectly safe."

He glares murderously at me, but his wrath is quickly refocused when Elder Nypan starts to laugh.

"She has a point there, Phillip," he tells Elder Balfour before turning back to me. "You can trust us, Vinna. We are your elders after all."

"And exactly what is it that you think you've done to earn my trust? You've moved me around like a game piece with no consideration for how I'd feel about it or what I'd want. You look at me like an experiment you're not sure is going wrong or right, and you just sat by and watched someone *you* brought here attack me."

"We didn't know that's what was going to happen," Elder Cleary jumps in to defend.

"Oh, come the fuck on. You think I'm too stupid to notice when you're talking to each other in your heads?" I glare at each of the elders in turn. "I caught every time he communicated with you mentally over the last three hours, and that's exactly what he was doing before he tried to choke me to death. For a culture that claims to revere females, you sure do have a fucked up way of showing it!"

I catch the faint sound of gravel crunching under tires. My gaze sweeps my surroundings quickly to gauge how difficult it will be to get the fuck out of here. Pebble is still lying unconscious on the ground, and the thought that someone should really check on him runs through my head. The elders are clearly having another mental conversation, and Nash, Kallan, Becket, and Enoch are gathered about five feet away from me. Paladin Ender catches my calculated assessment and gives me a small smile, mouthing the word *go* to me.

I don't question his instructions or hesitate for even a second. I take off and sprint toward the house, ignoring the commotion it causes behind me. I run my finger over the runes on my head, behind my ear.

"Make room for me and be ready to speed the fuck away from here."

I race through the house to the front door and fly out, not bothering to close it. Ryker's white SUV sits idling, and the back door is open and waiting. I jump in and find myself instantly pulled onto Bastien's lap. The door slams behind me, and the car peels out of the circular driveway back toward the gate.

I wrap my arms around his neck and snuggle into him, immediately feeling more relaxed than I have in the past twenty-four hours.

"I fucking missed you guys."

8

I fit myself against Bastien's neck and breathe him in. Peace and safety dull the panic and anger simmering inside of me, now that I'm surrounded by all of them. Sabin and Valen offer comforting caresses to my legs, and Bastien brushes stray strands of hair from my messy bun away from my face. His hand stills, and I know he's just spotted the damage to my neck that Marilyn's magic left behind.

"What the fuck, Bruiser? Who did this to you?"

Bastien lightly pushes against my shoulders, dislodging me from my current snuggling position and looks me over. Valen runs a gentle finger down my neck, and I catch a deep yellow crackle of magic rush across his forearm. It's the first time I've ever seen any of them lose control of their magic. I stare at it, shocked. He takes deep, measured breaths, and his leaking magic stops.

"Ryker, pull over when we're clear and it's safe. She needs you," Valen announces, his thumb grazing my cheek tenderly.

I don't look for Ryker's eyes in the rearview mirror, but I can sense them on me. The weight of his stare and the close proximity of all of them makes me feel lighter in a way I haven't felt since I watched the paladin force them away from me. I twirl a strand of Bastien's hair around my finger, liking that it's down and accessible. I stare at the rich cocoa-colored strands wrapped around my finger and release a resigned sigh.

"The elders came to test my magic today."

I find Sabin's green eyes, and the hard look he's wearing softens when our gazes meet.

"It was going great at first. They brought this teacher from the Academy, and he really helped me understand how to separate the different branches of magic in order to recognize them. A couple of hours into the testing, I was able to do things I couldn't before. I was finally starting to figure out how my magic worked, and it was incredible. It was the first time I didn't feel like some kind of failure or magic flunky. Then, the instructor attacked me."

Valen pulls me from Bastien's lap onto his own. He runs the palms of his hands up my arms, and Sabin and Bastien twine their fingers in each of my hands.

"I don't care if they're our elders. This is bullshit. They yank her from Lachlan's house because she's unsafe, and then they allow this to happen to her!" Knox growls from the front seat.

Tension wafts from all of them, and somehow it allows me to let go of some of my own; I purge it on a long exhale.

"Well, I stabbed Paladin Ender, told the elders to fuck off, and magically strangled one of them to prove a point."

The car falls into silence, the hum of the tires on the pavement the only sound brave enough to fill the car. Sabin, of all people, breaks the uncertain quiet when he starts to laugh. Slowly laughter fills the car as the other guys join in, and before I know it, everyone is howling. I don't personally think it's as funny as they clearly do, but their mirth is undeniably contagious, and a couple of wayward chuckles make their way out of my mouth.

"By the stars, Bruiser, the craziest shit happens around you! What did Paladin Ender do when you stabbed him?" Bastien asks, his hazel eyes filled with humor, and the corner of his lips tip up in a smile.

"Surprisingly, he seemed more impressed than mad. He helped clear the way for this little getaway here, so I don't think he's harboring any resentment. I doubt Elder Balfour will be so forgiving though. I'm pretty sure I'm now on his shit list."

"Is that who you strangled?" Sabin asks me, and I nod.

"You didn't do anything that most of us haven't been dreaming about for years. He's a prick," Knox admits and starts to crack up again. "I just wish I could've been there to see his face when he learned not to fuck with our girl."

The car slows, and Ryker pulls off onto a barely visible dirt road. Everyone in the car starts to bounce and sway as we make our way down a pitted uneven path. He drives through a small clearing and stops next to a cluster of trees. As soon as I climb out of the back seat, Ryker grabs me and starts running his hands and sky-blue eyes all over me, assessing my injuries. He presses his hands against my neck, and they heat up as his magic begins to drive away the pain and the damage.

When he's done, he places gentle kisses everywhere there was a bruise, and I close my eyes and lean into him.

"I missed you, Squeaks," he whispers against my ear.

His breath against my skin makes me shiver, and I wrap my arms around his waist, pulling him tighter into me. A caress moves across my shoulder, and I look over to find Knox, his gaze filled with concern.

"Are you okay?"

He steps closer to me, and I look up into his deep gray eyes. I slowly shake my head *no*.

"It was awful. One minute we were all together, and the next they're shoving you roughly out the door. What do we do if they deny your claim? I'm pretty sure they are pushing for something between me and Enoch's coven. Although, who knows what's going to happen now that I've attacked one of them and gone AWOL. Fuck, are they going to try and bind my magic?"

Knox wraps me up in a tight hug and holds me that way for a couple of minutes. My panic slowly subsides, chased away by the reassuring contact. When he pulls back, he cups my face and leans in to give me a sweet kiss. His lips pull away from mine, and I find myself tilting toward him, not wanting the kiss to end. His chest rumbles against mine with amusement.

"Killer, do you really think any of us would let that happen?"

I'm pulled away from him and wrapped up in another set of strong arms. Each of my Chosen takes their turn to hold me, all of us needing the physical reminder that we're okay and together. I feel instantly comforted and protected and, once again, so grateful that in all this mess, I at least have them.

Knox's statement echoes in my head, but I'm struggling to find the comfort that I know he's trying to provide. What if they can't stop the elders from doing what they want? We're all just being tossed around at other people's whims and going with the fucked up flow of that, but when does it stop? At what point do we draw a line in the sand and say, *no more*?

I brush off the niggling concern and instead focus on everything we need to sort out so that we can be together. A place to live, where we're all safe and free, seems to be the biggest obstacle. I try to picture what it would be like to have a place of our own, but I don't let my mind wander too much into that daydream. Reality is, I won't be able to have any of that until I can get free of the elders' claim.

How am I going to survive three years until my awakening? Three more years of restrictions, rules, and being manipulated into staying away from my Chosen. I'm struggling to accept another three days without doing the things to them I want to do. I'm aware that my sudden urgency for deeper physical connection is an undeniable side effect of their bodies currently being pressed up against mine as we console and reassure each other. Just their presence all around me is making me rethink the whole group sex caveat I mentioned before.

Down, girl! This is not the time or the place for that shit!

I have to stop myself from scoping out our surroundings in search of a good place to lie down and encourage things to go further. Their call to me has always been strong, but after I marked them, there seems to be an extra dose of urgent desire. If it weren't for all the crazy shit that always seems to be happening around me, I would be pushing *much* harder to introduce their body parts to mine.

"Vinna, I know it probably seems even harder to accept after what just happened, but it's going to be okay. We have every right to submit a claim, and the elders should take that seriously. But if, for whatever reason, they decide to fuck around, we'll just move on to plan B," Valen tells me, his smile sweet and his words confident.

"What's plan B?"

"We run. Just until you have your awakening. After that, there's nothing they can really do to force you into anything you don't want," Sabin explains.

I run my hands over my face in exhausted frustration. "Fuck."

Valen kisses the top of my head. "I don't think it will come to that. But I don't want you to think that we're not considering our options, too."

"But how is that even an option? You guys have your last year as conscripts starting in two weeks. You can't just walk out on that. You've been working most of your lives to be paladin."

"None of us are saying that would be an easy choice to make, but we've all talked about it, and if it comes to that, then it comes to that," Ryker states, giving me a small smile.

I look at each of them in turn. The twins have their wavy dark-chocolate hair down today, and it frames their full lips and sable-lashed hazel eyes. Ryker's smile is sweet, caring, and it makes his bright-sunny-day-blue eyes all the more beautiful. Knox stands like the Sentinel he'll soon become. His tall, chiseled body ready for anything and his rainstorm-gray eyes radiating his happy-go-lucky attitude. And Sabin, tattoos climbing up one arm, perfectly styled hair, and forest-green eyes that are the windows to an old soul with a tender heart, looks at me warmly. There's no doubt or hesitancy in any of their eyes. I only find acceptance and calm resolve.

"I don't know if I'm worth this. I don't say that because I'm fishing for reassurance or an ego boost, but I don't know if you guys are really thinking this through. I mean, just look what I've done to your family already." I look at the twins. "I've destroyed everything you grew up having in just over a month. If we ever bind together, I'm basically handing over a death sentence. My world is fucked up, and that's what's going to happen to your world, too, if we all stay together. You can see it happening already; the power plays from the casters, the attacks from the lamia. I'm condemning all of you to that, forever!"

"Vinna, stop. Right now, stop." Sabin steps up to me, and

Valen moves over to make room for him. "You didn't ruin or destroy anything. Lachlan and his coven, they did that. They fucked everything up for their own selfish, deluded reasons. That wasn't you. You have no control over the actions and choices that other people make, for good or for bad."

Sabin's forest-green eyes are imploring. They plead with me to see the world the way he does, but I don't know if I can.

"I killed Talon, Sabin. If it weren't for me, my mom, dad, Bastien and Valen's mom and dad, their whole coven, Talon and who the fuck knows how many others would be alive."

Sabin snorts, and the odd reaction makes me pause.

"Well, now you're just getting a bit full of yourself there, Vinna. I knew you thought pretty highly of yourself before, and rightfully so. I mean we all think the sun and moon rise and set with you. But this god complex you've got going! Whew, it's impressive. And to think, you once accused me of having a big ego. Well, now I can chalk that up to projection."

Sabin's features stay serious, but he gets the slightest twinkle in his eyes. An amused scoff escapes me, and I shake my head at him. He laces his fingers behind my neck and pulls me ever so close to him, his lips just barely out of reach unless I stand on my tiptoes.

"Fucked up shit happens. It's not your fault or your responsibility. You can only take credit for your own thoughts and actions. You have no right to try and claim anybody else's." He gestures to the others. "You can claim us, because we give ourselves freely, but our thoughts and our actions are still our own, just like yours are."

His eyebrows rise, and the question in his gaze is clear. I nod my head in understanding and let what he just said soak into me.

"Now, if you ever try to convince us again that you're not

worth it, there's going to be trouble. So remember that the next time things fall to shit, and they will, because that's life. And all of us are more than okay with that."

Sabin leans into me and claims my mouth. His kiss is demanding and intense and everything I need right now. His lips tell me things my soul can only understand from this kind of communication. All the words in the world about acceptance, desire, and belonging fall short of the way Sabin's lips communicate those sentiments to mine. It's in the flick and twine of his tongue against mine, the way he gives and takes what we both need. He consumes me and allows himself to be consumed, and it's a kiss I never want to end or forget. It's the moment that my doubts about where I stand with Sabin, or how to move forward, burn away to nothing.

9

Our kiss slows, but neither of us seems in a hurry to put a stop to the makeout session that's currently going on out here in the middle of the woods, in front of the rest of the guys. We languidly pull apart, and Sabin's eyes dart back and forth between mine. He finds whatever he's looking for and gives a slight nod before unlacing his hands from behind my neck and stepping back.

This whole showing affection in front of each other thing is still fairly new. So I'm not really sure what to expect when Sabin steps out of my immediate line of sight, and I can once again see the others. None of them look like what just happened was too big of a deal. Smiles and some heated looks stare back at me, and I mentally tear up the *no group sex* rule into tiny little pieces and then set it on fire. I'll have some fun sorting out the logistics of how I want that to work, but I'm confident my dirty mind is up for the task.

"So, uh...what's going on with the house hunt?" I ask, attempting to focus on something else other than the image of all of us naked and fucking over by the grouping of trees to my left. "I hope you guys fired Lucy Barton."

"Yeah, she swore up and down that she didn't say a word to the elders about our looking for a property, but someone in her office did. We hired a new guy this morning, and he's already sent over some options," Ryker tells me, handing me his phone.

I start scrolling through the listings of houses he's pulled up.

"Your Jeep is in the shop. They should be done with it sometime today, so I'll make sure they drop it off to Enoch's house for you," Sabin tells me, with a small sweet smile that does a good job of hiding the dominating, sexy caster I know is lurking just under the surface.

I grumble and throw my head back. "I was really hoping I wouldn't have to go back there," I whine, my chin falling to my chest in frustrated defeat.

Sighs and chuckles sound off at my antics. Bastien flicks his knuckle under my chin playfully, and I lift my eyes up to meet his.

His hazel eyes sparkle with affection, and his eyebrows tilt down over them making his features serious.

"Trust me, we all want you with us. But until we buy a house, bringing you back to Lachlan's is not an option," Bastien reminds me.

"We'd happily get you situated at one of our family's houses, but the elders have anticipated that. Elder Nypan and Elder Albrecht made the rounds and had a chat with all of our home covens. Our families are aware of what's going on, and they are not going to aid or ignore any defiance of the elders' orders," Knox tells me, gesturing to Ryker and Sabin.

Fuck. What must their families think of me, of this whole fucked up situation? I am so used to not having anyone who would care about what I'm up to, that I forget that's not the case with these guys. Silva seemed really laid back and lenient when it came to the twins, but I know Sabin is close with his family. I realize that I never asked Ryker or Knox about their home situation or their families. I seriously suck at this whole relationship thing already.

"I saw Aydin," I announce randomly.

"What the fuck did he want?" Knox grumbles.

"To apologize. Again. He told me that he and Evrin left the coven. Is that true?"

Eyes drop away from mine, and several of them rub their temples or the backs of their necks. I once again feel like shit for my part in showing up and wrecking their happy lives.

"I'm sorry," I whisper.

"Don't, Vinna; you have nothing to be sorry for," Valen tells me sternly.

"This isn't your fault. The way Lachlan has been the past month or so is very different from the caster we grew up with. I mean, we knew that Vaughn's disappearance fucked him up. I know I'd never recover if I lost Valen, but what he's doing with you makes no sense. No one seems to be able to make him understand that. Who knows what his fucking problem is."

Bastien's eyes are filled with so much sorrow and confusion, and I wrap my arms around him, wishing I could somehow chase it all away.

"I think every time he looks at me, all he can see is what he's lost, and not what he could gain. Maybe my being here just opens all his wounds over and over again. I don't know."

Bastien's words about how horrible it would be to lose Valen make me ache. I can't even imagine how devastating that would be. I try to put myself in Lachlan's shoes; what would I do in his place? How would I feel and act? I want to think I wouldn't be mistrustful or cold, but I can't say that with complete certainty. It's a fucked up situation, and unfortunately, there's no getting around it.

Valen trails his hand down my arm and links his fingers with mine. "Things at the house are pretty tense right now. There was a huge blow up when everyone got back after the meeting with the elders. A lot of pretty awful things were said by everyone, and now we're all just quietly trying to avoid each other. Aydin and Evrin moved out. Silva has been keeping to himself, and Lachlan and Keegan seem more determined than ever to figure out what happened to Vaughn and the other paladin," he explains.

"Lachlan now knows everything that we do, from what Talon told you, and he's working on some new potential leads. We're steering clear of him, from all of it. We've been staying at either Sabin's or Knox and Ryker's house until we can find something more permanent," Bastien adds. "See anything you like?"

I look back down to where I'm still clutching Ryker's phone and the listings. "These two are good. They both have nice gyms and big bathtubs."

Sabin starts to laugh. "Did you look at anything else inside of them?"

I shrug. "What? My criteria is shorter than most of yours. I'm the least picky out of all of you guys when it comes to where we live. The one that's brick with ivy growing on the outside is pretty. Honestly, I just want somewhere safe, where we can all be together. I am super ready for some alone time."

I mumble the last part under my breath, but Knox begins to snicker, indicating I wasn't as quiet as I thought I was.

"What is it, sweet Vinna? Are you wanting something you're not getting?" Knox teases with a chuckle as he sidles up to me. He runs the back of his knuckles across my cheek, his chest brushing against mine, and I'm suddenly very aware of every part of me that's deliciously close to every part of him.

Slowly I lick my lips, and then I widen my eyes innocently and blink up at him. "Yes. Sex."

At my response, Sabin starts to choke on nothing, and Knox laughs even harder. Bastien forcefully pats Sabin on the back a couple of times, trying to hide his smile at his friend's reaction. I look at Sabin.

"What? You can kiss me like that in front of all of them, but the word *sex* freaks you out? Captain, you knew this was going to happen at some point."

A small smile sneaks across his face before he hides it. I give Valen's hand a quick squeeze and look at the others in turn.

"I don't want to force anyone to do something they don't want to. It's just, this pull you guys have over me has gotten a hell of a lot stronger since your runes showed up. It's driving me mental. And you're all fucking hot. Like, drool all over myself, my brain no longer works, hot."

They chuckle, but the smile falls from my face as my thoughts grow more serious.

"You all have been amazing. All the shit that's gone down with Lachlan, the lamia, and losing Talon. I've never felt more connected to anyone than I do to you guys. I'm ready. I want you, all of you. If any of you want to take things slower than I do, I respect that. I just want you all to know where I stand."

Valen's grasp slips out from my fingers, and the next thing I know, I'm being swung over someone's shoulder.

"Knox, where are you going?" Valen shouts after us.

"What? She's ready. I'm ready. Carpe diem, fuckers."

I laugh and slap Knox's ass, encouraging him.

"Knox, come back here with our female. You can wait until we have a house and a proper bed."

I press up against Knox's lower back and playfully glare at Sabin. "Captain, mind your own business! To the trees, Knox, I scoped out some soft looking grass earlier."

Knox chuckles but then starts grumbling to himself. *Fucking hell.* It looks like Sabin's admonishment hit its mark. After another minute, he huffs and changes direction, heading back toward the guys.

"Knox, the grass is that way." I point behind him and pull on the back of his shirt as if I can direct him like I would Darcy with reins.

"The Captain's right, you deserve a bed for your first time," Knox grudgingly admits. "But after that, Killer, it's an anytime, anywhere free for all. You got me?"

I clench my thighs and stifle the moan that wants to sneak past my lips. Fuck yeah, I am definitely on board for that!

10

Enoch's house sits dark and ominous as I approach the front door. I hesitate as I reach for the black door knob, my hand dropping to my side. I take a step back and stare at the darkened entrance, like somehow my glare will change what sits on the other side. I hear the shuffle of faint footsteps on the other side of the oversized wooden door, and I'm surprised that anyone is up this late.

I purposely stayed out as late as possible, hoping to avoid anyone who might be waiting here for me. Images of the elders pouncing on me as soon as I set foot back inside this house and binding my magic have played in my head from the moment Ryker navigated his car in this direction.

I watch as the oversized door swings open quietly, revealing Enoch on the other side. I can't read the expression on his face, and he says nothing as he takes me in. Our eyes meet, and I see relief and frustration swimming in them. His eyes soften when he looks over my neck, but that disappears as he watches the red tail lights of Ryker's car disappear through the gates of his property.

The air between us is heavy with concern, and a part of me feels bad that I caused it, while another part doesn't want to care. We stare at each other silently for what feels like forever before I step through the threshold and walk past him. I go still when I find the rest of Enoch's coven sitting stoically in the living room, clearly waiting for me. Fuck. There goes my plan for sneaking in and trying to avoid everyone until I can get the hell out of this house.

I spot Pebble in an armchair. He's conscious and injury-free. I try to discern how he's feeling about me, my arrival, and the fact that I almost ended his existence today. His face is expressionless, but his eyes spark with some unidentifiable emotion as he runs them down and back up my body. I stand and wait for someone to break the silence. Enoch passes me and steps down into the living room, reclaiming his place on the couch.

"You okay?" Nash asks, his eyes scanning my neck for injuries.

"Ryker healed me."

Becket snorts and shakes his head. "We figured that's where you ran off to."

I want so badly to ask what happened with the elders after I left, but I bite down on my tongue and swallow all the questions sitting on it.

"Caster Sawyer, Elder Balfour, and Paladin Ender are all okay, in case you were wondering," Pebble tells me, his hands tightening as they grip the arms of the chair he's sitting in.

"I wasn't," I respond, my body language automatically tensing up to mirror Pebble's.

I can't get a read on what he wants to do right now, but I can tell he's itching to do something. My magic slowly starts to extend itself from my center into my limbs, responding to the potential threat. I zero in on Pebble, reading every twitch and tightening of his body and features.

"So today was a clusterfuck of epic proportions," Kallan announces.

Chuckles sound off around the room, and a smile slowly stretches across Pebble's face. He looks over at Kallan, losing our staring contest, and it allows me to relax a little.

"Paladin Ender does have a lovely way with words, doesn't he?" Nash admits, an amused smile fixed on his face, but it's not lost on me that there's no amusement evident in his eyes. "Those were his exact words when everyone stopped fighting after you ran off. Well, that and...what else did he say, Pebble?"

Everyone turns to Pebble who rolls his eyes and snickers. "I believe it was something along the lines of, 'Well done —pissing off the strongest caster we've seen in centuries.'"

I don't know if I want to laugh or groan at what Paladin Ender said. It's nice to know he stood up for me, but I'm pretty confident that's not going to be seen as a good thing in the elders' eyes. Then again, I was doing a pretty good job all on my own of convincing them I was the threat Lachlan thought I was. I doubt the *they started it first* argument is going to carry much weight with them, regardless of how true it is.

"For what it's worth, the elders were incredibly sorry that things ended the way that they did. Caster Sawyer was distraught that you didn't want to work with him anymore," Enoch states.

I snort at his declaration and narrow my eyes at him. "Do you think that matters at all to me? They're sorry? For which part? Sorry they let someone *they* brought here attack me? Sorry they got caught lying about it? Or sorry that there's no chance I will do anything they want, now or in the future?"

"Vinna, it's not like that," Becket insists. "They really are just trying to do what's best for you."

"Thank you for your propaganda, oops, I mean opinion. But how is any of this *what's best for me*?" I gesture wildly at them, at their house, at the world in general. "I've been threatened, dictated to, attacked, and moved around, all without consultation or consideration. What's best for me isn't even a fucking afterthought at this point."

"Who threatened you?" Enoch questions, moving to the edge of his seat like he's getting ready to take action against anyone I name.

"Lachlan for starters. I was told if I didn't come here willingly, the elders would bind my magic and force me to cooperate."

Enoch scoffs and shakes his head, a look of disgust on his face.

"Don't go getting all high and mighty, Enoch. Your dad and the other elders have taken away my decisions just like Lachlan did."

Becket opens his mouth to argue, but I cut him off.

"Is everyone here just going to pretend that the elders didn't give their permission to attack me with magic today? How can you still buy the *casters care about females more than anything else* line after witnessing what happened today? Nothing I have seen here so far has convinced me that females are anything but a fucking commodity to be traded, cashed in, and destroyed when convenient."

I shake my head in disgust. These guys have sat in a position of power in this community because of who their fathers are and who they're connected to. How do they not see the truth? I can tell by the looks on their faces that they still honestly believe the elders have pure motivations and intentions. My gaze flits between all of them.

"They *let* that instructor strangle me."

I shudder at the memory and take a moment to compose myself.

"I watched each of you try to break through the barrier that was erected to get to me. But did any of you see what the elders were doing?"

"They were arguing about what to do," Pebble offers.

"Arguing. But which one of them lifted a finger to stop what was happening?"

Pebble's eyes drop from mine.

"Who erected the barrier? Was it Caster Sawyer, or was it one of them? Did you bother to ask, to connect the pieces, or is it normal to swallow the bullshit they feed you without question, and then ask for more?"

Becket scoffs. "If *my father* said what Caster Sawyer did was the only way to confirm your ability, then I believe him. I'm aware that you have issues with your uncle, but not all casters are like him, Vinna. You can trust the elders; you can trust us."

"Like the shifters trusted you that day at the cliffs, when each of you stood by and watched your friends bully them?"

"We can't go around policing everyone. Shifters have their own rules and ways. We can't step in when their own should be," Kallan tells me.

"I thought you guys were Paladin Conscripts? Isn't that in your job description, to police and protect, or does that only apply to your own kind?"

Becket scoots to the end of his seat, frustration coloring his features. "We aren't paladin yet, and we don't have free rein to do whatever we want. We follow the rules, just like everyone else! Well, maybe not you, since you seem to have no loyalty or respect for anyone."

I tighten my fists and fight not to take his bait. "I give respect where it's earned."

"Then you should give others a chance to earn it instead of writing them off at your earliest convenience. I'm sorry you were hurt. Everyone else felt just as bad. Give them a chance to show you that they're looking out for you. That they just might know what's best."

I narrow my eyes at Becket. How can he think that the elders or anyone else knows what's best for me when they don't even know me?

"My little sister was murdered that way," I tell him, my voice even, emotionless.

He was prepared for an argument, but I watch as the fight leaks out of Becket, like a sieve, at my words. His face fills with shock.

"She was thirteen when some fucking piece of shit wrapped his hands around her neck and stole her life. Should I write the elders and Caster Sawyer a thank you note for giving me a clear picture of what Laiken experienced before she died?" I shake my head and look away from Becket and the others, focusing on everything and nothing outside of the dark window. "But hey, I guess what happened was what's best for me, right? I should just figure out how to trust others, who know nothing about me, to make my decisions."

No one says anything. I turn and walk out of the living room, making my way down the hallway. I leave my rhetorical questions to float awkwardly amongst them in the living room. I'm too tired to continue this pointless conversation. I shut myself into my assigned room, pull off my pants, and climb into the bed, where sleep seizes me like a thief, stealing me away from my troubled and unsettling thoughts and memories.

11

My head feels heavy, and I groan as I lift it up off my chest. The cool air hits me, bringing with it the stale smell of mildew. I open my eyes and freeze. I'm in the same cellar I just escaped from. What the fuck is going on? I call on my throwing knives, but the familiar warmth and flow of magic is absent from my limbs. I try again. Nothing. I reach into the bright place that's always existed inside of me, wondering why my magic isn't answering my call. But it's like a dying star sits ashen and crumbling inside my chest.

Panic tries to take hold of me, but I fight it for control.

"Little Warrior."

Talon's voice brushes past my ear from behind, and I go still. I close my eyes and try to lock down the pain that surfaces inside of me. A sob escapes me, despite my efforts to keep it locked inside my chest.

"Little Warrior, what are you doing here? I told you it's not safe."

Talon's voice darts from one side of me to the other, and I frantically search for him behind me. The tears that are dripping down my cheeks are flung around me as I jerk my head from side to side in an effort to catch a glimpse of him. He's a flash behind me, never stopping long enough for me to take in his features. To see him. I growl out my frustration and struggle against my restraints.

My desperation shatters me, and I lose it. I thrash and scream with my efforts. I ignore any need to escape. I just need to see him. Urgency races through my veins, and it keeps me from focusing on anything aside from my need to find Talon's face. Nothing I do brings him into focus. No amount of begging holds him still long enough for me to see that he's alright. Slowly my energy drains, and eventually, my chin falls to my chest in defeat. I shake with the sobs that wrack my body, and I pant as I try to wade through the desolation and fill my lungs with air.

"Vinna, don't cry," a small, melodious voice tells me. A voice I haven't heard in almost eight years. Laiken? With that thought, goosebumps rise on every inch of my skin.

"Laiken?" I ask out loud, my voice shaky.

"Vinna, you can't cry. Vinna? Vinna, can you hear me?"

Her fragile voice grows more panicked with each unanswered question.

"Laiken! Where are you?" I shout helplessly.

I can't get out of my restraints. I can't see anything except the gray concrete walls of this room. I can't do anything. Why can't I fucking do anything?

"Vinna, you can't cry. You have to run. Do you hear me? Run!"

Laiken's blood-curdling scream echoes in my ears as I fling myself off the bed. I smash into the corner of the room, my back against the *V* where the walls connect. My sudden movement scares whoever was just standing over me, and they whirl to track me, keeping me in their sights. A ball of magenta magic grows between my palms before I even realize that I've conjured it. The pink light of my magic emits a soft glow which highlights Enoch's face, his features set in a worried frown.

A noise draws my attention to the doorway, where the rest of his coven and Pebble stand, looking tired and equally concerned.

"Are you okay?" Enoch asks, pulling my attention back to him.

I stare at him blankly, confused.

"You sounded like you were hurt. We came to check on you, but I couldn't get you to wake up. You were screaming and crying." He points to my face, and I swipe at the tear tracks there. "What happened?" he asks as he takes a tentative step toward me.

I try to process what he just said. My heavy breathing and pounding heart make it difficult to focus on much other than the adrenaline coursing through my veins. I scan the room, not able to stop myself from looking for Talon and Laiken, even though I'm starting to connect that none of it was real. *It was a dream*, I realize as the last of the drowsy confusion leaves me.

"I must have been having a nightmare," I croak out; my voice is deeper and heavy with sleep.

I'm not sure what to do or think about that. I've never been prone to nightmares before, not even when I was younger and stuck with Beth and her torture sessions. Sleep was always a safe place. Always an escape.

Kallan steps hesitantly into the room. "Do you want to talk about it?"

He leans back against the wall next to the head of the bed, his hands anchored against the plaster just behind his lower back.

"Why?" I ask, suspicion lacing my tone.

"Sometimes it helps to work through whatever is bothering you," Nash offers.

He follows Kallan's lead and steps into the room as well. He leans against the wall opposite me and crosses his arms over his chest. "It's always helped me when my nightmares got really bad."

I'm surprised by his confession.

"What are your nightmares about?" I blurt in a whisper.

I instantly realize how messed up my question is, but it's already out there, and Nash doesn't seem bothered by it.

"My parents died when I was ten. For a long time, my nightmares were about that, about them. They trickled almost to a stop as I got older, that is, until about a week ago."

"What brought them back? The lamia?" I ask before I can stop myself.

Nash shakes his head, his black hair swaying, and his ice blue eyes fixed on me. "No. You did. Or I guess I should say the keening noise you made when your friend died. That's what has been haunting me these days. I can't seem to shake that soul-shattering sound or how broken I feel every time it replays in my nightmares."

I look away from Nash's penetrating gaze, not sure what to say.

"Yeah, I thought all the killing would stick with me more, but when I think back on what happened, two things stick with me. How I felt when I woke up tied to a chair in that cellar, and what happened in the back of the SUV that night," Kallan confesses softly.

I look over to Kallan as his words taper off, but he's staring at the ground.

"I see ash and blood when I close my eyes at night...and you, curled as small as you could get in the back of the car," Enoch tells me, his haunted gaze fixed on mine.

The ball of magic in my hands fades to nothing, and the room falls silent as the confessions absorb the weight and pain of the memories they hold.

"I was tied to a chair in that same cellar," I monotone,

staring down at the runes on my hands. "I couldn't get free. Talon was talking to me, warning me. But I couldn't find him, no matter how hard I tried. Then, Laiken was there."

I rub at my chest as an ache begins to build behind my sternum.

"I couldn't get to her. She was screaming, telling me that I need to run. She was terrified." My voice falls to a whisper. "That's when I woke up."

My heart starts to pound with the memory of her voice and the terror that was in it. I look around the room for her cedar box, needing the reassurance that it offers me, but I quickly remember that it's not here. She's with Sabin.

I'm not sure why I'm telling them what happened. Maybe it's because Nash shared, and I feel obligated to do the same. Or maybe he's right, and I just need to get it out, purge the feel and impact of the nightmare, through my words.

"Do you think it means anything?" Becket asks me, as he slides down the door frame until his butt meets the polished concrete floor.

He rests his forearms on his knees and waits for me to respond. I shrug. I scrub at my face with my hands, tired and trying to work through my thoughts about everything. *I'm not safe here.* That pressing feeling has been growing more and more persistent since the lamia attack. But I can't sort out what it means exactly. I'm not safe in Lachlan's house? That's what I felt initially, but I'm not there anymore. I don't feel threatened by Enoch and this coven, so does this feeling mean I'm unsafe in Solace, amongst casters, or is it the elders that are setting off this unease?

"Where's your gym?" I ask no one in particular.

I know there has to be one here somewhere. These guys are too built and defined to not work out on the regular.

"I'll show you," Enoch announces, standing up from where he was sitting on the bed.

I move to follow him and realize that I'm still just in my underwear and a tank top. I slide open the closet door and snag a pair of yoga pants from a drawer. I pull them on and track down a sports bra. I push the straps of my tank top down and pull the fitted bra over my head. I secure everything in place and pull the straps of my tank back up. I turn around to try and figure out what box my shoes might be in and realize everyone is frozen and staring at me. They're acting like they've never seen a female's back before. I know I didn't show them anything else.

"What?" I ask irritably.

Why do I feel like I've just done something I shouldn't have? Enoch clears his throat, and it snaps the others out of whatever trance they're in. He walks out of the room, and one by one the rest of us follow.

12

I shut my door and glare at Pebble as he makes his way around the Jeep to me. I cross the street, quickening my pace to put as much distance between me and Pebble as possible. I grumble to myself as his heavy boot-clad steps sound off behind me. When my Jeep showed up this morning, I immediately jumped in, eager to put some space between me and the coven of casters I've shared too much of myself with over the past twenty-four hours.

Every single one of them worked out with me for hours this morning. I just wanted to work the feel of panic and death out of my system, but instead I was painfully aware of their eyes on me and a strange energy in the air. I set a punishing pace for myself in an effort to distract from whatever the hell was going on, but it didn't work as well as I'd hoped.

When everyone broke off to get cleaned up, I took the fastest shower ever and worked on a plan to get the hell away from all of them for a little while. The sight of my baby-tank Jeep being driven through the front gates was all the invitation I needed. I was on cloud nine as I made my unnoticed escape. Well, until a sneaky Pebble opened the passenger door and climbed in. I had to make the split-second decision to either try and get him out of the vehicle and blow my chance to get some time away, or just accept that today I'd have a babysitter.

I approach the tattoo shop, and I can't help but chuckle at the name. *I'll Get You, My Pretty* is stenciled on the windows in a green color that matches the face of the fictional witch that made the saying famous. I open the door, and instead of a chime, a shrill cackle announces my arrival. A short, bald man in a well-fitted aubergine suit gives me a quick once-over.

"Who's your appointment with, my sweet?" he asks me.

His voice would make James Earl Jones jealous. It's deep and smooth, and I'm completely taken aback. I would never have guessed that voice belonged to this pocket-sized man. He gives me a warm smile, and I match it. It's probably a safe guess that I'm not the first, and won't be the last, to show shock over the dichotomy of his size versus the depth in his voice.

"I'm here to see Mave," I tell him just as my svelte pink-haired shifter friend rounds the corner.

"Vin!" she greets excitedly, skipping over to me and pulling me into a strong hug. "You finally here for those nipple piercings we talked about?"

Mave gives me a cheeky wink and a teasing smile as we pull apart. But a choking sound has both of us looking behind me to find Pebble giving himself a hard slap on his chest and coughing to clear his airway. Mave gives him an appreciative scan, and me a questioning look.

"No piercings for me, but Pebble here has been begging for a magic cross. I thought you'd be just the girl for the job."

Mave's smile is blinding, and she shakes her head,

amused. "Just when I think I have your kink level figured out, you go busting out terms like magic cross."

She chuckles. I flutter my lashes at her innocently and give her a sweet grin. She looks back over at Pebble and gives him a wink, motioning for him to follow her. He blushes ever so slightly and does exactly as instructed—such an obedient little puppy.

Well, well, well, what do we have here? I muse as I watch Pebble's gaze fix on Mave's ass. His eyes shoot up to her face when she turns around and ushers us into a small, clean room.

There's a chair that looks like something I'd find in the dentist office, and Mave directs Pebble to have a seat.

"So, were you looking to have both piercings done at the same time, or one now and the other when you've healed?" Mave asks, her professional mask slipping into place.

Pebble looks at me for guidance, and it's all I can do to keep my face straight and not crack up.

"Um, what exactly is a magic cross?" Pebble finally asks.

"I'll show you," Mave answers sweetly, and she moves to get something from a cabinet in the corner.

When Mave gives us her back, Pebble shoots me a glare, clearly not appreciating being out of the loop. My overly sweet facade completely falls to pieces when Mave turns around abruptly holding a very lifelike replica of a man's lower torso; ass, dick, balls, and all. Pebble's eyes grow huge, and he freezes when she wraps a hand around the generous prosthetic member and proceeds to shove a needle through the tip. The first needle goes through vertically, and then she adds another needle through the tip horizontally.

"See, a magic cross," Mave announces, as she slightly wiggles the fake phallus at Pebble.

He scrambles out of the chair and as far away from the needle-tipped replica-cock as possible.

He covers his crotch with both hands and stares at the needles with pure panic. "Oh, fuck no."

He narrows his eyes at Mave and then at me, as we both burst into hysterical laughter. Just when the laughs start to die down, Mave shakes the needle-cock at Pebble, and the squeal that he lets out as he tries to get away from it would put a *Belieber* to shame. I wipe tears from my eyes as I get my shit together, and Mave pulls the needles out of the fake dick and drops them in a sharps container. Pebble winces and moves further back into the corner of the room.

"Oh man, that was too easy," I admit, my laughter finally beginning to taper off.

"You really should be nicer to the casters you're collecting for your harem, Vinna," Mave playfully scolds me.

"Please, he should be so lucky." I wink at Pebble as he glares back at me. "Mave, this is Pebble; Pebble, Mave. He's my assigned babysitter. Not a contender for future *mate* status."

Mave's smile falls, and her face becomes serious. "What's going on, everything okay?"

I run my fingers through my hair and huff out a resigned breath.

"The elders yanked me from my uncle's house. Things weren't going so great for me there, and it gave them a chance to start meddling in my life," I grumble and shoot a scathing look over at Pebble.

He's unfazed by my ire, too busy checking Mave out to notice my glare.

"I tried to convince them that I'm fine on my own, but apparently casters are treated like mindless children until they have their awakening."

I roll my eyes, and Mave gives me an understanding nod.

"You're going to love this part," I tell her, my tone overflowing with snark. "I've been sent to live with Enoch Cleary's coven and given Pebble here *for my protection*."

I'm sure to put exaggerated air quotes around the last part. I've already proven that I can take Pebble when push comes to shove. There's really no reason for him to still follow me around. Or pretend that he's here for any reason other than spying on me and keeping me from doing anything the elders don't want me to do.

"Why the fuck did they put you with that coven of assholes?" Mave exclaims.

I give an incredulous snort. "Why do you think?" I roll my eyes. "They gave Elder Cleary temporary guardianship over me. He felt that his son's coven was where I'd be most comfortable, being that they're big strong casters and their magic is the most *compatible* with mine."

Mave scoffs and gives me a knowing look. "Sounds completely innocent and not at all self-serving to me. I'm sure Elder Cleary and Elder Albrecht aren't hoping that you trip and land on one of their son's dicks, right in the middle of a bonding ceremony."

I laugh, and Pebble coughs, obviously uncomfortable with the direction of this conversation and our talking shit about his bosses.

"Oh come on, Pebble, put on your big boy panties and take off your blinders. You know as well as we do what's really going on here."

He shakes his head at me, but it's not lost on me that he doesn't say anything to refute our claims and suspicions.

"What are you going to do?" Mave queries.

"What can I do? The guys submitted a Bond Claim, but I'll give you one guess as to who decides whether I can be with them or not. If the elders deny it, I'm fucking stuck until my awakening and I come into my full power."

"Holy shit! That was fast. Those boys aren't wasting any

time trying to get you on lockdown," Mave exclaims with raised eyebrows and a look that's half impressed, half shocked.

"What can I say, my magic brings all the boys to the yard."

I start to sing the rest of the song and dance around. Mave laughs, and the tinkling sound of it breaks up the tension that was building inside of my chest. The thought of being stuck with no control over my life for the next couple of years sits heavy on me.

"Well, you obviously need to let off some steam, and lucky for you, my pack has a moon ceremony tonight. We can party it up, get drunk as fuck, and forget all about life's problems. Tru has been asking about you," she teases.

"Tru doesn't talk, Mave, and the last thing I need is another guy sniffing around where there's not a chance."

She laughs. "He talks in the pack link. No one wants to go running with him anymore because he just wants to recap you fucking up those caster pricks. I think it's less of a crush and more that he really wants to see you fight again."

I chuckle at that revelation, and Mave's look shifts from innocent amusement to saucy.

"But now that you mention it, if those delicious caster boys of yours are about to put you on a magical leash, maybe we should arrange a little *puppy pile* for you. You know what they say, once you go wolf you never go...well...fuck. I was going to try and come up with something on the fly, but nothing rhymes with wolf." We both crack up. "Seriously though, they're big, virile, bossy, and experts at coaxing out a good howl, if you know what I mean." She elbows me and wags her eyebrows.

"Is anyone in your pack going to care that some *witch* is crashing their party?"

"Fuck no. Not when I'm the one vouching for you. Plus, we both know you can handle yourself."

Mave winks at me and saunters over to Pebble. She runs a finger down the front of his black t-shirt and looks him square in the eyes. Her lips purse slightly, and I watch as Pebble's breathing speeds up.

"Now, are you going to behave yourself and be a good boy tonight? Because if you start any shit with my pack, I will make sure that Vinna holds you down while I officially introduce your dick to the magic cross."

Pebble visibly swallows, and his pupils dilate. I can't tell if he's nervous or turned on by Mave's threat. I have a sneaking suspicion that he doesn't know either.

This is going to be fun.

13

A cool breeze brushes past me, and chills rise up on my skin. I'm seriously regretting the white off-the-shoulder peasant top that Mave forced me into.

"Why can't I just wear my t-shirt again? It's kind of cold up here," I whine for the thousandth time since Mave started throwing clothes at me from her closet. I magically styled my hair straight, and a breeze catches the thick black-brown strands and pushes them back and away from my face.

"Vin, I don't care what you say, but a t-shirt that says *Tryna look like one of those rap guy's girlfriends* does not set the appropriate tone for how tonight is going to go. Now, stop with the whining. As soon as we get a couple of sips of Cyrus's moonshine in you, you'll be happy you wore something light and breezy."

Mave smooths out her maxi dress, grabs my hand, and pulls me along behind her. Pebble, my ever-present and obnoxious shadow, falls into step right behind me. We make our way from the cluster of houses that the pack resides in, through the trees, and toward a clearing. The meadow I'm half dragged to has fairy lights crossing high above it. The strands of twinkling white bulbs have been strung up in the tall branches of the surrounding trees. It is beautiful and creates a laid back, intimate vibe. Tables of food and drinks border the large crowd of people all standing and socializing in the center of the clearing.

I see Kaika's big frame with a group of younger looking shifters. He's playing with them, which surprises me. The one and only time I met him at the cliff diving outing, he was the wolf shifter version of Grumpy Cat. I run my palms over my jean-clad thighs, feeling a little uncertain as we approach the large gathering of shifters. Mave insists it's fine that I'm here. Her family has been nothing but welcoming since I showed up on their front porch this afternoon, but I can't help but worry that, at any second, my welcome's going to get worn out. I know that things are usually tense between shifters and casters, and I don't quite know what to expect tonight.

Mave's parents wave at us from across the clearing, but they stay standing with their friends, chatting and laughing. Mave's family is everything she described them to be: loud, chaotic, rowdy. But they're loving and supportive, bonded in a way that I'm envious of. Spending the afternoon with them while they joked and harassed each other has me missing my guys more than ever.

I went outside later in the afternoon to try and call them again, but there was still no answer from anyone. When I stole my small bit of freedom this morning, they were the first calls I made. None of them have been reachable all day, and no one has called me back.

I'm starting to get a little nervous about it, but every time I go to use my runes to contact them, I talk myself out of it. They have lives and are probably just wrapped up in something. I keep telling myself not to be *that girl*. The one who needs to know where they are and what they're doing every second of the day.

Mave tugs on our intertwined hands when I'm apparently not moving fast enough for her.

"I'll introduce you to the Alpha first. Once we get that out of the way, we can start the debauchery."

She tugs me straight toward a group of males, each taller and more ripped than the next. Mave elbows and shoves her way through, and they chuckle and slowly move aside to make way for her. She stops in front of a man who looks like he could be Idris Elba's brother. He's big and radiates a raw gruffness. His clothes are clean cut, he doesn't have a beard, and his hair looks like he just came from a barber, the lines and fade are crisp and clean. His black eyes land on Mave, and I notice that she looks at him, but their gazes don't actually connect.

"Alpha, this is my friend, Vinna. She is the one who helped Tru out when he ran into trouble. Vinna, this is Trent Silas. Alpha of the Silas pack."

Mave steps back from the large imposing figure of her alpha and lowers her head respectfully. Unsure of what to do exactly, I wait for him to say or do something that signifies a greeting: offer a handshake maybe, or give a grumpy nod of tolerance at least. But he stands there quietly. I take in his navy blue chinos and his short sleeve denim shirt that's buttoned all the way to the top.

His eyes rake slowly over me, eventually making their way up to mine. When his black irises meet my seafoam green ones, he stills. I have a sinking suspicion that I'm committing some kind of shifter faux-pas, and I want to punch myself and then Mave for not going over what was appropriate when meeting the Alpha of the pack.

I suspect eye contact with certain members of the pack is a big shifter no-no. But, fuck it, it's already happening, and there's nothing much I can really do about it now. A fleeting thought flashes through me that maybe I should play nice and drop my eyes, but he's not said a word to me or made any effort to make this introduction less awkward. He's looked me over like I was some chewed up dog toy covered in drool, and it bothers the shit out of me.

So I keep my eyes fixed on his.

"Are you challenging me for my pack, Vinna?" he asks, his body language calm and self-assured.

His voice is smooth and accent-free. Bummer, I was really hoping he'd sound British.

"No, sir. I'm simply challenging you for your respect."

He lifts one eyebrow in question.

"I saw what you thought of me when you looked me over, or maybe it's just my kind that pisses you off, but I'm not them," I explain, my easygoing tone matching his.

His nostrils flare, and the hint of a smile twitches at the corners of his mouth. "I suppose time will show if that's true."

He gives me an almost imperceptible nod, and I drop my gaze immediately. The strained silence that was cocooning us shatters, and the shifters surrounding us relax and pick up their conversations. The alpha gives a deep rumbling chuckle.

"Vinna, allow me to introduce you to my Betas."

Trent Silas puts a large hand on the shoulder of a big man in a green t-shirt. The large man ends the conversation he's currently involved in and turns around at the touch.

"This is my second, Mateo—"

"Torrez?" I interrupt.

Torrez's face shows his surprise, and I'm shocked at how different he looks from the last time I saw him. His mohawk of dreads is gone. His ebony hair is short now and trimmed cleanly in a stylish undercut rockabilly look. His beard is also missing, leaving smooth tan skin in its place. He's wearing dark jeans that look like they were made for him, and a t-shirt that says *Ripped for her pleasure.*

I turn to Mave after seeing his shirt and glare daggers at her. So he can wear t-shirts that say shit, but I can't? Following my train of thought, Mave rolls her eyes and smirks, mouthing the word *puppy pile* at me. I try not to snort and turn back to Torrez. His dark brown eyes light up, and a smile takes over his face.

"Bitchless Witch? Of all the gin joints, in all the towns, in all the world, you walk into mine?"

I chuckle at his butchering of the famous movie quote. "Well, you look a hell of a lot better than the last time I saw you."

Torrez laughs, and the eyes of everyone around us ping pong from him to me and back again.

"What am I missing here? How do you guys know each other?" Mave asks, the confusion in her voice matching the look on the Alpha's face.

"This little vixen and I went head to head in the ring a couple weeks back. She ended my undefeated winning streak by almost ripping my face in half," Torrez explains. He chuckles like the lunatic he is and rubs his jaw for good measure. "I just started eating solids less than a week ago," he tells me.

I dismiss his play for sympathy and stick out my lower lip in an exaggerated faux pout. I bring my hands up in front of me and mime playing a tiny violin. "Them's the breaks, Wolf-man. I did warn you about your imminent loss. It's not my fault you didn't listen."

Torrez lets out a roar of laughter, and Alpha Silas looks me over with renewed interest.

Questions and mumbles of disbelief sound off around us, and I look at Torrez, confused.

"Did you not tell anyone that you had your ass handed to you by a female?"

"I did, but I can't help it if they chose not to believe me." He gives me a wink and turns to the group surrounding the Alpha. "This little spitfire walked right into the ring and said, 'I'm going to fuck up your undefeated record.' I thought for sure one of you fuckers was playing a prank on me." He slaps the chest of the shifter standing next to him and gestures to the rest of them with his other hand. "I couldn't scent any trace of lies in the air. There wasn't even a hint of fear or hesitation. I didn't know what to think." He looks from the amused faces of the big male shifters around us, back to mine. "I want a rematch, Witch."

"Anytime, anyplace, Wolf-man," I say with a sweet smile as I pat his cheek.

His eyes heat up at my declaration, and I have to admit the thought of fighting him again excites me.

"Vinna, I'd like to invite you to run with the pack tonight," Alpha Silas announces.

Heads snap to him in shock. The conversation around us dies like someone went and turned the volume off at this party. Alpha Silas looks nonplussed by the reaction of his pack.

"We don't typically welcome outsiders, but something tells me you'll be able to keep up."

I get the sense that what he's offering is a big deal, but I'm not sure what to think about it. I feel a squeezing pressure at my elbow, and I look over to find a rigid-looking Pebble. I'd completely forgotten he was even here.

"I don't think this is a good idea," he admonishes.

He's not looking at me when he says this. Instead, he looks past me to the Alpha and the shifters that surround us. That alone helps me make up my mind.

"Well, it's too bad no one asked your opinion then, isn't

it, Pebble?" I pull my eyes from where he's gripping my elbow and meet his aggravated stare.

"This isn't a good idea, and I'm sure the elders would agree," he grits through his teeth.

"The thing is, I don't really care what they would and wouldn't agree with. If the elders have a problem with *my* choices, they can fuck off, and if you don't let go of my arm in sixty seconds, I'm going to give you and this group a demonstration of how I fucked up one of their Betas."

Pebble huffs out a sigh. "This isn't about the elders, Vinna; this is about your safety."

"I can take care of myself," I remind him again, yanking my arm out of his grasp.

He takes a step toward me, and a chain reaction of deep menacing growls begins to rumble all around us. Pebble's eyes shoot daggers at the surrounding shifters, and his body language tells me that he's getting ready to square off with them.

"Think about what you're doing. You're on their land and outnumbered. You can either start some shit you don't have a chance of winning, or you can step off and go back to babysitting me like you've been ordered... Your call."

He looks past me again and then at me. I plead with my eyes for him not to do anything stupid. I won't be able to just sit by and watch him get torn to shreds by shifters, and I sure as fuck don't want to die that way.

"Magic cross," Mave throws out nonchalantly.

I have to fight my smile at her veiled threat, but it breaks free when Pebble finally relaxes and steps away from me. Someone steps up directly behind me, and I feel the vibration of a growl radiate from them as their chest skims my back. I turn to find Torrez towering over me. I stare at him until he drops his eyes from Pebble's to mine.

"You of all people should know I can handle myself," I remind him.

"Oh, I know. Doesn't mean you should have to."

I expected a snarky comment or some other kind of teasing, witty retort since that's kind of been our dynamic up to this point when communicating with each other. So his declaration and the fierce look in his eyes when he says it throws me a bit.

"Mave. Mateo. Make sure our guest is well taken care of." Alpha Silas nods at them, then at me, before he moves away from us, disappearing smoothly into the crowd of shifters.

14

I quickly toss back the shot of moonshine that was just handed to me. I expected it to taste like battery acid, but the taste of gummy bears coats my tongue, and I let out a surprised squeak as I swallow it down. Mave hands me another shot right away, and we clink glasses and throw them back. Holy shit, this stuff must be lethal. It tastes like candy and kicks like a mule. Torrez tries to hand me another shot, and I glare at it like the sneaky fiend it is.

"Two's enough for me," I confess, with a shake of my head when he tries to hand off the shot again.

I'm warm and fuzzy from the six ounces I just consumed. There's no way I'm letting any more of that deliciously potent elixir past my lips. Mave shrugs and steals the shot from him, downing it first and then following it up with the shot in her other hand. She licks her lips appreciatively and wiggles her eyebrows at me.

"Sooo good, right?"

"Like I'm drinking super-sweet Kool-Aid," I admit, with a giggle that has me instantly judging myself.

Mave laughs at me and throws an arm around my shoulders. "How can you be a lightweight when you're such a badass? I thought fighting and drinking went hand and hand."

I shrug my shoulders, which Mave seems to find hilarious. Torrez throws back another shot and smiles at the both of us.

"So, Vin, you ready to run with the big dogs? I mean wolves. Like really big wolves. Huge ones. Bigger than you've ever seen." Mave's eyes get wider as her hands grow farther apart. "Have you seen how big they are? Sooo big." She looks at her outstretched hands and starts to crack up. "I'm not talking about that, you dirty birdy. Although the dick size in this pack *is* above average." She wags her eyebrows at me but seems to get distracted by the movement of her hands again.

"And you're cut off," Torrez tells Mave when she makes a grab for another drink.

He pulls the drink smoothly out of her reach. She huffs her disapproval but doesn't put up more fight beyond that.

Torrez motions between me and Mave, and leans down toward me. "So, how do you two know each other?"

I open my mouth to answer, but Mave beats me to it.

"Amazing people always find their way to each other. Our bestieship was written in the stars, that's how," she declares.

She throws her head back and closes her eyes to the starlit sky, like she can feel fate looking down on her at this exact moment. Slowly she starts to tilt back, and I rush to catch her before she falls off the chair. I get her straightened out as she chuckles and pets my face. I laugh. Apparently, looking for a better explanation than the one he just got, Torrez looks to me for a coherent answer to his question.

I smile at him and point my thumb at Mave. "What she said."

Mave hugs me and then throws her head back and

howls. Answering howls sound off around the party, and something about it comforts me. What would it be like to call out like that and know that there's always someone there to answer you? I realize that Torrez is watching me as I blink away the thought, and I get the sudden desire to activate my runes and reach out to the guys.

"What?" I ask him as he continues to look at me with that same intensity he had right after my chat with Pebble. I wipe at my face, wondering if I've got something there.

"Are you really going to run with us?" he asks.

"Why wouldn't I?"

"I don't know. I've just never known a caster that would want to, let alone be invited to," he admits.

"Well, I'm not really a caster, so that probably still applies."

As soon as the words are out of my mouth, I want to grab them and shove them back down my throat. Why the fuck did I just say that? Torrez tilts his head, and I can see the questions written all over his face and spilling out of his gaze.

"What do you mean?"

"Uh...I...uh...just meant that I wasn't raised like one. I don't think like they do or have the same hang-ups."

He stares at me for a couple of seconds and then gives me an understanding nod. I don't miss the slight flare of his nostrils before he looks away at a group who's yelling and getting rowdy. *Shit!* Can he smell the half-truth in what I just said? I reign in my panic figuring he'll smell that, too, if I let it take over. I school my features and look around for a distraction.

I gape for a moment in shock when I look over and find Mave snuggled up in Pebble's lap. I'm not too surprised on Pebble's end, as he's been checking her out since the tattoo shop, but I didn't know she was feeling him too. I scan the shifters all around them to see if Mave and Pebble's closeness bothers anyone, especially after the dick move he tried to pull earlier, but no one seems to be paying them any attention.

A finger glides over the line of runes on my exposed shoulder, and a familiar wave of heat travels through me. I smile. *How the hell did they find me here?* A shiver rolls through me at the contact, and I turn, fully expecting to see one of my Chosen. I freeze when the finger trailing over my shoulder belongs to Torrez and not one of my guys.

I slap his hand away and push off of the tree stump I'm perched on. He rises at the same time, and I step to get in his face.

"What the fuck do you think you're doing?"

My aggressive stance has unintentionally pressed us closer together, and I see Torrez's eyes drop to my lips for a millisecond before they shoot back up to meet my glare. I shove him away from me before he can do anything that will get him stabbed. I push my way through the crowd and into the surrounding tree line. I stomp back toward Mave's house where my car is parked.

I debate for a quick second if I should tell Pebble that I'm ready to bail, but fuck it. He and Mave looked adorably cozy. Who am I to get in the way of the hot sex they'll hopefully be having later? Leaves crunch behind me, and I whirl around to find Torrez.

"You crossed a fucking line. What are you thinking? I was being friendly. Not giving off *make a move* vibes. Can no one tell the difference in this town?" I shout at him.

I throw my hands up in the air like I'm waiting for the universe to answer my question. When it doesn't, I turn back around and continue to stomp my way back in the direction of my Jeep.

"Vinna, I'm drawn to you."

I round on him. "Don't say that. Don't you fucking say that! I am not available. I'm not interested in drawing anyone else in. I have Chosen. I don't know where any of them are today, but that's beside the point. They're mine. I'm theirs. That's it. You need to go find someone else to scratch your witch itch, or whatever it is that has you interested."

Torrez doesn't look deterred at all by my rambling declarations. In fact, he just smiles and dares to take a step closer to me.

"I thought casters liked to share. I'm failing to see the problem with being drawn to you?"

"I'm not a fucking free-for-all. You flea-bitten ass licker. This is not a Vinna buffet." I motion to myself with a sweeping hand, but I'm pretty sure my point doesn't sink in when Torrez's brown eyes bank with heat. "You have to go to my Chosen to get to me. Wait, that's not right. Go through them? Go to them? Fuck, which one is the threat? I mean the threatening one because they will kick your ass. Fuck it; I'm going to kick your ass."

Torrez puts his hands up, palms out when I step toward him with clenched fists. "Okay, I'll back off until I can go to them."

"No. That's not what I mean. This"—I gesture from me to him—"is not up for discussion."

His smile gets bigger, confusing me even more. Why is he not getting it?

"What the fuck? Don't wolves mate for life? As in *one* mate for life. If you got involved with a caster, that would pull you away from your pack. You're what, second in line to take over? I think the moonshine has addled your brain. Or maybe you need a Snickers; you're not yourself when you're hungry—or at least that's what the commercials say."

I slam a hand over my mouth to keep any more dumb shit from dribbling out.

Motherfucking moonshine!

No more gummy-bear flavored alcohol for me. Ever. A laugh escapes him, and I can tell that he's trying hard to keep more in, but he's fighting a losing battle. Dick. A howl tears through the night, and then suddenly the air fills with the beautifully haunting sounds of other answering howls.

"Are you going to run with us, or run away scared, Little Witch?" Torrez challenges me.

"Please, are you going to double-dog dare me next and call me a sissy?"

He laughs again and shakes his head at me. "You might want to change into something that you can run in, unless you want to go naked. That's how we'll start; you could consider it embracing your inner wolf."

I glare at him, but his smile just widens. I look back in the direction of Mave's house. I should really leave, but judging by the word vomit I just spewed, I might be a little more under the influence than I thought.

"I'm sure Mave won't care if you raid her closet real quick," Torrez offers as if he can read the debate going on in my mind.

A run might be my best bet at sobering up enough to get the fuck out of here.

"Fine." I agree. "But you stay out here while I change, and keep your hands to yourself from here on out. That is the only warning you're going to get from me."

I turn around and close the distance between me and Mave's cabin. Here's hoping we wear the same shoe size because these sandals are not going to cut it for a run.

15

The night feels even colder than it did before, but I dismiss the bite of the chill air, knowing that as soon as I get moving, it will feel good. Everyone around me starts to casually strip down to their birthday suits. I train my eyes on the sky in an effort to avoid all the body parts that are none of my business. After a couple of minutes of looking like an immature idiot, I deem the situation safe and pull my head down and try to keep my eyes from landing on anything for too long.

A good portion of the shifters have already shifted into their wolf forms, where they eagerly wait to get going. I focus on them and the different features and colors of fur that mark them as individuals instead of looking too closely at those who are still standing around in the buff. Apparently, they like to shift more last minute or mid-run, Torrez informed me.

The wolves all vary in size and color, but each of them exudes a wild power and an undeniable predatory prowess. With each individual that shifts, more wild magic permeates the air, and I feel it start to soak into me. The feral power mingles with my Sentinel magic, and the swirl sends a chill running down my spine and urgency through my blood. I find myself feeling restless and ready to put my muscles to work. A wolf scuffle breaks out next to me, and the horse-sized gray wolf that is Torrez growls out a warning that puts an immediate stop to the aggression.

A distant howl rings out and rises to the stars, and all the wolves tilt their heads back and answer the call. Abandoning all self-consciousness, I point my face to the sky and let out my own answering howl. Torrez's gray wolf bumps up against me, and I push at his huge frame and grumble about him keeping his hands and paws to himself. I wonder offhandedly where Mave and Pebble are, but I have no time to focus on that as the wolves around me begin to lope in the direction that their Alpha leads the pack.

The pace starts out slow. The wolves in front of the group begin to lengthen their strides and pick up speed and soon the whole pack is hurtling through the densely clustered trees. I run full out, but their four legs easily outpace my two, and I start to fall behind. I call on some extra power from my runes, and as it spurs on my muscles, I start darting through the wolves that are bringing up the rear. Torrez stays with me the whole time, and I can feel his excitement as I push more magic into my legs and pick up speed.

Brisk wind whips my hair back behind me, and I feel a flush rise in my cheeks. All around me, wolf paws hit almost silently against the forest floor. The sound of fur brushing against trees, the thudding of my steps, and panting are the only sounds that surround me, as I find a steady pace in the middle of the pack. Out here, in the moonlight-streaked forest, I feel the pack's connection to each other and to the land in a surprising way.

My glimpse at their connection fills me with a keen sense of longing and accentuates how much of an outsider I am. Frost-kissed air moves in and out of my lungs, and I pump my arms and legs in a soothing tempo. The smile on my face is automatic, I love pushing my body, but this is so much more than that. I feel wild, predatory, and free in such a unique way. With each press of my feet into the rich soil, with each mouthful of crisp mountain air, I let go.

I shed the stress and confusion of the past few days. I press down against the longing for my Chosen. I uncoil the choking heartache of losing Talon and strip away the pain left by Lachlan. I feel it all just fall away as I focus on the here and now, on this moon-kissed run with a pack of shifters. I feel lighter and lighter with each stretched stride. Torrez pushes to move faster, and I meet his challenge, reveling in the power and speed. Soon I find myself weaving my way to the front, to run side by side with the Alpha and the rest of his Betas.

Torrez looks over at me, and I don't miss the hint of a wolfish grin as we make our way through the night in tandem. I resolve myself to the fact that I'm going to have to nip whatever he thinks is happening between us in the bud. I'm just not sure exactly how to do that. I thought I was being clear earlier when I told him that he had no chance, that I was taken.

But I'm getting the distinct impression that he's taking that as a challenge or some kind of game of playing hard to get. I have no idea what is happening in this town. Am I leaking some kind of magic pheromones or something? I know it's not my winning personality pulling all these guys in, so just what in the hell is it?

I notice the faintest change in the energy all around me, and Alpha Silas cuts across the pack and starts charging in a completely different direction. With ease, the pack falls into step behind him, but there's an edgy feel to the collective movement now. Tongues no longer loll happily out of the mouths of carefree and relaxed wolves as they enjoy a pack run. Focused eyes and tightening muscles replace the easy gaits of before. I start scanning our surroundings trying to pick up on what's setting them off.

I don't sense or spot it at first. But the sound of branches snapping and a gruff huffing as heavy steps move away from us, has me locating a cinnamon-colored mass about fifty feet in front of us. *Are they hunting a bear?* Alpha Silas begins to growl, and the hairs on my body immediately stand up and pay attention to the warning.

He presses harder to close the distance between the pack and the huge fleeing animal, which is no easy task. I had no idea that bears could move that fast. Although, a pack of hunting wolves could probably motivate the laziest of animals to Usain Bolt it out of their way. Torrez starts to press in against me, and I move away from him to keep from tripping and going ass over face into the dirt or getting trampled by the horse-sized gray wolf.

I realize after he does it a couple more times that I'm being herded away from the pack and their prey. I guess the invitation to run with them didn't include hunting with them too. I try to bat away my momentary disappointment. It would've been awesome to see how the pack dealt with such a ferocious challenger. Yeah, the bear is running now, but it'll start to fight when there's nothing else it can do.

Torrez gives me one more nudge in the opposite direction, and I turn to glare at him. *Alright! I fucking get it already.* The words die in my mouth as a flash of golden blond hair streaks away from me to my right. I immediately shift to follow it. Torrez doesn't seem to have caught what I just saw, and he breaks away to rejoin the hunt with his alpha.

I know I should call out to him, alert him to what I'm pursuing, but he's gone in a flash, and everything inside of me is demanding that I don't lose sight of *my* new prey. Flashes of the big, blond, Viking-esque lamia standing in the cellar when I was tied to a chair crash through me. I pump my legs and arms harder as I fight to keep up with Sorik as he careens through the trees away from me. I stay on him. It doesn't seem like he's trying to lose me, and that immediately sets off more alarms in my mind and has me on guard.

I pant as I press even harder in an attempt to gain on him, while simultaneously trying to be aware of anything that's sneaking up on me from behind. I activate the runes on the helix of my ear, so I have the extra advantage of being able to hear everything around me better. This is a trap. It has to be, but rage over what happened the last time I saw him in that cellar stokes me as I close in on the golden-haired lamia.

Sorik takes a sharp left turn and dashes behind a huge dead tree trunk. I follow without hesitation but slam to a stop when Sorik is suddenly crouched amidst a small copse. His arms are outstretched, and he mumbles something as he slowly rises from his hunched position. His arms steadily rise up until he claps his hands together. The sound is booming in the otherwise stillness of the night, and a magical barrier flashes up from the ground to dome over us.

What the fuck! Did he just use magic?

16

I stare at him in complete shock for a second before I get my shit together and call on some weapons. Twin short swords become solid in each of my hands, and Sorik's eyes dart to them before he fixes his gaze on mine. His eyes are filled with something I can't place.

"I'm not here to hurt you," he reassures me.

He raises his hands in surrender, like that somehow is all I'll need to trust him.

"How the fuck did you raise a barrier? I thought lamia didn't have magic like that?"

I should probably be asking him what the hell he's doing here or something along those lines, but all I can focus on is the fact that this hulking lamia just used magic like a caster.

"We can't. Normally. That's why I'm here."

Sorik drops his hands to the hem of his shirt and starts to pull it up.

"Whoa, Magic Mike. This isn't that kind of party." I avert my eyes just to the side so his strip show isn't in focus, but I can still track if he's going to attack. I'm not sure what the hell this lamia is up to. What the fuck kind of trap is this?

Get me alone and strip? Fucking magic pheromones, is no one immune?

"Sorry, it's probably just the easiest way to explain what's going on," he tells me, as he whips his shirt over his head. His long golden locks cascade behind him as he pulls his head free of the fabric.

I stare at him completely dumbfounded. "What in the actual fuck is going on?"

Sorik has runes.

He has three runes set between his pecs and runes that run down in a line on both sides of his ribs. I take an automatic step forward, my eyes wide with confusion as I try to take in what I'm seeing. I look down to his hands, seeking the runes that should decorate his ring fingers, but the skin there looks damaged—burnt maybe.

"How?"

I can only manage to squeak out that one syllable. I run my gaze over the runes on his body, over and over again. Does this mean what I think it does?

"Grier and I didn't think that a transference was possible. She had never heard of it occurring outside of either the Sentinel or a caster bond. We loved each other, and we thought we were being careful. No one knew. But then this happened."

He gestures to the runes running between his pecs.

"She marked you?" I ask, and he nods.

"We both panicked when the Chosen marks showed up. It meant that what Adriel had been trying to do for decades was actually possible. Up until that point, Grier had thought that no matter what he did to her, there was no way he could take from her what he wanted. But I was suddenly proof that everything she had been told was wrong."

Sorik's eyes fill with a deep sadness, and it reaches into me and tugs at my own.

"I tried to cut off the runes on my fingers. All the others could be hidden, but those runes gave us away. My skin kept regenerating until I finally burned the runes off and sealed the injury with shifter saliva, which is toxic to us."

Sorik's admission sends me back to the night that Talon died, when he told me something similar. *'They've been dosing me with shifter toxin. It's keeping me from healing.'* Talon's voice echoes around my head, and I have to shake myself out of the memory and refocus. Sorik's runes on his ribs are the same as mine, and it dawns on me that he must have weapons like I do. It seems my mother also passed Defensive magic on to him, too, judging by the good-sized barrier we're currently standing under.

I let go of my short swords, letting the magic in them get reabsorbed by my runes. I run my hands over my face, exhausted and exasperated, and not at all sure what to think about any of this. A howl breaks the silence surrounding us, and our meeting takes on a more urgent tone.

"Is my dad still alive?"

"I honestly don't know. I felt it when Grier passed, but I never felt anything like that after. Maybe the connection only works from Grier to her Chosen. If that's the case, I wouldn't have felt if anything had happened to Vaughn. I just don't know. I haven't seen him in all these years, nor have I heard Adriel talk about him at all."

At the mention of Adriel's name, I stiffen.

Another howl pierces the night, this one closer than the last. Are they done hunting already?

"Vinna, you're not safe here," Sorik tells me. "He's coming for you. I don't know how, but he's arranging something. You need to leave."

I look at Sorik for a minute and then out into the shadows just to the left of him, sensing something there.

"I have nowhere to go. Even if I did, what's to keep him

from finding me? Tell me where I am one hundred percent safe, and I'll consider running, but until then..."

Sorik looks away, and I'm not sure if it's because the answer is nowhere, or because he's trying to think of somewhere.

"Let Adriel come. I'm not without my defenses. I'll work and train. I'll be ready for him."

Sorik steps closer to me, causing me to automatically tense. I can see that the reaction bothers him, and he doesn't come any closer.

"You look so much like them both. I still can't decide which you take after more, Vaughn or Grier. The first time I saw you, I couldn't stop staring. You were laughing and dancing with your Chosen. It's good that you have them. Your mother hoped that somehow, someday you would be surrounded by such strength."

Sorik's voice grows softer as he talks about my mother. It makes me ache for not only my loss of her, but his too. He lifts his hand as if he's going to touch me but immediately drops it. To his left, out of the shadows, another lamia appears. He's the epitome of the unsettlingly perfect beauty that all lamia are. This one has olive-toned skin, stunning crystal-blue eyes, and brown hair that's short on the sides and spiked up and slightly over. I instantly flash my short swords back into my hands and crouch defensively.

"Sorik, we need to go," the new lamia warns.

"Who the fuck is this?" I ask, my tone accusing and suspicious.

"He's a friend, Vinna, and you can trust him."

"I'm not even sure I can trust you. So you vouching for some other lamia who just crept in on our conversation, is not doing a whole lot for me," I challenge.

Sorik seems unfazed by my words as his head snaps to the right and tilts in a way that tells me he's listening to something. I look in the same direction, my runes on the helix of my ear still activated. I try to pinpoint what has him pausing. I hear a couple growls and the soft sound of padded paws hitting damp dirt.

"Sorik, you need to go. If they find you on their land, they will probably tear you to shreds without question."

Sorik looks at his friend and then back to me, his face filled with an impenetrable sadness.

"I'm sorry about Talon," he whispers. "I couldn't stop them. Not without giving myself away."

Images of Sorik standing by while Faron tortured Talon in that cellar stab at my mind and heart. I stare at the big, golden-haired lamia, and I question if anything he says can be trusted. Why would it matter if he gave himself away? My mother is dead. Vaughn probably is too. Who is left to protect? I push down all the sudden doubts and suspicions that fill me. I'll look at them later, but right now Sorik and his buddy need to leave. Slowly, I nod my head in understanding, hoping the action will give him what he needs to go.

"I'll come back. When I have a better plan for how to keep you safe, I'll send for you. I have some things set in motion, but unfortunately, it's going to take more time."

"Sorik, now!" the blue-eyed lamia demands.

Multiple wolf howls pierce through the other lamia's order, and Sorik pulls his shirt on back over his head. He stares at me like he wants to say something else. But instead, he turns and runs through the barrier and out into the shadows of the night. The magic of the barrier shatters all around him, and the darkness gradually overtakes the light of the fading magic.

I release my hold on my weapons. I have no idea how to process what the fuck just happened or what Sorik's revelation means for me. Sentinels can transfer magic outside of Sentinel and caster bloodlines.

Holy shit!

Is this why Sentinels went into hiding and never resurfaced? Was it more than the fact that they were being murdered? Were they being forced to bind and transfer their magic to anyone strong enough to take it? Can Sentinels even be *forced* to mark and transfer their magic? *Fuck*! I really need to read that tablet the Readers left me!

Torrez is the first wolf to find me. He breaks into the clearing and drops his nose to the ground. He sniffs all around me, letting out a low growl followed by a whine. His huge wolf body nudges up against me, but I'm too numb and overwhelmed by everything that just happened to respond in any way. Alpha Silas breaks through the trees and skids to a stop next to Torrez. His wolf is black as coal, and his eyes glow yellow and reflective. Several other wolves lope in behind him and move to surround me. There's no sign of the rest of the pack.

Torres and Silas both shift in front of me, and I blame shock for not looking away.

"Are you okay?" Torrez asks me.

"Where is it?"

Torrez's question is flanked by Silas's, and I'm not sure who to answer first. I run my fingers through my hair, not sure what to say or how to respond. A brown wolf circles us, he gives a yip, and two other wolves break away from the cluster surrounding me and head in the direction that Sorik and his friend ran away.

Torrez places his hands on the outside of my arms and leans down. His looming face breaks up the image of the wolves who are now hunting down my mother's other Chosen. What does that make him to me? Another dad? An uncle? Lachlan's face flashes through my mind, and I immediately shut down my train of thought. I refocus on the smooth tan face and dark brown eyes in front of me.

"He's gone. It's fine. I'm fine."

I try to pull away from Torrez's tightening hold, but he doesn't let me. His grip is firm on my upper arms as he turns to his Alpha.

"Were they working together? One distracts while the other moves in on her?"

Silas looks me over as he contemplates Torrez's cryptic question. "What did the leeches say to you, Vinna? Why do you look so..." Silas's nostrils flare, and he breathes deeply before continuing, "unnerved?"

I meet his questioning gaze and debate what to do. They can smell lies, so there's really no point in trying to come up with some kind of cover-up for what just happened. I go with vague.

"It's nothing you should worry about. It has nothing to do with you or your pack."

Silas narrows his eyes at my lacking explanation. He folds his big arms over his chest, his stubborn body language matching the tone of my dismissive explanation.

"Leeches just breached our territory for the first time in pack history. I'd say that has everything to do with me and my pack. What just happened should've been impossible, and that's definitely something worth worrying about. I don't see or scent any ash, which means they were here with a good enough reason to convince you to let them live. Now, I'll ask you again, what did they want?"

Silas lets some bite come through in his tone as he demands an answer again. I can feel the threat in the air, and I know that I'm not going to get out of this unscathed if I don't cough something up. Seven wolves surround me, including Silas and Torrez. I try to picture what it would be like to fight seven versions of Torrez all at the same time. A part of me bubbles over with excitement at what a challenge it could be, to try and take them all on and win. But, could I do it without killing any of them? As much as a good part of me likes the idea of fighting my way out of this, I don't want to kill any of them or, you know, die.

"Fucking hell, I think she just got excited by your threat," Torrez groans, and his pupils dilate as he scents me.

He seems to be fighting internally with himself about something. A few whines sound off around me, and Silas gets an amused glint in his eyes.

"Definitely one of a kind," he grumbles quietly.

So quietly that, if I didn't already have my runes activated to increase my hearing, I would have missed it. Silas tilts his head as he considers me, and I decide to do the only thing that will satisfy his question and get me out of here as soon as possible. I tell him the truth.

"He was here to warn me. I have some history with his nest. He knew my parents, and he felt he owed them, so he came to let me know that I'm not safe here."

Torrez and Silas both scent my admission.

"And what did you say to that?" Silas asks me, a smile fighting to break across his face.

Why is he suddenly so amused?

"I said let the threat come. I'll deal with it when it does."

Silas gives me a nod of approval, and Torrez's hold on my shoulders tightens ever so slightly. I reach up and pinch his nipple in an effort to make him let go of me. Instead of it hurting him and causing him to flinch like I thought it would, the opposite seems to happen. I'm pretty sure he likes it, and the serious erection he's sporting supports that theory. He pulls me into him and shoves his face in the crook of my neck. He breathes in deeply, and I push against him in protest.

He nuzzles against me, either oblivious, or just not

giving a shit about my efforts to get away from him. Fuck, he's strong. So I do the only thing I can think to do in this situation. I call on a small dagger and move my hand to his overeager, rock-hard dick. I press the flat of the blade against the base of his hard-on and wait for him to notice. A few seconds pass, and he freezes with realization and then snickers with amusement.

Does he have any normal reactions to pain or threats?

Pfft, like you're one to talk, Vinna.

Not at all dissuaded by my clear lack of interest, Torrez runs the tip of his nose across the runes on the top of my shoulder. *This Balto-ass motherfucker.* I swipe my hand and the blade to the side, cutting him. He yelps and jumps back.

"Witch! What the fuck?" Torrez shouts, his hands flashing from my shoulders down to protect himself.

He pulls one hand back up and glares at me when he spots blood on his fingertips.

"Listen carefully, White Fang. I don't know what kind of sexual assault passes for affection around here, but I'm not interested in finding out. When a female pushes you away, you move the fuck away. And don't you ever touch my runes again."

Torrez flashes a knowing smile at me that has me seeing red. Fuck it. I take it back; I'm cool with killing at least one shifter tonight. In less than a second, the dagger I'm still gripping goes flying toward Torrez. Silas snaps his hand out, stealing the blade from the air, and keeps it from connecting with his Beta. The smug look that was sneaking across the Alpha's face falls when the second dagger I called and threw, lands in Torrez's shoulder. Torrez shouts and starts swearing, which effectively wipes the shit-eating grin he was just wearing right off his face.

I fucking warned him.

"Well, thanks for the run, the threats, and the complete

disregard for my body and boundaries. I think I've had quite enough of your hospitality, and I'll be on my way."

I give a terse nod to Alpha Silas, who doesn't seem to know if he should deal with me or tend to Torrez. I don't wait for him to decide before I turn around and start walking off. A gargantuan white and gray wolf growls at me when I step toward him, expecting him to move out of my way. Magenta streaks crackle over my skin when I call on my Offensive magic in response to the threat.

The wolf's eyes quickly dart behind me, and then he drops his lips back down over his canines and steps aside. I throw a look over my shoulder and give a nod of thanks to Silas for intervening.

"The lamia won't be back. Sorry my drama followed me here."

I give an absent wave but don't wait for a reply, before stalking my way back through the trees. Now to find my Jeep and get the fuck out of here.

17

I snuggle in deeper against the large body at my back. Morning wood pushes against my ass, and I rub my cheek against the muscular bicep under my head. Another arm coils tighter around my waist, pressing me in closer to whoever is behind me. Judging by the nicely tanned arms around me, it's either Valen or Bastien in here with me. They're lucky I noticed the runes on their finger earlier when I woke up cocooned by my surprise bed buddy.

I push my ass against the good morning going on in this twin's pants and fight off a smile. A big hand moves lower on my abdomen as one of the twins groans and grinds against me from behind.

"Fuck, Bruiser. You feel so fucking good," Bastien rumbles in my ear, before he nips at my earlobe.

I tilt my head to give him better access. My teasing laugh dies in my throat when Bastien sucks on my neck and thrusts his cock deliciously close to where I want it. I give an appreciative moan and grind back against Bastien a couple more times before I wiggle around in his arms so that we're facing each other. By the moons, he's gorgeous.

I give a quick thought about my morning breath, but the

concern flutters away when Bastien's lips take hold of mine. He runs his fingers through my hair and deepens the kiss. His tongue teases mine. His lips nip and suck me and every nerve ending in my body fully awake. He rolls me to my back, and I go willingly, spreading my legs wide in invitation.

He sucks my bottom lip hard and releases it with a pop. He kisses a trail down my neck while simultaneously pushing up my t-shirt. He grinds his hips between my spread thighs, and the friction has my soaked underwear delightfully rubbing against my lips and clit. My girly grunt of approval turns into a languid moan when Bastien takes my nipple into his mouth and sucks hard. *Fuck, he's going to have me coming from just that.* He alternates flicks of his tongue with deep hard sucks and pinches my other nipple hard with his fingers. He pulls away and softly brushes his full lips around my peaked, sensitive breasts.

"By the stars, I can't wait to wake up with you like this all the time. Even if it's not me, I'm going to get off every morning knowing one of the others is in here doing this to you."

Bastien punctuates his confession by trading nipples and resumes his ministrations. I arch into him, encouraging every single thing that he's doing. My hands are tangled into his dark waves as I pant and moan, and my orgasm builds. A purple flash of magic ripples down my arms and moves from me to Bastien. His head jerks up in surprise as the magic moves toward him. His eyes close, and he lets out a blissful moan as the violet magic soaks into him.

If I hadn't already experienced my orgasm-inducing, sexed-up magic with Valen, I'd probably be freaking out right now. But I know it feels fucking amazing instead of painful like I thought the first time it happened. That thought momentarily snaps me out of the hormone muddled moment.

"Bastien, where are the others, and how the hell did you get in here?"

He gives a deep moan and grinds against me again, as another ripple of purple magic soaks into him. Fuck. He takes a moment to process that I asked him something and tries to rein in his focus.

"The guys are all home. It was my night to come and try and break in, so that's why I'm here."

I stare at him confused.

"Knox tried to get in the first night, and Valen the second. Your paladin babysitter caught both of them and sent them on their way. I figured the same thing would happen to me, but last night when I showed up, he was nowhere to be seen. So I let myself in." He nuzzles my nipple with the tip of his nose. "The elders are fucking delusional if they think this place is safe. The gate opens for anyone, and I magicked the window open, and it didn't even set off an alarm. I'm sure Enoch and Becket probably think they're untouchable because of who their fathers are, but after what happened with the lamia, they should fucking know better."

Bastien leans down to get back to business, but I cup his stubble covered cheeks and pull his head up. Shit. Why does reality have to fuck with the needs of my libido?

"Bas, if so much shit didn't go down last night, I would be demanding right now that you bang me into next Tuesday. But a ton of shit did go down, so can we pause this fuckfest for like ten minutes?" He smiles at me, his eyes lighting up with humor. "I'm serious; it's just a pause, because this"—I reach down and palm his cock—"needs to be inside of me as soon as possible."

Bastien groans and grinds against my hand, and it's all I

can do not to reach into his pants and give his dick a proper hello.

"Bruiser, we're not having sex here in Enoch Cleary's coven house."

I sit up on my elbows and give him my best WTF face. "Uh...why the fuck not?"

"Because your first time and our first time is not going to be under his roof," he states matter-of-factly.

"Well...what the hell, you tease," I sulk and yank my shirt down over my exposed breasts.

Bastien chuckles at my indignation. "I was going to make you come. See what I could do to make you scream my name, nice and loud so everyone could hear the proof that you're mine."

His words streak right to my clit, and I have to fight off a moan and the sudden desire to let him do just that. Fucking hell.

"Listen, I've had enough of all of you pussyfooting around my pussy. I mean, yay for all your chivalry and consideration and shit. But let's get this show on the road! And, so there's no confusion, by show, I mean sex, and by road, I mean a lot of sex. You guys have been holding out on me since all the shit went down with the lamia. Now I'm stuck here in this house, and you guys don't want to touch me, what the hell?"

I decide to shut the fuck up before my tone gets whinier than it already is. Bastien cups my face and forces me to look at him when I try to look away.

"Bruiser, you had just been attacked and had to watch your friend die. We were all terrified and angry about what happened, and trying to help you through the horror show that you'd just experienced. Come on, you know that wasn't the right time to take things further. What's going on? Why the sudden urgency?"

I look back and forth between Bastien's hazel eyes and try to read what's hidden inside their depths. *Why do I feel so pressed about this?* I could easily blame it on my magic; there's definitely a pull there whenever the guys are around. Losing Talon could easily be a factor, too. Everything feels so finite in the wake of his death, and there's a lot of sadness and pain that I'd like to chase away with orgasms and mindless pleasure. But this need is more than that.

"I don't know. As weird as it might sound, you guys feel like home. There's so much chaos right now. I just want to feel settled, anchored in some way, I guess."

I try to cover my face with my hands. I'm not making any sense, and I sound like an idiot.

"Bruiser, don't do that. There's nothing to be embarrassed about." He softly kisses the back of my hands. "I get it. I never realized that you were a piece of me that was missing. Not until you were here. Until you fit into me in a way that made me realize that I wasn't really all of me without you. I'm *more*, in a way that's hard to explain. But I'm more with you, and now that I realize that, I don't want to go back to the way things were before."

I spread my fingers and peek through them to watch Bastien as he's talking. His expression and his words brand his name into my soul. And I know he's just marked me as permanently as I've marked him.

"We all hate that you're not with us, Bruiser. Trust me; we're doing everything we can to fix it as soon as possible."

"Even Captain Cockblock?" I tease, as I drop my hands from my face.

Bastien laughs and gives me a sweet kiss. "Even the Captain."

Bastien starts to say something else and then stops himself suddenly.

"Oh, you better dish it, Bastien. If you want to hear

everything that went down last night, and trust me you do, you better spill whatever you're holding onto."

He shakes his head at me, but his chest vibrates against mine with his laughter. "Fuck, the guys are going to kill me, but what am I supposed to do when you're pushing for sex and calling us *home*? Who can stand up to that?"

I laugh and tighten my thighs around his hips.

"We bought a house yesterday. That's why we all went radio silent. We wanted to surprise you."

I sit up so fast that I almost headbutt him. "Are you serious? Was it one of the ones you guys showed me the other day?"

Bastien mimes locking his lips and throwing away the key. I squeal in excitement, not even caring that he's not going to give me any more details. *This is huge.* This means that even if I get stuck being forced to live with Enoch and his coven longer, I can still go be with the guys in *our* house.

Holy shit, it feels weird to say that. We're an our and an us now. I bounce up and down on the bed.

"When do you guys get to move in?"

He shakes his head at me, and I glare at him.

"Oh, come on, you can at least tell me that."

He chuckles again and gives a relenting sigh. "This week. But I'm not saying anything else. I'm going to get my ass kicked enough as it is. Now your turn. What's all the shit that went down last night?"

I run my fingers through his hair and down the back of his neck.

"So, remember that blond lamia, Sorik, that I told you about? The one that seemed like he was trying to help me in some weird way in the cellar? Well, he and I had the craziest fucking chat last night. You are never going to guess the mental shit that I found out."

Bastien pushes himself off of me and doesn't stop until

he's off the bed. He looks pissed, which was not exactly the reaction I was expecting.

"What the fuck are these idiots doing? I mean how far does your head need to be up your ass to let another fucking lamia get close to you? Where the fuck is your paladin? I'm going to fucking strangle him."

I stand up on the bed to try to quiet Bastien, who's practically shouting at this point.

"Bas, shut the fuck up. If you wake up the whole house, I can't tell you what I learned. It's Sentinel shit."

He angrily paces at the end of the bed but doesn't say anything else, which I take as a good sign.

"Okay, so long story short. Mave invited me to some moon thing her pack was doing last night, so I went. The Alpha invited me to run with them, so I did. Mave and Pebble disappeared on me, and I'm pretty sure some dirty sex was the reason why. That's also the reason you were able to get in here last night, because I'm pretty sure they are passed out together somewhere. Shifter moonshine is no joke."

Bastien tries to say something, but I put my finger over his mouth to shush him.

"Okay, so I ran with the pack, which was beyond amazing. I'm ninety percent sure they'll never let me do it again because I stabbed one of the Betas and threatened to cut off his dick. But the run part was fucking incredible."

Bastien opens his mouth to ask all the questions brimming in his eyes, but I cover his lips with the palm of my hand to keep him quiet.

"So that's where I ran into Sorik. The pack went off to hunt, and I wasn't allowed to hang for that part. On my way back, Sorik went streaking by me. When I caught up to him, he whipped off his shirt—and guess what the fuck he had on him?"

Bastien narrows his eyes at me and points to the hand covering his mouth. I leave it there because he's never going to guess anyway.

"He has fucking runes, Bas. *Runes*. Sorik was one of my mom's Chosen. Can you fucking believe that?"

Bastien licks the palm of my hand, and I jerk it away at the contact.

"What the fuck? A lamia can be a Chosen?"

It takes me a minute to process Bastien's question, because all I can think about right now is all the other places I want him to lick.

"Fuck, Bastien, why'd you have to lick me, now all I can think about is your tongue and that whole screaming your name goal you mentioned."

"Vinna, focus."

The fact that he just called me by name, and not the pet name he's used practically from day one, snaps me out of my dirty thoughts.

"Right. So apparently, Sentinel magic isn't confined to just casters and Sentinels. We can bond and transfer with anyone."

Bastien runs both of his hands through his hair and stares at me. "Holy shit."

"My sentiments exactly. Bas, there have to be more Sentinels out there. There's no way they were all wiped out. I mean where the fuck did Grier come from? I need the tablet. I need to start going through everything that's on there. Maybe there's a way to find them. Something in there only a Sentinel would know or be able to make sense of."

He starts to pace again as he thinks about everything I'm telling him. I wait for him to come back around, and when our eyes lock, he stops.

"Bastien, I might not be the last Sentinel."

18

Someone pounds against the door, and I break away from the hopeful kiss Bastien gives me, my head snapping in the direction of the door. What the hell? I walk over and fling it open just as Enoch's hand goes up to pound on it again. He looks me over quickly.

"Sorry to wake you up, but is Pebble in here with you? He missed his check-in this morning, and his coven is here to see what's going on."

Enoch clenches his jaw, and I take in his tense body language and tightening fists.

"No, I haven't seen him since last night. What do you mean he missed his check-in?"

"He's here on assignment, Vinna. His whole coven has been tasked with your protection, but he's acting as lead. He hasn't checked-in since yesterday morning."

The doorknob I'm still holding onto gets pulled from my grasp when Bastien yanks the door all the way open.

"You're telling me she has a whole coven of fucking paladin for protection, and a lamia still got through to her last night?"

I elbow Bastien hard in the ribs, and he gives a satisfying

pained *umph*. Fucking hothead. He really needs to learn to keep his mouth shut.

"What the hell is he talking about, Vinna? And what the hell are you even doing here, Fierro?"

"I'm her fucking mate! That's what I'm doing here, and it's a good thing I am because the security around here is a joke. No alarms. No barriers. Are you guys *trying* to get her killed or taken again? Is this joke of a secure setup intentional, or are you guys just that incompetent?"

"Watch your mouth, asshole! Who the fuck do you think you are inserting yourself—"

I tune out the rest of Enoch's indignant shouting and step out of the line of testosterone-fueled fire. I grab some leggings and pull them on and slip on a bra under my t-shirt. I swipe my phone off the side table and open Mave's contact as the yelling and threats escalate to a louder decibel behind me.

Me: Tell Pebble he needs to get back here ASAP.

My phone dings with an incoming text seconds later.

Mave: He left twenty minutes ago. Hang soon to talk shit and rehash dirty details?

Me: You know it.

I don't have Pebble's number, so I have no way to give him a heads-up, but if he's missed his regular check-in, he has to know he's going to be walking into a shitstorm. I walk back over to the doorway where Bastien and Enoch are chest to chest, one practically daring the other to throw the first punch. I pinch Bastien's ass as I squeeze my way past them out into the hallway where the rest of Enoch's coven are standing by.

The fact that they're just standing by, lending silent support but not ganging up on Bastien, raises my respect level for all of them. I give a two-finger salute to the group, walking past them and out into the living room where

Pebble's coven waits. They're on edge, which makes sense given the missed check-in. The yelling down the hallway sure as hell isn't helping things, but clearly, Bastien and Enoch have some shit they need to sort out, so it is what it is.

"You guys want anything to drink or eat?" I ask the group of seven paladin all standing awkwardly in the living room.

They stare at me like I just said something in another language.

"Suit yourselves." I shrug and turn toward the kitchen. "Pebble will be back soon. We ran into a couple lamia earlier this morning, and he chased them off. We were near Silas pack territory when it happened, and he was just there giving them a heads-up."

Pebble's coven all tense up at my explanation, and I'm grateful as fuck that they aren't shifters and can't smell the dose of lies I'm feeding them. If it were just Pebble involved here, I'd probably let him face off against the firing squad on his own, but my cover-up is for Mave. She explained before that her Alpha—Trent Silas—worked with the caster Elders Council. I don't want any trouble there for him because of whatever happened between Mave and Pebble. I also don't want to take away Mave's new toy, not when she just started playing with him.

I pour a bowl of cereal and lean against a wall in the living room to eat. The yelling coming from the hallway has quieted, but I don't hear any telltale signs of fighting, so I take that as a good sign.

"Why didn't Paladin Rock call us to say he needed backup?" a gruff voice belonging to an even gruffer looking man, asks.

"You'd have to ask him," I offer unhelpfully, as I shovel another bite of cereal in my mouth.

Fuck, I miss the sisters.

"Why didn't you call us and tell us what happened?" a

lanky paladin queries, as he leans back against the arm of the sofa.

"Up until five minutes ago, I didn't know you existed. And before you go asking me why I didn't immediately alert Nash, Enoch, Kallan, or Becket, the answer is because I can take care of myself, and there wasn't shit any of them could do at that point."

I crunch down on another mouthful of cereal and stare at the door, willing Pebble to walk through it. Hopefully, he'll be smart enough to catch on quickly and just play along. Kallan, Becket, Nash, Enoch, and Bastien all file out of the hallway. Bastien still looks pissed, and judging by the look Enoch's wearing, they didn't quite sort out their issues. Bastien walks over to me and redirects a bite of cereal headed for my mouth into his instead.

"You're lucky you're so hot, ya thief."

I glare at him playfully, and his scowl morphs into a teasing grin. He swallows his bite and gives me a quick peck before he steals more of my cereal. I turn my back on him to guard the rest of my breakfast, hissing at him like a cat.

"The sisters make your every meal, and you're going to rob me of my Captain Crunch? You're not the man I thought you were."

Bastien chuckles and tweaks my nose. "That's because I'm a caster, baby."

The front door swings open, and Pebble walks in. He doesn't seem shocked to see the large group that's waiting for his arrival. I step forward, and Pebbles eyes land on me.

"Did the pack catch the lamia?" I ask casually, while I try not to be too obvious with the *play along* look I'm giving him.

He pauses for a beat. "No. The trail led out of town. They stopped tracking at the boundary."

Well, at least he's aware that there was a lamia issue last

night. Hopefully, he can use that info to pull himself out of the hole he's dug.

"Why didn't you call for help?" The gruff paladin from Pebble's coven asks, his eyes laced with suspicion.

"My phone was dead."

The room grows quiet and stuffy with unspoken doubt.

"We'd like to have a word with Paladin Rock outside," another paladin announces, his eyes trained on Enoch, but his words and suspicion aimed at Pebble.

Enoch gives a nod, and Pebble and his grumpy coven all file outside slamming the door behind them.

Nash steps forward, looking confused. "What the fuck is going on, Vinna? What happened last night?"

"You'll have to talk to Pebble about what happened with him. But I hung out with a friend and ran into some lamia, and that's that."

"Oh, *that's that?* I just ran into some supes who belong to a race that tried to abduct me a week ago, but hey, no biggie." Kallan blows on his nails and wipes them on his chest with mock indifference. "I mean, who cares that they're not even supposed to be able to get through the town barrier right now, but it's all good, guys."

I glare at Kallan, not at all amused by his high-pitched impersonation of me.

"Fuck, I need to call my dad and let him know there was a breach. You need to go."

Enoch gestures to Bastien with one hand while the other pulls his phone from his pocket.

"He can stay however long he wants," I defend, finishing off the last of my cereal.

"It's fine, Bruiser; I should go let the guys in on what's up anyway."

"Fine," I grumble, already not looking forward to his absence.

I'm so much more comfortable when one or all of my guys are around. I hate feeling like a guest and tiptoeing around this house because I don't belong here. Outside of my Chosen, I don't trust anyone's motivations, and I hate needing to be on guard all the time. It's fucking exhausting. I follow Bastien over to the door like a puppy that doesn't want its owner to leave. He tucks a strand of hair behind my ear and cups my cheek.

"Don't look so sad, Bruiser. You're killing me. We can hang later. And don't worry, this will all be over soon."

I nod. Bastien leans down and kisses me. His hands slip to cup my ass, and the kiss morphs into something that ranks between *fuck me now* and *bye dear*. I'm completely aware that Bastien is embracing his inner caveman and enjoying the show he's putting on as much as he's enjoying me right now. He's thoroughly marking his territory, and I like it. I start to chuckle at the glint in his eyes as we pull apart. He throws me a shit-eating grin and turns to open the door.

"Oh, I almost forgot," Bastien calls over his shoulder. "Knox told me to tell you that he's picking you up tonight for a thing at his family's coven house."

With that, Bastien leaves. I catch a glance of Pebble and his coven still locked in a heated discussion outside before the door closes, shutting them and their conversation away. I'm once again left on my own to deal with Enoch and his coven, none of whom look too pleased by everything that just went down.

Enoch's phone rings, and he answers it without taking his eyes off me. I'm not really sure what to say to any of them at this point, so I walk past their impersonations of tourists at a zoo viewing some kind of caged, wild animal and head toward the kitchen to clean my now-empty cereal bowl. My skin prickles from the eyes I can feel tracking me at my back.

"We're supposed to start tutoring you on magic use today. Caster Sawyer explained that with your ability to mimic, we mostly need to show you what's magically possible with each branch. Once you see it, you should then be able to replicate it."

My eyes narrow at Becket's mention of Marilyn Manson's real name. But my irritation at having to think about that asshole dissipates with the plan to train my magic. I turn around to find that Kallan, Becket, and Nash have followed me into the kitchen, all eyes still uncomfortably trained on me. I narrow my gaze at them.

"Sounds good. But consider yourselves warned. If any of you try to pull what the elders and that asshole did the other day, I'll fucking kill you. I don't care who you're connected to. I am done with being attacked. You either have my back or you don't."

"We have your back. You *can* trust us."

Enoch walks in from the living room, his eyes intense. His declaration hanging in the air amid the nods of confirmation from the rest of his coven. I release a deep breath. *Looks like it's time to see if that's true.*

19

I stare at my reflection critically one last time, wondering again if I should change. I initially thought a dress was the right thing to wear to meet the parents of the caster you've claimed and permanently marked as your own for time and all eternity. Then, I thought maybe that looked like I was trying too hard, so I changed into jeans and a t-shirt, but that made me seem like I didn't give any fucks at all. So I now stand here in dark jeans, a white fitted tank, and a lavender kimono-style cardigan that I've layered on top of it.

I twist from side to side, watching myself in the full-length mirror, trying to take in all angles of my outfit. The pale-purple, almost sheer cardigan, has large maroon and white blooms on it. I'm hoping it says fun, loving, and sorry I marked your son and unknowingly forced him into a relationship with me.

Fuck! I've never put this much thought into anything I've worn before.

I run my fingers through my loose curls, smooth down my middle part and huff out a sigh. By the stars, I hope they don't hate me. I don't know why that's the direction my mind automatically takes me when I think about meeting any of the guys' family. Maybe it has something to do with the less-than-stellar response I've gotten from anyone claiming to be *my* family, but I've spent the whole time I've been getting ready convincing myself that if their families hate me, somehow we'll figure out a way to survive it.

Deep down in my gut, I don't believe a word of my delusional reassurances, but I keep repeating them to myself anyway. Maybe if I say it enough, put it out there in the world, it just might come true. I look outside to the annoyingly cheerful blue sky—where's a star to wish on when you need one?

I can just see the weird arena that's in the backyard, and the sight of it triggers memories of the shitshow that was my first magic tutorial.

"Vinna, you're not even trying. Enoch, show her again," Becket insists.

Enoch huffs out a resigned sigh and once again focuses on a patch of sand just to the left of me. It slowly begins to churn, circling around until a tiny whirlpool occurs. Then the sand lifts up off the ground and becomes a cyclone. Above my head, ominous smoke-colored storm clouds form, and out of nowhere, a bolt of lightning strikes the center of the sand tornado, which then immediately crumbles to the ground.

Sweet Home Alabama fucking lied because there is no pretty glass structure left in the wake of the kissing lightning and sand, and I once again feel ripped off, even though this is like the sixtieth time I've witnessed this magical trick.

"Okay, now you try it," Becket instructs, and for the sixty-first time today, I focus on my well of magic and call to my Elemental power. The Kelly green slippery strand puts up a fuss, but eventually, I get an imaginary white-knuckled hold on it. I show it the sand tornado that I want, not even bothering with the extra pressure of the lightning show. I release the magic so it can

go be one with the epic sand cyclone I just commanded it to make, but once again all that happens is a tiny little cone of sand forms in the most pathetic and painfully slow way.

Fuck, I'd take an epic sand castle at this point, but no, I once again get the fucking cone of shame. Finicky damn magic.

Becket and Kallan groan their disapproval, and Enoch throws his hands up in the air in frustration. Nash gives me a sympathetic smile, which only makes me want to kick him in the balls. I don't need sympathy; I need to figure out why my magic hates me and thinks it's hilarious to make me look like a raging idiot.

"They said if you see it, then you should be able to do it, so what is the disconnect? Are you just not into this, or what is the problem?" Kallan demands.

"Do I have white hair?" I ask, lifting a wayward dark strand that's escaped my messy bun. "Are my eyes suddenly glowing white and I'm just not aware of it?"

Kallan shakes his head no, confusion flooding his features.

"That's right, because I'm not Storm or some fucking X-Man. I don't know how to make sand tornados and shoot lightning bolts from my ass!"

Kallan rolls his eyes, and Enoch throws his hands out challengingly. "Oh that's right, ass-knives are more your style."

"I'll take my ass-knives over your wannabe Zeus light show any day of the week."

We both take a threatening step toward each other before Nash rushes in between us and tells us both to cool off. Keeping things mature, I flip Enoch off as I walk away, abandoning the magic lesson that's not going anywhere, and head back into the house.

"We're not done with this, Vinna. You have to keep at it until you figure it out," Enoch shouts at my back.

"Go sit on a lightning rod," I shout over my shoulder, as I slide open the glass door that leads back into the house and disappear through it.

I shake myself out of the memory and smooth down my cardigan. The doorbell rings, and the sound works like a defibrillator that's just sent an electrical current straight through my heart, making it beat into a worrying frenzy. I quickly apply lip gloss, throw the tube into my bag, and make my way out of the room to the front door. I round the corner just as Nash opens the too big door and then proceeds to frown at my Chosen on the other side. Knox gives me a huge smile, and I find the happiness that's radiating from it contagious.

Momentarily, the worry that's riding me falls away, and excitement takes its place as I walk toward Knox in the doorway. He gives me a purposeful and appraising sweep of his eyes, and when they meet mine again, I see the want there, and I can't help but grin. With Knox, there has never been a single moment where I haven't felt wanted and devourable.

"Hello, beautiful!" he coos at me as I reach him.

He snakes an arm around my waist and pulls me into him, placing a soft and appreciative kiss on my lips. It's the kind of kiss that steals a little of my lip gloss but doesn't smear it all over my face, which impresses me and makes me give him an approving eyebrow raise and nod as his delicious lips pull away from mine. A light glossy sheen now accentuates his plump lips, and I chuckle at the thought of leaving it there, unbeknownst to him.

I try to keep my smile from giving me away as I picture this beefy jock of a male walking around looking like he's dipping a toe, or his lips rather, in the metro pool and flirting with a glossy feminine side.

Out of nowhere, the image of an apron-clad woman slapping a rolling pin into her open palm while glaring at me flashes through my head. I cringe at the mental image of Knox's disapproving mom and quickly reach up and wipe away the residue of clear gloss. Knox doesn't acknowledge his makeup wearing or the sheepish look that sits on my face as I try to tell the grumpy mental image of Knox's mom *sorry*.

"You ready to go, gorgeous?" he asks, not bothered or worried in the slightest about introducing me to his family.

I really shouldn't be surprised by his casual tone and *no big deal* attitude. It seems to take a lot to ruffle his feathers. His *rolling-with-the-punches, down-for-anything* crown sits firmly on his handsome head, and he keeps his arm around me as he leads me out of the house. We pass Nash who's standing there in all his grumpy glory, the disapproval rolling off him in waves. I can't be bothered to sort out whatever has crawled up his ass, so I give him a wave as I leave and then brush all thoughts of him and his coven out of my mind as I make my way to the white Range Rover parked in the circular driveway.

Why is Knox driving Ryker's car? I can tell it's definitely Ryker's and not just a Range Rover twin—which is a possibility given the caster hard-on for this make of vehicle—because of the music that starts playing when Knox turns the engine over. It's the same band Ryker was listening to the night I stole his car. Maybe Knox doesn't own a car... Hmm, I learn something new about them every day. I don't bother asking one way or the other, because it doesn't really matter to me. I wouldn't own one either if Aydin hadn't forced my hand.

"So we're the proud owners of a house now?" I try to ask casually, but a hint of giddiness peeks through.

We pull out of Enoch's driveway and head toward town. Knox chuckles at my question and then shoots a playful glare at me.

"It was wrong to use your feminine wiles against Bastien like that," he accuses.

I clutch my chest and feign innocence, "I did no such

thing, and I resent the implication. I can't help that this information happened to spill out in the heat of a *close* moment. Maybe he just sucks at secret keeping." I shrug my shoulders and bat my eyes coquettishly at Knox. He's not buying anything I'm selling, judging by the incredulous snorting noise he makes.

"Speaking of pillow talk, I want to know every detail of what happened with Sorik. He seriously had runes?" Knox exclaims, and his effort at changing the subject doesn't go unnoticed.

"Knox, give me more credit than that, I can't be so easily dissuaded."

He laughs.

"It's cute that you guys are trying to surprise me with this whole house thing, but now that the cat is out of the bag, I'm dying to know every little detail. I'm too nosey not to know exactly what's going on."

I turn so my back is against the car door, and I'm facing his profile, giving him the full effect of my pout. Since Bastien let the big secret slip, I've been picturing what our new place could look like. I've had to stop myself from getting too detailed in my daydream, because what if what they chose doesn't live up to the picture I'm painting in my mind?

I should just be happy with whatever they bought, because it means we all get to be together when we want to be. So what if it doesn't have a diving board? Is that really something to swoon over or get disappointed about if it's not there? It will still be the place that I can eventually call home with my Chosen, and really, that's all I need. Well, that and a gym, and maybe we can get a pool and add a diving board—you know, if it doesn't have that already, which it might.

"Just tell me one thing," I try to negotiate.

Knox gives me the side-eye.

"Does it have a diving board and a gym?"

He laughs and shakes his head at me. "You never said you wanted a diving board before."

"I know, I didn't even know I wanted one until today."

I throw my hand up in a *what can you do* motion and roll my eyes at myself.

Knox tilts his head for a moment, and then he sneaks a look at me.

"Fuck. Now I know how you got to Bastien so fast. Stop being so fucking adorable."

"I am not adorable. I am a vicious beast who can only be tamed by a diving board and a gym...and an occasional fight, maybe with a shifter, because as of right now, I've had the most fun fighting them."

Knox laughs even harder. "Killer, give me a shot at taming your beast, and we'll see if you still need all the other stuff."

His voice somehow grows thicker with sensual promise, and the combination of his deep tone and his smooth words works a spell over me that has me drooling and ready to ask him to pull over. I sneak a glance out of the window and send a silent challenge out into the universe that if it really loves me, the perfect pull-off spot will be just up ahead. I know the others voiced their opinions about beds and first times, but I know I can convince Knox to abandon all that nonsense in an effort to tame the need coursing through me right now.

I throw an angry grandma-style closed fist up at the universe when, instead of the perfect pull-off spot revealing itself just up ahead, I notice that we're in a suburban neighborhood and surrounded by houses. *Why does the universe want to keep me from getting laid?*

Knox cracks up and leans forward, howling with laughter. "What are you talking about? How is the universe keeping you from getting laid?" he manages to get out between bursts of laughter.

I narrow my eyes at him, not at all amused by the escaped thoughts that I apparently just voiced out loud.

"How close are we to your parents' house?"

"About five minutes."

"See, the powers that be are working against the needs of my libido. You can't sexy voice me and say shit like *let me tame your beast* and then not follow through. That's fucking wrong on so many levels. And now I have to go meet your family after you've got me all riled and shit! I was already fucking nervous, but now I'm fucking nervous, and I get to add horny and twitterpated on top of it."

"Fucking hell, don't say *horny*, not when there's nothing right now I can do to fix it," he groans and shifts in his seat. I grin. "Don't you smile about that, Killer, I can't walk in to introduce you to my family with a hard-on."

My smirk grows wider, and I try to bite down against the laugh that wants to come out. "Fine, no more horny talk," I concede, and he groans again. "Tell me about your family then. What's going down tonight, and how nervous *should* I be?" I take a deep breath and try to calm the swarm of angry bees in my stomach. "I've never met anyone's family before, and our circumstances are not exactly usual. What do they know about me already? Do they hate me for marking you?" I press down against memories of Silva and his obvious disapproval over my marking any of *the boys*.

Knox reaches over and grabs my hand, giving it a reassuring squeeze.

"We haven't exactly told anyone about the whole *marked* or *Chosen* thing."

An adorably sheepish look takes over his masculine

face, and the angry bees in my stomach soften into butterflies.

Then his words sink in.

The calm that started to prematurely bubble up inside of me fizzles out, and my heart sinks.

20

"Don't look like that, Killer. It's not like we're hiding it. Okay, it *is* like that, but not because we're ashamed of you or have any issues with what's happened. It's just that we don't know how smart it is to clue anyone in on how *different* you are, or exactly what that means for us as your Chosen."

Knox's words tumble out hurriedly, and I can see the worry on his face that somehow I'm taking this all the wrong way. He focuses back on the road for a minute, and the silence permeates the car.

"I love my family, but they trust the elders. They'll think our keeping secrets from them is wrong. They won't see things the way that we do, and will be suspicious of the way that we are. We're still hopeful that the elders will make a decision that is in everyone's best interest, but with them moving you into Enoch's house, we're divided on whether or not that will happen. We all agreed to keep this quiet until we know more."

I nod, understanding that handling what I am like this is for the best for all of us, but when I look down at Knox's hand in mine, I see one huge flaw in the plan.

"So how did you explain these?" I ask, lifting his hand and pointing to the runes on his ring finger.

"Well, we've been playing a solid game of avoidance. If we have to speak face to face with anyone in our families, we have something covering our hands like a towel or clothing. So far it's worked, but tonight is a mandatory family night, and there's probably not going to be any way for us to avoid what's about to go down."

I snap my head toward Knox and glare at him.

"Knox, are you kidding? Please tell me you're kidding! You can't take me to meet your family for the first time, knowing that we're going to blow up their lives. We're supposed to convince them of my awesomeness, not shatter everything they thought they knew. It was already going to take a miracle to get your mom to like me! I can't cook, I say *fuck* like every other word, and I like to fight...a lot! Now you want to go in and announce the whole *marked*, hey she's not a caster but a *Sentinel* thing, too? If we do that, then there's really no way I'm ever going to win your family over. I'm fucked! You totally just fucked me, and not in the way I was wanting."

Exasperated, I drop my head back against the tan leather of the seat. Fucked is an understatement; I'll be lucky if I can walk away from tonight without having to fight members of Knox's family, which I'm sure is going to go over really well.

Knox chuckles, but I fail to see what about this situation is even remotely funny.

"Don't stress, Killer, everything is going to be fine."

We pull into the driveway of a large Victorian house, it's modest compared to Lachlan's showy chateau and Enoch's modern ranch, but it's still big by any normal person's standards. The house and surrounding land seem well cared for, and Knox pulls the Range Rover in behind a line of other cars.

Knox rests a large hand on my thigh and gives me one of his mind-stopping smiles. It's all straight white teeth and full kissable lips, and it makes his gray eyes light up in this delicious way that makes me want to dive into them and never come out. If only getting out of this disaster-destined night were that easy.

"Don't worry; they're going to love you. Just go with the flow and trust us."

I just barely keep from rolling my eyes at his attempt at reassurance that doesn't manage to reassure me at all. Of course he thinks everything is going to be fine; this is Knox. We could be in the middle of a zombie apocalypse, and this dude would be all smiles and excitement as he cuts off heads and casually discusses what's for dinner.

Knox closes his door, and I hop out as he rounds the front of the SUV, coming toward me.

"You're supposed to let me be all chivalrous and shit in front of my family," he playfully scolds me.

"Pshhh, please! You're about to throw me to the wolves, I can't give off the needy damsel vibe, not when it's about to be survival of the fittest up in here."

He chuckles, and I slap his chest playfully. He snatches my hand and presses a kiss into my palm, and the pure sweetness of the gesture has me momentarily all aflutter. Our gazes settle on each other, and I'm so overwhelmed with gratitude for who he is and how he lightens the heaviness that perpetually pushes down on my shoulders. A soft smile lifts his lips, and he laces his fingers with mine. He tugs my hand, pulling me out of the moment that's swelling with feelings I'm not sure I'm recognizing correctly and sure as hell don't know how to navigate.

He leads me away from the car, but instead of moving

toward the plum-colored front door, Knox leads me around the side of the house and into the enormous gated backyard. Boisterous conversation and laughter bounce toward us as we walk to a group of people gathered around long tables loaded with food. I'm so focused on my breathing and trying to calm the nerves scurrying through my body, that I'm surprised when my eyes land on a face I recognize. Ryker's lips turn up in a beautiful and welcoming smile, and he puts down a plate of food and comes toward us. I look around quickly to see if any of the other guys are here, but only strangers stare back at me from the remaining faces.

Ryker reaches us, and he cups my face and plants a kiss that's just a bit more than a peck. It's a perfect hello and leaves me wanting more as his soft, cushioned lips break away from mine.

He pulls me into a hug, but Knox keeps my hand in his so it's a little weird.

"Bastien told us about what happened with the shifters. Are you okay?" he asks, leaning down with his mouth close to my ear, so only I hear his question.

He pulls away, and I reach up to place my palm against his cheek to soothe away the concern I see there. I nod, but it's all I can get out before people surround us, and I don't dare say anything more about Sorik and what happened. Ryker steps back, and I'm immediately inundated with handshakes and hugs until Knox picks me up, removing me from all of the commotion, and demands that they stop freaking me out. I laugh as he puts me down and rests his beefy arm over my shoulders protectively.

"Bunch of animals, you'd think you'd never seen a pretty female before, acting like that!"

Chuckles bounce around the group, and they settle with Knox's chastisement. He points to a dark-skinned man who steps forward from the group of casters and offers me his hand. I take it; his grip is firm, and his smile is reassuring.

"Killer, this is Blake, my dad; Dad, this is Vinna," Knox introduces.

Blake's eyes are a rich umber, and his gaze feels deep and comforting. Another male, this one looking like he has some sort of Mediterranean ancestry, steps forward and replaces Blake's hand with his own.

"I'm Rodrick, dad number two," he offers, with a cheeky smile.

I match it but don't get the chance to do more than that as Rodrick is boxed out, and dad number three takes my still outstretched palm.

"I'm Jason," he tells me.

His deep brown eyes are lit up with warmth and curiosity, and I have a feeling he has just as many questions brewing in his mind as I currently do.

Knox points to a Native American caster, who steps forward answering Knox's summons. He pulls my hand from Jason's and gives his compeer a teasing smile as he bumps his hip and body checks Jason out of the way.

"Don't go hogging all the pretty," he teases, and my smile grows even wider. "We've been dying to meet the female who captured our boys' hearts, but you're not allowed to pick a favorite dad until the end of the night, okay?" dad number four tells me with a wink. "I'm Merlin, but everyone calls me Lin."

A snort escapes me unchecked, and I immediately feel like an asshole for laughing at his name. He gives my hand a reassuring squeeze and an accompanying smile, and my chagrin fades slightly.

"It's okay; clearly my parents had a sick sense of humor," he whispers to me conspiratorially, and I laugh.

"Was he a real person—Merlin, I mean?" I ask, not able to help myself.

Merlin's face blushes ever so slightly.

"No, his origins are firmly in the land of make-believe. My older brother was a huge *Sword in the Stone* fan, and my name is his contribution to welcoming the new baby," he tells me with a *what can you do* shrug of his shoulders.

"Could be worse; you could have ended up an Archimedes," I tell him with a cringe.

Merlin bellows out a laugh, and the group around us does too. He pulls me into a hug that squeezes the air out of me and then steps back laughing and mumbling, "Archimedes, that's a good one," to himself and the others.

He hugs Ryker and Knox, one after the other, announcing, "Oh, she's definitely a keeper, boys!"

His announcement confuses me for a minute, and I once again wonder why Ryker is here and no one else; didn't Knox say this was a family thing? Another dad steps forward on a chuckle as he wipes a laughing tear from his golden-hued eyes. The tone of his irises is stunning, the molten shade one in a million. He smiles, and a familiar twinkle shines in his golden gaze. It's a dead ringer for the cheeky glint I've spied in Knox's stare from the first day that I met him.

I would bet anything that this man is Knox's biological father, although I'm getting the distinct impression that all the men in this coven claim daddy-ship, regardless of genetics.

"I'm Trace," dad number five tells me with a hug. "And these are our other two sons. Kace is the oldest, then Kiere, Ryker, and Knox," he explains.

We exchange hellos and waves, as I try to stay in the moment and not focus on the fact that apparently Knox and Ryker are brothers, and I had no idea. Kace looks like a skinnier version of Knox but with a little lighter skin tone and a reddish-bronze tone to his hair. Kiere is dark like dad one, Blake, but somehow has Merlin's Native American features and bone structure.

I tuck all my pressing questions away, not wanting to give their family a front row seat to how little I clearly know their sons. Especially when the plan is to drop the *Sentinel* and *marked for life* bomb. Letting them in on just how much I don't know about anything, including myself, might not be the most reassuring move.

After the introductions are made, I'm led to two long tables stuffed with food, and my mouth immediately begins to water at all the amazing BBQ fare in front of me. I start to load up a plate, already making plans for what plate number two is going to have on it, when I spot two females making their way down the steps of the wrap-around porch, with pies in their hands. I'm not sure who the one female is, but I know right away the other is Knox's mom.

Her gaze lands on mine and, where Knox's eyes are a stormy gray, his mother's are the rich gray-brown of a flash flood. Their skin tone is the same, water-kissed-sand color, and I know right away from just one look, that you don't want to be on her bad side.

Her face softens as she takes me in, and I set down my plate and step back from the food to greet her. Without missing a beat, she hands the pies off to one of her mates, and next thing I know, she's wrapping me up in a firm hug. She doesn't say a word to me, and yet, I can *feel* the welcome, the worry, and the hope in her embrace. I don't shy away from the contact with her. Instead, I squeeze her tighter, hoping she can feel my promise and commitment to be everything her boys deserve. I don't know how a hug can be filled with all that this one is, but she gives me a warm nod as she pulls away, and I know we both experienced the same phenomenon, that we understand each other.

"I'm Reese, but I think it's best if you just call me Mom."

Reese gives my shoulders a gentle squeeze before she pulls Knox's big hulking frame into her arms and then grabs Ryker for a squeeze, too. They both get kisses on the cheek before she steps over and reclaims the pies from dad three's hands. With that, the jostling around the food commences, and the heavy weight of rejection that's been sitting in my heart lifts and flies away like the unwelcome interloper it is.

21

I watch the flames consume the new logs that were just added to the fire pit. The wood chars and blackens as the fire consumes it mercilessly, taking everything the wood has, whether it's freely given or not. Knox and Ryker's family laugh and joke, and the jovial sounds fill the night air as everyone eats and enjoys the fire under the star-kissed sky.

I lean back into the camp chair I'm perched in, trying to make a little more room in my stomach for my fourth piece of peach pie.

"How you doin' over there, Squeaks?" Ryker asks, wiping a spot of pie filling from the corner of my mouth with his thumb.

He draws his hand back toward his mouth, and I watch transfixed as he sucks off the dash of peachy goodness from his thumb. *Fuck, that's hot!* Absently, I shove another delicious bite of flaky, buttery crust and sugar-and-spice glazed peaches into my mouth, and give Ryker a dopey pie-loving smile. He laughs, and I can feel Knox's matching rumble on my other side.

"I think we got her drunk on happy; what do you think, Knox?"

He tilts his head from side to side as he takes me in, making a show of contemplating Ryker's questions. "Yup, she's happy-pie drunk. I'd say it's a pretty severe case of the mellows we've got on our hands."

I laugh and elbow them both as I shovel the last of the piece of pie into my greedy mouth. I hum my approval and wonder if I'm close enough with their family to be able to unbutton my pants and let my food baby out in all its glory.

"No wonder you and your brothers are so massive; with food like that, you'd have to spend all day in the gym just to work the calories off of one meal."

Ryker and Knox chuckle, and I kick my legs out, getting as comfortable in my chair as I can. I look around us to make sure no one is paying attention to us and dive into the question that's been eating at me since I met the family.

"So, don't judge me too much, but how did it slip past me that you guys are brothers?" I ask, dropping my voice to almost a whisper.

Ryker smiles sweetly at me and chuckles as he shakes his head. "We're not related. We're brothers by soul and circumstance, but not blood."

He and Knox touch knuckles, and I wrinkle my eyebrows in confusion. Ryker pulls me into him and sweetly kisses my furrowed brow.

"My mom and one of my dads died in an accident when I was four; she was pregnant," he starts. "My two other dads didn't take it well. One left Solace for reasons unknown to me, and my sole remaining parent just didn't really know what to do with me. He tried, in his own way, but he was depressed and had lost so much. Unfortunately, it seemed to break him in a way that he just couldn't come back from."

I lean toward Ryker, drawn to the hurt that I hear just

under the casual words of his story. I know what it's like to talk about something like it's normal, because it is normal to you, and yet you know the wrongness of it, feel the ache of it, in a way that can never be undone.

"I was seven when the elders rescinded my father's claim on me. I was friends with Knox through school, but we never had any contact outside of classes because of my home issues. But when I needed a place to go, they stepped up and asked to be given guardianship. I've been with them ever since. Reese is my mom, and they are my dads in every way, aside from biologically."

"Do you see that dad at all, the one who stayed?" I ask hesitantly.

Ryker's eyes drop from mine for the briefest of seconds, and when he looks back up, I fall into the depths of his blue-tinged pain.

"He killed himself a couple of weeks after he lost me."

I'm up and out of my chair before I even know what I'm doing. I move into his lap, and he pulls me into him and secures me there.

"I'm so sorry," I whisper to him, and the words are filled with all the ways that I wish I could take the hurt away.

He gives me a small smile, the broken kind you give when nothing can be done or said to change the fucked up shit in your life, so you try to dismiss it and tuck the pain back into yourself. I know that smile. I give it every time I talk about Beth or Laiken...and now Talon. It's the smile that gives the others that know it a peek at the scars you wear on the inside. I hate that he wears this smile.

I smooth back his almost shoulder-length blond hair from his face. I run my fingers through the soft strands and wish I could say something that would make this better. But I know that words can never smooth away the gouges that life gives us. I lean in and claim his lips. Gently and purposefully, I let my kiss tell him how incredible I think he is and how much better he deserved from life. It's not enough, but it's all I have to give; it's all I have to show him, that I'll care for his heart and soul and treasure him the way he always should have been.

Ryker's hands run up my back, caging me in and keeping me from moving too far away as I pull my lips from his. He gives me another smile, and this one radiates happiness and appreciation. I vow to myself that, whenever that broken smile returns, I'll do everything I can to fight for *this* smile instead. Knox clears his throat, and I look over to him, realizing that Ryker and I, at some point, have acquired an audience. Reese is cuddled up to the side of dad three, but the whole family is looking at me and smiling in a way I can't interpret.

I give them an awkward close-lipped grin and a weird wave, not sure what else to do. Ryker chuckles, and Knox comes to my rescue.

"So, uh, should we play some music or something?" he asks, that cheeky twinkle I love in his eyes.

His words must be laced with magic because they pull everyone out of their fixation on Ryker and me. Skylar—the other pie-toting female caster and Kace's mate—starts clapping and begging Knox and Ryker to play "Photograph." She comes over and grabs my hand, pulling me away from the guys and down into a seat next to her.

"Have you seen them play together yet?" she asks me, her excitement contagious.

"No, but I've been told they're both amazing."

"It's like having Ed Sheeran himself give you a private concert. I can't wait to see your face when you hear Knox and the others. It's my favorite part of family get-togethers!"

Skylar lets out an adorable squeal of excitement and keeps a firm grip on my hand. I laugh as she bounces in her chair, and Reese walks over and claims the chair on the other side of me. Kiere comes from the house and hands Ryker an acoustic guitar, and then he proceeds to sit down on a white wooden box next to Knox. Ryker pulls a pick out of the strings and plays a chord before adjusting the tuning of the instrument. When he finds the sound that he's looking for, he gives Knox a nod and then starts to play.

I don't recognize the song until the first line of lyrics flow out of Knox. My mouth falls open of its own volition, and I'm completely blown away by the incredible voice pouring out of Knox. Skylar giggles, and I can feel her eyes on me, but I can't take mine off of Knox and Ryker. Ryker plays like he was made for it. There's soul in Knox's voice, smooth, silky tones touched by a hint of grit. He's incredible.

One is the perfect complement to the other's talent. Just when I think it can't get any better, Kiere starts pounding a rhythm into the box that he's sitting on, and it takes the song to a whole other level. Knox's voice goes up, and Kace starts singing, his lower tone creating a perfect harmony with Knox, and goosebumps rise from my skin.

They sing and play together, and I'm now in complete agreement with Skylar, this is my new favorite part of family night. The song ends, and she turns to me, expectantly.

"Incredible, right?"

"Understatement of the century. I definitely owe Knox my panties now," I mumble, and she breaks into a fit of laughter.

Reese chuckles, and I'm suddenly painfully aware that their mom is sitting right next to me and just heard me say that. I give her a sheepish look, and she chuckles even harder. I debate whether I should explain what I mean, but I figure pointing out Knox's panty melting skills might not be the best topic to discuss with his mother. She pats my leg and gives me a sweet look that tells me I'm off the hook.

Skylar runs a finger over the runes on my hand and leans in ever so slightly toward me.

"Are you guys going to tell us what these mean and why you all have matching ones, or are we all still supposed to pretend that we don't see them?"

Alarm shoots through me as her words sink in.

I turn to her, not sure how to answer, but as I look into Skylar's sweet gaze, I realize that I don't want Knox and Ryker to feel like they have to keep anything from people who obviously care so much about them. I also don't want them to feel responsible for anything that might happen if we reveal my secrets and it goes wrong. If *I* put it all out there, the risk and consequences will hopefully land mostly on me.

"They're runes. They do a lot of different things like create weapons and channel different types of magic." I pause for a moment. "So...uh...my magic works a little differently, we've discovered, and it marked the boys as mine, which is why we're all matchy and shit now."

I look from Skylar to Reese as the hushed confession seeps from me to wrap around her, changing her world with each reverent and nervous word I speak. I'm worried about what I might find in her eyes as my truth comes out, but all I see is the same hope and acceptance that's been there all night.

"How did you get them?" a deep voice asks me, and I look up to find that the voice belongs to Merlin, and he's not the only one watching the exchange. They all are. I take a deep breath and get ready to drop the bomb on all of them. Reese must feel and see my hesitancy, and she takes my other hand and gives it a squeeze.

"I am a Sentinel. It's a different race of magic user from casters. There aren't a lot of us around anymore, or so I'm told. According to the readers, I might be the last of my kind, but I'm hoping somehow they're wrong."

"So the runes just marked my sons, and now you *have* to claim them?" Reese asks, her eyes tracing the symbols on the hand that she's holding and then moving up to meet mine.

"Yes. I didn't know the runes or my magic worked that way, but even if I had, I wouldn't change my claim on your sons. They're incredible, and I care very deeply about them. I would choose them regardless of my magic beating me to the punch. I am theirs, they are mine, and I wouldn't have it any other way."

My confession hangs precariously in the quiet that blanketed the group. The silence is only breached by the sound of crackling, fire-touched logs, and the crickets that are serenading us with their night song.

"Just tell us one thing, Vinna, and I want you to think long and hard before you answer..." Trace tells me, his golden gaze serious and intimidating. "Are you Team Edward or Team Jacob?"

His question takes me completely by surprise, and I have no idea where he's going with this.

"Totally Team Jacob," I announce with only the smallest amount of hesitancy.

He shakes his head at me, disappointment swelling in his gaze.

"Did you even read the books? How could you choose Jacob? Edward is superior in every possible way!"

And just like that, the bomb I was worried was going to mess up everything for me and this family, turns into a war between glittering vampires and hot werewolves.

"Edward was a dick. He just made all these decisions without really thinking them through! Oh, let me just abandon you because I decide that it's best; what's that about? Jacob was there for her; he loved her in a beautiful way that built her up and made her better."

"How dare you attack my Edward like that. He loved her more than himself; he was willing to make the hard decisions!"

My eyes betray the laugh that I'm trying to stifle at Trace's passionate confession and clear fangirl love for Edward Cullen. Slowly a chant of *sumo* echoes around me until the demand is deafening, and Trace raises his hands to quiet the demanding members of his family.

"We sumo!" he announces, and the rest of the family hoots and cheers their approval. I look to Knox and Ryker, not sure what the hell just happened, and Knox gives me a *cat that got the cream* grin.

"Oh Killer, our dad has no idea the pain he just unleashed on himself! This is going to be epic!"

Thirty minutes later, I'm laughing so hard I'm worried I'm going to pee my pants inside the massive sumo suit I'm wearing. I push the black bun-haired-helmet out of my face and watch as Trace rocks from side to side, trying to figure out a way to get up from where he just landed sprawled out on his back. He looks like that little French Bulldog puppy on YouTube that can't figure out how to get off its back, so it just rocks side to side in a hysterically adorable way.

From the minute I was forced into the sumo suit, to the first time I body slammed dad number five and watched him go flying, I haven't been able to stop laughing. I wobble over to Knox, who's bent over chortling away. I do the pee wiggle, although in this sumo suit, I probably look like I'm shimmying my large man breasts in his direction.

"Knox, I have to pee! Help me out of this thing before I defile it and break your dad's heart."

Knox laughs even harder, but he and Ryker start to pull the Velcro apart and unzip it.

They both wipe tears out of their eyes and then trade pecks on my cheeks as I climb out of the suit and unbuckle the massive helmet.

"I demand a rematch!" Trace shouts from where he's still wiggling side to side on his back.

"Know when you're beat, Old Man," Knox shouts at his dad through his tear-streaked laughter.

"Who said that? Old man? I'll show you old... I demand a sumo!" he shouts from the ground.

"I walked right into that one," Knox admits with a groan as he takes the suit from me and starts climbing into it.

Best family night ever.

22

"Again, Vinna," Kallan shouts at me.

He may look like a young Jared Leto, but the resemblance is only skin deep. I've had the *pleasure* of discovering that Kallan's true calling in life should be a drill instructor. He has an uncanny knack for insults, yelling, and pressure-tested results. He's been relentless when it comes to my training.

Initially, it was just when I trained with him, but now he's taken to joining me in my other tutoring sessions and yelling at me all through those too. If he wasn't so fucking effective, I'd have ripped his vocal cords out by now. To my utter displeasure and annoyance, I've discovered that I perform better under pressure. Apparently, a constant heightened state of stress and anger are the key ingredients I need to master my magic.

Over the past week, I trained every day with all of Enoch's coven. I spend the mornings with Becket, training in Defensive magic. Mid-afternoon is spent training in Offensive and Elemental magic with Enoch. After lunch, the resident drill instructor, Kallan, works me through Elemental, Offensive and Defensive magic, and then I get to spar. Sparring is my favorite time of the day. I'm paired up with one of the others, and we work through various obstacle courses that Kallan creates. We make our way through as if we're in a battle, and we simultaneously attack and defend against the rest of the coven as they come at us.

It feels more like fun than work, and after a week of mock battles, I'm discovering that all of us are starting to act like a well-oiled battle machine. After the magic battles are complete, I work on healing with Nash for the rest of the evening. By the time dinner rolls around, I'm so exhausted that I barely have the energy to chew. It's getting significantly better, but yesterday Kallan insisted that I start training to use multiple branches of magic at the same time, and I've since then reverted back to a zombie-like state by six p.m.

"Vinna, you're distracted. Focus! Now, try again."

I glare at Kallan, but he's unfazed by the empty threats simmering in my eyes. I scan our surroundings and spot the perfect weapon. I don't let my eyes rest on it too long; I don't want to give myself away. I maintain the appearance that I'm still scanning my surroundings, and Kallan maintains the appearance that he's only watching me and not preparing for whatever I'm about to throw at him.

I call on my magic and work to keep it contained and focused on what I want, instead of allowing it to spark all over my body. I previously thought that standing around like a harbinger of doom while colorful magic crackled all over me was the definition of badass. Now, I realize that it's actually evidence of lack of control. I've been working like crazy not to let my magic *leak* out, but I've been doing it unknowingly for so many years, it's a hard habit to break.

My fingers twitch, and I strain to keep them still. It feels natural to use gestures to help direct my magic, but it also shows me for the amateur caster that I am. *Man, Harry Potter made this look so much easier than it is.* If only it was all about using wands and incantations. Magic floods my limbs, and just when it's about to spill over and out of my body, I taper my pull on it.

Almost out of nowhere, the dead tree trunk that was lying on its side goes hurtling toward Kallan. I open the tap on my magic and let it flow, causing the long-dead tree to pick up speed. Effortlessly, Kallan magics the trunk to explode, and dry bark rains down on both of us. Rocks begin to fly, and large chunks of tree bark stop mid-fall as Kallan and I start to attack each other with nature-supplied projectiles.

I look like some video game character as I dodge, incinerate, explode, and redirect the things Kallan sends at me. A man-sized boulder comes hurling out of nowhere, and my instincts are screaming at me to dive away and avoid being crushed. Instead, I grit through the rush of magic it takes to force the boulder to change directions. It slams down against a tree that snaps and falls toward Kallan.

Kallan's focus moves from me to the tree tumbling toward him. I press my advantage by throwing the huge boulder at him as well. In an attempt to distract him further, I open the soil beneath him and then close it, trapping his feet. Kallan magically flings the trunk away from him and does the same with the boulder. He releases the ground's hold on his legs and turns to renew his attack against me. He freezes when he takes in the sharp levitating pieces of bark surrounding him. The pieces of the exploded tree, that I've magically sharpened, inch closer toward him, making the threat clear.

"Well done," he offers with a proud smile on his face.

I drop my magical hold on the wooden weapons surrounding him. They fall to the forest floor with light thuds, and Kallan and I both try to brush the evidence of this battle from our clothes.

"Your Elemental control has improved a lot over the past couple days, and your ability to improvise with what's around you is excellent."

I try not to smile at the praise as Kallan makes his way over to me. He pulls out a piece of tree bark from my hair, and we start making our way to whatever obstacle course he's created for the day.

"What did you and Becket work on this morning?" he asks me, using his teacher voice.

"Shielding other people, sensing others, and illusions."

"And Enoch?"

"Water, creating clouds, directing lightning, and weaponizing magical barriers."

Kallan angles toward the house, and I look at him confused.

"It's Sunday. Elder Cleary invited us over for dinner," Kallan reminds me.

I wrinkle my nose in distaste and bite back the groan that wants to escape.

"Come on; it's not so bad. All of our families will be there tonight. You missed last Sunday, and that didn't go over too well, and technically, Elder Cleary is your guardian, so just suck it up," he teases.

Missing the dreaded Cleary Sunday dinner last week was completely unintentional. But I need to figure out a way to do it again, because I can't think of anything I'd rather do less than go sit and pretend to be friendly with any of the elders. Maybe getting captured by Adriel, but honestly, they're about neck and neck at this point. The issue with my going AWOL for last week's dinner seemed to get lost in the *Pebble, lamia* drama that came out the next morning.

Pebble was pulled off lead duty, and now he and his

coven guard me from afar. Apparently, it was decided that I was a bad influence on poor sweet Pebble, and his coven felt protection at a distance was the best way to move forward. I had to bite the inside of my cheek to keep from laughing when his coven came in and announced this to me the morning of his missed check-in. If they only knew what he was really up to, but the secret is safe with me. I move around under the adopted delusion that I no longer have a babysitter. At least not one I can see all the time like I used to see the ever-lurking Pebble.

Not that Enoch and the others have given me any time to myself or a chance to get away and have any kind of a life. It's been training, training, and more training. I start running through excuses and scenarios that might get me out of this dinner, but I come up empty-handed. *Fuck.* Why can't I think of anything?

"I know what that look means, Vinna. Don't even think about it. Enoch has already told all of us that we're not to let you out of our sight for even a second today. You are not going to get the chance to sneak off again. Everyone is on high alert, which means you are coming to this dinner whether you like it or not."

I glare at Kallan and mentally curse Enoch and his dad.

"You don't know me well enough to know what the looks on my face mean," I grumble. "All I was thinking was that I'm tired, and I want to take a nap."

It's as if speaking the words have magically given them some kind of hold on me because even more exhaustion washes through me. I suddenly feel completely lethargic and groggy. I pause mid-step, not sure of what just happened. My limbs feel heavy, and there's an ache to my body that wasn't there seconds ago. What the hell?

Kallan bends down, bringing his face even with mine.

His blue eyes dart back and forth between my light-green unfocused irises.

"What just happened? You okay?"

Just as quickly as the exhaustion swept through me, it's suddenly gone, and I shake off the echo of it in my limbs.

"Yeah, I'm fine. Just...tired."

Kallan's concerned look stays etched on his face, but he gives me a nod, and we both continue toward the house. Maybe I need to eat something. All this magic use has definitely been catching up to me this week.

Another yawn escapes me, and I clap a hand over my gaping mouth to prevent the tired groan that wants to accompany it. It's all I can do to keep my eyes open as we wait for the gates to open and grant us entry into the Cleary Mansion. I crack my neck from side to side and try to get my shit together. Elder Cleary is too sneaky and calculating for me not to be on my toes. I need to be ready for whatever he's going to throw my way.

I just need to shake this exhaustion. Magic seriously has been taking its toll on me this week. I swear I haven't been this tired since I started training to fight with Talon when I was fifteen. Maybe not even then. Talon's face pops up in my mind, and I find comfort in his familiar and strong features. I've been working hard to see this version of Talon when I think about him, instead of the gaunt and tortured memory of how he looked before he died.

The ache I feel over his loss sits ever present in my mind and heavy in my soul. Just like with Laiken, I'm coming to accept that the sadness and pain will never really go away. I know, with time, I'll learn to function with it, and some days, that will be easier than others.

Enoch pulls off to the side of the colonial monstrosity, columns and all, and I release the deep breath I've been holding. Car doors slam all around me, indicating everyone's exit from the car. I sit and stare out the window at the siding of the house as I once again try to come up with some kind of way to get out of this dinner. My door flies open, and Nash gives me a look that says, *don't even try it*. I huff and unclick my seat belt, taking his warm hand as I step out of the car.

We make our way to the front door. I almost expect Enoch to ring the doorbell, but he grabs for the doorknob and lets himself in. I remind myself that he probably grew up here. The entire inside of the house is cream and gold, and no matter how hard I try, I can't picture a young Enoch and his friends running through these halls. We walk into a formal living room, and the noise of multiple conversations lowers.

Elder Cleary and Elder Albrecht are talking to each other on one side of the room, and there are clusters of other casters spread out through the rest of the lavish room. Kallan and Becket both move further into the room and receive hugs and kisses from women I would assume are their mothers. I suppose that would make the rest of the older males in this room part of the different covens Becket, Kallan, and Nash come from. Elder Cleary's eyes fix on mine as I walk into the room before his gaze slowly moves down my arm and settles there.

It takes me a minute to figure out what he's staring at. But I soon realize that Nash is still holding my hand from when he helped me out of the car. *Shit*. How the hell did I not notice that? I yank my fingers out from between his.

Nash looks over at me, but I don't answer his questioning glance.

Fucking hell.

I can practically feel Elder Cleary's smugness from here. I clench my teeth and berate myself for being so stupid. I can't help but think that somehow I've just fucked everything up. If the elders believe there's even a hint of a possibility that my guys aren't the mates that I choose, then they could deny their Bond Claim. I might have just given them the fuel they need to continue to try to control me and force me into a match with Enoch and his coven. Motherfucker!

23

I take an involuntary step back from Enoch and Nash, trying to create as much separation as possible between them and me. They don't seem to notice, or if they do, they don't react. A short woman with strawberry-blonde hair and a burgundy dress walks in and makes a beeline for Enoch. She grabs him in a hug and then sandwiches his cheeks in both her hands.

"You look tired. Are you not sleeping?"

Enoch chuckles and pats her hands on his cheeks.

"I'm good, Mom; you worry too much."

Her eyes scrunch up ever so slightly with concern, but she nods her head and gives Enoch's cheeks a squeeze before releasing him. She turns to Nash, and she showers him with similar maternal affection before her eyes land on me. I'm not sure what to do exactly or what I really expected when it came to Enoch's mother. I figured she'd be a lot like Elder Cleary; cold, calculating, worthy of only mistrust, but first impressions lead me to believe she's quite the opposite. I almost find that even more unsettling. Why would a female like this be with someone like Elder Cleary?

"Mom, this is Vinna. Vinna, this is my mother, Isla Winifred." Enoch offers.

Isla's smile brightens, and she stretches her hand out to me. I take it, and she places her other palm on top of our joined hands and gives a gentle squeeze.

"It's a pleasure to finally meet you, Vinna. You've been quite the talk of my mates since your arrival, and I'm thrilled to be able to put such a beautiful face to your beautiful name."

Her words make me pause ever so slightly before I smile back and tell her it's nice to meet her too. I know casters are polyandrous, and I have no idea why I thought the Elders would be any different, but I did. I pictured Enoch in this stuffy pristine house eating quiet and awkward dinners with his scheming, power-hungry father and his equally thirsty and grasping mother. I'm starting to realize that I couldn't be more wrong.

A familiar face walks into the room, and his presence brings a reassurance that I'd been lacking up until now.

"Ah, there's one of my mates now. I believe you two have met already?"

I stare at Isla Winifred and just barely manage to keep my jaw from unhinging and my mouth from falling to the floor. Paladin Ender saunters into the room and makes his way over to us. He snakes an arm around Isla's waist and kisses her cheek affectionately. She beams up at him, and I'm completely floored by the interaction. I turn to look at Enoch with my best *what the fuck* look. He shrugs and goes back to scanning the room, unfazed by the affectionate display. Isla is bonded to an elder and the leader of the paladin. Damn, who else is in her coven? Dumbledore?

"It's nice to see you again, Vinna." Paladin Ender gives me a friendly nod. "It will be nice to get to know you better and under far friendlier circumstances than last time," he offers.

I give him a noncommittal *hmm,* and my eyes find Elder Cleary as he floats around the room, speaking to his other guests. I bring my attention back to Paladin Ender and give him a bland smile.

"Friendly would be a nice change, but I'm not holding my breath."

He chuckles, which for some reason makes me like him even more. I suddenly realize that I've just insulted Isla's mate, and I turn to her, ready to receive a glare or some other offended look. I'm surprised when she doesn't seem bothered at all by my comment. Maybe she didn't hear me. She's chatting with Nash about something I don't follow, and her arm is settled around Paladin Ender's lower back.

"Thank you for your assistance the other day with my escape," I tell the scarred and grizzled leader of the paladin.

"It was the least I could do after what happened. I am sorry about what went on that day. It was not the right decision, to do what they did."

The light of the gilded chandeliers gleams off his snow-white hair and deepens the tan of his skin.

"How are you his compeer? I don't get any of the same *manipulative prick* vibes from you that I get from him. Are you just better at hiding it?"

Nash elbows me in the side, the movement a clear warning. I'm not sure when he tuned in to the conversation, but apparently, he caught enough of my question to decide I need his censure. Paladin Ender chuckles, and he rubs the hint of a five o'clock shadow on his cheeks.

Before he can offer an answer or tell me to mind my own business, a man in an ascot and tails appears in the doorway and announces that dinner is served. The large group begins to stroll toward the formal dining room, and I find myself once again surrounded by Enoch, Nash, Kallan, and Becket.

I'm guided to a spot just a few seats down from the head of the table, and Kallan pulls out my chair. I sit and watch the twenty-five or so other guests all settle in comfortably in the enormous dining room. Enoch sits to my left, Becket to my right, and Kallan and Nash bookend our grouping. I watch them sit and adjust their chairs closer to the table and wonder why they aren't sitting with their families.

I glance around the table again and realize that each of the female casters now sits in the middle of their mates. Isla is seated at the end of the table, Paladin Ender on her left and Elder Cleary on her right. Another man sits next to Paladin Ender, and he and Isla are laughing about something. Nothing about the seating arrangement is lost on me, and I look for a distraction from my rising frustration. I lean toward Enoch and whisper harshly.

"At what point were you going to tell me that Paladin Ender was your second dad?"

He looks down at me, and I can't tell if he's feeling chagrin or amusement.

"You didn't ask," he merely supplies.

"So, let me get this straight; I'm supposed to supply you with every detail of my existence, but you can't be bothered to tell me who your family members are? Cool, good to know."

"It's not like that. I thought you knew. Everyone knows who my family is."

Enoch's statement and the arrogant tone that accompanies it makes me snort.

"Oh, well, *sorry*. I'm not in the know of who's who in Solace. My bad."

"You didn't ask about us after our run in at the lake?" Becket asks me, inserting himself into the conversation.

"No, I didn't. Why would I be interested in finding out about a bunch of assholes who just stood by and watched their friends behave like dicks? You think I saw that display of cowardice and thought to myself, '*Oooohh,* I bet they're fun to hang out with; I wonder who they are.'"

I attempt to sound as shallow as possible as I finish my rant. I take a sip of water from a pretentious crystal goblet, and all I can think about is that I would love to shatter this thing in the middle of the table and walk the fuck out of here. But as much as I hate this situation, I still have to live in this community, and temper tantrums sure as hell aren't going to solve anything. Elder Cleary stands, and a crescendo of tapping on crystal moves around the table until everyone falls silent.

He smiles, and it's as if I can see the charisma wafting off of him.

"I speak on behalf of my coven when I say how honored and pleased we are that all of you could join us tonight. This is a rare treat, and we're thrilled that we could all come together to celebrate our incredible children. So let us raise a glass and toast. To them and their bright futures where, together, the hope and possibilities are endless."

Crystal goblets rise all over the table, and chants of "here, here" work their way around. A glass of water is held firmly in my hand, but I don't bring it to my lips. That would feel too much like surrender, and that's just not my style. Light chatter sprinkles the table as servers flood the dining room with plates of fancy food. After a couple of courses have come and gone, I've concluded that I am not a *fine dining* kind of girl. I am dying for something that looks edible. If I'm handed one more plate with more artful dollops of reduced *whatever the fuck* rather than food, I'm going to lose it.

"So, Vinna. How are you finding Solace? I'm sure it must be quite the adjustment from, where was it again…"

The platinum blonde woman, who I'm pretty sure is Becket's mother, turns to her mate and gives him a questioning look.

"Nevada. Las Vegas, to be exact," he supplies with disinterest.

"That's right, Las Vegas."

She looks over to me and offers a smile. There's nothing warm or friendly to be found in its depths. It looks like I might not be the only one unhappy with this arrangement, but that seems strange since, if she is Becket's mother, then one of her mates is Elder Albrecht. I glance around her and spot him a couple of seats down from her.

"Yes, quite the adjustment," I offer vaguely and equally as cool.

"Shame, that business about your uncle. It's been quite the shock around town."

Her murky blue eyes give a spark of delight, and I know I'm not going to like wherever she's going with this.

"And what business would that be?"

Everyone around the table is watching the exchange. There's a mixture of tension, disapproval, and excitement floating about. The whirlpool of emotion in the room makes it hard to pinpoint who disagrees with what she's trying to do, and who wants to see me brought down a peg.

"Well, between the crumbling of the coven and his rank being stripped—"

She pauses mid-sentence and looks to her mates and the others around the table. Some meet her eyes, mirroring her amusement. Others maintain blank facades, not offering her the validation she's so obviously seeking. She lets out a little, amused huff.

"It's no wonder he's gone into hiding. I wouldn't show my face either."

Bitchy Witch Barbie gives me a smile that's meant to look innocent but misses the mark by a mile.

"Well, with a face like that, no one would blame you if you wanted to spend more time indoors."

Nash chokes on the wine he's drinking, and Becket tenses beside me. His mother's face scrunches up indignantly, making her even uglier than her personality alone accomplished. Becket's lucky he got his looks from his dad.

I gesture in her direction with my fork, keeping it classy and mature. "See, that face right there. No one should have to live with the nightmares it must cause."

She begins to turn a deeper shade of purple.

"That's enough," Elder Albrecht chastises as he turns to his ever-reddening mate and mumbles something in her direction.

"I'm sorry. I'm confused. I thought we were starting the shit-talking portion of the evening. Don't tell me she can dish it, but she can't take it?"

I meet his glare with a blank face and a slight tilt of my head. Enoch slaps Nash's back a couple times as he tries to rein in the coughing fit caused by the aspiration of his wine. Becket's mother throws her napkin on her plate and shoots a murderous glare my way. Her chair scrapes loudly against the marble floor as she stands dramatically and stomps out of the room. None of her mates move to join her.

I lean back in my chair and look around the table at the remaining guests, half of whom I haven't been introduced to.

"Anyone else want to have a go? Unlike some, I promise I can hang with the best of 'em. Give me your best shot."

"No, I think that's quite enough dramatics and entertainment between courses." Elder Cleary raises his eyebrows and gives me a patronizing grin.

"So how is training coming along?" he asks, quick to change the subject.

I roll my eyes at the fact that he's asking about me but not at all talking to me. His question is addressed to his son as if Enoch is my master. Like the good little soldier that he is, Enoch begins to fill everyone in on what we've been doing and my overall progress. I tune him out.

I do all I can to keep from showing that what Becket's mother said hit its mark. I'm not going to show any weakness around these people, but I can't keep her words from swirling around my head. What did she mean Lachlan's rank was stripped? Is he no longer a paladin? Why the hell would they do that? I make a mental note to call the guys as soon as I'm out of here and away from Enoch and the others. I need to know what the hell that bitch was talking about.

Since the elders removed me from his house, I've tried hard to keep from thinking about Lachlan and the others in his coven. I guess I felt that there was no point picking at that wound by wondering the *whys* of it all; that sure as hell isn't going to help heal anything. Lachlan never struck me as the type to hide or mope. So if he's disappeared, that sets off a few alarms for me. I would assume that the guys would have said something. But maybe not. With my intense training and their moving into our new house, news about Lachlan could have easily been pushed to the back burner. It probably doesn't help that talking with me about Lachlan and the others is still weird. We all kind of try to avoid it at all costs.

The rest of the dinner passes uneventfully. Thank fuck, dessert looked and tasted like cheesecake, or I'd be way more pissed as I wait for Enoch and the others to say their goodbyes so I can get the fuck out of here. I'm starving. With the exception of dessert, I only had a couple of bites of the nine thousand different courses they served tonight. I debate whether or not these assholes will stop somewhere so I can grab something to fill the gnawing hole that is my stomach, or if I should call one of the guys and see if they'll bring me something.

Elder Cleary moves to stand next to me, and I try not to visibly stiffen at his proximity.

"You've made the night much livelier than it typically is," he tells me, amusement sparkling in his eyes. "We usually have smaller, more intimate gatherings for Sunday dinner, but everyone was dying to meet you, and we couldn't resist getting them together for your first official dinner. Next week won't be nearly as intense."

I snort. For people who were *dying to* meet me, only a handful of them actually introduced themselves. This is supposed to be the upper crust of casters? They have shit manners, and I'd be thrilled if I never had to see most of them again. As if he can read my mind, Elder Cleary chuckles quietly.

"You'll get used to them. Enoch and the others will teach you how to navigate things better for next time."

I open my mouth to argue when his words and tone suddenly make me realize something. I turn and look into Elder Cleary's cunning cobalt-blue eyes.

"You're going to deny the Bond Claim, aren't you?" A hollow chuckle escapes me. "I should have seen that coming. But the guys were so certain you and the other elders would be fair and impartial."

I take a step closer to him, squaring off, but he only seems to grow more amused by it.

"Allow me to clarify something for you, and feel free to pass it along to the others. I am not yours to command.

Nothing you *ever* do or say will make me choose your son or his coven. What you're pushing for, what you're trying to force me into, is never going to happen."

Elder Cleary's smile drops ever so slightly, and he lowers his voice ensuring that no one can hear him but me.

"Come now, Sentinel. You of all people should know how possible the impossible can be. Your mere existence proves that one should *never* say never."

The blood drains from my face, and every muscle in my body goes taut from fear. How does he know what I am? I knew that the *Baby Sentinel* nickname Faron called me could make it back to the Elders, but I didn't expect them to know what it meant. I shutter away the panic and the questions buzzing inside of me and slip a blank mask on.

"I would strongly advise against threatening me. It's never gone well for anyone who's done it in the past."

Elder Cleary tsks me. "Now, now, Vinna. I think you misunderstood me. I only seek to reach a mutual understanding. I am your guardian, after all; I only have your best interest at heart."

A flash of magenta crackles over my hands as Elder Cleary and I stare coldly at one another. The color of the magic deepens to violet the longer our standoff goes on, and I don't bother to try and rein it in.

"What seems to be going on over here?" Isla asks.

The sound of his mate's voice pulls Elder Cleary's challenging gaze from mine. His hard eyes soften as he offers her a smile, and she tucks herself into his side. I sneak in a couple of deep breaths while they're focused on each other. I need to calm down and keep this from escalating.

"We were just talking, darling. Nothing to worry about," Elder Cleary reassures his mate, and they both turn expectantly to me.

I give a noncommittal shrug.

"Talking, threatening, it's probably all the same to him."

I put my hand out to Enoch's mother, and she takes it automatically. "It was nice to meet you. I have no intention of ever coming back here. Just like I have no intention of taking your son as a mate. That has nothing to do with you, however. You've been very kind, and I appreciate that more than I can say." I squeeze her hand and walk away from both of their shocked faces.

The cool night air caresses my face as I make my way outside. I don't get more than five feet away from the front door before Enoch and the others are calling my name and rushing after me. I'm fed up with them, this nightmare of a dinner, and this entire situation. When Enoch catches up to me, he reaches out and places a hand on my shoulder to stop me. I whirl on him, shoving him away from me.

"How long have you fucking known what I am?" I shout at him.

"What are you talking about? What just happened in there?"

"Don't fucking lie to me, Enoch. There's no way your dad knows, but you don't. Who else knows? The other elders? You guys?" I look at the rest of the coven. "Did you really think you could threaten me into a bond?

Enoch steps toward me again, and I shoot him a scathing look that warns him not to get any closer.

"Who threatened you? What the hell are you talking about?" Nash shouts as he motions to the others in his coven.

"I will *never* choose you. You will never have access to *my* magic. So, all of you, keep the fuck away from me!"

A flash of purple magic shoots out from my core and pulses away from me. It passes through Enoch and the others and disappears into the night. The pulse mutes my anger and steals the last of my energy. My knees buckle, refusing to hold me up any longer. Enoch darts forward and catches me before I crumple to the ground. He wraps his arms around me, securing me against him, and I start to shiver and shake in his hold.

What the fuck just happened?

My teeth are chattering so hard I can't speak, and my head feels like it's wrapped in a thousand layers of cotton, muffling everything. Enoch and the others are shouting around me, but I can only make out bits and pieces of it. Enoch scoops me up in his arms, and my head lolls limply against his chest, as he wraps one arm behind my knees and another behind my back.

He moves toward the house, and it takes everything in me to try and get away from him. I don't care if I die out here on the manicured lawn—and with how I'm suddenly feeling, that's a possibility—but I am not going back into that house. Enoch seems to catch on to what's distressing me, and he stops walking. More shouting goes on around me, but I can't focus on them. I fight the need to pass out, knowing that if I do, they'll take me back inside, and I can't let that happen.

My shivers start to morph into convulsions, and judging by the terrified look on Enoch's face, something is seriously wrong with me. My breaths are quick and shallow, and I'm trying so hard to speak, but my mouth won't cooperate.

Have I been poisoned?

Thoughts of Talon and toxic shifter saliva float through my foggy brain, and I try to think of when someone could have slipped me something. The only thing I really ate was dessert. Fucking cheesecake, and fucking Elder Cleary for ruining cheesecake for me. It had to be him. Car doors slam around me, and I realize that I'm being cradled in the back seat. I feel the car start to move, and Nash leans in and places his hands on my head and chest.

When they warm to try and heal me, it feels like a brand against my skin. I can't bite back the pain-filled scream that tears out of my throat. He pulls his hands away, but the pain doesn't go with him. I'm flooded by it and drowning, I can't breathe or grit through it, and I realize at that moment, whatever this is, I think it's going to kill me.

24

Everything hurts. I don't know if that's good or bad. It means I'm not dead, but it's getting harder and harder to keep from wishing that I were. The pain is unyielding. Sometimes it feels like I'm burning alive, other times I feel like I'm being flayed. I thought getting my runes was bad, but this—whatever this is—is infinitely worse. Whoever is holding me brushes hair away from my face and speaks close to my ear. Their breath feels like needles against my neck, and their words are lost in the pain that saturates every inch of me.

I can't control the screaming. My throat is raw from it, my voice slowly giving out. My body can't decide if it wants to crumble in on itself or arch to escape the pain, and I twitch from one position to the other. Cool air brushes against my skin, and I feel myself being passed over to someone else. I force my eyes open, hoping to see one of my guys, but Becket looks back at me instead. He shouts to the others, and suddenly we stop moving. Enoch, Nash, and Kallan peer down at me, asking me if I'm okay, but I'm about as far from it as I can be.

I will one trembling hand over to the other and run a

shaky, pain filled finger over the runes that will call my guys. Becket and the others watch me, confused, but I'm not capable of giving them any answers. It's all I can do to keep my eyes open, to focus on the task of calling my Chosen. They'll come. I just hope I can hang on until then.

Becket starts moving again. I close my eyes against the pain the jostling of his movements spark, and grit my teeth against the scream trying to force its way out of me.

"We should have taken her to our dads, at least they might know what the hell to do! What the fuck are we going to do for her here?"

"Becket, shut the fuck up! For all we know, they did this to her. She didn't want to go back into that house for a reason!"

"Fuck you, Nash! You can shove your bullshit accusations up your ass!"

Something cool presses against the back of my body, and I realize that I'm being placed in a bed.

"Both of you, stop! Becket, she's here now, so figure out something more helpful than bitching about it. Until we know what the hell is going on, Nash, keep your issues with the elders to yourself. Kallan call Aydin, see if he has any idea what's going on." Enoch's voice booms around the room, and the others fall silent at his commands.

The bed presses down next to me, and he runs his hand over my forehead and down my cheek. I try to turn away from him, but I can't move. I can't speak. My scream-abused voice has finally abandoned me. All I can do is whimper and hope, one way or another, this ends soon.

"What the fuck is going on? Get away from her!"

Knox's deep baritone breaks through the silence, shattering it like glass and pulling me from the blackness I've been floating in and out of. My heart rate picks up, knowing he's near, and I try to fight through the pain and my body's sluggishness to get to him.

"What the hell are you doing here?" several voices ask simultaneously, and I hear movement around the room.

"I said get the fuck away from her!"

The body taking up space next to me is ripped away. A scuffle seems to break out, judging by the shouts and movement. The mattress dips down next to me again, and I'm pulled into big strong arms and surrounded by a scent I would know anywhere. Knox.

"Killer, what's going on?" His voice caresses my face, and I hear a slight break in the tone as his arms tighten around me.

"What happened?" Ryker asks, his voice close. I feel him lean over me as he places his hands on my head and neck.

Before anyone can stop him, Ryker's palms heat up, and he tries to press Healing magic into me. It burns through me like lava. My back arches in agony, and my mouth opens in a silent scream.

"Don't fucking do that; it hurts her! You think we haven't tried that already?" Nash shouts at Ryker, who yanks his hands away from me.

"Fuck, Squeaks. I'm so sorry! What the hell is going on?"

"She can't talk. She was screaming in pain up until twenty minutes ago, but I think her voice is gone now. We don't know what happened. One minute, she was yelling at us; the next, magic is pulsing out of her, and she's been like this ever since," Enoch recounts.

"She's going through her Awakening," Aydin announces from somewhere else in the room.

"What are you two doing here?" Bastien growls out.

"We called him for help. You guys still haven't explained what the hell *you're* doing here," Kallan sounds off from the corner.

"She called us!" Valen counters.

"You guys can measure magic and dicks later. When did it start happening?" Evrin asks.

Another pulse of magic rushes out of me, and the rushing sound that fills my ears blocks out everything else that's said. Ryker runs his fingers through my hair, and every time his hand skims my scalp, my pain recedes a miniscule amount. Each hand stroke brings a millisecond of relief from the constant agony. I try to lift my hand, but I can only manage a couple of inches before it drops limply into my lap.

"What is it, Bruiser?"

Bastien lifts my uncooperative hand into his own. He presses his full lips into my palm and laces his fingers with mine. The contact chases away any doubt I had in my mind. When they touch me, it hurts less.

"Vinna, can you hear me? I can see you're hurting, but it shouldn't last much longer. You're going to be okay. You're experiencing your Awakening."

Evrin's words float around the room and me, and they mix and get lost in the pain. I try to grasp them, but all I can hold onto is the need for my Chosen.

"Isn't she young for an Awakening? She should have a couple more years at least," Nash inquires.

"Yeah, um, with Vinna, things tend to be different," Aydin offers awkwardly.

If I could tell Aydin that my secret's out, I would, but I'm just trying to focus on Valen and Sabin and somehow bringing them closer to me. It's not working. They're too focused on whatever discussion is going on now between

Aydin, Evrin, Enoch and the others. I focus on the runes on my sternum. So far, when I've activated them, I've used touch, but I know if I focus enough, I can call them just like I do the runes for my weapons.

I picture each of the symbols in my mind and match them with the unique individuals that they represent. I imagine pulling the magic into me and then feeding it back into those specific marks on my chest. Groans and shouts of pain suddenly surround me. I hate that I'm sharing this agony with them, but I can't think of any other way to get them to understand what I need. I can't talk, I can barely move. It's a struggle just to keep thinking through this torment.

"Fucking hell, what's happening?"

Knox is crumpled on top of me, and Bastien holds my hand tightly as he grits out a response.

"Bruiser, is this you? Fuck, is this what you're feeling?"

"Moons, it's going to kill her! Are you sure this is an Awakening? It feels like something is trying to tear her apart," Ryker groans out.

"If she goes, I think we're going with her," Valen announces.

Ryker steadies his hand on my forehead, and the pain recedes slightly. I hope against hope that one of them feels the change. But I just slammed them with a fuck ton of suffering; maybe they won't pick up on the subtle difference.

"What just happened? Something affected her. Not a lot, but enough. What did one of you just do?" Sabin shouts out the question.

His voice is lower than it was before, and it makes me think he's on the floor now instead of standing like he was before. I feel horrible for putting them through this, but I need them to figure it out.

Ryker's hand falls away from my forehead, and I feel his

body sink to the ground next to me. The pain intensifies at the loss of contact, and the guys groan and yowl at the new level of searing torture. A hand presses flush against my chest, and again the pain withdraws just a fraction.

"Ryker, put your hand back on her," Sabin grits out, and Ryker's hand presses back against the clammy skin of my face.

The pain ebbs.

Groans of relief echo around me, and without needing to be told, I feel Valen push his hand under the hem of my shirt to rest on my clenched stomach. The anguish loosens its grip even more.

"Knox, you're holding her, but find skin. Skin to skin seems to work the best," Ryker instructs.

My pants are unbuttoned and slowly pushed down my hips. Knox rests one arm over my thighs while the other snakes under my shirt and rests against my back. As soon as Knox settles against me, the agony dulls to a manageable throb. The change is so drastic that a surprised gasp immediately escapes me. Slowly, as the minutes pass and the pain plateaus at this level, my rapid, shallow breathing starts to even out as my lungs expand and cooperate.

I don't know how much time passes as we all snuggle against each other, greedily taking in the respite. I open my eyes to find five sets staring intensely down at me, and I've never been so grateful to see them as I am in this moment. The corner of my mouth tries to twitch up in a smile, but I probably look more like a bad Elvis impersonator.

"It's okay, we feel it. We're so fucking glad to see you, too. We're sorry it took us so long to figure it out, to help you."

I focus on Valen's hazel eyes as his words soothe me, and I try to pull my hand up to my chest. I'm surprised when it works, and I graze Sabin's large hand on my chest as I disengage my runes. Each of them relaxes even more as I steal the pain back into myself.

"Everyone out!" Bastien shouts, and I flinch at his booming voice as it punches through the heavy silence blanketing the room.

"Who the fuck do you think you are, telling us what to do in our own house?" Becket demands.

"She needs skin to skin contact from us to manage the pain. You don't need to be there for that. So get the fuck out!"

Before anymore arguments can ensue, Aydin and Evrin start herding Enoch and the others out of the room.

"Show me what you've got around here for food. She's going to need a shit ton of calories if her Awakening is pulling in enough magic to cause pain like that," Aydin instructs.

He ushers them out against their small noises of protest, and the door clicks shut behind them.

"Squeaks." Ryker's voice pulls my attention to him, and I lethargically refocus on his sky-blue eyes. "We're going to strip down, and then do the same for you. That way we can get as much contact with you as we can. Each of us is going to try to keep a hand on you, so the pain is not as bad, but this is probably going to hurt until we can all get positioned around you."

I nod slowly in understanding, and Ryker flashes his hand away and strips off his shirt as quickly as he can. A new wave of agony hits me at the loss of his touch, and everything around me is thankfully swallowed by blackness.

25

I wake up with a dull ache in every inch of my body, but it's a welcome feeling compared to the agony I was experiencing before. I'm warm and almost naked, pressed against bodies that are equally warm and almost naked. I inhale deeply, and immediately I know Knox is pressed to my front. He has this incredible smell that is all him, and I'm obsessed with it.

A scruffy chin nuzzles into my neck from behind, and a satisfied hum spills out of me.

"How are you feeling?"

Ryker's voice trails up from below me as his hand strokes gently up my calf. It's then that I realize that each of my Chosen are wrapped around me like I'm wearing my very own outfit of hot men. I'm lying on my side on top of Sabin. Knox is snuggled into my front, Bastien is at my back, and Valen and Ryker are each holding my legs like they're body pillows.

"I'm okay," I croak out, surprised that my voice can do even that much.

"I healed your throat," Ryker explains, reading my confusion. "Once we were all channeling the massive amount of magic flowing through you, my magic didn't hurt you like it had before. I think, when I tried earlier, it was just adding to the overload of magic you were already dealing with."

I give him a weak smile, and I have to look away from the concern and sympathy in Ryker's eyes.

"How long was I out?"

"Almost an hour."

Sabin's chest rumbles beneath me, and his hand threads gently through my hair. "Most Awakenings don't last more than a couple hours, so you should be in the final stretch. Although, it could be different for Sentinels. You're an early bloomer by caster standards, so honestly, we have no idea what's normal or not."

I nuzzle his muscular chest and absently play with the line of hair that trails from his belly button into his boxer briefs.

"I'm pretty sure Enoch knows what I am. I was in the process of finding out when this whole Awakening shit happened."

"What do you mean?" Bastien queries, his breath warming my back between my shoulder blades.

"Elder Cleary threatened me tonight. Pick Enoch and his coven, or my Sentinel status might not stay under wraps. I'm not sure if the other elders know, I'd be surprised if they didn't. I also figured if Cleary senior was in the loop, he probably brought Cleary junior in, too."

Grunts and huffs of frustration sound off all around me, and the atmosphere grows taut with rising tension.

"I'm going to fuck up that whole family if something happens to you because they're power hungry," Valen declares.

"Fuck waiting for them to make a move; I say we start laying a foundation of *don't fuck with us* now!"

I run my hand over the muscular forearm Bastien has wrapped around my waist.

"Let's wait and see what Cleary's next move is. I'm pretty sure I just fucked what they thought was a sure thing."

I look up into Knox's storm cloud gray eyes and see confusion.

"Elder Cleary thought, as my assigned guardian, that he'd have control over me for the next couple of years. They have no intention of taking your Bond Claim seriously." I rub my palm against the stubble on his cheek. "If I had to wait until my Awakening at twenty-five-ish, there wouldn't have been much I could do to keep the elders from moving me around like the pawn they see me as, but now I'm officially considered independent according to their rules. They can't force me to stay here."

Knox's eyes light up as the pieces fall into place for him, and a beautiful smile stretches across his face. He chuckles and leans down, claiming my lips in a sweet kiss.

"Hey! No making out with our half-naked mate while we're all cuddling and she's still going through her Awakening!" Bastien complains.

"Bas, don't hate that I have access to these delicious lips and you don't."

"If I move my hand down six inches, I've got access to a whole other set of lips that I'm sure are just as delicious," Bastien challenges.

Valen coughs out a laugh, and the sounds drown out the small moan I'm pretty sure just escaped me. I'm still achy, but I'd have to be dead not to get wet at Bastien's words. It's no surprise that my awareness of the close proximity of these delectable males suddenly becomes the only thing I can focus on.

A knock on the door pulls me from my thoughts, and I feel everyone slightly freeze around me. Aydin pokes his head into the dark room. I can tell it's him because he's a giant, and he's currently doing this awkward duck under the doorway thing.

"I heard voices. Is she awake?"

None of the guys answers, as if they're giving me time to decide what I want to do. Sabin hands me a shirt, and I quickly pull it over my head.

"I'm up," I announce after I get myself resettled amongst the guys.

Aydin steps into the room, followed by Evrin. The door closes behind them as they shut themselves in with us.

"How are you feeling, Little Badass?"

His question hangs in the room for a second longer than is comfortable. I'm not sure how to interact with them after everything that's happened.

"Is it normal for Awakenings to hurt like that? Everything I've read until now made it seem like a surge or a rush, and that sure as hell isn't what happened to me," I ask.

"It's not talked about a lot, probably because no one wants to freak young casters out about what they may or may not go through, but it happens. The more magic that awakens in you, the more painful it can be." Evrin scrubs the back of his heavily tattooed neck with his palm. "No one really knows why it happens to some and not to others."

Aydin inches closer to the bed as Evrin answers my question, and I suddenly find myself wishing that things between us could go back to the way they were before. I hate that he couldn't give me the benefit of the doubt and see me as I really am, not the fucked up threatening version that Lachlan believes. And I hate that his presence feels like an awkward intrusion now instead of the easy friendship we had before.

We stare steadily at each other for a minute as questions I'm tired of swallowing bubble up into my throat.

"Why, Aydin?" I ask softly. "You should have known me better than any of them. You asked me to trust you, but why would you ask for something that you weren't willing to give in return?"

Aydin wears a helpless look, and his hands scrub his face before falling defeated at his side. "Little Badass, I feel like whatever I say at this point is just going to tiptoe in the land of excuses."

"I need you to try and help me understand. Because if you never do, I will always think that how you were with me was a lie, some kind of trick. I don't want to think that way about you. But I can't crawl out of the pit of hurt and mistrust on my own."

Aydin's eyes are still on mine, but I can feel a sudden disconnect. Like even though he's here in front of me, his thoughts are somewhere else entirely. He drops down to the edge of the bed as if whatever he's carrying has suddenly grown too heavy to continue to bear. The guys all tighten their hold on me almost at the same time, gearing up and literally supporting me for whatever Aydin is about to unload.

Aydin looks up at Evrin, and Evrin gives him a nod.

"A little over ten years ago, we were tracking some lamia. They had been glamoring humans out of money, and we were tasked with eliminating them. When we finally caught up to the nest, things took a weird turn. There were eight lamia, and it wasn't much of a fight, but when Lachlan went to kill one of them, they recognized him.

"The lamia kept asking how he was there. At first, it sounded like nonsense. We had looked everywhere for Vaughn and the others with nothing to show for it. I think most of us, at that point, had come to terms with the fact that they were gone, killed somehow. So when the lamia started rambling questions about how Lachlan was there, none of our thoughts went directly to Vaughn.

"It wasn't until he said the name Adriel that it clicked. This lamia wasn't seeing Lachlan. He was seeing Vaughn in Lachlan's face. It was the first scrap of a lead that we had come across that might give us some clue about what happened to Vaughn, Eden, and Lance, and their bond mates." Aydin nods toward the twins, and it registers that Eden and Lance were the names of their parents.

"We worked on that lamia for almost a month, but he was like the fucking Joker and Riddler in one. Nothing he said made any sense. He would scream on and on about how they were going to steal our magic, but we easily dismissed that as an empty threat. Toward the end though, he started going on about how a *baby* destroyed Vaughn. Or that the *baby* was not what we thought.

"We never got anything but nonsense out of the lamia, and Silva ended him when none of us could take the nonsensical bullshit anymore. We walked away from that situation even more defeated. Lachlan wasn't the same after Vaughn went missing, but the month we spent with that fucking crazy ass lamia seemed to break something in him.

"Years buried those memories, and then one day, out of nowhere, you popped up. As soon as your name spilled out into that car, it dug up the crazy ramblings of that lamia. None of us knew what to make of it, what to make of you, and it put all of us on guard."

Aydin shakes his head, and he looks down at his big hands before looking back to me, his eyes pleading.

"You're so powerful. You were before your Awakening, and only time will tell what you'll be capable of now that all of your magic has opened up. Every time I tried to see you as an innocent female in all this, you would do something incredible, and I couldn't help but wonder what that lamia meant. It was clear you were the baby he was talking about, so what did he mean when he said you weren't what we thought?

"It felt almost impossible not to be suspicious, and therefore, cautious around you. We were missing so many pieces of the puzzle before, then there you were, more or less dashing everything we thought we knew to the ground. What were we supposed to do, Little Badass?"

I look away from Aydin's pleading eyes and find Bastien's hazel orbs waiting for me. His emotions are masked, and I can't get a read on exactly what he's feeling right now. I suspect he doesn't want how he feels to influence my decision about how to move forward with Aydin, or whether or not I even think that's possible.

"I was a baby, Aydin. If somehow my existence killed Vaughn, and it probably did, what would I have known about it? How could you guys look at me, or *the baby,* as the villain in that scenario?"

"It wasn't that, Vinna," Evrin pleads.

I raise my eyebrows and tilt my head, giving him *the look,* and he immediately rephrases his words.

"I mean, maybe that is part of Lachlan's problem, but that wasn't the issue with me or with Aydin. It was the warning that somehow you weren't what you seemed. After your reading, what you were became clear. Our suspicion morphed from the possibility that you were some kind of spy, to understanding that you were more than any of us thought possible—a Sentinel. For the first time, what you were wasn't a threat, at least not in the way we had been thinking. We finally had some answers."

I release a deep breath, not sure how I feel about anything they've just told me. It does help me understand, but it doesn't help me feel better. I was hoping whatever it was Aydin had to say, that somehow it would magically erase all of the hurt. I should know by now that there are no quick fixes when it comes to shattered trust; when something breaks, you can't always glue the pieces back together.

"It doesn't make how you guys behaved acceptable. This doesn't excuse any of you from acting without compassion and empathy," Valen tells Aydin, voicing how I'm feeling perfectly.

Aydin meets Valen's stare. "I know. Like I said, I don't want this to sound like I'm making excuses. I'm not perfect. Evrin's not perfect. None of us have been in this position before; we fucked up. But we learn and do better, that's how life works, or should anyway."

I try to put myself in their shoes. Would I have been any different? Could I have seen through the suspicion and doubt to the truth? *Fuck.* I didn't even know what the truth was; how can I expect them to have foreseen it? I want to bitch about how he should have told me, but would I have done that, would I have just laid all my cards out there for someone I wasn't sure would use them against me? I just don't know.

I look around as I consider what they've said, and land on Evrin's deep, brown gaze.

"Why did you never heal me? Ryker asked me once, and I could never figure out the answer."

"I tried to, a couple of times, right after Lachlan attacked you, and after that incident in the car when you blasted Keegan. You didn't want me to come near you." He takes a hesitant step closer. "There was so much going on, and the last thing I wanted to do was force something on you just because I thought it needed to be done. I didn't want to push or take away your choice, not like I saw Lachlan do. Maybe I should have tried harder to explain. I didn't know how to go about forming a connection. I've just always been quiet, and I tend to stick to the background. I figured you knew I could heal and would come to me if you decided you needed it." Evrin offers me a small smile.

I think back to the library when he tried to approach me after the attack, or how I reacted after I walked back to the car after I magically tased Keegan, or any of the other times Evrin healed Aydin when we sparred. He's right, I told him I didn't want him or anyone else coming near me. I was hesitant and distrustful around him because of everything that was going on with the others, and around me in general.

"Is there anything else I need to know before we work to move past all the shit?" I ask them both. "Think hard before you answer, because I can't deal with any more secrets from here on out. Not after what happened with Talon, and you guys. I've hit my limit. So if there was ever a time to get it all out, it's now."

The room falls silent, and I feel the rise and fall of the guys' chests all around me. The steady synchronized rhythm soothes me, and I find more comfort in the simple contact than I ever thought I could. We're connected, and the certainty of that steadies me in a way I'm in desperate need of.

"There are no more secrets, and I promise there won't be any more again," Aydin tells me.

"We'll do better, Vinna."

I nod my head at their statements. As awkward and stiff as this whole conversation is, it takes some of the hurt weighing me down with it, too. There's now hope where there was once only bitter hurt, and I suppose with everything that's happened in the past month or so, that's something.

26

My stomach lets out a yowl a feral cat would be wary of, and everyone looks at me with some form of shock on their face.

"Lay off me; I'm starving." I laugh at my joke, but it's lost underneath another vicious growl from my angry, empty stomach. Aydin chuckles and shakes his head.

"They don't have shit here to eat, so we'll go get something for you, Little Badass."

He doesn't give me time to answer or request anything before he and Evrin are ducking through the doorway and disappearing down the hallway.

"Well, as much as I love this pile of almost nakedness that's happening right now, I feel better, and I want to get the fuck out of here," I announce.

I move to get out of the cocoon of my Chosen, and bodies around me vibrate with chuckles and grunts of agreement. Valen and Ryker are the first to climb out of bed. I pull Sabin's shirt over my head and hand it back to him. Valen gives me my bra and shirt, and I slip both on while the others scoot out of bed around me, pulling on their own pants and shirts. I button up my jeans and give myself a quick once over. I don't look any different as far as I can tell. I don't spot any new runes, and aside from being a little shaky and a lot starving, I feel like me.

I look around the room for the first time and realize that I'm not in the assigned room they had me in before. I'm not sure who this one belongs to with its warm burnt orange tones and textured rugs and furniture set about the sizeable space. There's a wall of bookshelves filled with books, and I'm tempted to go check out the collection, but a kiss to my neck pulls me away from that plan. I look up into Valen's warm hazel eyes and match his tender smile.

"You scared the shit out of us." He punctuates the statement with another short kiss to my lips. "I'm so relieved you're okay. We all are," he tells me, his lips against mine.

"Just keeping you on your toes. Wouldn't want you to get too comfortable and secure, thinking things are just going to be smooth sailing from here on out," I tease.

Valen chuckles. "True. The craziest shit does seem to happen around you." He kisses the tip of my nose.

"Yeah, and I fucking love it!" Knox announces, as he snags me out of Valen's grasp and lays a noisy quick kiss against my lips. I laugh, and he gives me a wink.

"Now, let's get you the fuck out of this house so we can get you settled into where you belong," Bastien declares before he also pecks me all too quickly on the lips.

Alrighty then, looks like kissing in front of the others is officially a thing now. Good to know. The guys start to spill out of the room into the hallway, and I find myself sheltered right in the middle of them. They're once again in that protective mode that I first witnessed on the night of my reading. Their positioning warms my heart just like it did the first time I noticed it and every time it's surfaced ever since.

Our group makes its way to the living room where

Enoch, Nash, Kallan, and Becket shoot up from where they're sitting on the couches and chairs.

"Are you okay?" Nash asks, taking steps toward me like he can only be reassured if he can see for himself.

The guys tighten around me infinitesimally, but it's not lost on Nash.

"I wouldn't hurt her," he defends, and the rest of his coven close in next to him in a show of support.

None of the guys say anything as they do their best impersonation of the fucking Secret Service.

"Are you okay?" Kallan asks, reiterating the unanswered question.

"I will be..."

"Vinna, we need to talk," Enoch interrupts, stepping forward to take point for his coven.

Bastien and Valen move in closer to one another in front of me, cutting off Enoch's line of sight.

"Will you guys cut it the fuck out! We're not going to hurt her, so stop treating us like we're threats!" Becket shouts at the guys.

"Vinna, what happened at the house? Why did you storm out, what got you so upset?"

Enoch's question cuts off the mounting fight that is itching to take place between these two groups of casters.

I reach forward and pinch both Valen's and Bastien's asses. I get a good hold on both of their butt cheeks and use it to guide them over so I can have some space to move forward. I get that they're feeling territorial, but talking to Enoch and the others like they're disembodied voices floating in the ether isn't going to work for me. I need to see their faces when this conversation goes down.

My eyes land on Enoch's.

"What has your dad talked to you about when it comes

to me?" I ask, keeping my emotions in check and my face blank.

His eyebrows dip down slightly in confusion. "Nothing."

My blank look turns incredulous. "Well, I guess if we're going to just lie to each other, this conversation is over."

I try to move to leave, but I'm boxed in by big muscular bodies, so I end up kind of bouncing around until the guys get the hint and start moving toward the door. We're definitely going to have to work on our synchronized stomping out.

"You're powerful. Probably the most powerful Sentinel anyone has seen since *The Forsaking,* which is what my ancestors called it when the Sentinels broke from the casters and disappeared," Enoch confesses, and I whirl around.

His body language is resigned, but his eyes are pleading.

"How long have you known?" I ask him. At the same time, Kallan and Becket turn to Enoch and demand to know what the hell he's talking about.

It's not lost on me that Nash doesn't seem as confused as the rest of his coven.

"I suspected when I first saw you at the beach that day, but I *knew* when you picked Harris up by his neck and threw him down. My ancestors have been passing down stories about the magic users of old for forever. When I was younger, they were fairytales my mom would tell me at bedtime. But when I saw your markings and what you could do, the fairytales I loved as a kid became real."

Enoch's explanation doesn't surprise me as much as it would have before his dad's threat. I figured his family had seen and interacted with my kind recently enough for the knowledge to still be fresh, or somehow the stories of another race of magic users weren't as dead and buried as the readers seemed to think.

"Seriously, what the fuck are you talking about?" Kallan demands again, looking from Enoch to me when his question isn't immediately answered.

"I'm not a caster," I tell him. "I'm apparently from a different race of magic users called Sentinels. That's why I can do the things I can, and why the lamia are after me."

Kallan stares at me. His aqua-blue eyes run over every inch of my face, and I think he's trying to gauge if I'm fucking with him. He turns back to Enoch.

"You knew this the whole time, and you didn't say anything?" Kallan questions, his voice overflowing with hurt and swirling with anger.

Enoch sighs and runs a tired hand over his face. "My dad told me not to."

"We're your fucking coven!" Becket shouts at him. "You're telling me you don't trust us?"

"It wasn't like that. This information is dangerous. He was trying to protect you, as is his duty."

"Do you really believe that, Enoch?" I interject, speaking over the bickering and accusations that are flung between each other.

"Was it my safety your dad was concerned with when he threatened that I either pick you and your coven, or risk being exposed as a Sentinel?"

I watch Enoch carefully, looking for any sign that he knew this was his father's plan. He's either an incredibly talented actor, or the shock he's currently wearing is genuine. Man, what I wouldn't give to be able to scent a lie like the shifters can. My stomach shouts its displeasure at me, sounding a lot like the growling wolves I was just thinking about. Ryker presses a hand to my lower back and leans into me.

"Let's get you fed and rested. We can deal with all this shit another day."

I nod and give him a tired smile. I would kill for three burgers the size of a plate and a hot soak in a tub.

"Well, it looks like you guys have some shit you need to work out between yourselves. And if I don't eat soon, the hangry is going to kick in, and with the extra batteries my magic just acquired, that's probably not going to be enjoyable for anyone. I'll come and get my stuff this week if that's cool, and then I'll just see you guys around, I guess?"

I get all awkward and fidgety as I try to say goodbye. It comes out more like a rambling question, and I all but wink and shoot them a gun finger while making a weird clicking sound with my tongue. Why is this weird as fuck?

"What do you mean get your stuff?" Nash asks, speaking for the first time since the Sentinel truth bomb exploded all over this room.

"I'm all awakened now, so no more manipulative magical guardians for me. I can go where I want to go now, and that's always going to be with them."

Nash looks at each of the guys surrounding me one at a time and then back to me. He parts his lips to say something, but Enoch cuts him off.

"You still need to train and work on your magic, especially now that you'll have access to even more of it. This is the best place to do that. Look at how far you've come already. What did they teach you the whole time you were at your uncle's house? We are the best coven to help you." He gestures to the guys around me. "Don't let them convince you that they are your only option."

"Listen, you arrogant piece of shi—"

I step in Sabin's path as he moves from behind me to square up with Enoch. I reach back and grab Sabin's hands and place them firmly on my ass, hoping that will give him something else to think about aside from wanting to rip

Enoch to pieces. Knox moves to step forward, and I grab his hand in mine. I hold it up for Enoch and the others to see.

"If you know what I am, then you know what they are to me." I point to the runes on Knox's ring finger. "They're mine. I'm theirs. It's a done deal." I lower Knox's hand but keep my fingers intertwined with his. "Thank you for bringing me back here instead of to your dad's house." I pause. "Maybe your dad didn't have the best intentions, but he was right in saying knowing about me is dangerous. You guys said I could trust you. I really hope that's true."

"Vinna, wait!" multiple voices shout out at me, as I turn toward the door.

I look over at them and the step toward us they all seem to have taken. "It doesn't have to be *us* or *them*," Kallan tells me, his eyes darting to Enoch for the briefest of seconds.

Enoch's gaze drops at Kallan's words, but when the room grows quiet again, his aqua eyes fix back on me.

"We're here no matter what happens," he offers.

His hand reaches out toward me for a beat, but he forces it down. Enoch's body language changes as some kind of decision or acceptance takes place inside of him. He looks up at me, and I don't see the pleading or apology that I saw before; determination stares back at me, and I'm not sure what to think about that.

I give him, Nash, Kallan, and Becket a nod, not sure what else there is to say. This time when I turn for the door, no objections or pleading words pull me back. I squeeze Knox's hand and look up at him, beaming.

"Take me home."

27

Darkness kisses everything around me, and I lean back against the headrest, happy to watch beams of moonlight flit across Valen's face as he drives the Jeep to wherever *home* is. This moment feels surreal to me, but I hold tightly to that *too good to be true* feeling, knowing it may be fleeting and hard to find again, or at least it has been for me in the past.

Each of us stares out into the night, lost in our own thoughts, and feeling no push to invade the quiet calm of the moment with words. The road we're on winds up and then down, and a mailbox appears in the distance. Valen slows as we get closer to the mailbox, and we turn down a long paved driveway toward a house that's lit up like a beacon in the dark.

The outdoor lights paint the two-story brick home with warm, gold tones, and I spot touches of ivy climbing up the sides of the structure. The brick's been treated with something, and it has more cream tones to it than the deep red it probably once was. We pull toward two garage doors, and one of them rises, lighting up the empty space my Jeep now gets to claim.

We pull into the garage, and I realize there must be another set of garage doors on the other side of the building because there are plenty of open garage spaces in front of me. The space can easily hold more than six cars, and I spot ATVs already parked in the corner. I immediately think of all the fun things we'll add here over the years, the toys we'll acquire and the life we'll build.

I feel Ryker's gaze on me and catch Valen staring at me from the corner of my eye too.

"What do you think?" Valen finally asks, and I can hear a touch of nervousness in the question.

"I love the ivy and the brick. I can't wait to see it in the daylight if it's already this pretty in the dark," I exclaim as a huge smile takes over my face.

Valen's worry slips out of his features, and he gives me a killer grin that befuddles my brain and scrambles my hormones. I reach out a hand to caress his cheek, marveling at how incredibly beautiful he is. I run my thumb over his full lips as my eyes rove greedily over his features.

My hand is shaky, and I pretend it's more from low blood sugar than the realization that all of the obstacles that have kept me away from my Chosen just became obsolete. Finally, it's just me and them. Valen grabs my hand and kisses the inside of my palm, his eyes filled with something deep and infinite that I'm not sure I'm ready to name yet.

Ryker climbs out of the back seat and circles around to my side of the car. He opens the door, and I watch Sabin, Knox, and Bastien pile out of Sabin's Bronco in the spot next to the Jeep. Ryker takes my hand and leads me through a door into the house. We pass through a small hallway with doors that he doesn't point out or explain, into the kitchen where Birdie, Lila, and Adelaide are busy making something that smells like heaven.

I pause in the entryway and watch as the sisters bustle

around the kitchen, moving seamlessly around each other as they work. It gives me such a sense of rightness that goosebumps rise up on my whole body, and my eyes well up. I don't wait for them to notice that they have an audience; I walk right into the middle of the melee and open my arms wide. A gasping squeal echoes around the large kitchen, and three of my favorite people in the whole world crash into me as I'm seized up and surrounded by sister love.

We hug, and cry, and hug, and say nonsensical things to each other about how sorry we are and how much we've missed each other. I'm not sure what the apologies are about; I catch murmured tear-stained mentions of Lachlan, the coven, Talon, my parents, them. But none of it matters right now to me. I've missed them so much, and they're here, and right now in this moment, everything feels like it's exactly the way it should be.

We all wipe tear tracks from each other's cheeks and then laugh at our own silliness. I look over to the guys who've gathered around the edge of the kitchen to observe our particular brand of crazy, and they're all beaming.

"Thank you!" I tell them, beyond grateful that somehow they managed to convince the sisters to be here tonight.

Inside, I'm hoping it's forever, but even if it's only for tonight, it's exactly what I needed to feel complete and at home here. Knox lifts his shoulders in a shrug.

"Don't thank us, thank them." He gestures behind me.

I turn to see Aydin and Evrin leaning against a wall that leads into the dining area. I don't know how I missed the ginger giant's hulking frame or Evrin's tattooed presence. I hesitate for the briefest of seconds before I push past the uncertainty and act on the instinct that's driving through me. I walk over to where Aydin is standing, look up into his dark-blue eyes, and open my arms. His eyes flash with surprise, and his Adam's apple bobs in his throat as he tries to swallow down the emotion now simmering in his gaze.

"I'm sorry, Little Badass," he tells me again, and he bends down and scoops me up in a giant hug. Tears fall freely down his cheeks into his auburn beard and get crushed against my shoulder. He squeezes me tightly and straightens up, lifting me off the ground and up to his height.

"I'm so fucking sorry," he mumbles over and over again, and I let his apologies wash over me.

I can't tell him that it's okay, because it's not, but I can feel and hear how sorry he is, and it's enough to turn that sliver of hope I've been grasping into a window of possibility. We can work to get back to a better place, and I know that he will. I hang in Aydin's hug for a while until we're both brimming with the silent reassurances that we needed to be able to truly move forward.

Aydin sets me down, and I immediately move to stand in front of Evrin, my hands outstretched and offering the same forgiveness. Maybe that hug-it-out theory isn't so fucking weird after all. Evrin looks unsure for all of one second before he accepts my offer and steps into me, giving me a strong, reassuring hug. He utters his apologies too, making promises to do better and try harder. It seems easier for me to let go of Evrin's part in all the bullshit. I don't know why that is, but it gives me hope that I can do this forgiveness thing after all.

Everyone is sitting at the table, full, happy, and leaning back after consuming the massive spread that the sisters laid out for us. I went full-on wild, rabid badger as soon as the food was within reach, practically growling at anyone who got too close to my full plate. I think I emptied and refilled it five times, but the food coma I'm currently suffering from makes it difficult to recall the details accurately. Everyone is laughing and joking, filling me in on old stories or calling each other out on embarrassing things, and it all feels so perfect that I'm fighting off my exhaustion tooth and nail so that tonight doesn't come to an end.

I yawn loudly, slapping a hand over the sneak-attack betrayer of my fatigue. One yawn quickly morphs into another, and my body demands that I wave the white flag on this night and immediately crawl into somewhere soft and warm and sleep for a week. I lean into Ryker, who wraps an arm around me to support my suddenly leaden upper body. I offhandedly wonder if I can convince him to carry me to wherever I'm supposed to be sleeping tonight, because I just don't think I can convince my legs to work.

"I think Squeaks is ready to call it a night you guys," Ryker announces.

I give a small, tired smile because he's absolutely right, but at the same time, I don't want this night to end. It's like I'm afraid if the fun and ease of tonight suddenly stops, somehow I might never get it back. I just want to stay here, locked in this moment where nothing bad is happening, and everyone is happy and laughing. As if Valen can read my mind, or sense the battle raging inside of me not to let tonight become a yesterday, he comes up with a plan to keep everyone here.

"Why doesn't everyone stay here tonight? We have plenty of room and beds, thanks to the sisters and their awesome furniture ordering skills," Valen chuckles, and the rest of the guys join in. "Knox and Ryker, you can show Vinna her room. Bastien and Sabin, why don't you get Evrin, Aydin, and the sisters settled, and I'll clean up dinner...and that's not up for debate," he playfully scolds the sisters, who simultaneously open their mouths to argue about the cleanup part of the plan.

I laugh and shoot the sisters a victorious grin while adding a tally in my favor to the mental scoreboard I keep for our dishwashing war. Their margin of defeat is still massive, but I have high hopes that I'm going to flip the script on them now that I have better control over my magic, and I've been working on some sneaky skills that will aid me in the war.

Knox gets up from the table and puts his hand out for me to take. He helps me up from my chair and then turns around and crouches down, giving me his back. I smile and leap up onto him, wrapping my arms around his neck and my legs around his waist. He wraps his arms under my thighs and knees, giving me extra support, and I kiss the side of his neck in thanks. Everyone stands up from the table, stretching and groaning and thanking the sisters for another amazing meal.

My smile grows even bigger as Knox takes me around to everyone to say good night. Hugs are dished out, and I get soft, sweet kisses from Bastien, Valen, and Sabin before Knox carries me through the living room, past the front door, and down a hallway. Ryker leads us all the way to the end and stops in front of the tall, black door there. With dramatic slowness, he grabs the door handle and pushes the door open. Ryker gestures for Knox to go first, and I'm carried into the room just as the lights blink on.

Just like in the rest of the house, the floors are a light hardwood, and the walls are incredibly tall and painted a soft tan. My eyes move up to the high tray ceilings that have beautifully intricate white patterns on them. A chandelier hangs above the bed, giving the room a definite feminine touch that compliments the light and airy feel of the space. The bed is humongous. It has to be custom-made because it looks just shy of two king-sized mattresses pushed together. The headboard is cream, and the bedding is a peach-and-cream pattern that looks soft and incredibly inviting. The long, cushioned bench at the foot of the bed and the side tables are cream, and everything sits atop a large area rug in the same color.

There are two sets of French doors that lead out to a spacious patio. In front of one set of doors is a beautiful sitting area with comfortable looking couches and chairs. I can easily picture the lazy days of lounging on the cozy furniture—napping, reading, or just enjoying the warm sun that is guaranteed to pour into the room during the day. It's gorgeous and perfect in ways I would have never thought of, and I love it.

I slip down Knox's back and step further into the room, catching even more gorgeous details. Ryker rubs the back of his neck as he looks from me to the room and back again.

"The sisters helped us choose the colors, but all of us picked everything else out. Once we got everything in here, we were a little worried it might be too girly. Is it okay?"

Ryker's admission surprises the shit out of me. I assumed that I had the sisters to thank for this perfection, but knowing that they selected everything in this room makes it even more amazing than I already thought it was. My stunned face turns into a beaming smile, and I find Ryker's worry about whether I like what they've done adorable.

"Well, I am a girl, so girly works for me," I tease, as I take one last look around the room. "It's perfect! Beyond perfect, really. I love everything about it, and then I love it a million times more because you guys did it."

Ryker and Knox shoot matching prideful grins at each other, and their sudden excitement makes me chuckle. I step over to Ryker and push a lock of blond hair away from his face. I soak in his beautiful blue eyes and run the back of my fingers over his cheek.

"Thank you," I tell him softly, gratitude and appreciation radiating from my gaze.

I reach up on my tiptoes and pull his lips to mine. He tries to get away with a quick peck, but I'm over these *all too quick* kisses, and I let my mouth demand more. I claim his top lip first, deliberately slow as I cup the back of his head and nape with my hands. My fingers sink into his thick, golden hair. He hesitates for the slightest of seconds before wrapping his arms around my back and pulling me in closer. I deepen the kiss and bite back my moan of satisfaction when Ryker finally stops holding back.

I push for more with each stroke of my tongue and nip of his lips before diving back into an all-consuming kiss. All too soon, I feel him start to shut the kiss down and begin to pull away. I huff out my irritation against his soft lips, but it doesn't stop him from stepping away. I turn to Knox, and the heat I see in his eyes sends a delicious twinge between my thighs. I move toward him, and in two huge steps, he meets me, cupping my face in his strong hands and crashing his lips to mine. Knox wastes no time kissing me mindless. He owns my mouth with no hesitation or reservation, and I match his claim and fervor.

The words *thank you* never make it out of my mouth to Knox, so I put them in my kiss instead, and I can taste them on his lips and mine. I reach down to the hem of my shirt and start to pull it up.

"Vinna," Ryker calls, and Knox stalls our kiss, giving me one last little nip before stopping.

I look over at Ryker, not missing the conflict in his features.

"Squeaks, you just went through your Awakening. You need to rest and recover. There's no rush, we're not going anywhere, and there will be plenty of time to escalate things when you're one hundred percent and not coming down from a traumatic experience with your magic."

I consider Ryker for a moment. I know he means well, but I'm done hitting the brakes. I was tired before, but I'm sure as fuck not now, and if these two walk out of here after getting me this wound up, I just might lose my mind. I look from Ryker's apologetic face to Knox. My king of going with the flow, down for anything, the one who always supports me in whatever I want to do. I step out of his arms, ignoring the tiny flash of disappointment I see there before he covers it up.

I take a couple steps back so I can see them both. I grab the bottom of my shirt and slowly pull it up and over my head. It lands on the ground next to me. I reach down and unbutton my jeans, lower the zipper, and push them down my thighs, past my calves, and off my feet. I look up, the intensity in my eyes matching what I see in Knox's and Ryker's heated gazes.

"You guys in or out?"

28

I hear Ryker murmur something along the lines of *fucking hell,* but it's drowned out by a charging Knox. He grabs my ass, lifts me up to straddle him, and announces "in" before kissing me. His grip on my ass is bruising, his kiss punishing, and I love every second of it. No holding back, no more fucking hesitation, just raw, aggressive need at its finest. I suck on his tongue, and he grinds up into my spread legs, making me moan at the contact. I push away from him, hopping down out of his hold, and go right for the button of his pants.

He chuckles and whips his shirt over his head, dropping it to join mine on the ground. He kicks his pants off and reaches for me again, pulling me into another deep, panty-melting kiss. I squeak in surprise when I feel Ryker press against my back and slowly run his hands over the side of my hips and up my ribs. I honestly thought he was going to leave after telling me he thought I should wait. I look over my shoulder at him, the question clear on my face.

"In. I'll always be *in* when it comes to you."

His declaration seeps into me as he leans down and

kisses me with such tenderness and devotion that it sends my soul singing.

Knox reaches around my back and unhooks my bra. The straps slide off my shoulders, and he pulls it the rest of the way off. I reach down to Knox's boxer briefs and push the top of them down. Ryker pulls his lips from mine, and his kisses move languidly down my neck and over the runes on my shoulder.

When his tongue snakes out and connects with my runes, a flash of purple magic breaks out across my skin. It's as if Ryker's tongue is somehow in direct contact with my clit, instead of running across my runes, each kiss and flick sends a zing of pleasure straight between my thighs. I'm soaked with desire and want, and I grind my ass back against Ryker's erection which is still frustratingly trapped in his jeans. I moan as he switches from the runes on one shoulder to the runes on the other, causing more magic to spark all over me.

Knox cups my breasts and runs his thumbs in tandem over my peaked, sensitive nipples.

I arch into his large hands and watch as a flash of violet streaks up my torso to connect with his palms. He groans as he absorbs the magic and grinds his hips forward against me. Ryker lets out a short moan of pleasure as he also gets his first dose of orgasm-inducing power.

"What is that?" Ryker asks, his voice deep and sensual.

"No idea, it just happens when you guys get me really turned on or really pissed off."

Ryker's hands replace Knox's on my breasts, and he pinches my nipples between his fingers and grinds into my ass.

"By the stars, you feel so fucking good!"

I gasp, and my magic flares at all the incredible sensations his hands and mouth are creating. Knox steps back and finishes what I tried to start, by pushing his underwear off. He stands in front of me, proud as a peacock, happy to let me look my fill. My eyes greedily take him in. All that perfection is definitely something to be proud of. His mocha skin is smooth and soft, his frame large, muscular, rippling, and defined. His cock juts out invitingly, and I want him inside of me so badly I could scream.

I feel Ryker behind me start to undress, and nerves begin to break through my lust. I've been pushing for this and wanting this practically from the moment I first saw them, but it feels weird that it's about to morph from fantasy into reality. Knox stalks forward and kisses me so thoroughly that all I can think about is his incredible body against mine and how to get more of him. He lifts me up again, but instead of perching me against his chest, he throws me onto the bed.

I go airborne with a squeal. Both of them chuckle as I bounce down onto the large bed. *Fuck, that was hot.* Knox climbs up my body and hooks his fingers into the top of my underwear, deliberately pulling them slowly down my legs. He takes a moment to soak in my nakedness before his gaze rises to meet mine.

"You're the most beautiful thing I've ever seen."

His gray eyes stay locked on mine, the adoration and warmth I find there slowly seeping into my soul, claiming a piece of it.

I open my mouth to respond, and I'm shocked by the word that wants to slip out. *Love?* That can't be right. It's way too fucking soon for me to be making that kind of declaration. I'm not even sure if I know what it means. I try to find something else that fits how I feel about Knox, Ryker, and the others, but nothing fits. Nothing captures what they mean to me while still leaving room for things to come.

Unfazed by my lack of response, Knox spreads my legs, dips his head down and sucks my clit into his mouth.

"Holy fuck!" I groan loudly.

He chuckles, spreads me even further and licks me from the bottom of my opening all the way up, swirling his tongue in tiny circles around my clit.

Holy shit!

The bed dips down next to me, and Ryker's gorgeous, naked body crawls to me. He pushes his blond locks out of his face and seizes my lips, kissing me deeply. I fight not to come from what both of their mouths are currently doing to me.

I moan into Ryker's kiss when Knox does moons-knows-what to my clit; it has me squirming and grinding myself onto his face as I try to capitalize on my building orgasm. Purple magic flashes wildly all over me, and Ryker and Knox match my moans and groans as they absorb it and feed the pleasure back to me.

Ryker sucks on my bottom lip, releasing it with a pop and moves to do the same with my nipple. Knox flicks my clit with his tongue, and I feel his finger circling my opening, pressing in more and more with each revolution. I arch off the bed and cry out my release as both Ryker's and Knox's mouths send me over the edge.

Ryker switches to my other nipple, simultaneously sucking and tonguing one and pinching the other with the perfect amount of pressure. Knox slips a finger inside of my clenching pussy and starts pumping in and out, working to extend my orgasm. My clit gets sensitive as my orgasm ebbs, and I squirm in an effort to separate my clit from Knox's mouth.

He chuckles but relents, pulling away from my now sensitive nerves. But he slips another finger inside of me and continues to pump in and out of me. I clench and unclench around his fingers, loving the friction and feel of him. Knox croons his approval and begins to move even faster. The heel of his palm hits my clit and the surrounding nerves every time he thrusts in. And even though I'm sensitive there, the repeated, fleeting touch of his palm against my clit causes another orgasm to build quickly.

I mewl out encouragement as Knox fingers me roughly.

"Mmmmm, that's it, Killer, come for me again. Get nice and wet and ready for us," Knox orders, as he leans down and nips at my inner thighs, his pace deliciously aggressive, his words and tone promising so much more.

Ryker sucks hard on my nipple and then pulls off to claim my mouth just as another orgasm crashes through me. He swallows my shouts greedily, and when I'm spent, he begins to nip at my earlobe. Knox pulls his fingers out of me, and our eyes lock on each other. He brings his fingers up to his mouth and sucks on them, his storm-gray eyes never leaving mine.

"Fuck, that's hot!" I admit, and he smiles as he continues to lick my orgasms from his fingers.

"She's ready for you," Knox announces to Ryker.

He moves from between my legs and lays on his side next to me, watching me with so much heat banked in his gaze, I can practically see steam rising off of him. Ryker replaces Knox between my legs and runs his hands up my inner thighs as his eyes roam over me. His cock is hard, the tip glistening, and as much as I want it buried deep inside of me, I can't help but feel a little nervous too.

"Do we need protection or something?" I ask, my voice breathy with nerves and desire.

"I'll make you a birth control potion in the morning if that's what you're worried about," Knox explains.

Ryker runs a hand up my abdomen, over the runes between my breasts, and then caresses back down, running his fingers lightly over the lips of my pussy. Knox's hands stroke softly up the runes on the outside of my arm, and their touches have me and my magic going wild.

"I can get condoms if you're not sure about unprotected sex," Ryker offers.

"No, I was worried about babies, not you guys," I admit.

I sit up on my elbows a little and watch Ryker run his fingers through my wetness as he parts my lips.

"Is it going to hurt as bad as some girls say it does?"

Ryker's blue eyes fill with warmth, and he gives me a sweet smile. "I hope not; I'm going to try and do everything I can so that it doesn't."

I reach for his cock, run my thumb through his precum, and swirl it around his tip as I think about what I'm about to do. It twitches in my hand, and Ryker gives a low hum of approval.

I lie back and spread my legs further in invitation.

"Let's find out if this is going to suck or be awesome," I announce, and Ryker and Knox both snort out a chuckle.

Knox leans in and kisses me slowly, tenderly. I close my eyes and get lost in the sensation of his lips and tongue sucking and coaxing me out of my nervousness. He pulls away, and I can practically taste the adoration and want on his tongue. He lies back down on his side, seemingly happy to watch Ryker claim my virginity, and he palms his cock and slowly begins to stroke it.

Ryker kisses leisurely up my torso. He traces the runes on my sternum with his tongue as he pinches my nipples in both of his hands, and I almost come again just from that. My moans grow louder, my encouragement more forceful, as he positions the head of his cock at my entrance and starts to shallowly pump in and out. I stretch slowly around him as he dips inside of me more and more, and it feels different but good. I thought Knox's fingers inside of me felt incredible, but this, feeling Ryker make his way inside of me, this could be addicting.

He pulls his talented tongue from the runes on my chest, and our gazes lock.

"Are you okay?"

"More than okay," I tell him and pull him into a kiss.

He thrusts deep inside of me. I tense at the slight stinging sensation, and Ryker stills. He pulls his face back and looks at me, measuring my reaction.

"I'm good," I reassure him.

He stays still, deep inside of me, giving me time to adjust to the feel of him. He reaches a hand down between us and sets it low on my stomach. His hand heats up, and it steals away any discomfort I'm experiencing from having him inside of me. I stare at him in awe.

"Whoa, that's a cool trick."

Ryker chuckles, and it morphs into a deep groan as he pulls out and thrusts back inside of me. I cry out my approval as his movements take on a steady rhythm. He kisses, nips, and sucks on my lips and tongue, my neck, my breasts, my runes, while steadily moving in and out of me. He feels incredible, and I'm lost to the sensations of his thrusts, tongue, and my magic flashing all over me, heightening everything to a level I never want to come down from.

The sound of skin slapping against skin gets louder and faster, and my shouts and exclamations match it. I reach a hand out to Knox, and even his groans increase as my magic flows into him, enhancing everyone's sensations.

"Fuck, Vinna!" Ryker growls out as he grinds into me slowly a couple of times before resuming that incredible faster pace.

"I can't last much longer with your magic doing that to me," he admits, and I cry out and demand he keeps going, when his thrusts hit a sweet spot inside of me.

"You're good. I'll finish her off, just hurry up! I fucking want inside of my mate!" Knox insists.

Ryker pumps into me three more times before he growls out his release and stills as deeply inside of me as he can get. Violet strikes crawl all over his skin, and he kisses me sweetly before pulling out and collapsing on the bed beside me. His muscles twitch as he absorbs my weird sex magic, and he gives me a lazy smile as he presses back into the pillows.

Knox climbs over me, and the grin he gives me is salacious and filled with all kinds of promise.

"Are you sore? I'm dying to be inside of you, but if you're not up for that, I get it."

I smile at him and sit up. I cup his beautiful face in my hands and kiss him. Purple magic flicks from my hands to his face, and he moans into my mouth. I lean into him, and he dips back to accommodate me until he's on his back and I'm leaning over him. I climb on top of him, and he caresses me gently all over; I can feel the worship in his touch, and I revel in the intimacy of it. I straddle his hips and reach down to palm him and position him at my entrance.

Knox's eyes follow my every move, and he licks his lips as I take hold of him and slowly lower myself onto him. I moan in appreciation of how he feels inching into me. My thighs meet his hips as I fully connect us, and he lifts up off the bed, pushing even further into me. We both groan in tandem, and I place my palms on his chest and lean forward a little, using his strong body as leverage.

Knox runs his hands up my sides as he leans up to steal my lips for another deep, passionate kiss. I grind my hips down against his, and the kiss tapers off as we get lost in the moans and sensations of me riding him. I chuckle a little, and he looks up at me with lidded, questioning eyes.

"I have no idea what I'm doing," I admit. "Am I supposed

to use my legs and do this *pogo stick* style, or just grind on you to my heart's content?"

Knox laughs, which makes me start to crack up too. No amount of romance novel reading has prepared me for the real thing. I'm trying to be all sexy, but I realized after I slipped down onto Knox that I have no idea how to even go about accomplishing that. He lifts his hips up off the bed again, pushing deeper into me, and my laugh morphs into an exclamation of appreciation.

"Just do whatever feels good to you. I promise you'll hear no complaints from me," he encourages.

With that, he leans forward and steals a nipple into his mouth. I throw my head back absorbing the ecstasy his mouth and cock are creating, and pump my hips up and down on top of him while occasionally grinding my clit against the black curls settled at the base of his shaft. Knox releases my nipple, replacing his mouth with pinching fingers, and I increase my pace. Knox grips my hips and starts to grind up into me every time I slam down onto him.

Our heated gazes connect, and we watch each other's pleasure as we chase our release. Knox's hands trace up my back, and out of nowhere, he flips our positions. I open my mouth to object, but he covers it with a kiss, shifting out of me and then roughly back in. He slams into me relentlessly over and over again, and my objections die amidst sensations I don't ever want to end.

"Fuck, Knox!" I exclaim with a shout, unable to string together anything more coherent.

He hums, satisfied, into my ear. "Mmmm right there, Killer, is that where you want me?" he asks, grinding deeply into me and circling his hips against mine before pulling back out and slamming punishingly back into me. I gasp and pant, and he growls into his thrusts. He reaches down between us and thumbs my clit, and it's all I need to go over the edge. With a shout, I climax and tighten around Knox's cock, and he roars out his release, sinking deep inside of me.

He gives me a couple more shallow thrusts before he kisses me again and pulls out. He collapses on top of me but scoots down, so I'm not crushed under his weight or size. He rests his head between my breasts and lets out a contented sigh. With one hand, I run my fingers and palm over his buzzed hair, and with the other, I reach out for Ryker.

Ryker moves in closer to my side and steals a sweet, tired kiss.

"You okay, Squeaks? Do you need anything?"

I give him a slow, satisfied smile. "I need us to take a quick nap and wake up to do that again."

They both chuckle against me, and I close my eyes, succumbing to the calm and peace that's beckoning me to sleep.

29

I wake up surrounded by heat. I'm clammy with sweat and tucked tightly between two large muscular bodies. Knox's forearm and hand rest on my stomach, and he's curled into my side, his deep breaths sinking into my hair and neck. Ryker is on his back on the other side of me. He's draped a leg over my thighs, and our fingers on one hand are laced together and resting on his abs.

Soft light floats into the room from the large windows, and I would guess it's very early morning. I'm tempted to try and fall back asleep, but I feel kind of sticky and gross, which makes my only goal right now a shower. I get out from underneath Ryker's leg first and carefully move Knox's arm toward his chest. I get out from underneath the covers, and thankfully neither of them stir. I scoot slowly toward the end of the bed, slip off, and head for the closed doors at one end the room, one of which I'm hoping leads to a bathroom.

Jackpot!

The first door I reach for takes me exactly where I'm wanting, and I step into the dim room and fumble against the wall for the light. I flip the switch up and gasp at what the illumination reveals. Directly in front of me is a tub that's probably better classified as a small pool. All the guys and I could fit in there at one time and still leave room for probably both of Sabin's horses. There's a large shower that practically takes up a whole wall to the right of the tub, and a long vanity with two sinks to my left.

I step into the massive shower and twist knobs until the shower head above me turns on, and the water becomes molten just the way I like it. I step under the spray and stand as it washes away any evidence of last night's activities. I take stock of myself, once again feeling for my magic and trying to determine if anything is different now that I've had my Awakening. Where I once used to visualize a ball of tangled magical threads, now sits a dark hole.

The depthless chasm in my chest surprisingly doesn't worry me. It doesn't represent emptiness, but more of an endless source that I can now pull from. I reach for my Elemental magic, and the Kelly green power surges into my center like a legion ready for war. I focus in on the water around me and weave my intent with the abnormally eager magic. A ball of water floats in the air chest high in front of me, and I watch it grow in size at my command. I jump up and down with a huge smile on my face, ecstatic that my Elemental magic didn't fight me as much as it has in the past.

Strong arms snake around me from behind, scaring the shit out of me. I squeak-yelp in alarm, and my giant ball of water bursts and disappears down the shower wall and floor. I twist to see who's behind me. Ryker's soft lips half turn up in apology, but his eyes sparkle with amusement as he pulls me closer to him.

"Sorry, Squeaks, I didn't mean to scare you. You just looked so wet and inviting, and I couldn't resist climbing in here with you."

"Warn a girl next time. What if I had zapped you or punched you or something?"

He chuckles and leans down to kiss my neck. "Sorry. I consider myself warned. If I get punched in the future, I'll take full responsibility for it."

I run my hands up the damp golden skin of his arms, appreciating the dips and peaks of his muscles as they flex and pull me even closer. I step back into the spray and bring Ryker with me—he yelps and immediately jumps back.

"Shit, sorry!"

I scramble to adjust the knobs and cool down the steady stream flowing from the shower head in the ceiling. I guess boiling isn't his preferred temperature setting. Wisely, Ryker sticks his hand under the stream of water before stepping back underneath it. I watch, mesmerized as the water darkens his golden hair, and he tilts his head back appreciatively and closes his eyes.

Ryker is breathtakingly beautiful, and I can't seem to snap myself out of the staring I'm currently doing. My eyes trace the trails of water that streak past his long lashes, sculpted nose, chiseled jaw, and plump lips. He tilts his head down and catches me creeping out on him.

"Stop looking at me, swan," he imitates, and I crack up at the spot-on Billy Madison impersonation.

He kisses my nose and hands me a bottle of shampoo.

"I'll do yours if you do mine," he offers.

I can't help but give a salacious waggle of my eyebrows, happily going right for any and all innuendo in that statement. He chuckles and pops the top of the shampoo, squeezing some into my hand. I reach up and work the shampoo into his hair until it's lathered and white and I can make shapes with his almost shoulder-length locks.

"How are you feeling today?" he asks, as I whip his hair

into a dollop that any Who from Whoville would be proud to sport.

"Good. My magic doesn't feel tangled anymore. My center, or core of magic, or whatever it's called, feels different, less limited maybe." I try to explain, but it sounds more like a question than an answer. "Other than that, everything feels the same, but I also have no idea what I'm supposed to be looking for."

He nods in understanding. "How about physically? Do you need any healing? Anything sore?"

I can't help the chuckle that escapes me. "My vagina is fine, if that's what you're asking." He laughs and reaches up for some bubbles from his hair and proceeds to flick them at me before stepping into the spray and letting the water steal away the shampoo and his sudsy hairdo.

The shower smells like honeysuckle, and I breathe it in appreciatively.

"You're going to smell so girly and flowery today," I tease.

He holds on to my hips and leans into me as I proceed to work conditioner into his strands.

"I'm good with that. Hell, this might be my new favorite smell," he admits with a chuckle. I look at him confused. "Now, when I smell honeysuckle, it will remind me of you naked in the shower, dripping wet and beautiful."

He brings a hand up and skims my cheek with his thumb, as the rest of his palm cups the side of my face. There's so much depth to the tender affection in his eyes. Before I can say anything, Ryker twirls me around and squeezes shampoo into his hand. He works it into my hair, and it's impossible to ignore the muscles of his chest as they brush against my shoulder blades, or the hard cock pressed into my lower back. I lean into him, loving the intimacy of this moment even if the intensity of the feelings swirling in here make me nervous.

I rinse shampoo out of my hair, and Ryker's hands start to rub all over me under the guise of spreading body wash. I'm impressed he let me clean up a bit before pouncing. I've personally been working out the logistics of shower sex from the minute he waltzed in here.

Ryker rubs his soapy palms in a circular motion up the runes on my sides and then reaches around my front to generously lather up my breasts. He doesn't spend as much time there as I'd like, moving up and over my shoulders to massage some of the stress that's been sitting there for way too long. I pull us both under the spray, washing away his efforts, and then spin around in his arms, done with the leisurely pace he's setting.

I reach down and grip his hard cock, stroking it easily as the water pours down onto both of us. His eyes are heated and locked on mine as he lets out a sexy groan and shifts his hips forward, thrusting into my hand. He slowly starts to back me up toward the shower wall, and a zing shoots down through my stomach and straight between my legs as my body starts to anticipate how good it's going to feel to have him back inside of me.

"Wrap your arms around my neck," he instructs before he grabs my ass and lifts me up, pressing me in against the wall of the shower.

The marble is cold against my back, but his full lips crash down on mine, and all I can think about is his tongue, mouth, and dick and where I want all of them to be. I moan into his mouth as he lines up and starts to press into me. I stretch around him, and he takes his time filling me up as he kisses me thoroughly. He nips my bottom lip just as he pulls out and thrusts deeply back in, and I sink my hands into his hair and demand more.

I hold onto him tightly as he grips my ass and drives in and out of me at a pace that has us both panting already. He thrusts in deeply and suddenly freezes. I nip at his jawline and grind against him with my hips, encouraging him to keep going, but he doesn't move. Every muscle in his body is rigid and tense, and I'm not sure what the hell is going on.

"Ryker, are you okay?" I ask, trying to pull back and get a look at his face, but he's pressed his head into my shoulder.

He groans, but it's not the sexy kind you hear when someone is enjoying themselves. I shove against his chest, trying to push him out of me so I can figure out what's happening, but his grip on my ass becomes bruising, and something about it makes me start to panic. I call on extra strength from my runes and shove hard against Ryker pressing my back into the marble of the shower wall to give me even more leverage.

I slip out of Ryker's hold, and he crumbles to the ground as my feet touch the shower floor. I scramble to him, brushing wet locks out of his face. His eyes are squeezed tightly closed, his jaw clenched, and he's scaring the shit out of me. I shout for Knox as my fingers try and fail to sooth away whatever the fuck is happening to Ryker. I run a hand down his arm, and I can feel every inch of muscle locked up and rigid. I scream for Knox again, but the doorway remains empty. I run a shaky finger over the runes behind my ear and mentally scream for help.

"Ryker, can you hear me? What the fuck is happening? Are you hurt? Did I hurt you somehow?"

My hands flutter over him, but I don't set them down anywhere for fear that somehow it might make whatever's happening worse. A strained scream starts to bubble out of Ryker's clenched teeth, and the agonizing sound fucking kills me. Heavy footfall pounds just outside of the bathroom, and I hear shouted voices coming closer. Valen runs through the doorway first, and with no hesitation, he heads right for me and Ryker.

"I don't know what happened. One minute he was fine, and then he just froze up like this. He's hurting, Valen, but I can't tell from what."

Valen's worried gaze leaves mine as he crouches down next to Ryker and tries to talk to him to no avail.

"Whatever it is, it's fucking with Knox, too; we found him writhing in the bed when we ran in here."

Valen's words are punctuated by Bastien running into the bathroom.

"Knox is in agony. I don't think he can talk."

I open my mouth to ask them what the fuck is going on when the realization hits me like a sledgehammer. *Oh fuck, I did this!*

30

I take in Ryker's body, frozen in pain, his clenched eyes, his inability to respond or interact with anything beyond what he's feeling right now, and I recognize it from when it happened to me at sixteen. He's going to come out of the worst of it, and that's when the screaming will start, and the runes will sear themselves into him and Knox, the magic altering them forever.

Fuck! I thought we had to bond or whatever the fuck it's called for this to happen?

"Valen, it's the runes!" I tell him, the panic clear in my voice.

Valen turns to me, and worriedly his eyes run over my runes.

"Not mine, they're getting runes," I gesture frantically down to Ryker who's still rigid with agony on the shower floor.

Bastien hurriedly steps in and turns the water off.

"I thought we had to be bound or something for me to transfer my magic, but apparently not. That's what's happening to them. It's the transference!"

Understanding dawns on the twins' faces, and it immediately mixes with shock and then worry.

"Let's get him to the bed," Bastien announces, and without any further discussion, Valen and Bastien both bend down and lift Ryker off the floor.

He makes a pained noise, and I break a little, knowing how much he's hurting right now. Bastien and Valen easily maneuver Ryker out of the large shower, and I quickly grab a few towels and wrap him up. They take him out to the bed where my heart splinters even more at seeing the agony that's taken hold of Knox too.

He's not as locked up as Ryker, at least his body isn't, but his face is frozen in a silent scream as he fists the sheets beneath his hands and writhes as much as his pain-filled muscles will let him. They set Ryker on the massive bed, and I scramble onto it, dampening everything I touch. I'm panicked and frustratingly clueless about what to do now. This moment reaffirms that watching someone I care about suffer is infinitely worse than any amount of pain or suffering I've ever personally experienced.

"It's going to be okay, you guys. It'll be over soon," Valen tells them, and the words sit more like a prayer in the room than an offer of reassurance.

Bastien and Valen stand helplessly on the side of the bed, and I can hear Sabin talking to someone on the other side of the door. A thought races through my mind, and I reach out to both Knox and Ryker, setting the palms of my hands on both of their chests. I was hoping just my touch might offer some relief like theirs had during my awakening, but if they're feeling anything good from my damp hand against their skin, they aren't able to show it.

I close my eyes and tap into the chasm in my center. I beg my Healing magic to help me do something. I release a grateful whimper when the thick, soft-teal strands of power cooperate without hesitation. The stream of hope that runs through me when my magic answers my call quickly dries up when I feed the Healing magic into Ryker and Knox and nothing happens. I feel raw and gutted at having to watch them go through this. I know it will end. I know they'll be okay. But it offers zero comfort as Knox screams through a clenched jaw, his voice giving agony a sound that will haunt me for the rest of my life.

I know from personal experience that as soon as you can scream through the pain, you're in the final stages of this fucked up process, but that doesn't make it any less brutal. I kneel between Knox and Ryker on the bed refusing to take my eyes from them. I did this, and I deserve to have to live with the memories of how it hurt them. The other guys call my name, but I can't look at them. The picture is now crystal clear for them, and there's no more denying that what I am is going to hurt them. Just like it's hurting Knox and Ryker. Just like it hurt Talon. I can't bear to see that knowledge and understanding written all over their faces.

I want to beat the shit out of myself for letting something like this happen. I have a fucking tablet with information that might have clued me in on how transference works, but have I opened it even once? Nope. I look from Ryker to Knox and back again, letting their cries of pain scar me the way that I deserve. I can't keep hoping that somehow life is going to mellow out and resemble anything close to normal. I'm a Sentinel, and pain and fighting are written in the stars for me and everyone I care about. *I'm a fucking plague.*

Black marks float to the surface of their skin like the suffering has somehow boiled to the surface. The color deepens slowly, and the runes take on more and more clarity as their pained shouts reverberate around the room. A droplet of water drips from me onto Knox's side, and it traces a path past the runes forming on his ribs. Another tear follows, and I wipe furiously at my face to keep any more of me from tainting him or Ryker.

The yells dull to aching moans, and if I wasn't so angry and disgusted with myself, I might be able to feel some form of relief that this is almost over. I wipe sweat from Knox's brow and try to cover Ryker with the sheets and comforter so he doesn't get cold when he comes out of this. Part of me wants to trace their runes—I've never seen them this close on anyone but me—but I kick that part of me in the face and tell it to fuck off.

Knox and Ryker begin to settle, the tension seeping out of their clenched muscles and the writhing becoming more of a rocking. They both pant with shallow breaths, and I watch the rapid rise and fall of their chests until it starts to smooth out. The staccato rhythm of their breaths becomes quieter, their inhales becoming deeper, as each of them is released from the pain at precisely the same second.

"Vinna," Valen calls to me, but I ignore him.

I'm only able to focus on Knox's brow smoothing out, and the lines around Ryker's eyes disappearing as the pain leaves them both, and the need for furrowed brows and clenched lids evaporates. Ryker is the first to open his eyes. He brings his hands up and twists his arm to take in the line of runes that now exist there. His eyes find mine, and he gives me a half smile.

"Ouch," he chuckles, and I hear a relieved breath and strained chuckle escape Bastien and the others.

I wish I could appreciate his attempt at levity, but that simple word might as well be a hammer, and too much of me is made of glass right now. The back of a strong hand strokes down my arm, and I turn to look at Knox. He takes one look at my face and his fills with panic. He rushes to sit up as I scramble away from him and Ryker. His movements are shaky, and there's a touch of stiffness still in his limbs.

An echo of what he's feeling resonates in me as I recall how I felt after my runes showed up.

"Why are you crying? What happened?" Knox asks, confused.

I climb off the bed, and an angry and indignant snort escapes me. His eyes track me and narrow when I flinch as Bastien moves toward me.

"What the fuck happened?" he demands more forcefully, glaring at the others as he tries to scoot on unsteady arms out of the bed's comfortable embrace.

Ryker looks around confused, slower to take in that everything is not even remotely close to okay right now.

"What do you mean, what happened?" he asks.

"Vinna. Look at her. She looks like she did after the lamia attack. That same broken, pained, and lost look that killed us, the one we just started to chase away."

Ryker's eyes snap to mine, and he takes me in. I feel all of their scrutinizing gazes as they run over my still naked body. Collectively, they all take a step toward me, and I back up, trying to maintain the distance that suddenly feels vital right now. I quickly realize that I'm cornered and there's nowhere for me to go, and I find myself suddenly choking on panic. I claw at my throat desperate for air, frenzied to escape the terror crashing into me. I gasp around huge mouthfuls of nothing as I try to find oxygen, but it seems like the air is suddenly devoid of it.

Arms seize me tightly, and I'm pulled into Valen's chest. Bastien sandwiches me in, and they both press in tightly against me. The space between where I exist and they exist disappears, and the line between *I can't get away* and *I don't want to get away* dissolves so quickly that I can't really gauge what I want or what I need right now. I suck in huge gasps, fighting for air, fighting for control over the massive and consuming emotions trying to escape me right now.

How can I do this to them? How can I condemn them to this life? I didn't want to be alone, so I opened myself up to what we could be, but how could I be so selfish?

My self-loathing rises even higher as I battle against how good it feels to be surrounded by all of them as they attempt to soothe me and understand what's happening. Knox cradles my face in his hands, and the furious look on his face gives me pause. It's then that I realize I've been babbling that *I was sorry, and I couldn't do this to them.*

"You fucking stop that shit right now. Do you understand me? You are mine!" Knox smacks a closed fist against the runes on his chest, and his eyes are filled with fire and frustration. "You are here, you are in my soul, and there isn't shit you can do about it. You are not a fucking plague! You are ours, and we want it that way!"

"But I'm hurting you!" I yell at him, somehow hoping the volume helps embed the truth of what I'm saying into him.

"No, you're tempering us. We will be stronger because of you. Connected because of you. Better because you are ours and we are yours. But not if every time things get difficult, you cut us out. Why don't you trust us?"

His voice breaks on the question, and the argument in my mouth crumbles to ash.

"I do trust you."

"No, you don't. If you trusted us, you wouldn't dismiss what we say and want so easily. We tell you that we understand what it means to be with you, to be Chosen, but you throw that away because *you* decide you know better. You decide for *us* that being together is not worth it. Each of us has told you that we're in. Did you think we made that decision lightly, that we didn't think through what that meant for us, for you?"

I stare at him, and his words rumble like thunder through me.

"You didn't have a choice. I marked you and forced you to make the best of a messed up situation."

"Oh, is that what we are, a messed up situation?"

"That's not what I meant, and you fucking know it!" I growl at him.

Knox steps even closer to me. He brings his face even with mine, his lips a hair's breadth away, his long eyelashes kissing mine as he blinks once before his eyes lock onto mine.

"Now you listen to me...you may be one badass Sentinel, but guess what, so am I now. Stop questioning your place in our lives. Stop doubting us when we say that, no matter what, this is what we want. You are what we want. The scorching I just got from those runes? That's nothing compared to the hurt when you doubt me, doubt your place with us. So get your shit together, Killer. Either you're in, or you're out."

Knox's face remains serious, but a twinkle enters his eyes. He knows he's got me, *cheeky fucker,* using my own words against me. I stay silent, and my eyes bounce back and forth between the gray storm clouds in his gaze. *In or out*. The challenge resonates through every part of me, and it stomps out the fucked up pieces in me that insist I'm not worthy or deserving of what they're offering me. I kick at the doubts and useless insecurity and decide once and for all.

"In."

31

I walk into the open kitchen, taking in the details that I failed to notice last night. Cream-colored cabinets and countertops are set against exposed brick walls. There's a mixture of old and new throughout the entire house, and it somehow feels perfect and complimentary.

The sisters are leaning against the counters in the kitchen, conversing about something that has their hands flying around passionately and the looks on their faces intense. I perch against my own counter space and try to catch on to what they're talking about, but as soon as I'm spotted, the conversation dies.

"Hello, my Love, how are you doing this morning?" Birdie asks me, her sweet smile and kind eyes running over me, assessing the situation herself.

"I'm good. One dramatic freak-out down, and hopefully not many to follow," I offer casually, punctuating it with a slightly hollow chuckle.

Adelaide's smile turns empathetic, and she tilts her head just slightly to the side, as she takes me in. "Don't be too hard on yourself, Love. With everything that's happened, all of it in such a short amount of time, it's a wonder that you're handling it all as well as you are."

We all fall reflectively silent for a couple of seconds.

"So what're you ladies talking about?" I ask, grasping for something that changes the subject and steals me away from my thoughts about everything that's happened since I ran into the paladin almost two months ago.

The sisters shoot each other a loaded look, and it's as if I can see the silent conversation that's playing out in their gazes. Lila takes a deep, fortifying breath and looks at me in a way that tells me she just selected the short straw.

"We were talking about Lachlan, Love, and the others, and what we're going to do."

I nod my head, even though I have no idea exactly what that means.

"Lachlan, Keegan, and Silva all left about a week ago to pursue some leads. The house is empty, and aside from keeping it clean, there's really no need for us there, at least not while they are gone. But we're discussing whether or not we should stay when they return, however long that may take."

I look at them confused. "Why wouldn't you stay? I thought you'd been working for the Aylins for a long time?"

Birdie nods at me, and her smile grows pained. "We have, that's true, but given everything that's happened, staying there while Lachlan behaves the way that he does feels like we're giving our permission, and that doesn't sit right with us."

I look away from her earnest blue eyes and process her words. I can't help but wonder what the leads are that Lachlan and the others are looking into.

"Was Lachlan's paladin title stripped?" I ask, suddenly recalling what Becket's bitchy mom insinuated at the dinner from hell.

"He was given a demotion for behavior not in line with the beliefs of the paladin. When the elders wouldn't sanction reopening Vaughn's case, he stepped down altogether."

I rein in the snort that tries to tumble out of me at Adelaide's mention of the beliefs of the paladin. So far, the majority of paladin I've met reek of sexist, controlling bullshit. Lachlan's behavior seems right in line with that.

"Why aren't you married?" I blurt, since apparently every thought that pops into my head now has to come out of my mouth. "I mean, you can tell me it's none of my business, and I'll shut up, but I thought caster females are supposed to be rare and precious and all of that—not that I really think anyone actually believes that. At least, I haven't seen any evidence that casters revere females. Does *revere* mean control here? Is there a language barrier that I'm not aware of? Does *precious* actually mean commodity in caster?" I look over at the sisters' bemused faces and realize I'm rambling. "Yeah so, how did you get out of the whole *encouraged* binding thing?"

The sisters chuckle, and their previously troubled features smooth out with their tinkling amusement.

"We're Nulls, Vinna," Lila tells me, as if I should know what that means.

Reading my baffled expression, she continues, "We have almost no magic. And no magic means no interest in bonding with us or forming a coven."

My eyebrows crinkle, and my mouth falls slightly open with the frustration I feel for Lila's statement.

"But you're fucking awesome!" I exclaim. They all give me a sweet smile, and Adelaide just shrugs her shoulders. "How is that overlooked and buried under what your magical abilities may or may not be?"

This time Lila gives me the shrug.

"Fuck casters then, let's go find you ladies some silver foxes of the human variety."

I push off the counter like I'm ready to go get them some love right this minute, but their chortles make me pause, and the fact that none of them have moved to follow me also clues me in that maybe they're not as into my plan as I am. Bastien walks into the kitchen, takes in my expression and the laughing sisters, and walks over to me like he's my reinforcement for whatever's going on.

"What's got the sisters all a-cackle?" he asks me before pressing a kiss to my temple.

Knox, Ryker, Sabin, and Valen all pour into the room, Evrin and Aydin bringing up the rear. Their synchronized arrival makes me momentarily wonder what they were all doing together. Last we spoke, everyone was heading off to get dressed before breakfast. But the sudden group entrance makes me feel like I missed some kind of impromptu meeting. The sisters' giggles taper off, and it distracts me from my suspicious thoughts.

"We like our life, Vinna. We're happy with what we have, and no male, human or otherwise, could make things any better," Lila tells me with a warm smile.

"Sex!" I exclaim. "Sex can make a lot of things better."

Aydin spits out the water he just took a gulp of and starts to cough uncontrollably. Evrin gives him a couple hard slaps on his back, and I can feel Bastien's laughter rumbling in his chest next to me. I realize that maybe the sisters might not exactly be down to talk about their sex life, or the lack thereof, in front of all of these guys, but seriously, I'm not wrong.

Not that I'm some kind of expert, being that my first time was last night and resulted in two out of three parties writhing in pain, but I'm trying not to focus on that. Aydin recovers from his coughing fit, and the sisters start to bustle about the kitchen getting things together for breakfast. My statement is left hanging in the air like we weren't just having a conversation. I turn to Sabin.

"Casters claim that females are valued and treasured, but how can you believe that when they're traded like prize stock if they're powerful, and dismissed as insignificant if they're not?"

Sabin opens this mouth to say something, but I can tell by the look on his face he's going to defend the beliefs he was raised with. I do everything I can not to roll my eyes and try hard to hear him out. I want to know why so many of them say they believe one thing, but the action of the culture shows something very different.

"Our ways all revolve around magic and keeping it strong. It's the foundation of our traditions and practices. It may seem archaic, but where would we be if magic died off?"

"I'm not saying that magic isn't important, but why does it seem to be the only thing that is? The elders are pushing me toward the coven of *their* choice because they want a powerful match, but why is our match"—I gesture to him and the others—"any less powerful than what I would have with Enoch and his coven?"

I watch Sabin as he gives what I'm saying some thought.

"I don't for a second believe that it would be," I tell him. "I honestly think they assume that Enoch and his group would control me better, which in turn gives the elders more direct access to me and what I can do. You can't tell me that what they're trying to do is all about keeping magic safe and strong."

Sabin doesn't say anything, and I can tell that he's searching for some other explanation or way to show me that what I think is not the way it is at all, but I don't think he's going to find it. I'm sure it can't be easy questioning things and people that you've never had to question before. The doubt I see on his face doesn't make me feel triumphant; it makes me feel sad. Sad that the world he thought existed is crumbling before him under the weight of its bullshit facade.

I turn to Knox. "Speaking of *delicate flower broodmares,* let's get that birth control potion you mentioned sorted."

He gives me a warm smile, but when it drops slightly, an alarm sounds in my head.

"I don't think I should try and make the spell, not with whatever new magic you've just given us. I don't want to make something and find out later that it didn't work because my magic isn't functioning the way I'm used to."

"Uh, okay, so what does that mean? Can we have someone else make it?" I ask and look around the room for volunteers, because I'm sure as fuck not having any babies.

Sabin rubs the back of his neck awkwardly, looking away and then back to me. "We can go to my family coven's shop; they'll have something for you there," Sabin offers, and I don't miss the tips of his ears getting redder or the blush that sneaks across his cheeks.

It's tempting to tease him about it, until I realize that I'm about to possibly meet some of Sabin's family for the first time, and it will be when he takes me to pick up birth control.

Well, this should be fun!

32

I run my hand over the creamy leather interior of Sabin's old and lovingly restored Bronco. We sit in companionable silence as the familiar grouping of buildings that make up Solace's main part of town looms closer in the distance. I spot the bell tower of the Academy and realize I've never heard it chime the time once since I've been here.

"Your last year of training starts what...next Monday? Are you ready to start training again?" I ask.

Sabin's features morph into an indecipherable look as he searches for an answer to what I thought was an innocent question.

"Yeah, I'm not sure, to be honest. Most of my life, I've been picturing a future as a paladin, but now I wonder if that's really going to be a possibility for us."

I turn to him perplexed. "Why wouldn't it be?"

"Elder Cleary knows what you are, and now, so does Enoch and his coven, and Knox and Ryker's family, but as far as we know, that's it. If all of us get runes and start manifesting magic we've never had before, how long will it take before the secret's out and you have an even bigger target on your back?"

I sift through his words for a minute, looking for an out or a way to keep the future he's describing from happening.

"Right now it's just Ryker and Knox that have the runes. The three of us can just go the recluse route, which wouldn't be too hard since the house has everything we could want. We can make sure that you, Bastien, and Valen don't acquire any new runes or power. You guys can fulfill your paladin dream, while I train Knox and Ryker. And when you graduate, we'll be a half-paladin, half-vigilante, kickass crime-fighting coven." I tell him with hopeful eyes and a reassuring nod. "We can totally make that work."

He chuckles and reaches out a hand to caress my cheek.

"I'm learning that maybe this isn't the place I've spent my life believing it was. I hoped that somehow when what you are and what you can do comes out, that the community would simply embrace you and treat you like you're one of them. But even if most of them did, the small number that didn't or that wanted to use you, like Adriel does, like maybe the elders do, they'd always be a threat to us. We would always be looking over our shoulders."

Sabin's admission sucks to hear. It's made all the more worse by the truth that sits heavy in every syllable. He's told me not to take on guilt that doesn't belong to me, but what do I do with the guilt that does?

"Sabin, how do I not feel guilty about that? I don't want your life to become this unrecognizable thing that has you always on the run, always looking over your shoulder. Don't you think you'll eventually resent me for that? I don't want to steal away everything you've always wanted. I'm not enough to fill the holes that would leave in who you are."

I know, out of all of them, this relationship and the way I up the ante with the Sentinel aspect of it, is probably the hardest for Sabin to come to terms with. The loss of control that seems so important to him and the speed at which I'm pushing things forward is an issue for him. I'm confident that Sabin is here by his own choice and that he cares for me, but I still worry that I'm pushing him too far and too fast out of his comfort zone.

"Vinna, your presence in my life is not creating holes. It's just opening up possibilities I never saw before. Maybe the goal of paladin shifts to badass, vigilante peacekeepers. Maybe there needs to be more balance out there when it comes to who makes the decisions about what's right and what's wrong. I don't know, and I don't think we'll know what the best move for all of us is until we're faced with it."

"But what about your families? What about your home here?" I press.

Sabin shrugs.

"I don't know. I have no idea how to fit all the pieces together yet. We all talked about it this morning, but none of us think we've reached that tipping point where we know, one way or the other, which way things are going to go down."

I throw my hands up in exasperation. "You guys did have a super-secret meeting without me, I fucking knew it!"

Sabin laughs.

"We just didn't want you to feel guilty or put too much on yourself. All that shit just happened with the guys and the runes, and we didn't want to push you over the edge by bringing up a bunch of hypotheticals that none of us are sure could even happen. You're dealing with enough; we don't want to keep adding to the stress."

I run my eyes over Sabin's profile as he drives and confesses why they kept me out of the loop. My initial reaction is to get mad, but when he talks about what happened with Knox and Ryker this morning, I realize that I was doing the same thing to them. Making decisions that I thought were in their best interest, cutting them out of the stress, putting the weight of it on my back, so they wouldn't get bogged down.

"I get why you all made that decision, but I don't want you guys to do that again. I'm also going to make sure that I'm not doing the same thing to any of you."

I reach over and grab his hand, and he relinquishes it willingly to me. I set it in my lap and trace the lines of his palm as I work through how to explain to him what I need.

"What we're all dealing with is a lot. It sucks. It isn't easy, and there's a strong likelihood that not much in our lives ever will be. But I realized that we need to look at things like my Awakening. Alone, I felt like I was dying, I couldn't take the pain, but when we shared it, it was manageable for all of us."

Sabin's hand closes around mine, and he brings it to his lips and presses a soft kiss to the back of my hand. I smile at the gesture that exposes the romantic hiding in the body of a bad boy.

"You're right; I'm sorry we left you out, and I'll make sure it never happens again," he tells me, and my heart swells.

"Well, that was easy. I thought I'd have to put more fight into getting my way," I admit.

Sabin laughs and navigates the Bronco onto the main street of Solace.

"I'll make it harder next time," he teases, and I bite down on the *that's what she said* joke.

The struggle must be obvious, because Sabin laughs even harder. "I walked right into that one, didn't I?" he asks, and I crack up.

I close the Bronco door behind me and walk through the side parking lot to the front of Gamull's Spell Shop. The front is all pristine glass, and it's the corner shop attached to a strip of other shops located on the main road in the center of town. Sabin leads me into his family's spell shop, and the scent of clove with the faint undertone of something woodsy fills my senses. It's not overwhelming or headache-inducing, but welcoming and soothing. I look around the well-organized space and the shelves of different things available for sale. Sabin was right; it does resemble a bath and body shop.

"Bean!" a girl squeals and tackles Sabin in a way that would make an offensive lineman proud. Sabin stumbles backward as he catches her and absorbs the momentum of the hit.

"What are you doing here? Don't you have school today?" Sabin asks the green-eyed ball of energy currently attempting to separate his torso from the rest of his body via the tightest hug I've ever seen.

"I got sent home," she pouts, and it's like I can see all the previous excitement drain out of her.

"For what?" Sabin demands, and the little girl and I both cringe at his tone.

"The Alson sisters mess with me all the time! They talk crap and shove me around. Today I threw water on one of them to get them to back off, and I'm the one who gets into trouble!"

"Cyndol, we talked about this; if they start something, you tell an instructor." Cyndol rolls her green eyes at Sabin and focuses on me like she just now noticed me next to him.

"You look tough; if some girls were picking on you, what would you do?" she asks me.

"I'd go for the nose."

"Vinna!" Sabin scolds me.

"What, Bean, I would." I look back down to Cyndol, who I've deduced is either Sabin's little sister or related to him somehow.

She looks to be maybe eleven, but I'm shit when it comes to judging ages. Her green eyes are more emerald versus Sabin's forest-green color, but the rest of their features and coloring are too similar for them not to be closely related somehow.

"If they physically touch you first, they're fair game," I tell her.

Cyndol gives me a wide smile, and Sabin rubs his hands over his face in exasperation.

"Tell an instructor first, Cyn; they'll keep them away from you."

Ignoring Sabin, Cyndol steps closer to me. "Will you show me how to punch?"

I open my mouth to answer, but Sabin's resounding "no" cuts me off.

A man calls Sabin's name, and he looks over to the caster that's making his way toward us. As soon as Sabin turns his head, I nod my head *yes* at Cyndol, and she lights back up with excitement. Like a born pickpocket, she slides an unlocked phone into my hand. I quickly type in my number and name while Sabin greets the other man with a hug. I slide the phone back to Cyndol, and she tucks it away as Sabin turns to introduce me to one of his dads. He narrows his eyes at me, his gaze filled with suspicion. I just blink innocently at him.

"Vinna, this is my dad, Luke. Dad, this is Vinna, my mate. And this is my little sister, Cyndol, whom you've already corrupted in the three seconds you've known her." He glares playfully at his little sister, and I chuckle at his teasing tone.

Luke's eyes widen a bit in shock, but he does a commendable job covering it up as he shakes my hand.

"Anyone else here?" Sabin asks his dad as he looks around.

"No, they're out doing deliveries; they won't be back for a couple more hours probably. It's just me and…"

Luke looks to Cyndol, who's trying to look inconspicuous just behind Sabin.

"Missy, you're supposed to be stocking shelves as punishment, now get to it."

She pouts, and her shoulders hunch as she side hugs Sabin and walks toward a doorway I'm assuming leads to a back room. Sabin and his dad are talking about what happened with her at school, and I raise my hand in the universal sign for *call me*. Cyndol nods enthusiastically and disappears through the push door. I tuck a lock of hair behind my ear trying to mask my movement when I notice Sabin look over at me.

Nothing to see here, Captain. I shrug innocently.

"So what brings you here? Since I'm assuming you're not here to make introductions," Luke teases.

Sabin's ear tips redden again, and I find it completely adorable until I remember why we're here.

"We need a birth control potion," he mumbles, and Luke's eyes fill with humor.

"I'm sorry, I didn't catch that, what did you need?"

I laugh, already deciding that Luke and I are kindred spirits, and Sabin gets even redder. Before I can join in on the teasing, I spot the bottle of honeysuckle shampoo and conditioner that my shower was stocked with.

"This came from here?" I ask, reaching for the bottle and taking a deep inhale of the incredible scent.

"Yes, that's from our premium line. Spelled Honeysuckle with a hint of Jasmine; it's great for sharpening your intuition, stimulates creativity, attracts and increases love, and is useful in increasing sexuality."

I look over to Sabin. "Captain, you gave me sex shampoo?"

He rolls his eyes at me. "Of all the things he said it does, of course that's the one you focus on."

Luke, being my kindred spirit and new dad bestie, pounces on the opportunity to harass his child. "He totally gave you sex shampoo."

"He did!" I agree.

"So about that potion," Sabin interjects, stopping us before we can really get started harassing him.

Luke chuckles. "Come with me."

33

Luke runs Sabin's card and pulls out a handled box that holds all the spells and potions we're buying. I'm like a kid in a magical candy store; there are so many cool things in here. I'm stocked up on birth control for the next year, and I only have to take a potion that tastes like sweetened tea once a month. I loaded up on sex shampoo and conditioner, bought a potion called Copal for Knox when Luke told me it helps with spelling, and some hair dye spells because that's a prank I'm going to love pulling.

"Alright, Vinna, you are all set," Luke tells me. "Let's set up a dinner or something with the family soon; they're going to be so jealous that I'm the first to meet your amazing mate!" Luke tells Sabin as he wraps him up in a goodbye hug and kisses his cheek. Luke opens his arms to me, and I step into them.

"Heads up that Knox's dads are going to make you sumo when I tell them you're my new favorite."

Luke cracks up and gives me a beaming smile. "I'll take 'em all down, don't you worry, your favoritism is well placed! Oh, and I slipped in a delicious spelled apricot, juniper, and dragon's blood massage oil in there; it's a very potent aphrodisiac that promotes virility, passion, and love."

"Ooh!" I coo at Luke, and we both chuckle when Sabin's ears turn red.

"First Cyndol picks her over me, and now you two are cohorts. Perfect...just perfect!"

"Aww, Captain, we love you too!" I tease and then instantly freeze when I realize I just let the *L* word escape.

I try to cover up my *oh shit* reaction by shouting a goodbye to Cyndol who's still stocking shelves in the back. I don't risk looking at Sabin to see just what he thinks of my slip up. I was joking, but will he think I'm serious? *Fuck*. Out of all the guys *that* could have slipped out to, it has to be the one who wants to take things slow.

Nice, Vinna.

Cyndol shouts back a goodbye, and Luke walks us to the door. We make our way through the parking lot toward the Bronco. Sabin takes a quick inhale, the kind people do when they're about to say something, something that you may or may not want to hear, and it sends my adrenaline pounding.

"Vinna!" Someone shouts my name. I turn to track who and see an older female caster with three males speed-walking toward me.

"Are you Vinna Aylin?" She shouts at me again.

Before I can so much as part my lips to respond, Pebble is in front of me in a defensive position. I have no fucking clue where he just came from, and I turn to Sabin to ask him if he saw where, and I spot the rest of Pebble's coven closing in around us. It's like they just appeared out of nowhere. I actually completely forgot that they were still even assigned to guard me. I'm not sure where the threat is right now, it could be the female still barreling toward me, or honestly, it could be these paladin too.

Sabin pivots so that his back is against mine, and I

immediately feel a warm reassurance run through me. I call on my magic, and I feel him do the same. I experience an intense rushing sensation as I pull Defensive magic from my source, and it comes to me like a freight train. Holy shit, my magic has some serious kick to it now. Thank fuck Sabin is behind me, his large frame keeping me from going anywhere; otherwise, I'd probably be on my ass right now.

The woman coming straight at me sees the appearance of the paladin and seems to be just as shocked as I am at their sudden appearance, but I see a set determination on her face as she continues forward.

"Stop, ma'am, don't come any closer," Pebble warns, and the three casters surrounding her pull her to a stop.

She does not look happy about that, and she snaps at one of them something that I can't hear. The male looks torn between pissing off who I assume is his mate, or her getting lit up by the paladin surrounding me, because she looks like she wants to barrel right through them. I look her over, trying to see if I can place her face or the faces of her three mates, but she doesn't look familiar. Who knows what I could have done to piss her off.

"Are you Vinna Aylin?" she asks again, winded, and she shoots another glare at her other mate when he puts a hand on her shoulder.

"Yes, can I help you with something?"

One of the paladin in Pebble's coven, a shorter bald man, moves a step closer to me. I don't like it, so instead of focusing on the woman as she attempts to catch her breath to answer my question, I turn to him.

"Too close, Phil Collins, way too fucking close," I warn him.

"We're here to protect you, not hurt you," he counters.

"You were assigned by the elders, and I don't trust them, so sorry, not sorry, that means I don't trust you either. Back up, or you and Pebble can trade bedtime stories about how good my knife skills are."

Pebble snorts. "Back off, Brody; trust me, you don't want to find out."

I smile at Pebble.

"Aww, Pebble...you *can* be taught. How you doing, buddy? Long time no see. Are you still in a time-out?"

I feel Sabin chuckle behind me, and Pebble sighs.

"Can we deal with this first before the gossip session starts and you try to braid my hair and paint my nails?"

I roll my eyes at him. "Fine, but when this is all done, I get to do your fingers and toes."

I return my focus to the female who was the catalyst for this whole reunion, and when my eyes land on her, she starts talking like she's just been waiting for me to call on her.

"My name is Olivia Steward; you saved our son, Parker Steward."

An image of me crouched over Parker as I desperately try to heal his lamia inflicted neck wound, flashes through my mind.

"I just saw you come out of the store and wanted to thank you. I didn't mean to cause all this," she gestures to the paladin.

I move to step around Pebble, but he anticipates the move and blocks my path.

"Pebble, relax, take it down to Defcon...whatever is the non-threatening number. I know her son."

"Yeah, but you don't know her."

"I thought you guys are here to protect me from lamia; why would I need protection from casters? What am I missing here?" I ask, confused.

What is it about the situation that set off their alarm bells so much that they would come out of stalker mode and show themselves? I look around at the paladin around me, taking in their positioning. Pebble is in front of me, his back to me, facing what I assume is the *threat*. The rest of his coven is giving me their profiles, which means they're watching *me* and this group of casters that just approached me.

I sigh and step closer to Pebble. Sabin follows my move so that our backs stay in contact. I drop my voice so only Sabin and Pebble can hear me.

"Pebble, are you in on the *Vinna can't be trusted* part of your mission too, or is it just your coven?"

Pebble turns his head slightly toward me but keeps his body squared off with Mrs. Steward and her mates. "What are you talking about?"

"Look at your coven. If they were guarding me, they'd be giving me their backs right now. Do you see any backs?"

Pebble's gaze flits over the members of his coven that are in his line of sight, and his eyes narrow.

"Yeah, you should probably look into why they're not telling you what's up," I advise.

I reach back for Sabin's hand so I can somewhat communicate where I'm going to move, so that he can go with me. We need to do some field training as a group, I realize. Yeah, we can talk to each other in our heads, but until we master mental talk in the middle of a fight in a way that doesn't distract or get anyone hurt, we need to work out a communication system outside of that.

I clear my throat and raise my voice so all of the surrounding paladin can hear me. "I'm going to step past Pebble and talk to my friend's family. I am not a threat to them or to you. But if any of you try to stop this innocent interaction from happening, I'll make you sorry that you did. We clear?"

A couple of incredulous snorts sound off around me, but

Pebble steps aside to let me by. As I pass him, I lean down and mumble.

"I don't know if you're okay, or what's up with your coven, but if you need a place to stay, my house is a safe place. Sabin will give you the address."

Sabin quickly lists off the numbers and road info, and Pebble gives an almost imperceptible nod of his head. I move toward the Stewards, and none of the paladin attempt to stop me. I would guess they're not allowed to engage with me unless I start something; I doubt my little threat had any real effect. They think they're big, badass paladin assigned to babysit some too-full-of-herself little girl. They're not going to take me seriously until they're recovering from a lesson in *I say what I mean and mean what I say.*

I put my hand out to Mrs. Steward, but when I get closer to her, she forgoes my offered handshake and pulls me down into a fierce hug. I wrap my arms around her to keep from tumbling over from our height differences. I rub her back, and she proceeds to whisper *thank you* to me over and over again.

She pulls back after a couple of minutes and wipes at the wet tracks on her cheek. Sabin pulls a handkerchief from his pocket and hands it to Mrs. Steward. The sight of it suddenly stirs a memory in me, when a kind stranger offered me a handkerchief when I was younger. I don't know why this memory has stuck with me, but I remember thinking people who carry handkerchiefs are good people.

I catch Sabin's eyes with mine and give him a huge smile. I can tell he's trying to figure out why I'm looking at him like this, but his eyes fill with affection and he grins sweetly back at me.

"How's Parker? I've been meaning to check in on him, but things have been a little crazy."

To prove my point, I motion back toward where the

paladin just were and find that they're gone. It's all I can do not to scan my surroundings and pick them out from wherever they're hiding and watching right now.

"He's doing very well, thanks to you. He's not going to continue with the paladin program. I think the experience with the lamia showed him that it's not what he wants to do," she tells me, and I nod with understanding.

"Sorry I'm so flustered, I didn't even introduce you to my mates. I just saw your markings, and I knew it had to be you, and I just had to say thank you. Truly *thank you* doesn't even begin to cover how grateful we are and how much we owe you for saving him."

She grabs my hand in both of hers and looks at me with such a beautiful motherly ferocity that I feel my eyes start to sting a little.

"I owe him, really," I admit. "He carried my friend out, and it gave me a chance to say goodbye." I pause so I can get control over my emotions, and Mrs. Steward pulls me down into another hug. "I'm sorry Parker was even in that situation in the first place," I tell her, and she shushes me and squeezes me tighter.

"Well, Vinna, you are a member of our family now, and if you ever need anything, you come to us, okay? I don't care what it is; you can count on us. Now give me your phone, and I will put our numbers in there," she tells me as we break away from our hug.

We exchange phones and numbers, and when it's all done, she gives me an approving nod and smooths down her dark hair.

"Thank you for talking to us, we won't steal up the rest of your day, but we mean it. You need anything, you call, okay?"

She gives me a stern mom face, and I parrot *okay* back to her.

"Tell Parker I say hello, and if he needs to talk or anything else, he can call me anytime."

We say our goodbyes, and they continue on with whatever they were doing before they spotted Sabin and me coming out of the spell shop. I pick up the box of spells at my feet and scan everything around us, spotting three out of the five members of Pebble's coven. I look over to Sabin, and he's doing the same thing.

"You're a good guy, Sabin Gamull," I tell him, a huge smile taking over my face.

He looks at me confused for a moment before leaning down and giving me a sweet kiss.

"You look like the kind of guy mothers should hide their daughters from, but inside you're a handkerchief-toting, *Pride and Prejudice* loving, stargazing romantic, who has my back...literally. I am one lucky girl."

Sabin pulls open the back of the car and takes the box of spells from my hand to set them inside. I let out a surprised squeal when he suddenly grabs me out of nowhere, pivots me so he's supporting my weight, and dips me back until I'm a foot off the pavement. He kisses me deeply and thoroughly as he dips me, like we're part of some grand dance finale from the 1950s.

When he's kissed me nice and properly mindless, he swoops me back up, steadies me and boops my nose. "You're just now realizing how lucky you are?" he asks, a cheeky tone in his playful voice. "You've got to get quicker on the uptake. Now let's get back and figure out what to do about the elders and your set of stalker paladin."

He twirls his keys around his finger as he swaggers to the passenger side and opens the door for me. I watch his ass as he moves, and when he turns around, I run my gaze lasciviously and with no shame up his body.

Fuck, lucky girl is a serious understatement!

34

"Shit!" Knox exclaims as he calls a short sword into his hand, and the blade appears in his palm instead of the grip.

He jerks his hand back, and the sword tumbles toward the ground, disappearing before it can make contact with the dirt. He eyes the cut on his hand, staring at it like it's a traitor that's betrayed him in the deepest of ways, before reaching his palm out to me. I take it, trying to fight my smile, and push Healing magic into him. I watch as my magic cooperates and the skin knits together. I feel bad that he's having trouble figuring out the magic weapons, but it's been good for practice for me with my Healing magic.

"Why does that keep happening?" Knox asks, a hint of a whine in his tone.

"It's the sequence you're calling. If you push too much magic, too fast, into the runes you want to activate, then the sequence gets fucked up. That's why you keep getting blade first, or the whole weapon sideways. You have to slow the flow down, feed it into each rune until you get the combination you want. Don't flood the sequence."

Knox lets out a frustrated huff and twists his arm to stare

at the runes there. The muscles in his arm tighten with the movement, and it sends a flutter of desire through me. Seeing his gorgeous body with *my* marks all over it sparks something in me in a primal, Neanderthal-ish way. *By the stars, I want to get him naked.* I clench my thighs against that thought. *Not the time or place, Vinna.* I pull myself away from my sex-filled plans for later and refocus.

Knox is staring at the runes on his arm, and I'd swear he's giving them a lecture. I chuckle because I talk to my magic too. He looks up at me, chagrin leaking into his features at getting caught.

"How the fuck do you make it look so easy?" he asks.

I snicker and hold up my index finger. "One, because I'm a badass, and two, I've got six years of practice on you. The thing is, I didn't have anyone around with Healing magic to fix all my booboos, so Sentinel up, and let's fucking do this!"

I swat his chest with the back of my hand and raise an eyebrow at him in challenge. Bastien's laugh bounces toward us from the chair he's perched in on the back patio, and Knox aims a glare at him.

"Laugh it up, chuckles, we'll see how many cuts you end up with when you get your runes," Knox threatens.

"I'm pretty sure I'll be able to figure out which end of the sword not to grab," Bastien retorts.

"Them's fighting words, Fierro! Should we bet on it?"

Bastien's grin widens. "Yes, Howell, I think a friendly wager is in order; name your stakes."

"Shit's getting real if they're using last names," Valen announces as he strides through the sliding glass door and plops into a seat next to his twin. "What'd I miss?"

"Knox likes the sharp and pointy side of his weapons, Bastien's ego is on a level that should concern us all, and Vinna is a badass."

I grin at Ryker as he sums up what's happening for Valen, but he seems singularly focused on the task I just assigned him. Bright yellow-orange magic crackles across his skin as he tries to activate the runes on his back that create the staff. He's done really well with calling his short swords and daggers so far, and has graduated to what I find are the harder of the sequences, the long sword and the staff.

"You're leaking," I tell him.

Ryker furrows his brow in concentration, and the crackle of magic sparks out, but no staff appears in his hand. I walk over to him.

"These weapons were harder for me; it helped sometimes if I physically touched the first couple of runes, like it helped my instincts or brain realize which set of runes I was needing. You can try that if you want, but be careful; it's become a habit for me now to call these runes that way, and that might not be a good thing. You still want to make sure you can call them without touch. So focus on how each rune feels as you call it, memorize that feeling, and it will be easier to call that particular rune or put it in a sequence when you need it."

He nods and refocuses on the task, and Knox's adamant bellow of *hell no* steals my attention back to him.

"I'm not giving up any time with Vinna, and we haven't even sorted if we're even doing a schedule," Knox argues with Bastien. "I still think you should have to shave your head when I win."

I picture Bastien with a buzzed head. He's gorgeous, and I'm sure he could pull it off. But the thought of no more long waves to run my fingers through, or the loss of my fantasy about his dark silky strands caressing my skin as he kisses his way up from between my thighs to claim my mouth, is not a world I want to live in.

"That's not fucking happening," I chime in, trying to rein in the desire and panic ringing out in my voice.

They turn to me. "I like his hair just the way that it is; he's not cutting it!"

Bastien and Valen exchange grins.

"I mean, cut it if you really want to, who am I to stop you, but if it's all the same to you, I like it long," I offer more casually, hoping it covers up the desperate way I just announced that I don't want them to have bodily autonomy when it comes to their hair.

"Just have the loser concede to the winner's greatness every time they call a weapon or something," Sabin announces, setting the tablet the readers gave me on the outdoor coffee table he has a foot resting against. "You're right, Vinna, nothing in here about the transference or even how Chosen are really selected. There's some small mention of Chosen bonds, but it's in relation to injury or death. The rest is genealogy, information on investments, and a lot of stuff about possible origins for Sentinels, casters, and some other supernaturals."

"Right! I don't know why I was expecting more of a *how-to*, but most of what's in there seems irrelevant. Yay, Sentinels used to have holdings in Kazakhstan and Russia, but how does that help me figure out anything about what I am and what I can do?"

Sabin nods as he stares at the tablet, as if just the weight of his demanding gaze can will more information to magically appear in the text that the readers left.

"I'm going to track down the number they left you. See if they have any information they can send that might be more useful."

"Follow your gut, but if they had anything, you'd think they would have included it in there," I tell him, gesturing to the tablet. "They knew I had no idea what I was, maybe this is just all that they have."

"That's a good point. It didn't exactly sound like they were in the Sentinel loop anymore," Sabin adds, thoughtful.

Bastien picks up the tablet and starts to scroll through it.

"What do you mean 'concede to the winner's greatness?'" Knox asks Sabin, bringing us back to the undecided terms of the bet.

Sabin shrugs his shoulders. "I don't know, maybe whoever loses has to shout out Hear ye, hear ye, the great and formidable winner has called on his weapon; let us bathe in his glory and cower in fear. Or some other equally asinine thing."

I laugh at Sabin's suggestion and how ridiculous it is, but when I turn to Knox, the smile on his face tells me he likes it. I look at Bastien, and he's wearing a similar grin.

"Fuck yes!" Ryker shouts, and all eyes snap to him.

His smile is electric, and the pride in his eyes shines like the sun as he holds up the staff in his hand. We all whoop our support and encouragement, and Ryker in his excitement gives the staff a twirl. It makes half a revolution before smacking his forearm and slipping from his hand. Ryker tries to catch it before it falls too far away and disappears, but that only gets him hit in the face somehow before the staff evaporates into nothing and his runes reabsorb the magic. A small laugh escapes me before I slam my palm over my mouth. Maybe I was lucky there wasn't anyone around to see me try and figure these runes out.

"You are not allowed to laugh," Ryker scolds me as he rubs at the red spot in his cheek where the staff just bitch-slapped him.

Of course, that only makes me laugh even harder. He steps toward me, and his gaze is playful and filled with naughty promises. A flash of the same look on Ryker's face as he slid deep inside of me makes me wet, but another flash of his pain-filled features and clenched muscles as he laid on the shower floor, punches my lust in the face and replaces it with panic. I call on my staff as Ryker stalks forward, and twirl it in the same way that Ryker just attempted.

"Show off," he lobs at me, coming to a stop when I point the end of the staff at his throat.

I bite down on the smile teasing my lips.

"Whatever you have in mind for punishment, table it. We have to train. That means no distractions. You guys have to know how to use your new magic. You're Sentinels now, which means you're targets. If you can't defend yourself when the time comes, we're all screwed. The day you can get this staff out of my hands is the day we can relax a little, but until then, we're going to go hard every day."

Knox snickers, but it stops when I give him a stern look.

"And there will be no *going hard with me* until you two can do everything that I can...as well as I can," I tell him.

That should buy me some time to sort through whatever sex-related PTSD I seem to be suffering from after watching Ryker and Knox get their runes. Sabin already wants to take it slow, and I'll just figure something out for Bastien and Valen. My eyes land on the twins of their own accord, and they're both watching me in a way that makes me think they can read my thoughts like they're written in the air around my head. I look away before I get too sucked into their over-observant hazel orbs.

Knox's cheeky smile drops. "Whoa, that's not cool, Killer. I've been working at this all day. Who knows how long it could take to get to the level you're at; like you said, you've got six years on us."

"Then work harder or come at me, bro. Maybe you're like me, and you perform better under pressure?"

"I'm not going to fight you. You'd kick my ass, and even if

I could do everything that you can, I would always pull my hits. And you can just forget about me coming at you with weapons, that's never going to happen," Knox announces.

I glare at him.

"Fighting me is the only way you're going to learn. I'm the only teacher you're ever going to have, so you're just going to have to get over yourself."

He shakes his head. "No, I don't. I'll fight Ryker until the others get their runes. Then we'll fight and train with each other. You can coach and correct us, but none of us are fighting you."

Knox crosses his arms in front of his chest, in a *this is final* pose. I look around at the other guys, and they are all wearing similar *there's nothing more to discuss* looks on their faces.

"You all agree with him?" I ask, surprised.

They don't answer, but they don't need to, I can see it written all over their faces and body language.

"Fine, get yourselves killed or taken by some psychotic, power-hungry lamia, all because you don't want to fight a girl. That makes a ton of sense." I throw my hands up and turn to stomp toward the house.

"Don't run off because you're mad. I thought we were training?" Knox challenges.

I whirl on him. "How can I fucking train you if you've already decided what you will and won't listen to or do?"

"I can't hurt you. I wouldn't be able to do that. It would make training like that ineffectual!" Knox declares.

"Oh, but I can hurt you, and that's fine because it's making you stronger. What's the word you used? Oh, that's right, I'm tempering you."

"That's different, Vinna. You're not actually searing the runes into us. Hitting you or actually trying to stab you with a knife is on a completely different level!"

"How can you look at my runes as a good thing, but not see training with me the same way? If you get a hit in, then I'll learn to keep that from happening again. It's not like we don't have a healer. Nothing is permanent; it's just pain, and temporary pain at that!"

"I just can't fucking do that, Vinna; why are you pushing for it? Are you seriously mad because none of us are okay with hurting you?"

"Talon trained with me; I learned tons of what I know now from taking hits and getting back up."

"Well, that goes hand in hand with Talon being an asshole!"

Knox's words are spoken in the same calm and authoritative way he's been using this whole argument, but he might as well have yelled them at me and then punched me in the stomach, because that's what it feels like just happened. I wait for a look of apology to come over his face when he sees how hurt I am by what he said, but it doesn't come.

"Knox," Valen calls out in warning.

"No, you guys all think it too, don't even try to deny it. How much fucking time did he have to tell Vinna the truth? He never did, not until he *had* to." Knox turns back to me. "You were killing off lamia since you were fourteen; you honestly think he didn't know? He taught you to fight, but why didn't he tell you who you were fighting against and why? Don't make him a martyr when he wasn't, Vinna."

Knox's statements echo some of my own frustrations, but it sounds so much more vicious coming out of his mouth than it does in my head. He didn't know Talon. Maybe I didn't either, but it's killing me to know that these guys think so poorly of him. They don't know what he saved me from or helped me become. My eyes fall on Sabin.

"Where are Talon's ashes?"

"I put them in your room. They're in a green fabric box next to Laiken's box."

I nod and turn to walk away.

"All of you, come with me, please," I call over my shoulder as I make my way back into the house.

I grab a bag from my closet and walk over to the shelf that holds the two boxes. I set Talon's box in first and then Laiken's on top of it before I close up the bag and position it on my back.

It's time to say goodbye.

35

The rumble of the ATVs all around me blocks out the sounds of nature that greeted me the first time I was here, but the little white flowers sprinkled throughout the unkempt grass still feels like a happy hello. A slight breeze carries strands of my hair out toward the cliff's edge, where the dark lake sparkles back at me.

I turn the ATV off and climb down as the other guys all pull up around me. I tuck the map that I had the sisters draw me into my back pocket, and I watch all the guys climb off their ATVs and glance around at our surroundings. I walk out into the welcoming flower-sprinkled grass and open my bag to pull out Laiken's box. I decided on the way over here that Laiken should go first to her final resting place amongst the wildflowers that feel free and peaceful in a way I don't think Laiken ever did.

The guys keep their distance, staying quiet and watchful. I know Knox's words are floating around everyone's mind. Maybe they're not sure what to say, or if I'm interested in hearing it, or maybe they can feel my need for peace, but up to this point, no one has questioned what I'm doing, and I'm grateful for that.

I kneel on the ground and open Laiken's cedar box. I pull out the bag of ashes and open the top, setting the bag in the grass as I think about what I want to say to her; how I want to say the goodbye that I never got a chance to say. I've thought about this moment a lot in my hunt for the perfect place for her, but now that I've found it, I'm not sure where to start.

"When Laiken was born, Beth wouldn't let me touch her," I tell the guys, because somehow talking about her right now feels easier than talking to her. "She was so soft looking and fragile, and I hoped that she wouldn't see all the bad things that Beth did. One night Laiken wouldn't stop crying, so Beth came into my room and handed her to me and left to get some sleep.

"I was five, and I didn't know what to do with her. I thought maybe she was sad because she wanted a friend, just like I did. So I laid her in my blanket on the floor and cuddled up next to her. I promised her that I would always be her friend, and I would make sure my bad didn't rub off on her. I promised if Beth ever found any bad in Laiken, I would steal it away and make it so Beth couldn't find it anymore. Laiken burped and calmed down, and my five-year-old self took that as a sign we would be friends forever."

I smile as I think about all the times I made up stories to help Laiken sleep, or we sang silly songs back and forth and laughed and laughed until we got into trouble. Laiken would sneak me food, and as she got older, she would tell me stories and say comforting things if I was too hurt to talk after one of Beth's beatings. I don't think I would have emotionally survived Beth as well as I did if it hadn't been for Little Laik.

I stand up and bring her with me. I walk further into the grass and slowly tilt the bag and watch as what's left of

Laiken meets the small white flowers that peek through the lush grass.

"I love you, Laik. I'll love you forever, to infinity and beyond, more than you can ever say times a billion." I pause as a shuddering sob works its way through me. "I am so fucking sorry that I failed you. I'll never stop being sorry that I couldn't find you. That I couldn't protect you."

Tears drops down my cheeks, and I let them fall unchecked. I watch as pieces of me mix with the essence of my sister. "You'll always be my best friend, and I will never forget that you were the first to love me and show me that I wasn't made of anything bad."

The bag empties, and the wind carries pieces of Laiken to rest with the surrounding trees. She would love it here, and even though I'm hurting at the memory of her loss and all that she was to me, I also find comfort that she's here, and I can still come and be with her in this place that soothes my soul, and I have no doubt will soothe hers as well.

I wipe my ache for my little sister from my cheeks. I take a deep breath and walk over to take the green box that has Talon in it. I set it next to the cedar box that used to house Laiken, and remove the fabric lid. I take out the bag of Talon's ashes and stare at it a moment before I look to the guys.

"Laiken was the first person to teach me that I wasn't made up of bad things, but Talon is the one who taught me what I *was* made of. He was tough and brutal, and because of that, I discovered I could ask more of myself than I ever thought possible. Talon taught me balance. He let me rage when that was the only way I could get the taint of Beth out of my soul, and then he showed me how to find peace and calm, and the power hidden within them."

My eyes rest on Knox, and I watch as he wipes a tear away.

"He was an asshole." I pause as a small smile lifts my lips, and then the sobs start again in my chest. "I don't know why he didn't tell me what he knew until I watched him die. I'm sure there are a million ways we can look at what happened and find a better way to have managed it, but there's no point in doing that. I don't want to be mad at him for not telling me. I don't want to be mad at him for leaving, even though I know he didn't want to. So, instead of focusing on what he didn't do right, I'm going to focus on all the right that he did."

My eyes drop to the bag in my hand.

"You can think he's an asshole, but I also want you to realize that there is no way that I'd be standing in front of you right now if it weren't for him. Everything that I am, everything that you say is worthy of you, Talon helped me to find."

I turn and walk over to the edge of the rocky cliff. I open the top of the bag, and I tilt it out over the edge. The breeze picks up the ashes and carries them out over the water.

"Talon, we got to say goodbye, which felt like the end of me, but I will live the rest of my life grateful that I got to look into your eyes and tell you what you meant to me. You were an asshole, but somehow you were my asshole, and I will live the rest of my life missing you."

The empty bag somehow feels heavy in my hands, like instead of empty plastic, I now hold the dense weight of loss.

"I'm going to kill Adriel, for my mother, my father, and for you," I tell Talon's ashes on the wind, as it carries my words and my friend forever away from me.

Strong arms wrap around me from behind, and I lean

back into Valen. We stay like that, quietly watching the sun dip lower until my legs are numb with the lack of movement, and I hurt a little less from the sad memories playing through my mind. My muscles groan in protest as I turn in Valen's arms and look up into his beautiful face.

"Thank you," I whisper, grateful for his quiet comfort.

He leans down and rests his forehead against mine.

"I wish I could take it all away," he whispers back, and the sweet sentiment brings a small smile to my face.

"I wouldn't be who I am without all of it."

"I know, but it's hard to watch you hurt, to know what you lived through, what you're still living through. Thank you for bringing us here, for letting us see and understand you better."

The wind forces his hair into his face, and I brush it back.

"Thank you for coming and for wanting to see and understand me better."

Valen runs his thumb across my cheek, and the look in his eyes pierces my soul. "Always, Vinna, we'll always be here; we'll always want you and to understand you better. I've got you, we've got you. It's us against the world forever, and none of us would have it any other way."

Anything more that Valen tries to say gets lost in my kiss as I take his lips, his reassurances, and his promises, and let them take root and bloom inside of me. I can taste the truth of his *always* on my lips and tongue, and without question or hesitation, I return it. Valen ends the kiss before I want to, and he chuckles at my squeak of protest as he kisses the tip of my nose. He takes the bag from my hand and sets it inside Talon's box and places the green box and the cedar box back in the bag.

"Any plans for what you want to do with these?" Valen

asks, as he closes the bag and slings a strap over his muscled shoulder.

He tucks me into his side and underneath his other arm, and we make our way over to where the others are sitting. Knox's eyes trace our path, and I see the apology and sorrow written all over his face.

"I'm going to burn them at the next family night at Knox and Ryker's house, while they sing a beautiful song that steals the sadness away for a bit."

Knox gets up and reaches for me. I squeeze Valen's side for a quick second and sneak out from under his arm to go to Knox. I wrap my arms around his thick neck, and he lifts me. "I'm sorry, Killer…"

"No, Knox, you didn't say anything that wasn't true, I just wanted you to know the other side of it, too."

He peppers playful kisses all over my cheeks and my neck, his scratchy stubble tickling me, and I squirm and squeal to get away from him. He laughs and starts doing it more, when a movement in the trees catches my eye. Knox must immediately feel the change in my emotions or body as I try to hone in on what just caught my attention. He puts me down, his face now all business as he follows my gaze out into the surrounding trees.

We both scan the encroaching forest, but I'm the one to catch the hint of gray as it slowly, almost imperceptibly, weaves through two close-growing trees.

I break into a run, and Knox is close on my heels.

"Don't run, wolf," I shout out in warning, as I see his muscles go still with the realization that I'm coming right for him.

So what does he do? He runs.

Motherfucker!

I call on my runes and push power into my legs. I reach the tree line and weave dangerously fast through the large trunks in pursuit of Torrez. He's fast as fuck, but I learned on the run with his pack that I can be too, and I ask even more from the muscles in my legs as I inch closer and closer. The large gray head of Torrez's wolf looks back to gauge how close I am, and it gives me the opportunity I need to close the last few feet to him. I push off the ground and fly into Torrez's back legs. I wrap my arms around his wolf version of a waist and tuck my head to protect it from the tumbling we're about to do against the unforgiving ground.

Torrez growls, but thankfully we go rolling before he can reach back and sink any of his sharp teeth anywhere. We skid to a stop, and gravity does me the favor of landing on top of him and half pinning him down. In seconds, Torrez flashes into himself and glares up at me, his muscles taut and rippling and not a stitch of clothing on him to hide any of it.

"Well, that was rude, Witch."

"What the fuck are you doing here? Are you following me around?" I demand, as I push against his shoulders. So far he's not putting up a fight, but if this is an act to lull me into complacency before he strikes, I'll be ready.

"Yes. I like to call it watching your back, but I guess following you around is accurate, too."

Torrez shrugs nonchalantly.

"Why did you run? Who else is out here with you?"

A throat clears, and my eyes snap to the left to find Knox standing there, chest heaving from the chase he just gave. I see the other guys running through the trees just behind him.

"Who...the fuck... is...this?" Knox asks between gasps for air, his narrowed gaze running over Torrez.

I look back down to find Torrez beaming a salacious smile at me. In a flash, his hands move to my hips, and he leans up toward my face.

"Running was the easiest way to get you on top of me. I *let* you tackle me, Witch, but next time it's my turn to get nice and rough!"

His grip on my hips tightens, and his eyes fill with fire, his nostrils flaring as he scents me. I shove against his shoulders and scramble off of him. He chuckles, but lets me go.

Knox reaches out and plucks me away from the shifter, stepping slightly in front of me. I brush dirt, pine needles, and leaves from my shirt and leggings and feel the other guys arrive and position themselves around me.

"Remember that shifter that I beat the shit out of?" I ask Knox.

"Yeah," he answers.

I point to Torrez who's leaning back on his hands, still sitting in the dirt.

"That's the big bad wolf?" Knox asks, and I snicker at the unintentional storybook reference.

Torrez gets an indignant look on his face and stands up. Someone clamps their hand around my eyes, blocking Torrez's naked body from my view. I don't know if I want to laugh or be annoyed by the gesture.

"Now that we've established who I am, who the heck are you guys? A little overprotective for bodyguards, don't you think? I mean, this isn't anything that she hasn't seen before. Isn't that right, Witch?"

I swat away the hand shielding my eyes, and it drops to my shoulder. I glare at Torrez. "What the hell are you doing here?" I ask at the same time Bastien announces, "We're her mates!"

Torrez ignores my question and the threatening look I'm giving him and addresses Bastien instead.

"Oh, perfect, just who I was looking to speak to."

"About what?" Sabin growls from behind me, his hand flexing on my shoulder.

I should have known that Captain Cockblock would have been the one to literally cockblock Torrez by shielding my eyes.

Torrez gestures to the guys. "How do I go about applying to be one—you know, a mate?"

36

"Wait, what?" Valen asks, just as confused as I am.

"She said I had to talk to you guys about getting added into the group. How does that work? Shifters usually do the one on one thing, occasionally we mix it up with a two on one, but I don't know how you guys establish the group. In the pack, we'd probably fight it out and choose based on the winners, but I don't get the impression that's how you casters do things."

All eyes turn to me like somehow I'll offer clarification to whatever in the hell is going on here. I narrow my gaze at Torrez.

"I did not tell you that you could *apply* to be my mate. I said I already had mates, and then I'm pretty sure I threatened to kick your ass. So feel free to go blow some other house down; this one is brick."

To punctuate my *run along* message, all the guys take a step toward me.

"Now, Witch, I have to disagree with your version of events. I remember things very differently. I touched the runes on your shoulder, and you liked it, but that got you all worried, so you stomped off. I followed you to make sure you got wherever you were going safely, and that's when you told me that I had to go to your mates to get to you."

My eyes dart back and forth between Torrez's brown irises. I can't tell if he's trying to start shit or if that's really how he thinks things went down.

"He activated your runes?" Bastien asks me, and I don't miss the anger-tinged hurt in his voice.

"I didn't know it was him. I thought one of you somehow showed up. I turned around and saw it wasn't one of you, and told him not to touch me again. We don't know shit about how my runes work; it could happen anytime someone messes with them. Don't read more into it than that."

"Witch…"

"Stop calling her that!" Ryker demands.

Torrez takes a deep breath, and I wonder what he's scenting now. Is *this group of casters is about five seconds from giving me a beat down* a smell?

"Vinna, you want me. You might be in denial about it in your head, but the rest of you screams *desire* loud and clear. I can see you're worried about your mates, but that's why I'm coming to them so we can all figure it out. So…what happens now?"

The guys start arguing with Torrez and, for some reason, each other. I grab Knox's phone out of his pocket and dial Mave's number, and she picks up on the third ring.

"Hello?"

"Mave, it's Vinna."

"Heyyy, how's it going? You free for lunch? We seriously need to catch up!"

"Not right now, but later this week would probably work."

"Cool, I'll check my appointment schedule and get back to you. What's up?

"Can you call your Alpha and have him call off his watchdog? I don't need another stalker, especially one that thinks he can apply to be my mate."

I expect Mave to laugh or something, but when the line is quiet, it freaks me out.

"Hello, you there?"

"Yeah, I'm here. You're talking about Torrez right?"

"The very one."

"Um, Vin, Torrez left the pack. He had to in order to pursue you. I thought you knew."

"He did what?" I shout into the phone, and my eyes snap to Torrez's.

"You left your pack? Why the fuck would you do that?"

"You're not a shifter. I can't claim my rank and also claim you," he tells me casually, like somehow I should know that's how this works.

"But weren't you second in line to take over or something?" I ask, shocked that he would walk away from that for any reason.

Torrez shrugs again. His blasé attitude about this whole situation is really starting to irritate me. Mave calls my name from the phone, and I tune back into her voice.

"Did you hear what I said?" she asks.

"No, sorry, I was a little busy freaking the fuck out."

"Vin, Torrez can't come back to the pack. If you don't accept him as a mate, he'll have to find somewhere else to go, and there's no guarantee another pack will ever take him." She's quiet for a moment. "Basically, what I'm getting at is this is a big fucking deal."

I release a hollow laugh and run my fingers through my hair. "More like, this is a big fucking nightmare."

"He's a good male. You guys could be really amazing together."

"Mave, I already have five mates...five!"

"And now you can have six!" she snickers.

"Why do shifters act like I'm just adding fruit to a basket? He's not an apple. He's a being, a male, an individual."

"Yeah, an individual any female in their right mind would want to take a bite out of," Mave grumbles.

"You're not helping," I tell her, exasperation seeping out of every word.

"Come on, Vin," Mave teases seductively. "Let him take a bite out of you, or better yet, a nice long lick. Get a taste for how shifters like to do it, and then call me and tell me you don't see the benefit in adding a sixth to your collection of gorgeous males. I don't even know why you're complaining; it's a tad ungrateful if you ask me. I'd switch places with you in two-point-five milliseconds, and I'd spend the rest of my life fuc—"

I cut Mave off. "I'm hanging up on you now."

"Good, I'm going to go have some *me* time while I fantasize about the group orgy I'd be having right now if I were in your place."

Mave hangs up on me, and I shake my head at the phone as I hand it to Knox and watch him slip it back into his pocket.

What the fuck am I going to do?

I thread both of my hands into my hair and fight the urge to start pacing. He can't go back to his pack, but he can't join my Chosen either, so where the fuck does that leave him? My troubled gaze finds Torrez's warm brown eyes. I stare into them, and it's like I can smell the rich soil my feet sink into as I run through the forest on a moon-kissed night.

I can feel the crisp air whooshing past me and the laughter and joy bubbling up in my throat. Why am I drawn to him?

Torrez takes a step toward me, but I'm pulled from the moment when Bastien steps in front of me, cutting Torrez off from my line of sight. I snap back into reality. Our life is complicated enough. There is no chance I can add this on top of everything else we're already dealing with. I sidestep Bastien, and Torrez's eyes snap back to mine. His chest falls at whatever he sees in my stare, and he shakes his head.

"Don't decide this now. Not like this. You need time to see the truth your worry is hiding from you. I can wait."

I open my mouth to argue, but before I can so much as inhale in preparation of a response, Torrez flashes into his wolf and darts away through the trees.

I shout for him to come back, there's no point delaying the inevitable. But my call echoes through and around the trees and then falls to the forest floor unanswered.

"What the fuck just happened?" Sabin asks.

But any answer, or more likely the lack of one, is lost in the sound of the ringtone from someone's phone. Valen pulls his phone out and brings it to his ear. He answers and then grows silent, his eyes locking onto mine, his look searching.

"We'll be right there," he tells whoever's on the other end before disconnecting. "That was Aydin; I guess there's someone named Pebble at the house. He's saying he needs to talk to you right away."

I follow the guys into the living room where Aydin and Evrin stand, arms crossed, lording over Pebble as he sits stiffly in a chair. Pebble spots me as we pour into the room, and he stands up.

"Are you okay? What happened?" I ask, stepping toward him.

"I didn't know they had been ordered to move against you if they considered you a threat, but I know who issued the order."

Everyone in the room seems to hold their breath as we wait for Pebble to continue.

"Elder Cleary was who I heard on the call, giving instructions. When you took the ATVs through the forest, we couldn't track you, and a member of my coven called him. They must have forgotten that I wasn't in the loop, or they figured the cat was out of the bag after what happened in the parking lot. But it was definitely him on the phone."

"Are any of the other elders aware of this, or do you think he's acting alone?" Aydin asks, his eyes hard and his body language screaming that he wants to hurt someone.

"I don't know. When he took the call, he made my coven leader wait until he was somewhere more private he could talk. He could be hiding this from the other elders, or he could have been around casters that aren't privy to what the elders are doing as a collective, it's hard to say. As soon as I knew though, I came to tell you."

"What's your coven going to do when they find out you were here?" I ask, aware that Pebble is risking a lot to be here.

"I don't give a fuck at this point. I don't know what's going on, but tracking and being ordered to move against citizens who haven't broken any laws, is not what I signed on for when I became a paladin. If this is how it's going to be, then I'm out."

Pebble moves toward the door. He's clearly eager to

leave, and I don't blame him. I wouldn't want to be on the elders' radar if it was avoidable either.

"Do you have somewhere to go?" Evrin asks as Pebble reaches for the doorknob.

"I'll figure it out," he calls over his shoulder.

"Thank you, Eli," I shout toward him as he takes a step out of the house.

He stills for a moment and turns back to me. "It's Pebble if you don't mind, and I'm sorry for being such a prick before." He smiles that arrogant smile that's all him, and I chuckle.

"Be good to Mave, asshole!" I yell as the door starts to swing shut. Pebble flips me the bird before the door clicks closed, and I can't help the grin that takes over my face.

Who would have thought he'd grow on me? Mave is going to eat him alive.

"Now what?" Ryker asks.

"Now nothing," I say and then hold up my hands in a *just hear me out* gesture when all the tense eyes in the room turn their irritated gazes on me.

"We already knew Elder Cleary was an issue." I motion to the door that Pebble just walked out of. "He didn't really give us new information. We still don't know if the other elders are involved, and we already have *plan B* set up in the event things go to shit here."

Everyone nods their agreement, but I can tell they all hate not being able to do more. This whole waiting game is brutal. Who will make a move first; will it be the elders as a whole or just one of them? What does Adriel have up his sleeve? He was putting something together that had Sorik nervous enough to come to warn me and risk getting caught, but I haven't seen any lamia here, outside of Sorik and whoever his friend was.

I find myself antsy with anticipation.

"Knox, Ryker, and Sabin. Why don't you guys set up bank account backups for us and your families, and make sure there's enough money in multiple places that any of us can access it if needed. Pick out a place your families can run to, if needed, and a password we can tell them that will let them know to hit the road."

They nod and separate to grab whatever they need to start working on that. "Aydin and Evrin, you guys do the same if you have anyone you want to keep safe. Bastien and Valen, it might be time to reach out to Silva and find out what he, Keegan, and Lachlan are doing. If they have a lead on Vaughn or Adriel, that info could come in handy down the road. Not that I think they'll share it, but it might be worth a shot."

I head in the direction of my room.

"What are you going to do?" Valen asks me.

"I'm going to call Enoch."

"Why the fuck are you calling him?" Bastien demands.

"Because Enoch's dad wants me to choose him. Maybe if Elder Cleary thinks I'm considering it, it will buy us some time and a little temporary protection from anything else that might be coming our way."

"Bruiser, you can't trust Enoch and his coven."

My eyes move back and forth between Bastien's green-ringed pupils and the earnest concern radiating from his features. Weeks ago I would have agreed with him, but my gut and head are at war on this. Logically, given everything that's happened, I probably shouldn't trust them, but my gut is telling me differently, and I always listen to my gut.

"Let's hope you're wrong, Bastien."

37

I connect my phone to the speakers wired throughout the whole room. Imagine Dragons' "Believer" fills the room as I walk over to the treadmill and power it up. I choose the run that I want and start a slow jog as the drum beat in the song helps to get my blood flowing. I'm not sure how long I run, but Linkin Park's "Hit the Floor" is just getting started when it suddenly stops, and the only sound now filling the gym is the whirring of the treadmill track as it moves and the thump of my long stride as my feet connect with the machine. I look over at where my phone is docked to find Bastien leaning against the wall there.

"What are you running from, Bruiser?"

"What makes you think I'm running from something?"

"Because you only run like that when you're upset. What's bugging you?"

I turn off the treadmill and wind down my run. When the track stops, I step off and take a moment to catch my breath.

"Take your pick. I'm not even sure if I know anymore, there's so much to choose from."

Bastien gives a humorless chuckle and walks toward the

black mats in the corner of the room. He picks up some pads designed for punch-kick combos and nods for me to come to him.

"You want to kick the shit out of something?" he teases, and I snort.

"I don't know, Bastien, can you hang with this?" I joke back and motion down my body.

Bastien takes his time looking me down and back up before his eyes return to mine.

"I think I can hang; I am a Paladin Conscript after all."

Bastien puffs out his chest and takes up a defensive stance. He starts calling out punch combos, and I'm impressed to discover that he knows what he's doing and can keep up. He starts adding in kicks, and we both fall into a rhythm. Me punching and kicking the shit out of the pads, and Bastien calling out different ways to help me release my aggression while he absorbs the hits.

I'm surprised by how easily he falls into sync with me. I haven't seen the guys in their element, training to be paladin, but I can see that Bastien probably excels at the physical aspects of it. A twinge of guilt shoots through me at the thought that he and the others will probably have to leave that behind, but I shut the guilt down. Just because their training at the Academy stops doesn't mean training in general stops. We'll be working *together* to become a team of unmatched skill and power.

He calls out a jab, hook, roundhouse combo and I must be going too fast because I realize too late that my roundhouse is about to land on his torso instead of on the pad since it's not in place yet. My kick lands brutally hard against Bastien's ribs, and he lets out a pained grunt and crumbles to the floor.

"Fuck! Bastien, I'm so sorry! Are you okay?"

Bastien grunts out a response, but I don't speak caveman

and have no idea what this particular grunt means. I rest a hand against his side and call on my Healing magic, pushing it into him. I don't feel anything broken, but I can feel the deep bruise there as it heals. Bastien lies back against the mats, and I watch his pained face smooth out, and his breathing deepens as his body adjusts to the sudden absence of pain and injury. I crawl toward his head and brush hair back from his face.

"Are you okay? I'm so fucking sorry; I was going too fast!"

He opens his eyes, and I'm relieved to find humor in the hazel depths.

"You know what this means, right?"

I look at him confused. "That you can't hang with this?" I tease.

He cracks up and out of nowhere pounces on me. Bastien declares *retaliation* as he pushes me onto my back and blows raspberries against my neck. I squeal and wiggle to get away, tickling his side in an attempt to try and gain the upper hand.

"Can you hang with this?" he mocks, as he tickles me back mercilessly. I try to kick him off of me, but I'm laughing so hard I can barely breathe, and I can't put much strength behind my efforts to escape.

"Truce!" I half gasp, half squeal until Bastien relents and falls back down on his back, chuckling.

We both ride out our giggles, and the room grows silent as we lie side by side.

"Bruiser, why didn't you tell me about Torrez?"

I turn to my side so I can see Bastien's face as his question hangs in the air between us. His tone doesn't give any emotion away, and his face just shows curiosity and not the hurt that I was afraid I might find there.

"I didn't mean to *not* tell you. There was just so much going on that morning. What happened with him didn't rise to the top of the priority list; not after Sorik, and the house news, and then Enoch knocking down the door, and all the drama with Pebble's coven."

Bastien gives me an understanding nod and falls quiet again. I run my finger across his jawline and begin to trace the beautiful angles of his face absently. He closes his eyes against my touch, and I get lost for a moment in how gorgeous he is. His full lips call to me, and I lean into him and taste them the way that they're begging to be tasted. He moans deeply into the kiss, and the sound of his pleasure vibrates through me to land right between my thighs. I deepen the kiss, needing more from him, and he answers my demand by pulling me on top of him as he masters my lips and my tongue.

He pulls my shirt up and over my head, forcing his lips from mine, and runs both of his palms up the runes on my ribs. His touch sets my runes ablaze, each caress shoots right to my clit, and I pant out an approving moan at the sensations.

"Did it feel like this with Torrez?"

His question throws me off, and I go still. Bastien continues to stroke my runes as he watches me.

"I was turned away from him. Mave was in Pebble's lap, and I was worried that the other shifters might take issue with that. He ran his finger across the runes on my shoulder..." I pause as the sensations from the memory run through me. "Yes, it felt like this when he touched me. That's why I thought it was one of you."

Bastien rolls us, switching our positions and pressing me into the cool mats. "Do you want him, Bruiser?"

He grinds himself against me, his hardness rubbing perfectly against my clit.

"Bastien, I'm sure as fuck not thinking about *him* right

now. Why are you asking me this?" Irritation peeks out of my words and eyes, and Bastien gives me a cheeky smile.

"Because if he's right, and you do want him, but you're too worried to admit it even to yourself, then it's something we need to deal with."

"I'd rather you deal with getting my bra off. Then I can deal with getting you naked, and then we can both deal with you giving me a couple orgasms, while I do the same in return. That's about all the dealing I'm interested in doing right now."

Bastien chuckles but doesn't require any more convincing as he pulls my sports bra over my head and off my arms. He pulls his own shirt off, and we both take our time appreciating each other's naked torsos. I run my eyes and then a fingertip over the indentations of his abs, and he runs his heated gaze over my breasts. He hooks his fingers into my leggings and pulls them down my hips, taking my underwear with them.

The fabric skims down my thighs and calves, and I'm beyond turned on just from his removal of my clothes. I lie spread out before him, and I hungrily watch as he pulls his sweats down. His hard cock springs free, and it sends a jolt of anticipation straight to my opening. I lean forward and, without thought or hesitation, flick my tongue out and lick the shine of precum from the head of Bastien's erection. Bastien moans and pumps his shaft with his hand as I steal another taste of him. It's saltier than I was expecting, and he laughs at the face I make as I catalog the taste.

Bastien kneels and cups my face, pulling me into a kiss so deep that there's no longer a separation between where he begins and I end. He pushes me back against the mats as he sucks and nibbles my lips. He grinds into my spread legs and dips his tongue back into my mouth. Our moans tangle together and intertwine, mirroring our tongues. Bastien lines up with my entrance, the tip of him shallowly thrusting in and then out of me. He teases me, refusing to sink into me any deeper. I claw at his lower back trying to make him give me what I want as I grind against him.

He pulls away from my lips and nips his way to my breasts. He stimulates one nipple with his tongue and rubs circles around the other with his fingers, tickling and teasing and driving me deliciously mad. His mouth and hand trade places, sucking and applying the perfect pressure to call to the wetness between my thighs. I run my fingers through his hair as he sucks on me, his lips and tongue waking up every nerve ending in my sex.

Bastien looks up at me, and we watch each other as he moves lower down my body until his head hovers over my slick slit. It's hot as fuck when he stares at me as he extends his tongue and takes a long lick, coating his mouth with my arousal. He wraps his massive arms around my thighs and hips, trapping me against his mouth, and he starts to devour me. I gasp when he sucks my clit into his mouth, but I don't drop my head back and get lost in the sensation, because watching Bastien bury his face in my pussy is a sight I want to remember.

I moan and encourage him when he hits the perfect combo of suction and pressure, and an orgasm surges inside me, so close to tipping over the edge. I press his head against me and grind against his face, trying to ride into my release, and he groans his encouragement. He nips my clit and shakes his head from side to side quickly, and sensation explodes through me as he pushes me over the edge and straight into an orgasm that has me moaning out his name and riding his face.

I pinch my own nipples as Bastien sucks on my pussy lips and then moves back up my body. I spread wide to accommodate his large muscular body, and he brings his elbows to rest on each side of my head. He kisses the runes on the top of my shoulder, and I feel his hardness line back up with me, and he thrusts deep inside of me. We both moan, and I run my hands up the muscles of his strong back as he pulls out and grinds back into me.

His lips take control of mine, and he swallows my desire as he increases his pace.

"Fuck, Bastien!" I shout when he pounds into me, and the sound of our skin slapping together echoes around the gym walls. He suddenly slows the punishing pace I was enjoying and trades it out for a slower deeper thrust. He swirls his hips against me which hits my clit in this perfect way that has me begging for more.

"Come for me again, love," he demands, grinding in and against me a few more times before a new orgasm rushes through me. I start to call out my release, and Bastien moves his arms underneath my knees, pushing them up by my shoulders. I ride the explosion of sensation shooting from my clit throughout the rest of my body, and then he rocks my fucking world when he starts to pound into me, hard and fast from this new angle.

"Yes, love, tighten around me, just like that! Yes, that feels so fucking good!"

I hold tight to Bastien's biceps as he fucks me deep and hard, his pace and angle extending the orgasm he just gave me, and it all feels so incredible. His breaths grow ragged, and his moans and exclamations grow louder, his pace growing even more, punishing inside of me until he suddenly stills, shouting his release as he comes inside of me. I'm just coming down from my orgasm, and my walls clench and constrict around his thick shaft, and he grunts his approval.

Bastien kisses me deeply, content to stay buried inside of me. He reaches a hand between us and circles my clit, and immediately it sets me off again. I arch into him, and he pinches a nipple between his fingers, still massaging my clit with his other hand. He whispers all kinds of things against my lips as I moan through another orgasm, telling me how beautiful I am, how good I feel, and how happy he is. I lose myself to his words and the sensations he's coaxing from me, wishing somehow this would never end.

38

Why I do anything other than just stay in bed with my Chosen or on gym mats like I currently am, I will never know. I run my hands through Bastien's dark waves as he rests his head on my stomach, running his fingers leisurely over the various lines of runes on my body. I'm not sure how long it will take before the pain starts. I feel nervous for him, but he seems relaxed. There's a calm and contentedness radiating from his every move right now.

"What made you change your mind about sex?" Bastien asks me, as he lazily traces the patterns of my runes.

"What do you mean?"

"I got the impression that you were going to try and avoid marking any more of us if you could."

I snicker and shake my head.

"You, Bastien Fierro, are way too observant."

He chuckles.

"I get that a lot. What can I say? I'm an emotionally sensitive guy."

I laugh, but even though he's trying to play it off as a joke, I realize that he really is. He picks up on little things that most people miss, and reads me and the others around him with an eerie accuracy I've never seen before. Behind his spontaneous actions and live-for-fun attitude, is an incredibly sensitive soul.

"I'm trying to not be Edward Cullen."

He looks up at me confused. "Who is that?"

I smile. "We are so downloading some books and reading them together."

He shrugs and kisses my stomach.

"Edward is a sparkly fictional creature that was full of angst and made all these decisions that just fucked everything up. I'm trying not to do that. I don't want you guys to hurt, but there's nothing I can do about it. I can think of ways to put it off, but at some point, it's going to happen. I said I was *in,* and that means for the good things and the hard things. You all know what will happen when we're intimate. If you're initiating sex, then I'm taking that as you're telling me you're ready for the next hard step. Who am I to tell you that you're not?"

The barely-there stubble on Bastien's cheek rubs against my skin as he nods his head.

"Plus, I've discovered I really like sex. So there's that, too."

We both crack up and then fall back into companionable silence for a while, just touching and learning the intricacies of each other's bodies with our fingertips.

"What's your favorite color?"

I grin at the random question.

"Purple. What about you?"

"Blue, I really like gray, too, but Valen said that's not a color so he'd never let me pick it as my favorite when we were younger," he chuckles.

"Gray is totally a color," I challenge. "You can have that as your favorite; I won't tell Valen."

Bastien smiles and nuzzles my abs. The light of the setting sun peeks through the windows and brightens his features, making him glow and look even more breathtaking.

"Favorite food?"

"Ooh, that's a hard one," I admit, thinking about it for a moment. "Maybe burgers, I am always down for a burger. And carrot cake, ooh, and a good gooey cinnamon roll."

He laughs. "Well, I guess that covers favorite dessert too."

"What about you?"

"Pasta, all kinds of pasta. Dessert...probably brownies and ice cream."

"Mmmmm," we both groan at the same time and then chuckle.

"What was it like growing up here?" I ask, tracing the dark hair of his eyebrows.

"When Silva wasn't on assignment, he was always doing stuff with us, teaching us things. We all love the outdoors, and he taught us how to fix cars and fight. He was preparing us to be paladin before we even understood what that was," he chuckles. "The sisters, Lachlan, and the others, they're family, at least the only family Valen and I have ever known. Our upbringing was pretty laid back. For the most part, we could do whatever we wanted as long as we did well in school and didn't cause too much trouble. "

I laugh at that, and Bastien looks up at me, a cheeky twinkle in his eyes.

"Why do I have a feeling that you and Valen caused more trouble than you ever got caught for?"

He chuckles. "Because you'd be right. You'd be surprised what you could get away with when people can't tell you apart, or they feel bad that you're a poor motherless child and can't help your feral ways," he snorts.

"Do you remember your parents at all? I know you were young when they went missing... "

"I have some memories, but it's hard to know if they're authentic or if it's a mash-up of my brain's wishful thinking and images I've seen in pictures. Silva would always tell us stories about our mom. She was wild, always getting into one thing or another, and she gave her mates a run for their money. She was independent and opinionated, and I think if she were around, she would have loved you."

Bastien's eyes widen suddenly, and at first, I think it's because he dropped the *L* word and feels weird about it, but his breathing suddenly becomes rapid, and he presses his face into my stomach and grabs tightly onto my hips.

"I think it's happening!" he grits out, and I sit up and wrap myself around him.

"Do you want me to talk, or shut the fuck up and just be here?" I ask, trying to figure out what will help him most while attempting to hide the panic in my voice.

"Talk...give...me...something...else...to...focus...on!"

Bastien's jaw clenches, and he pulls his knees underneath him. He folds in on himself while he also leans into my chest and wraps his arms around my waist. I push his hair out of his face with one hand, and hold him to me with the other.

"Breathe, Bas. It'll be over soon. It won't last, I promise. I'm here. I'll always be here. Just breathe through it."

I repeat my attempt at comfort over and over again and watch Bastien struggle against what's happening inside of him. The door to the gym flies open with a large *boom* that echoes around the walls. Valen rushes in, his face radiating pure panic as he searches the room. He spots us on the mats and realization sinks into his features.

"My adrenaline spiked out of nowhere, and I knew

something was wrong," Valen rushes out, and I can tell he's not sure if he should go or stay.

"Fuck, I'm sorry, Valen. I didn't even think about how it would feel to you when his runes showed up. I didn't factor in the *twin* aspect, or I would have warned you."

Valen hesitates for another second and then walks over and kneels down next to us. He puts his hand on Bastien's shoulder and leans down toward his twin.

"I'm here, Bas."

"Fuck!" Bastien shouts out in pain and tightens his grip around me.

I try to soothe him with more promises that it will be over soon as black runes swirl into solid symbols forming one line and then another up Bastien's spine. He screams out again as the black marks stamp themselves all over him, and the burn of the magic settles permanently there.

"I'm sorry, Bruiser!" he grits out, and I lean back to get a look at his face.

"What the fuck are you sorry for? I did this to you!"

"Worth it!"

I snort at his pained declaration.

"I'd do it...a...mill...ion...times...over...for...you...Bruiser! You...are...worth...it!"

He bites down against a groan, and I fight against the sudden stinging sensation in my eyes. Leave it to Bastien to be worried about me when he's the one going through hell right now. Valen leans down toward his brother and places his hand on the back of Bastien's neck.

"Out of the night that covers me,
    Black as the pit from pole to pole,
    I thank whatever gods may be
For my unconquerable soul.

. . .

In the fell clutch of circumstance
    I have not winced nor cried aloud.
    Under the bludgeonings of chance
My head is bloody, but unbowed.

Beyond this place of wrath and tears
    Looms but the Horror of the shade,
    And yet the menace of the years
Finds, and shall find, me unafraid.

It matters not how strait the gate,
    How charged with punishments the scroll,
    I am the master of my fate:
I am the captain of my soul."

"**A**gain!" Bastien demands of his brother, and Valen complies, repeating the poem over and over again until I also have it memorized and join in on the poetic chant.

Slowly Bastien's grip around my waist softens, and I can feel the taut muscles in his back start to loosen. Valen gives me a huge smile, and I'm filled with tender affection for how relieved he is.

"Whose poem is that?" I ask, unable to quash my curiosity.

I would have never pegged either of them as poetry buffs.

"It's by William Ernest Henley. It's called 'Invictus.' Silva didn't know any lullabies or nursery rhymes, but he knew poems. At night when we were young, we would fall asleep to him reading or reciting things to us. This one was always one of our favorites. It just became a thing we did for each other when we were scared or struggling with something; we'd pick out a favorite and recite it until the other felt better."

Valen flashes me a shy grin and then looks down at Bastien when he grunts and starts to sit up. They make eye contact, and I watch as an unspoken conversation happens between them; it's filled with worry and reassurance and love. It's like I can physically see the unique and incredible connection they have as they communicate and reassure each other, without ever saying a single word.

Bastien turns to me. I'm not sure what I'm expecting to see in his eyes, but the awe I find there is not it. He pounces on me, and my surprised squeak gets lost against Bastien's lips when they crash into mine. He follows me back down to the mat and kisses me so thoroughly that I stop questioning why he's kissing me and just go with it. He pulls away, and his hazel eyes bounce between my light green ones.

"Holy shit, you are fucking powerful! I mean, I knew, I thought I did anyway, but not really. Now that I can feel it here..." He rubs the runes in between his pecs. "I could have never comprehended that *this* was what was in store for us. Thank you, Bruiser, thank you for choosing me...us."

He gestures toward Valen who's just grinning at us, not at all phased by our naked display. He slaps Bastien's ass hard and gives me a wink.

"You need to go eat, Bas; you'll need the calories right away just like Ryker and Knox did. I see that look in your eye, and no, I don't mean eat Vinna."

Bastien laughs and gives me a peck. He climbs off me and stands up, offering me a hand while he rubs his ass cheek with the other. He teeters slightly, and both Valen and I rush up to make sure he doesn't fall over.

"Fuck, head rush."

I pick up his sweat pants and help him step into them while Valen holds him steady. I pull on my clothes and look up to find both of them watching me, heat banked in their eyes. I point to Bastien.

"You go eat and then rest; you'll be shaky the rest of the night, but we'll start training tomorrow. And you..." I point to Valen. "I need your help coming up with a training schedule. I need to know what you guys have learned in your paladin training, and we need to combine that with what I know and how I use my magic."

They both smile and salute me at exactly the same time. Valen helps a slightly trembling Bastien out the door, and I shamelessly watch their asses as they leave. Three down, two to go.

39

"Motherfucker!" Bastien shouts.

He snatches his hand out of his pocket and glares at the throwing knife he currently holds in his hand. Everyone in the car tries to keep from snickering, but Knox and Valen are close to losing their battle. Ever since Bastien woke up this morning spooning a long sword, he's been having trouble accidentally calling his weapons, and the rest of the guys are having trouble not giving him shit about it.

"I'm just reaching for my phone, *magic*, I'm not calling any weapons, for fuck's sake," he argues with the new power now flowing through him.

He glares at the small dagger in his hand before letting it fall toward the ground and watching it disappear. He throws a glare around the car, daring anyone to have a go at him, and that's what ultimately tips me over the edge. I burst out into a fit of laughter. He looks at me, his features incredulous, but it just makes me laugh harder.

I howl out my amusement, and it becomes contagious throughout the vehicle, not even Bastien can keep from letting some chuckles escape. It's exactly what we need to help break up some of the tension that's been mounting ever since I announced that we're going to train at Enoch's house this morning. No one seems happy, but after explaining about Enoch's training ring and the plan Valen and I came up with, there wasn't much they could argue with.

I'd prefer to leave Enoch and his coven out of it. I'm still not sure how things stand with them, and their connection to the elders is not ideal either, but the guys and I need help. I'm struggling with trying to explain how Sentinel magic works well enough that they can work to master it, and I'm in serious need of training on all aspects of magic in general. My time with Kallan, Nash, Enoch, and Becket was filled with all sorts of craziness and uncertainty, but one thing we did well together...was train.

When I spoke to Enoch yesterday, he seemed surprised to hear from me but willing to get back to work. I haven't talked to anyone else in his coven, but I'm hoping they all feel the same way. The last thing we need today is drama, or a bunch of hotheads and egos clashing, when three of my guys have spazzy Sentinel magic and no idea what they're capable of. I'm also oddly nervous of what Enoch and the others are going to say when some of the guys show up with a matching set of my runes all over their bodies.

Enoch and his dad know what I am, but I don't know if they know the ins and outs of being a Sentinel and what all it entails, or how much Enoch has shared with the rest of his coven. Some of them seemed pretty pissed that he had been keeping secrets, and if I were them, I would have demanded to know everything before even considering forgiving him for keeping shit from me. He's lucky I'm not in his coven; I'd have probably stabbed him.

I reach over and pull Bastien's finger from his mouth. I heal the small cut on the pad of his finger and then kiss the spot where the cut disappeared from. I give him a sweet smile, and he pulls me in toward him and places a gentle peck on my lips. He nuzzles my nose with his own, but the opening of Enoch's gates pulls us back into reality. He huffs out a deep breath, and I sneak another kiss.

"You'll get it. It hasn't even been twenty-four hours since you got your runes, and you're doing better than I ever did; I stabbed myself for weeks. My magic still does shit I had no idea it could do, so cut yourself some slack."

He smiles against my lips. "Thanks, Bruiser, I just can't lose this bet with Knox."

I laugh, having forgotten all about their shit-talking to each other and the subsequent bet that ensued.

"Well, maybe that will keep your mouth from writing checks your ass can't cash."

Bastien's eyes fill with mirth.

"Let's blow off this meetup with douche and his asshole coven, and I'll cash your ass right now."

I roll my eyes at him. "We're training, Bas, not having a tea party. I thought you lived for all that training and paladin shit. That's all this is. Well, better, because now you get to be a badass Sentinel, and let's keep it real, that trumps paladin any day."

"Don't let Paladin Ender hear you say that," Valen teases.

"I don't know; I think I could take him."

All the guys chuckle, and Bastien tweaks my nose.

"Now who's writing checks her ass can't cash?" Bastien exclaims.

"What, I got the drop on him before."

Knox pats my knee. "Vinna, that man is a machine. I've never seen anyone do what he can, not even you or your sweet little ass."

We pull up in front of the house, and Enoch, Nash, Kallan, and Becket walk out to greet us. It gives me a sense of deja vu and pulls me back into the memory of the car ride with Pebble and his coven right after they forced me away from my Chosen. It's a weird full circle moment, and something resonates inside of me, making me feel like something about this is important or pivotal.

It's a strange feeling, like somehow I should be seeing something that's right in front of me, but I can't bring it into focus and catch the needed details. It's that annoying sensation when you know a word, but it sits on the wrong side of your tongue, and you just can't speak it into existence.

The light-hearted atmosphere that just filled the car evaporates. The guys get their game faces on, and there's a collective deep, fortifying breath taken before everyone climbs out of the car and faces off with Enoch and the others. There's a long awkward pause where it seems no one knows what to do or say. Like we're standing on opposite sides of a line and can't decide if it's worth crossing or dangerous in some way. Instead, both groups stand there taking each other's measure.

I cross the invisible divide first and head right for Enoch's door. I lived here, sort of, so I decide that means I can just walk into the house and right past whatever the fuck these guys are silently yelling at each other about as they square off, arms folded over chests, and glare at one another. I walk through the house and out the back doors, heading straight for the training pit.

The dick measuring contest ends sooner than I thought it would, and Enoch catches up to me. I can practically feel the debate going on inside of his head about what to say.

"I'm glad you called. I didn't know if you'd want to hear from me or us." He rubs the back of his neck, clearly searching for a way to make this interaction less awkward. "How are things going?"

I stop mid-stride, surprising him, and stare at him for a beat.

"Enoch, I'm not sure how to answer that."

His face fills with confusion.

"You can tell me anything, Vinna. You can trust me."

"That's the thing though, I don't *know* if I can. I'm trying to, but you ask me a simple question like *how is everything going*, and instead of just telling you the truth about all the crazy shit that's going down, I debate if I can tell you anything. Right now, I'm weighing the risks in my head about whether you or your dad can use what I want to say against me somehow, or if I'm being set up for something I can't see coming."

Enoch runs frustrated fingers through his blond hair and takes a step toward me. As Enoch moves closer to me, I see Sabin out of the corner of my eye move to intercept him, but I give him a small wave to wait and let whatever is about to happen, happen.

"He made a power play, Vinna; it doesn't make my dad evil or me untrustworthy."

"I'm not a chess piece, Enoch! Do you not understand that?"

"I know that...now. I didn't know *who* you were when I saw you at the lake. I just knew *what* you were and what that could mean for me." He gestures to the rest of his coven. "For us, if you were open to it. But then I started to get to know you, and it wasn't all about the power and the politics anymore, because I started to see *you*. You are what's important to me."

"To us," Nash chimes in.

"But then why not tell me what you knew? Why not just be honest?" I ask, frustrated and confused.

"Because you didn't seem like you wanted anyone to know," he points to where Sabin and the guys are gathered.

"I didn't know that they knew or that your uncle and his coven knew. When Faron called you Baby Sentinel, and you looked more panicked than confused, I realized that clearly you knew what you were, but I didn't want to freak you out by bringing it up."

I go to argue with that point, but Enoch beats me to it.

"What was I supposed to do, swagger on up to you and be all, *so you're a Sentinel, want to be friends?*"

"I mean, leave out the weird Eeyore, Elvis voice you just did, but yeah, that would have been a hell of a lot better than letting your dad blindside me at the weekly family dinner!"

Enoch throws his hands out to his sides in a half-defensive, half-exasperated pose. "I didn't know he was going to do that! I swear, I didn't know he was going to come at you that way. You're headstrong and don't bow down to him; I don't think he's used to that."

I take a step toward him, anger simmering just below the surface. "Don't fucking defend your dad to me, Enoch. He threatened to expose me because I wouldn't hop on your dick and hand over my abilities! I'm not going to find him redeemable because he's related to you or has issues with a female having a say in her own fucking life or who she chooses to be with!"

"Fine. Let's leave him out of it. This is about you and me anyway! I'm sorry I didn't just come out with the whole *I know what you are* thing. I didn't know how to approach it; I thought Sentinels were just stories, and then there you were, and you were...you."

Enoch motions up and down toward me and gives a slight shrug. Nash chuckles.

"What does that mean...I was me?"

"He means you're hot," Kallan tells me.

I roll my eyes.

"I saw the chicks you had with you at the beach; I'm not falling for the *I can't talk to pretty girls* bullshit."

Valen interjects by walking over and wrapping an arm around my shoulders. I stare up at him, and his hazel eyes burn with an unreadable emotion as they stay locked on mine.

"You're not pretty, Vinna...you're everything. Everything that we could have ever hoped for, and so much more."

Before I can shake myself out of my shocked stupor and think of a response, he turns to Enoch.

"It's great that you guys see that about her too, but she's our mate, and we're here to work, so let's get to it."

With that, Valen guides me away from Enoch, closing the distance to the training area.

Valen's jaw ticks as we walk, irritation radiating off of him.

"Valen, he knows what you guys are to me."

"Yeah, I don't think he does," he tells me, and a strained smile stretches across his mouth. "It's fine, your Chosen will be happy to clear things up for him; we'll remind him—and them—for however long they need it," he tells me, his strained smile smoothing out into something lascivious.

I laugh. "Don't start too much shit; we need them to help, okay?"

My plea gets swallowed up by his lips when he stops at the entrance to the training arena and kisses me. It's not an *I need inside of you right now* kind of kiss, but it hints at that, and I can taste the reminder on my lips of who he is to me and who I am to him.

Nash squeezes past us, mumbling, "Might as well just piss all over her."

His grumbling steals me away from the questions Valen's kiss has stirred up, and I chuckle.

"Nah, golden showers aren't my kink," I announce as

Valen pulls away from me, and we follow Nash further into the sand and stone training pit.

I clap my hands together once loudly, and everyone's eyes fall on me.

"Okay, here's what's going to go down." I focus on Enoch and his crew. "You guys are going to do what we normally do: build a course and try to keep me from getting through it."

Kallan smiles devilishly, and the rest nod their understanding.

I turn to the serious faces that each of my guys are wearing.

"I'm going to activate runes so that you can feel and hear what I'm doing when I call my magic. Valen and I think this will be the easiest way for you guys to get a feel for the different branches of magic and how I call weapons. I'll run their course until you feel like you're ready to join, and then we'll team off and try to take each other out. Sound good?" I ask, looking around at everyone.

They all nod to me, but everyone is quiet, and it's uncomfortable. The guys go sit on the stone benches, and I watch them get settled. Why are they treating Enoch and the others like they're a threat to what we have together? I don't mind the territorial gestures, but I do mind the fog of doubt that seems to have permeated my Chosen. Kallan walks over to me, and I set my questions aside to focus on what we're here to do.

He nudges me with his shoulder and smiles down at me. "If I give you a hug, is one of them going to stab me?" he teases.

"I'm not going to lie, it's a possibility," I admit, running my gaze over where the guys are seated.

Kallan chuckles and wraps his arms around me anyway.

"Worth the risk," he announces as he squeezes me tightly in a hug that pulls my feet off the ground.

I chuckle but shoot him a scolding look as he plants my feet back on the ground. We make our way out toward the tree line so the rest of his coven can work out the course they want to put together without me seeing or overhearing anything.

"So have they at least pulled their heads out of their asses and started working with you and your magic?" Kallan asks casually. "Are you keeping up with the drills that we set up, or do they have you working a different plan?"

"I've mostly been trying to help them to use their new magic. I haven't focused too much on what I need to develop."

Kallan lets out an annoyed grunt and shakes his head at me.

"Vinna, you can't let what they want get in the way of what you *need* to do. You can't always rely on brute strength or blades. You have to work on mastering your power, now more than ever after your awakening. You were doing well here; you need to keep that momentum going!"

"Kallan, I know that. There's so much shit going on, but I promise I've not lost sight of what I need to do. Why do you think I called you guys? I need help. I'm so out of my depth on figuring out what I'm capable of, and now I have to help them sort it out, too. That's why I'm here."

He pulls me in for another hug. He nods his chin toward my Chosen.

"Don't worry about them so much. They'll figure it out; they've lived their whole life knowing what magic is and how to use it. All they need to know now is how to recognize the different branches and separate them out. They're paladin. They know how to work hard, and it'll click into place for them. But who's going to help you do the same,

Vinna? I promise I'm not trying to start shit. I really am just trying to look out for you, but whenever you're with them, you back away from what you need to do. Why is that?"

"Don't make it sound like I'm walking away from what I need, for them. It's not like that. I just haven't figured out the balance of it all. Work, play, study, train, fighting off seen and unseen enemies, I'm figuring it out. If you've got an instruction manual that you want to hand over, I'm game, but if not, don't judge, just help me work through it."

Kallan chuckles and lets out a sigh. "Fair enough. I wanted to tell you how sorry I am about what happened at Elder Cleary's house, and I'm sorry that Enoch was keeping the truth from you...and from us."

Kallan's tone has a bitter edge to it, and I take a moment to look at him, really look at him.

Enoch is part of his coven and his future compeer, and I can't imagine how I would feel in his shoes.

"I'm sorry he did that to you. How are you guys? How are things?"

"To be honest, none of us have really been talking to each other. Well, Enoch and Nash are, but Nash wasn't in the same boat as me and Becket. Enoch told him what was going on. This is the first time we've all been around each other for any length of time since the night you left."

I'm surprised by his admission, and it takes me a moment to think of something to say to that.

"Do you think you guys will get past it?"

He shrugs. "If Enoch was keeping this from us, I can't help but wonder if there's more he's keeping from us. Becket feels the same way. I know some paladin and covens aren't close, and they treat working together more like a job, but we never wanted that to be us."

I look out at the trees. I scan our surroundings and nod at him. I empathize with the shitty situation he's in and wish there was more I could do or say to make the situation better.

A whistle from the practice arena sounds behind us, and Kallan turns to me expectantly.

"Should we do this first run through together since you're all rusty and shit and clearly need me to kick your ass into gear?"

I run my finger over the runes on my sternum and the ones behind my ear. I give Kallan a mock salute. "Yes, drill sergeant!" I yell in my best impersonation of a soldier.

He chuckles, and then I watch as his *take-no-fucks* persona shutters down over his face. His features harden, and his body language becomes rigid and unyielding.

"Let's fucking do this, now *move*!"

40

Sand flies at me from every possible direction, and wind whips my ponytail around my face and claws at my clothes. Enoch seems to be tapping into his sense of humor for this battle round, because he's been laying the sand tornadoes and lightning on pretty thick. I call on my Elemental magic and shove the sand away from my airway and face.

Fuck, cleaning this shit out of my every nook and cranny is going to be a pain in the ass, I grumble to myself. Maybe one of the guys will help me with that. My name is shouted, and the sound of it whips through the cyclone surrounding me, swirling around before the wind chases it away. Fucking hell, Kallan, how does he always know when I'm not focused? He has to have some kind of freaky radar or something.

I use the cover of the magical storm to track where Kallan, Becket, and Enoch are in relation to me. I reach out with my Defensive magic and get a feel for what they have waiting for me when I'm out of Enoch's current trap. Enoch has tendrils sinking into the earth in addition to the tornado he's creating, but they feel like back up and not an active effort to fuck with the ground beneath my feet. Becket has his Defensive magic focused on Kallan, which makes me think he has something particularly brutal waiting for me as he's being protected.

But I'm not falling for it. Kallan is an excellent strategist, but he hasn't been using any spells in any of the four previous battles, and that's the type of magic he has. I steal back the air around me, and the swirling stops as sand falls back to the ground. I don't go for Kallan or Enoch, the more obvious threats in this round, but instead, focus on Becket.

A pulse of fuchsia magic darts from me toward him, and Becket pulls the shield from Kallan and erects it around himself. My magic hits the barrier and starts to coat it. I reach for the tendrils of magic that Enoch has waiting in the ground and force my magic toward them, forcing a wall of dirt up and around him. Offensive magic fully surrounds Becket's barrier, and I force a streak of lightning into it.

The barrier-turned-cage lights up with energy, trapping Becket inside. I feel the shield-runes on my body go on high alert, and a shield explodes out of my side before a red ball of magic slams into it. I turn to Enoch and throw orbs of fuchsia magic in return, lighting up the atmosphere around us with Offensive magic as the orbs slam into each other and fight to connect with the other person.

Snake-like tendrils of the ground form around me, and they come for me, trying to wrap themselves and find purchase anywhere they can, to cage me in. I dodge and weave, running toward Enoch as I jump, spin, and dash through sections of the earth that try to claim me and keep me from my target. I pull the magic from Becket's barrier as I fight toward Enoch. I release throwing knives in Becket's direction and send a pulse of orange magic at Kallan, knocking him back from where he's running at me.

I look up just as Enoch is feet from me, and we slam into

each other at full speed. I let out a pained grunt at the contact and instinctively shove both of my hands against his chest. Power shoots out of my palms when they connect with Enoch, and as soon as I register the color, I try to pull my hands away and stop, but I can't move.

Violet magic slams into Enoch's chest, and judging by the look on his face, whatever I'm doing is hurting him. I scream out my effort to pull away from him and get control of what I'm doing. I reach into my core and try to constrict the flow of Sentinel magic flooding out of me. I close my eyes and focus everything that I have on reining myself in. Hands wrap themselves around my wrists, and my eyes flash open to find Valen staring at me, panic in his eyes.

"I can't stop," I shout to him, but I don't know if he can hear me past the loud rushing sound coming from the power I'm forcing into Enoch.

Suddenly all the Sentinel magic flooding Enoch pulses out of him, slamming into everyone else before it continues to flash out toward the trees, and disappears. I take shaky hands away from Enoch, and he collapses to the ground as I scramble backward away from him. Valen wraps his arms around me, keeping me from moving any further away, and the other guys rush to surround us. The guys crowd around me, running their hands and eyes all over me to make sure I'm okay, each of them wearing a look of alarm.

"Oh, fuck, did I kill him? Is he okay? I felt like I was killing him."

I'm terrified of the answer, but I have to know. Ryker joins Becket, Nash, and Kallan who are bending over and kneeling around Enoch.

"He's awake and breathing, Squeaks. It's okay!"

Relief floods me, and I stare down at my hands, feeling betrayed. I have no idea what just happened. I've never felt anything like that before.

"Fuck, that hurt!" Enoch announces.

I watch him try to sit up, and Nash helps him lean forward and into a sitting position. Enoch pats himself down like he's making sure everything that's supposed to be there is still there. His blue eyes search around him until they land on me.

"I'm so fucking sorry; I have no idea what just happened," I say, guilt flooding my body.

"Are you okay?" he asks me.

I nod that I am, and watch as Nash runs his hands over his coven mate, checking for any areas that might need healing.

"I don't feel any injuries. Anything going on inside that would tell you differently?"

Enoch stares down at his arms, torso and then his legs. "I'm good, just have a fuck ton of adrenaline pumping through me right now. Nothing hurts or feels different."

Knox steps into my line of sight, blocking Enoch from my view.

"Did you just mark him?"

His question shocks the fuck out of me, and it takes me a second to answer.

"No, it didn't feel like what happened with you guys. When I give you Sentinel magic, it feels good to you and to me. That's not what just happened."

The fury that fills Knox's face at my words takes me aback. He whirls on Enoch just as his coven helps him up off the ground.

"Did you just try to force her to mark you? What the fuck did you do, Cleary?" Knox accuses, stepping toward Enoch.

Bastien and Sabin grab onto Knox, keeping him from advancing too far.

"What the fuck? I would never do something like that,

even if it were possible, which I don't think it is!"

"We all felt what she felt; it was like someone was taking the magic and she couldn't stop it. So I will ask you again, and if I find out you're lying, I will fucking kill you! Did you or your dad do something to make this happen, to try and force her?"

Enoch's features darken with rage, and he tries to square off with Knox. His coven holds him back just like Sabin and Bastien hold Knox back.

"I already fucking told you that I wouldn't do that to her. If you question me one more time, we're going to have a serious fucking problem, Howell."

I step out of Valen's hold and move in between Knox and Enoch. I'm not sure what to say. Knox's accusation has stunned me silent. Before he said anything, I would have just chalked this up to another episode of spazzy magic, but I can't get the taint of Knox's words out of my head. Could they have done that to me? I try to shake off my doubt. If it were possible to force a marking, wouldn't Adriel have figured that out when he was trying to get magic from my mother?

I turn to Enoch. Whatever look I'm wearing turns his anger to alarm.

"Vinna, I wouldn't do that. My dad is a lot of things, but he wouldn't do that. You have to believe me."

"I believe you."

"Vinna, you can't..."

I cut Knox's argument off when I turn to him and reach up to cup his face. His eyes lock on mine, and I hate the desperate and worried look that I see there.

"My magic has done weirder things. I had Sentinel magic pouring out of me during my Awakening, and it didn't mark any of them. Okay?"

I nod my head up and down, and Knox mirrors the

move.

I pull his face down to mine and place a soft kiss to his lips, lacing it with all the reassurance I can. I pull away, and his gray eyes flick between mine, looking for any hint of doubt in my gaze. He relaxes in my hands and claims another kiss before stepping back and away from Enoch and his coven. Bastien gives me a small smile as our eyes meet before I turn back to Enoch and the others.

"Are you sure you're okay?"

"Yeah, it hurt at the time, but I feel fine now."

I look past him and scan the trees and house around us. I search for answers in our surroundings that I know aren't there, but I can't seem to help myself. Is Pebble's coven out there watching us right now? I know Enoch believes that his dad wouldn't do what Knox is accusing, but I'm not convinced.

The trill of a ringtone breaks up the heavy silence and doubt that's pressing down on me. I turn to watch Bastien pull his phone out of his pocket and bring it up to his ear, a curious look on his face.

"Hey, what's up?" he greets whoever is on the other line.

Everyone watches the phone call, and Valen takes a step toward his brother just before Bastien's face is touched by alarm.

"What do you mean; what happened?"

I walk over to him just as he tells the caller that *we're on our way right now*. The phone drops from his ear, and before anyone can even ask, he looks at us. "That was Aydin, something's happened, and we need to get back to the house."

"What?" Ryker starts.

"He didn't want to say over the phone, but it has to do with Silva." Bastien's eyes land on his twin, and he communicates something silently before both twins turn to me. "And Lachlan."

41

Everyone is silent all the way home, lost in thought or running through all the possible scenarios of what could be going on. Did they find a lead, something solid, and Aydin's about to fill us in on what they've been up to? My heart rate speeds up. What if they found Vaughn? That would definitely be something you wouldn't reveal over the phone. I push back against the hope that tries to roost in my soul. *Don't get your hopes up, Vinna. Don't set yourself up for the crash if you're wrong.*

Ryker reaches over and takes my hand. He offers me a sweet smile and laces his fingers with mine. He turns onto the road that leads home, and my adrenaline spikes. I squeeze Ryker's hand unable to help myself, and we pull up to the front of the house, not bothering with the garage as we're all too eager to find out what's going on. We pile out of the car and into the house, calling out for Aydin. He comes out of the kitchen and waves us in. I round the corner and screech to a stop when I find the sisters there dabbing at red, tear-filled eyes. I look to Aydin and his haggard, worried face.

"Silva called," he pauses, clearly struggling with what he's going to say next.

My heart drops in my chest.

"Lachlan and Keegan were taken. Adriel has them."

My brain stutters for a moment, recalibrating from thoughts of my father and processing what Aydin just said.

"How did they find him? Does Silva know where they are?" I ask rapid-fire, trying to sort through this development.

"They found a lead." He holds up his hand stalling the questions that sit on the tips of everyone's tongues. "I don't know what it was or how they ended up in Belarus, but that's where they are. Silva needs help and supplies, and we need to pack and get over there as quickly as possible."

"Did you charter something, or do we need to book tickets still?" Valen asks, falling into the battle plan mode I discovered he had when we hatched out our training plan.

"I've chartered a plane. The pilot and crew should get there about the same time we do if we leave in the next hour."

Aydin starts assigning tasks and supplies to everyone, and I step back out of the chaos and work through what the best plan of action here is. We're about to go up against a monster who has taken out covens of paladin and covets all things Sentinel. We're going to do that with three paladin who just split ways with each other, and not on good terms from the sound of it, and a group of Paladin Conscripts, three of which have new runes and magic they don't know how to use yet.

This is a really fucking bad idea!

"Wait!" I shout out as everyone bustles around me, making plans and lists of supplies they need to get before we leave.

"We can't go in there magic blazing, thinking that it's

going to get us anywhere. Look at all the evidence there is that shows doing that isn't effective. We need to be smart about this. Smarter than the others that never came back, and smarter than fucking stupid ass Lachlan who thought he could do it all on his own."

"What do you suggest then?" Aydin asks.

"I don't know, but we need time or more help, maybe both."

Evrin steps forward, shaking his head. "We don't have time. We don't know what he'll do with them."

"He'll use them to his best advantage, either that or they're already dead either way." I point to the guys. "They can't go into this fumbling with their magic and abilities. That's a fucking death sentence." I pause, trying to figure out the most delicate way to say what I need to say next. "Fuck it; there's no *nice* way to say that Lachlan isn't worth their lives."

The room fills with the weight of the arguments I know are mounting in all of their minds. I get that Lachlan holds a different place in their hearts than he does mine, but I'm not about to throw my Chosen to the lamia for him.

"Bruiser, we have to do this. We can't leave him to the same fate that our parents and your parents had. It's not right. You told us that we can't stop you from fighting the battles that you need to fight, and now the same applies to us."

"I'm not trying to stop you. I'm just trying to make you see that you need to train more and be ready. This fucker is no joke, and we can't come at him the way every missing paladin and caster has."

"Fine, let's get there and then work out a plan of attack. Hopefully, Silva will have more information for us then. If Adriel is going to use them as bargaining chips, then we may have time to train and get ready."

I nod my head, conceding to the fact that as much as I hate this, I have to trust the guys when they choose their battles. If that's what I expect, then that's what I have to give, no matter how much it sends my instincts screaming and my heart begging me to come up with a better way.

Sabin sidles up next to me and traces the line of my jaw with the back of his hand.

"I need to go to my family's warehouse to pick up some shifter saliva, do you want to come with? It might be good to step out of the chaos for a moment and take a breather?"

I give him a hollow smile and a nod. He takes my hand and leads me away from all of the noise, planning and scrambling around, and as the door that leads out into the garage shuts behind me, I'm instantly enveloped in silence. We climb into his Bronco, and I try to snap myself out of this numb state I'm currently floating in.

"Sabin, you have to see that everything about this is a horrible idea."

I turn to watch him as he drives to wherever it is that we're going.

"Yeah, nothing about it is ideal, but what choice do we have? As long as Lachlan and Keegan are alive, we have to fight for them. Just like they did for your dad, and the twins' parents, and family coven. This is what we're about, what we've been training most of our lives to do, kick ass and bring supes who break the laws to justice."

He gives me a cheeky smile that I'm more accustomed to seeing on Knox's face or Bastien's, and it lifts some of the weight of worry that's pressing down on me. I can't help but give him an answering grin. I sigh and lay my head back against the headrest. The sun is starting to sink closer toward the horizon, and this day suddenly feels way too long. The threat of many more days to come, endless in all the worst ways, looms in the air.

It's getting colder at night, and it seems summer is finally relinquishing its hold as autumn forces its way in. I try to think about mundane things like what the trees around here look like as their leaves change color, instead of focusing on the gnawing pit that was once my stomach. We pull off on to a small road that's so obscured by trees, you'd miss it if you blinked. It takes us to an area cleared of trees where a small warehouse sits.

Sabin parks near a door, and I climb out of the car and follow him into the building that has rows and rows of shelves filled with inventory for his family's shop. Fluorescent lights blink angrily above us, their irritated buzzing the only sound in the space. Sabin finds what he's looking for and begins to put jars of shifter saliva in a box that he must have grabbed when I was too busy looking at other things.

I could probably spend all day here learning about all the items on the shelves. It'd be fun to come out here and learn as much as I can someday when things calm down. Sabin clicks off the lights, and I follow him out the door. I make sure that it clicks shut behind me and turn around and promptly slam right into Sabin's back. He swears as he stumbles forward, and my apology turns to vinegar in my mouth when I take in what had him freezing in place.

Between us and Sabin's car are four fucking massive grizzly bears. They watch us as we watch them, and it doesn't take long for me to piece together that there is nothing normal about this gathering of grizzlies. I quickly flip through my memory banks, trying to remember if there are bear shifters that live here, but I only remember being told about wolves and pumas.

I slowly lift a hand to activate the runes behind my ear so I can talk to Sabin without whoever these shifters are knowing, but a deep growl from a bear makes me pause. A grizzly that's way bigger than it would be if it were just a bear stands up on its hind legs, and the next thing I know, the bear is gone, and in its place is an average-sized man. I wait to see if he's going to explain why they're keeping us here, when another grizzly stands up and blinks into a person.

Recognition sucker punches me in the face, and all thoughts that this bear hold up is going to end well vanishes. I step out from behind Sabin but don't step in front of him like I want to, because one of the bears steps closer to us, and I decide not to push it...yet.

"You better be here to say thank you, because if you're here for what I think you are, you're going to join your buddies," I warn and glare at the big, burly douchebag.

I rescued this fucker from Lachlan and his paladin the night I first met them, and now he's back, proving that no good deed goes unpunished. *Fuck my conscience!* He chuckles and takes a step toward me. I call on my short swords, and they flash solid in my hand.

"Watch it, Yogi, I gave you a shot to get away before, but there won't be a repeat of my mercy if you come any closer."

The other shifter that's in man form chuckles, and it earns him a glare from the guy I saved.

"An old friend reached out to me in hopes that I would help him procure something he'd spent a very long time searching for. Imagine my surprise when I get the description of the precious cargo, and I know exactly where to find her. So thank you, pet, you just made me a shit ton of money. I'd say fate handed your sweet ass right to me, but I don't believe in that shit."

The memory of Lachlan telling me that the shifters they were killing were traffickers flashes through my mind, and I'm ninety-five percent sure that I have Adriel to thank for the reappearance of this asshole in my life.

"Now put your pretty knives away, pet, and be nice and

sweet with us, and we won't slowly rip your friend into tiny little pieces."

With that, the two shifters who are still bears move in toward Sabin and me, and we have to decide quickly if we fight or comply. I focus in my mind on the runes that represent each of the guys and feed magic into them, activating the link in our heads. I'm so used to touching the runes to activate them that I have to focus entirely too much on the process of doing it without touch, and a bear gets within striking distance.

"Fuck, Sabin, do you think you can take a shifter? Or at least hold your own against one until help arrives?"

The bear steps even closer, and pink and orange magic flashes across my skin in warning.

"Be good, pet. If you fight, it will be all the more painful."

The Big, Burly Douche licks his lips, and his meaning isn't lost on me.

Sabin's voice is silent in my head, and I realize that he can't activate the runes without touching them.

"Guys, we're in trouble. We're at Sabin's warehouse and surrounded by bear shifters. Tell Aydin it's the grizzlies from our first fight together, he'll know what I mean. We're going to fight, so don't start screaming in my head. Just get here!"

Sabin nods his head almost imperceptibly, and I call on my Elemental magic and throw up a wall of dirt in front of us. A growl vibrates through me as a grizzly the size of a car slams into the dirt wall, clawing through it to get to us. Sabin is using his Elemental magic to defend us just behind me, but I can't focus on what he's doing as teeth and claws come at me. I trade my short swords out for a long sword. I clap my empty hand against the hilt to create two of the weapon.

The bear roars out its challenge, and I scream in answer as I run toward it. I push magic into my limbs and take two huge strides before I leap high into the air, just missing the claws aimed for my torso. I pivot midair and slam my swords into the back of the grizzly. They slide deeply into the shifter, pulling me out of the air and onto his back. He snarls in pain, and I immediately call on new swords and get to work trying to cut this fucker's head off.

I am barely able to avoid the claws as he reaches around his back, trying to dislodge me as I stab through the thick muscle and fur protecting his throat. His bellows turn to pained yowls, and just when I think he's going to collapse to the ground and accept death, I catch another bear coming straight for me.

I make one more last-ditch effort for a kill shot on the beast beneath me and prepare myself to go toe-to-toe with another elephant-sized grizzly. What have these assholes been eating, fucking Mutagen? I tense, my body preparing for a bite that's unavoidable; I just hope the promise of a big payday will keep it from ripping me in half.

42

Out of nowhere, a massive dark gray wolf barrels into the bear, knocking it off balance, and they both go down in a tangle of teeth, paws, and snarls.

I dismiss the shock and the *thank fuck* that fills me at seeing Torrez, and I call on my longsword, giving one last swipe at the injured bear's neck. His head rolls away from his body, and I send out a silent plea that help is coming as I look up and see two bears closing in on Sabin. I run for him and unleash throwing knives at the bear closest to him, aiming for the eyes and nose. Firing one blade after another, I hope Sabin can hold off the other bear because there's no way I can take two at a time.

My target swipes at the small knives sticking out of its face, and it rears up to protect its head. I call on my short swords and fall to my knees, sliding past the legs of the bear as I slice through the muscles holding it up. My blades meet bone, and I release them calling on immediate replacements to shove up into the belly of the bear as it comes crashing down on top of me. My lungs give up all their air as the furry mass that weighs a fuck ton slams me into the unforgiving ground. I force myself to focus through the panic and hack away at the underside crushing me as much as I can.

I'm covered in blood and gore, and my hold on my knives becomes slippery as I give one last stab and feel the bear on top of me die. I gasp in need of oxygen and magically muscle my way out from underneath the massive shifter. I get up on my hands and knees as I pull myself all the way free, and I'm just in time to look up and watch as the grizzly bear Torrez was fighting rips his stomach open. I try to scream, but nothing comes out as my lungs work to inflate and serve my oxygen-deprived body. I shatter inside as Torrez yelps in pain, and the grizzly bear moves in to finish him.

Desperation and rage surge inside of me as I watch Torrez's wolf try to crawl away through puddles of his own blood, his organs spilling out from where they're supposed to be inside of him. My runes light up with violet fury. Sentinel magic pools inside of me and then blazes out, slamming into the bear. The shifter is engulfed in purple flames, and the magic blasts him away from Torrez. I run-crawl toward my bleeding wolf, but when I get near him, I don't know where to touch or how to offer comfort, he's so battered and covered in gouges and bites.

Oh, fuck! Oh, fuck! Oh, fuck! I cry to myself as I scoop up Torrez's intestines and try to press them back into his body. He's not moving, and I'm terrified of what that might mean. A strangled sob bubbles out of my throat, as I run my eyes over his tattered chest, trying to detect any movement there. I force Healing magic into him, but it won't take to any of the injuries, and I scream out my frustration. I scramble toward his face and, with blood-covered hands, run my palms over the fur around his eyes.

"Stay! Please stay!" I beg, helplessly petting his face and realizing I'm a fucking idiot.

He was right, I am drawn to him, and it's not in some mysterious *where is this coming from* kind of way. I like him. I want him. And now I'm going to lose him.

"Mark him, Vinna," Bastien shouts at me in my head.

"I don't know how!" I shout out, the confession slamming into the trees just in front of me and bouncing back to tear at my soul.

"Weave your intention with the magic, Vinna. I read it in that stuff the readers gave you. Chosen have a connection that could save him, but you have to decide what you want."

I call to my Sentinel magic for the second time tonight and beg it to save Torrez. I don't weave my intention. I fucking demand obedience. My hands glow deep purple as I place one against Torrez's head and the other on his battered body. I flood him with Sentinel power and claim him as mine. He jerks against my hands as I flood him with magic, and I watch as he starts to knit together. I seize onto the small amount of hope that swells inside of me that somehow this will work.

A snarl demands my attention, and my head snaps up as the singed bear I blasted comes barreling back toward me and Torrez. A possessive war cry sounds off inside me, and I refuse to let this fucker anywhere near my wolf again. I send one more strong pulse of magic into Torrez and hope it's enough as I rise from his body and square off with the shifter. I call on the runes on my toes, and two spiked maces form in my hands. The metal of the weapon is missing the blue sheen of my rune magic that it normally has, and instead is saturated with the purple of my Sentinel magic.

This piece of shit is going to bleed.

I run toward the bear, violet magic streaking in my wake,

and I skid to the side as I slam both maces into the bears face in a one-two combo that sends him reeling. One mace gets stuck in the side of his skull, and I let the magic go and call on another. They're not the most practical weapon in my arsenal; I could make this fast by slicing him up with blades instead, but I need him to suffer. I need him to know with every spiked point that brings this piece of shit closer to death, that you don't fuck with what's mine!

He swipes at me, but I don't even feel the claws as they shred my side. I slam him in the head with my mace and follow up with an uppercut to his muzzle. I bring a spiked ball down on his paw as he swipes at me again, and the bones shatter first in his hand and then his forearm as I bring the other mace down hard there too. I twirl around and use the momentum of my spin to slam one mace into his face and the other lands in his throat. His skull gives way to my spiked vengeance, and the bear collapses to the ground. I raise my weapons for the final blow when I notice two people walking slowly toward me.

My haze of rage clears just long enough to see that it's Sabin, and he has a knife to his neck.

I immediately release my hold on the maces, and they evaporate into nothing as my runes reabsorb their magic.

"Ah, ah, ah, pet. If a new weapon so much as blinks into existence near you, I will slice his throat!"

Big, Burly Douche punctuates his statement by applying pressure to the blade, and Sabin's eyes widen in fear. He tries to lean away as the blade nicks his throat, but with the shifter standing behind him, using him as a shield, there's nowhere for him to go to escape the knife, and it moves even deeper into his skin.

"Stop!" I demand and hold up my hands. "No more weapons. I'll come with you wherever you want, just stop.

He gives a self-satisfied grunt and jerks his chin toward the road that leads into the warehouse. "Start walking, pet. Stay where I can see you, and Harry Potter here won't die an agonizing death right here in front of you."

I start walking in the direction that he tells me, and about five minutes later, I see a black van parked on the side of the road.

"Open the doors and take out the tape and the hood."

I do as I'm told and then hand them to Sabin as instructed. I hold out my hands as Sabin wraps thick, silver duct tape around my wrists and then my forearms. My eyes stay locked on his as he tapes me up, and it breaks my heart to see how helpless he is right now.

"I'm sorry," I tell him mentally, and I work hard to blink back the tears that fill my eyes. *"I didn't protect you. I'm so fucking sorry, Sabin!"*

A sob wracks my chest as Sabin pulls a hood over my head, and my world goes black.

"I don't know how close you guys are, but we're being taken. We're in a black van, but I can't tell where we'll be going from here."

"Can you stall? We're less than five minutes away!" Knox begs me.

"He has a knife to Sabin's throat. I'm taped up in the back of the van. I can't do anything without risking Sabin."

Tears stream down my face, and I bite back the shuddering lament that wants to escape me.

"I fucked up. I tried to save Torrez, but I don't think it worked, and I got so wrapped up in wanting to punish the shifter that hurt him, I didn't watch Sabin's back. I just left him to fend for himself."

"Vinna, don't do that. It's not your fault; we're going to get you two out of this. Evrin and Aydin are in a car behind us,

they're going to go check on Torrez. We'll look for the van and follow you guys to wherever he's taking you. We're here, you're not alone, and as soon as we can, we'll get you."

Valen's words pierce my desolation, and I try to calm my breathing and get control of my emotions. I don't know where we're going, but crying about how I fucked up can happen later. Right now, I need to keep it together and help the guys to get me out of this. I try to recall how far away the nearest airport is, and I wonder if Big, Burly Douche will try to bring us to Adriel himself or if he'll hand us off to another group of lamia like Faron did.

A small spark of hope kindles inside of me at the thought that somehow Sorik might be part of the group responsible for bringing me in, maybe he'll be able to help, and the guys will have better odds at a rescue. He tried to warn me that Adriel had something planned, but I thought it would somehow be another lamia attack of some sort.

With that thought, a flash of wolves chasing a bear on their pack run pops into my head. I growl in frustration at myself. How the fuck did I not make the connection? Just how long have these fuckers been watching me?

My body tilts forward as the van makes a turn and slows slightly. I'm not sure how long we've been driving, but it doesn't seem long enough to have left Solace's boundaries. The brakes squeak as the van comes to a stop, and the van door is thrown open. Someone reaches for me, and I move to get away from their grabbing hands, but the shifter holding Sabin at knifepoint tsks me.

"Pet, same rules apply, be nice or else."

Sabin gives a pained gasp, and I picture the knife pressing into him even deeper. All resistance leaks out of me, and I go limp with compliance. I'm pulled out of the van and thrown over someone's shoulder. My hood flips up slightly, freeing my mouth, but gravity doesn't help it lift any further, and my surroundings are still a mystery. I'm carried into a quiet house or building, and scuffled footsteps echo around me as I'm lugged up a flight of stairs. I'm taken off of whoever's shoulder I'm on and unceremoniously dropped to the ground. I grunt in pain as my shoulder and hip connect with the floor.

I smell floor cleaner of some sort, and it makes me think I'm definitely in a house. I don't reach out to the guys; instead, I strain to listen to what's going on around me, trying to piece together any clues as to where I am and who is here. A door clicks closed, and muffled voices start up on the other side. I can't make out anything that's being said, and I tune it out.

"*Sabin?*" I ask mentally.

He doesn't answer.

I push back against the panic that bubbles up inside of me, and instead I call on a small throwing knife and slowly angle it in toward the tape on my wrists. I get the blade against the tape with serious effort, but I can't get the necessary friction needed to damage the tape and free my hands. I abandon the plan to cut myself free and reach up to pull the hood off my head so I can get a look at where I am. Sabin taped my wrists and forearms, but luckily I can still move them. I reach for the hood, and footsteps sound on the other side of the door. I yank my hands down, just as the door squeaks open and heavy footfall makes its way into the room.

"As promised," the Big, Burly Douche exclaims.

"Yes, I can see, thank you," a man's voice deadpans, and something about it sparks recognition in me, but I have no idea where I've heard it.

"I want double what we agreed upon."

At that, a scoff fills the room.

"She practically killed my entire sleuth!"

"Then you should have acquired her cooperation sooner! Your incompetence is your own, and I bear no responsibility for it," the familiar voice exclaims.

"Well, then maybe I should see who else is interested in my pet. At the lengths you've gone to procure her, I'm sure there are others out there who would be more than happy to meet my price."

Footsteps move toward me, and the word *stop* is bellowed out. The footsteps do as commanded and the familiar voice moves toward where it sounds like the shifter is standing.

"As appreciation for your services, please accept this as a token of my gratitude," the familiar voice coos.

A gasp fills the room, and the sound of fabric moving against fabric feels strangely loud in the space. It goes on for a couple of minutes, and then the room grows quiet. A thump sounds in front of me, and the loud noise makes me jump.

"Filthy shifter," another male irritably exclaims, and then the room grows quiet again.

"*Sabin?*" I try again, but the silence in my head and around me is deafening.

The air next to me shifts, and the presence of someone next to me is now all I can focus on. The hood over my face is gently tugged off, and I blink against the dim lighting in the room. I turn to track whoever is in here with me, but I spot an unmoving Sabin in a large chair that's pushed up against one wall of the dark wood-paneled room. Before I can even think about springing an attack, air rushes past me, and I watch as Sabin's eyes fly open, and he starts grasping at his throat. I push up on my feet and scream for them to stop, when I feel a knife pressed flat against my throat.

"Just tell me if he's okay," I beg as a figure steps out from the dark corner.

As the shadows fall away from Elder Albrecht's face, confusion wars with anger inside of me. Looks like the question of *where I stand with the elders* just got answered.

43

Whatever they're strangling Sabin with relents, and he starts to cough and struggle to suck in large lungs full of air. Helpless rage slams through me, and I glare at Elder Albrecht. He gives me a polite smile and motions toward a grouping of green velvet chairs on the opposite side of the room. The knife falls away from my neck, and I'm tempted to make a move, but I need Sabin more recovered and ready in case I can't get to Elder Albrecht and the bald guy fast enough.

So I follow Elder Albrecht to the designated cluster of chairs and sink down in one with exaggerated defeat.

"He took an unfortunate bump on the head, but he's alive and well as you can see," he reassures me as he sinks into his own chair, crossing his legs and leaning back like he's the fucking king of the world.

The knife-toting bald man saunters over to Sabin and looms over him, the threat clear. I sneak one last glance at Sabin, as his breathing smooths out a little, and I cling tightly to the momentary relief that flashes through me. I turn my attention to Elder Albrecht, ready for him to explain just what the fuck the elders want now.

"Vinna, I must remind you that it is completely in your control if Conscript Gamull continues to stay alive and well. I hope that our unfortunate acquaintance made at least that much clear to you."

Elder Albrecht turns to look at something on the floor, and I follow his gaze down to find the grizzly shifter that brought me here dead by the door. I feel no sympathy for the wide, lifeless eyes that were clearly filled with fear in his last moments. I only wish that I could have dished out the justice myself.

The door opens to the room, and Elder Balfour walks confidently in, closing the door behind him and barely sparing a glance at the dead shifter on the ground or at Sabin on the couch.

"I called him; he'll be here soon, although I want it noted that I don't like the lack of planning on your part for *this*." Elder Balfour announces, flicking his fingers in my direction, indicating that I'm clearly the *this* he's referring to.

I swallow the retort that snakes up my tongue. I want nothing more than to mouth off to these pricks and then fucking kill them, but I've already failed Sabin once. I won't let them hurt him again because I can't rein in my temper.

"You worry too much. Everything is working out, despite having to move up our timetable; he won't be any different. In situations like these, you can't control everything. We just have to take things as they come," Elder Albrecht reassures Elder Balfour as the squat, balding elder sinks down into a seat across from me.

I fix him with a murderous stare and wonder how long it will take for the rest of the elders to show up.

"Don't answer back, I need to stay focused on what's happening here, but it's the elders who are behind this. I'm staring at Elder Balfour and Elder Albrecht right now," I tell the guys.

I don't know what they're going to be able to do with that

information, but maybe they can think of something I can't. I breathe through the mounting rage that's festering inside of me as I fight my need to act, to kill each of these corrupt men. Elder Balfour won't look at me, but Elder Albrecht watches me like a cat stalking prey.

"We'll be joined soon, and then you will need to make a very important decision," he informs me as he steeples his hands in front of him.

It makes every inch of him so much the clichéd villain, that I fight to keep from rolling my eyes.

"We know what you are, and subsequently what you can do, and your decision is simple, share your magic with us, or refuse and we'll kill your mates. Then, we'll hand you over to a certain lamia who has been keen to get his hands on you. I can't imagine that life would be very pleasant for you, but I suppose it's ultimately your choice."

Elder Albrecht flicks an imaginary piece of lint from the knee of his crossed legs, his casual tone and body language giving off the impression that talk of me handing over my magic or being tortured into it, is the kind of casual conversation he takes part in every day.

"I still don't understand why we can't just take it," Elder Balfour mumbles, still refusing to look at me.

Elder Albrecht glares at him, his calm, patient persona cracking, and the irritation he has for his fellow council member seeping out.

"If I chose to share, what happens then?" I ask, pulling Elder Albrecht's attention back to me.

"Once the transference is complete, you will be free to live life with your mates."

I lock my muscles against the shudder that tries to break free at the thought of what I'd be required to do with these disgusting, power-hungry parasites in order to give them my magic. If he thinks for one second that I believe that I'd just be free to go about my life after that, then he's a fucking idiot.

The door opens again, revealing the one elder I'm not surprised to see here. When he sees me, he pauses a couple of steps into the room, and I think I catch shock in his eyes. He pulls his gaze away from me, too quickly for me to read what's written on his face, and takes in Sabin and the dead shifter. He looks over to his fellow council members, and a small smile plays at the corner of his lips.

"Well, from the looks of things, someone's been having fun."

Elder Albrecht chuckles deeply and then gives Elder Balfour a self-satisfied grin that reeks of superiority.

While the elders are focused on each other, I look to Sabin.

"As soon as these fuckers are done kissing each other's asses and telling me their plans for world domination, I'm going to kill them. You take out the bald guy and slow down anyone you can, okay?"

Sabin's eyes are locked on mine, and he gives an almost imperceptible nod. Elder Cleary moves into the room and takes the seat next to me. I pull my gaze away from Sabin and refocus on my targets.

Elder Cleary runs his eyes over me, his gaze lingering on the tape around my arms.

"Want to fill me in on what's going on?" he asks as he reaches over and runs the point of his index finger against the thick gray bands.

With a touch, he cuts through the tape, and then he proceeds to pull it away from my skin. Thankfully it comes off easily; I guess there was too much blood coating me for the tape to adhere to my skin better. The methodical and casual way that Elder Cleary handles the liberation of my arms surprises me almost as much as his words.

"I'm sorry to spring this on you, in this way, but I know that we're like-minded individuals, and this is a once in a lifetime opportunity," Elder Albrecht explains.

Elder Cleary doesn't immediately respond as he balls up the duct tape in his hands and runs his gaze over the room.

"You mean, you need three casters for the binding and thought I was your best bet to bring on board."

Elder Albrecht's eyes narrow ever so slightly. "There is that, too."

The word *binding* sends fear running up my spine, and I look over the room more carefully, trying to see whatever clued Elder Cleary in on what's happening. The room is sparse with only the green velvet chairs in it, so I focus on the paneling of dark wood on the walls and floor, and that's when I see the runes carved into the ground. They form a large circle around where I was dropped when they brought me in here. I have no idea what the setup means, but based on what Elder Cleary just revealed, they're either going to bind themselves to me, or bind my magic—neither of which I'm going to allow to happen.

My arms are free, and no one is holding a knife to Sabin's throat anymore. If I'm going to make a move, it's better to do it now than wait and have to deal with the other elders when they arrive and I have more magic to go up against. I start to call on the runes for my throwing knives when Elder Cleary's words stop me in my tracks.

"How long have you been working with Adriel, Seth?"

Elder Albrecht's head snaps to Elder Cleary, and I can see him work to keep his nonplussed mask in place.

"I've suspected for some time now that Adriel's coven of lamia had inside help, but I could never identify the connection."

I have to swallow back the seething anger that rages through me, demanding action. He's been working with

Adriel this whole time, selling out his own people, and doing who knows what else?

"Sabin, now!"

With that, I'm out of my seat in a flash, slamming daggers into Elder Albrecht's chest. I pin him to the green velvet chair, staining it with the blood of a monster who's hurt the ones he was supposed to protect. A scuffle breaks out next to me, but the piece of shit I'm shoving my hate and blades in, has my full attention. He blasts me with maroon magic that activates my shields, and I press into him even further.

The twins' faces run through my mind, followed by Silva and their mother, smiling back at me from the framed photo that Bastien has in his room. I imagine Lachlan and Vaughn with their arms around each other laughing and talking shit, and then I picture my mother. This fucker ruined all of their lives! I pull my dagger out of Elder Albrecht's chest, and I cling to the faces of the ones I love—and never got to love—as I shove a blade through his ribs to pierce his lung.

"They fucking trusted you, and you sold them out for what? More power?" I shake my head at him, seething, and shove another blade slowly into the other side of his chest. "Well, they can look through my eyes now and watch you die…slowly…painfully…pissing yourself."

I stare at his face until it goes slack and the life in his eyes fades. I stand up to find Elder Balfour's body in a heap on the ground and Elder Cleary helping Sabin off the ground where the bald guy is lying in a pool of his own blood. I stride toward them, cock back my fist and punch Elder Cleary in the face. Sabin moves next to me as Elder Cleary pulls his hands away to protect his now broken nose.

"I'm not in on this, Vinna! I was trying to help!" he shouts, his voice pained and nasally as blood drips through his cupped hands.

"Don't convince yourself that you're the good guy! You took your shot at trying to play and manipulate me, too. Be glad you just have a broken nose; it could be worse."

Elder Cleary follows my gaze back to the dead Elder Albrecht. He looks back to me and gives me his best *I'm not intimidated* look. So I give him my best *I'm not fucking joking, I will stab you* look. We stand like that for a moment before Elder Cleary pulls his phone out of his pocket and calls for help. I guide Sabin out of the room, ignoring Elder Cleary's order to *not go too far*. Sabin hasn't said a word, and it's freaking me out, so I stop just outside of the room now coated in death. I cup his cheeks and stare up into his green eyes.

"Talk to me, are you okay?"

I don't ask where he's hurting, I push Healing magic into my hands and let it start working on his injuries.

He just stares at me, something unreadable in his eyes.

"I'm so sorry. I shouldn't have left you alone like that. I should have been more aware of what was happening around you. Please, say something, anything, even if you need to scream at me..."

"I love you, Vinna."

I don't know what I was expecting to fall out of Sabin's perfect lips, but *that* was not it. I send another pulse of Healing magic into him, certain there must be a serious head injury I missed somehow, but he pulls my hands away from his face.

"It's not a concussion-addled confession," he tells me, his mouth turning up in a smirk, but I don't miss the flash of insecurity in his eyes.

"No, Sabin," I tell him, and he looks at me confused. "Not when I'm covered in blood and reek of death."

He cups my cheek. "I know those words should be spoken under starlit skies and punctuated with soft kisses, but they're no less true when we're covered in blood and reek of death. I love you."

Before I can say anything else, Sabin leans down and kisses me. I may not want to hear him say *I love you,* not like this, not when I'm not sure I can say it back. But he tells me anyway, his lips on mine, his soul demanding its place with my soul. I may not know what love like *this* is supposed to be like, or if I'm ready to say those words, but I let what I do feel for him seep into my lips, and it surprises me when my kiss begins to feel just like his.

44

Sabin and I walk out of the front door of the palatial monstrosity Elder Albrecht called a house. We've been questioned and now released by the paladin sent to investigate and clean up what happened here tonight. I'm exhausted. The heaviness of my tired feet and limbs is made worse by the fact that the difficult times don't die inside this house tonight. There is still so much more death and destruction waiting for me out in the world, and we're about to take a direct flight right into the middle of it.

I spot the guys huddled just past a guard of paladin who've been instructed not to let anyone onto the grounds. I break into a run, pulling Sabin along with me, and I shove through the line of guards and jump right into the middle of my pile of Chosen. Ryker catches me, and I'm peppered with kisses as he runs his hands over me, confirming for himself that I'm alright. I already saw a healer inside, and I reassure him that the blood isn't mine and I'm okay.

I don't get any more explanation out before I'm stolen away and the kiss-slash-check-if-I'm-okay process begins again and gets repeated three more times. When the guys aren't checking on me, they're checking on Sabin.

"By the stars, that was awful. Knowing what was going on and not being able to do anything is by far the worst feeling in my life," Knox confesses, pulling Sabin into one side of him and me into the other.

We all take a moment just to breathe and try to rid ourselves of the anxiety and worry that has hung heavy around all of us throughout this whole ordeal. We climb into the car and head for home, and I try to sort through everything that's happened tonight.

"Did Aydin and Evrin make it to Torrez?" I ask, terrified they'll say *no,* and somehow equally terrified that they'll say *yes*.

Bastien turns to me, and I can't read what's written on his face. "He needed more healing, which Evrin took care of, and he's resting back at the house."

So many different feelings flash through me, and I'm not sure which one to cling to: relief, fear, intrigue, worry? I finally settle on guilt.

"I'm sorry, you guys," I announce into the quiet of the car.

"For what?" Bastien asks.

"For wanting to mark someone other than you guys. I didn't know, until I thought it was too late, that I even wanted to. But Torrez was right; it was there, and I just didn't want to look at it too closely. I was drawn to him, but it was different, I don't know how to explain it...I should have talked to you guys more. Tried to figure out what was going on, so we could all make a decision, and now I've gone and *forced* another thing onto you all," I confess, feeling horrible that once again my lack of self-awareness has made a mess of things.

"We'll just have to adjust, Vinna. We all trust your magic, and if it found him worthy, then we'll find a way to as well,"

Sabin tells me, and I'm shocked when each of the guys voice their agreement.

I feel like I should say more, explain more, but when I sift through the words in my head, nothing feels right. I don't know what sentences I could string together that would make me feel better about what happened. Or what I could say that would make it easier to believe that this transition will be as simple as Sabin's words make it seem. So instead of looking for a solution that doesn't seem to exist, I stay quiet and soak in the reassurance and acceptance that I always feel just being in their presence.

We park in front of the house once again, knowing that we're here to clean up, pack our bags and then leave for the airport. Aydin, Evrin, and the sisters pour out of the front door, and all of us are wrapped up into hugs and relieved greetings.

"Well, Little Badass, at this rate, we should probably stop letting you out of the house at all. Have you guys ever met a bigger trouble maker?" Aydin teases after he sets me down from a bone-crushing hug and wipes a few tears from his cheek.

Evrin wraps an arm around my shoulders as we head inside the house and gear up to leave again. I look around, nervous that Torrez will be leaning against a wall, smirking and demanding that our new situation is dealt with immediately, but he's nowhere to be seen.

"He's sleeping in a guest room. The sisters cleaned him up, fed him, and fussed over him. He passed out pretty quickly after that. I don't know how Sentinel magic works with other kinds of supes, but he seemed to be pretty wiped out."

I give Evrin a grateful smile. "Thank you for healing him. I didn't know if I had done enough, so thank you for making sure he made it."

Evrin gives me an awkward hug, and I chuckle.

"You're worse at that than I was," I tease, and he laughs. "Do I need to sic the sisters on you? They're good at hug-it-out therapy."

Evrin laughs again and points me in the direction of my room. "Go shower; you're gross."

I laugh but realize he's right. "Sisters, Evrin really needs a hug. He's feeling very emotional," I shout over my shoulder and dash into my room just in time to see the three of them surround Evrin.

"Thanks a lot! Payback's a bitch!" he shouts at me.

I laugh all the way to the bathroom where I promptly strip and throw everything I'm wearing away. I don't know how long I spend under the molten stream of water that falls from the ceiling of the shower, but no one comes to hurry me along, so I take my time. I magic myself free of most of the hair on my body and then towel off, dry and style my hair, and take a deep breath before I leave the sanctuary of the bathroom and step back into the real world.

I get dressed and head out to ask if I need to pack a bag, when angry yelling has me running down the hallway to the front of the house. I get to the living room and run right into complete chaos. Aydin and some of the guys are trying to pull Knox and Bastien off of...Enoch?

What the fuck is going on?

I rush to insert myself in front of Knox and Bastien as they're pulled back, and when I see the looks on their faces, it scares the shit out of me. I've never seen them so angry.

"You fucking shit bag liar, I'm going to kill you!" Knox bellows over me as he struggles to get out of Aydin and Sabin's hold.

It's a good fucking thing he has no idea how to use his Sentinel strength yet, or we would be in some serious trouble. I spin around, focusing on a swollen-eyed, bloody-lipped Enoch.

"What the fuck is happening here?"

"I swear on everything, Vinna; I have no idea how it happened. They just showed up."

I'm confused as fuck about what Enoch is rambling about. *They just showed up? Who showed up?* Enoch swipes at the blood on his lip, and everything inside of me plummets as I take in the black marks on his finger.

No. Fucking. Way.

I spring for him, my bloodlust demanding action. The betrayal I feel screaming through every part of me. I catch him with a right hook to the cheek, and he falls back, avoiding my follow up hit. I'm raging inside, but I say nothing as I pounce on him, ready to smash his face in. Kallan steps in front of me, and I move to go around him until I spot what's on his hands, too. My seething eyes find his, and the only thing that keeps me from killing him is the terror in his eyes.

"How the fuck do you have runes, too?!" I demand.

Arms wrap around me from behind, yanking me away from the people who need to give me answers right fucking now. My Chosen may not know what they're capable of yet, but I sure as fuck do, and I push magic into all of my limbs and fight to get away from whoever is holding me back. I writhe and flail and do everything short of hitting and stabbing my captor, but fuck they're strong. Lips press close to my ear.

"I can do this all day, Witch. But if you'd stop rubbing yourself all over me for just a second, I'd like to point something out."

Torrez's arms tighten around me, and the shock of his deep voice makes me pause. He pushes a hand out in front of my face and nuzzles my neck.

"They're not the same."

His words and silky tone reverberate through me, and it takes me a minute to figure out what he means. I stare at the dark-tan tone of his skin and the runes that mark his entire ring finger. The second rune, the one marking him as mine, sits black and prominent. Its presence pushes the other runes representing my Chosen down; the last rune resting on his knuckle. He moves his palm slightly, and I look through his large splayed fingers, honing in on Enoch's hand.

He's right... The runes on Enoch's finger aren't mine. So, whose the fuck are they?

The End of Book Two...

THANK YOU FOR READING

Thank you for reading

You've just finished the second book in The Lost Sentinel Series and I thank you so fucking much for that! If you loved Awakened and Betrayed, please take a moment to leave a review.

You can stalk me on Instagram, my Facebook Reader Group, my Facebook page, Amazon, BookBub, or my website for updates on this series and more.

ACKNOWLEDGMENTS

There are so many people who helped this book get past the finish line. Denise, Nichole, Robin, Megan, Nesa, Tiffany, Sara, and Dom, thank you for your time, talent, support, eagle eyes, and for being incredible!

Raven and Ann, thank you for being the most supportive, badajj birches—wink, wink— a girl could ever hope to find and call squad!

S & S, thank you for being amazing about the nights of eating out and weekends of staying in to write! Love you!

And to you, the reader: you have read, reviewed, recommended, and lifted me up in a way that's changed my life and made my dreams come true. Thank you, and know that I love and appreciate you more than I can say!!!

ABOUT THE AUTHOR

Ivy Asher is addicted to chai, swearing, and laughing a lot—but not in a creepy, laughing alone kind of way. She loves the snow, books, and her family of two humans and three fur-babies. She has worlds and characters just floating around in her head, and she's lucky enough to be surrounded by amazing people who support that kind of crazy.

- facebook.com/IvyAsherBooks
- instagram.com/ivy.asher
- bookbub.com/profile/ivy-asher
- amazon.com/author/ivyasher

Printed in Poland
by Amazon Fulfillment
Poland Sp. z o.o., Wrocław